COME
AND
GET IT

ALSO BY KILEY REID

Such a Fun Age

COME AND GET IT

A Novel

KILEY REID

G. P. PUTNAM'S SONS
New York

PUTNAM
— EST. 1838 —

G. P. PUTNAM'S SONS
Publishers Since 1838
An imprint of Penguin Random House LLC
penguinrandomhouse.com

Library of Congress Cataloging-in-Publication Data

Names: Reid, Kiley, author.
Title: Come and get it / Kiley Reid.
Description: New York : G. P. Putnam's Sons, 2024. |
Identifiers: LCCN 2023044408 (print) | LCCN 2023044409 (ebook) |
ISBN 9780593328200 (hardcover) | ISBN 9780593328217 (ebook)
Subjects: LCGFT: Campus fiction. | Novels.
Classification: LCC PS3618.E5363 C66 2024 (print) | LCC PS3618.E5363 (ebook) |
DDC 813/.6—dc23/eng/20231005
LC record available at https://lccn.loc.gov/2023044408
LC ebook record available at https://lccn.loc.gov/2023044409

International Edition ISBN 9780593716175

Printed in the United States of America
1st Printing

Book design by Ashley Tucker

For Caleb Way

I don't want to spend eternity with the lights off. I'll buy the most expensive, longest lasting bulbs, and charge them to my Amex.

—Lucy Biederman, *The Walmart Book of the Dead*

We're all working together: that's the secret.

—Sam Walton, *Sam Walton: Made in America*

COME
AND
GET IT

1.

AGATHA PAUL STOOD IN FRONT OF BELGRADE Dormitory at 6:59 p.m. One block down was an ice cream store with outside seating and young women holding paper cups. An Airstream trailer with a colorful pennant banner was selling tacos across the street. Two students with large backpacks walked past her toward the dormitory entrance. One said, "No, I've actually had oatmeal every day this week." The other opened the door with a key fob and said, "See, I need to start doing that, too."

A moment later, through a partially frosted glass door, Agatha saw brown Birkenstocks hustling across a tile floor. She didn't know what Millie looked like, but she immediately assumed that these shoes belonged to her.

"Hi, Agatha?" she said. She opened the door with an outstretched hand. On her chest was a lanyard weighted with keys, an ID case, and hand sanitizer.

"Yes. Millie? Hi." Agatha shook her hand. "Thanks for setting this up."

"No worries. Come on in."

Agatha stepped into the dorm. The paneled ceiling lights in the lobby were the kind that made her skin look transparent and baby pink. There was a front desk behind a glass window. An overloaded bulletin board: kickball sign-up, dining hall menus, and flyers for movie nights (*Beetlejuice*, *Pitch Perfect 2*). The dorm smelled both dirty and artificially clean. There was a faint Febreze scent and something candied in the air. It smelled like perfume purchased from a clothing store, like Victoria's Secret or the Gap.

Millie waved to a Black woman sitting behind the sliding glass. "Can I get the sign-in sheet, please?" she asked. The woman swiveled in her seat and said, "Yes, you can." Agatha signed her name beneath a few others: David. Hailey. Aria. Chase. She hadn't seen this many Black people (Millie and this security guard) in the same room since she arrived in Fayetteville. Millie walked to the elevators and pressed a button, but then she turned around. "Our elevator is super slow," she said. "Are you okay with stairs?"

Millie wore black cotton shorts and an oversized red polo with *University of Arkansas Residence Life* embroidered in white. She had rosy brown skin, a pear-shaped form, and an expanse of dark wavy hair in a lopsided bun at the front of her skull. Millie was cute with bright eyes and large, lightly freckled cheeks. From the neck down, she looked like an adult poking fun at campus life, someone dressing like an RA for Halloween. In one arm she held a clipboard and pen. A dated cell phone was behind her waistband at her hip. In a two-finger hold was the plastic loop on a wide-mouth Nalgene bottle. It was covered in overlapping stickers; one said *Save the Buffalo River . . . Again!* As Agatha followed her up three flights of stairs, she decided that Millie was probably twenty-two years old. She was the type of student that college student service centers swept up for pictures and profiles. Students paid parsimoniously to give brief campus tours.

Millie bent to use the fob on her lanyard to open the stairwell door. She looked back and asked, "So you just moved here for the school year?"

"I did," Agatha said. "Are you from Arkansas?"

"No, I'm from Joplin. But I used to camp here when I was little."

"Did you go to Devil's Den?"

"Yeah. Many times."

"It's lovely over there."

Millie dipped her chin. "You've been camping already? That's impressive."

"No no, long time ago. But I should go again."

Agatha followed her down a long, bright hallway past several doorways that had pool-themed cutouts taped above the peepholes. Written in Sharpie on paper sunglasses and palm trees were names like Sophia, Molly, and Jade. Agatha had lived in a residence hall for her freshman year at Amherst, but then she moved into one of the Amherst Houses, which felt more like a boardinghouse than it did a residence hall. Evidently, aside from her own age and the trend in baby names, everything else had stayed and smelled the same.

"Is this okay?" Millie led Agatha into a tiny room with white walls and a speckled tile floor. Near the door, a tall stool held a landline phone. There was a tilt-and-turn window at the far end, and in the center was a circular table and five chairs. Agatha was certain that whatever website boasted Belgrade Dormitory, and probably Millie herself, referred to this room as something like the Resident Lounge or Media Center. "This is perfect," she said, and she meant it. There was a gentle tug of wholesomeness, and she liked the lack of pretension. Millie removed a Post-it from the wall. *Reserved from 8–8:45. xo Millie.*

"You're welcome to sit in," Agatha said, "if weddings are a thing you're into."

"Oh, no. I can't," Millie said. She swiped at the table, pushed crumbs down onto the floor. "I have to do rounds in a minute. Oh wow, that's so nice of you."

She was referring to the items Agatha removed from her bag. A six-pack of lemon La Croix. A cutting board and knife in a gallon Ziploc bag. Two blocks of Manchego cheese. Raw almonds. A red apple and a flecked orange.

"Yeah? You think this will be okay?"

"Oh, for sure. They like anything free. I'm gonna grab them unless you need a minute."

Agatha pushed a chair toward the window. "No, that's fine. I'm ready now."

Millie left the room, but very quickly, she was back. The crumpled reservation Post-it was still in her hand. "Do you mind what they call you?"

Agatha leaned forward on her arms.

"Do you prefer Miss Agatha? Or—sorry. Professor?"

"Oh. No no," she laughed. "Agatha is just fine."

Agatha's first real writing assignment had been a campsite review, when, at twenty-five years old, she drove a rental car to six different states. In Georgia, she started a fire without matches. In Louisiana she was bitten by a dog on her lower thigh (she gave herself two temporary stitches to hold the wound closed). And here, in the Ozarks, she started writing her first book. She spent two nights each in Devil's Den, Tyler Bend, and Mount Magazine State Park. Perhaps it was silly to feel a connection toward a state she'd spent only six nights in, where she'd talked to fewer than four people, but this appreciation, however dormant it had been for thirteen years, was considerable enough to make her submit a recent change of address.

Fayetteville, Arkansas, had a screen-saver, campus-visit, Scholastic Book Fair beauty to it. There was a thirty-six-mile bike trail called the Frisco Trailway that crossed a stream not too far from Agatha's home. It was spotted with overly courteous biking couples ("On your right, ma'am. Thanks so much"). Every Saturday morning in the town square was quite possibly the cutest farmers market Agatha had ever seen. She walked with a weekend pace, drank iced coffee, and bought eggs the color of wet sand. One Saturday, she spotted a little bakery that said *Stop in for a bloody* on a chalkboard outside. The young man behind the counter said, "Would you like a to-go cup?" Agatha smiled under her sunglasses. "Yes. That would be great."

She lived rent-free in a two-story, three-bedroom house that belonged to a professor on sabbatical. The house sat on a grassy hill at Wilson Park: a large block of green with a basketball court, tennis courts, two playgrounds, and a winding walking path. The park, and Fayetteville in general, was teeming with hills and trees. In many of the latter were thick webs stitched into the branches with Gothic little worms that writhed in the shade. Agatha's street was filled with enchanting homes and people much like her: academics, liberal-seeming couples, families affiliated with the university. Two blocks behind her home was sorority row. Brassy-looking houses with porches, columns, and stairs, all created with group photos in mind. There were often cars parked along her street with bumper stickers of Greek letters in white. Inside, through the windows, Agatha saw Target bags and paisley duffels. Tangled leggings in back seats. Diet Dr Pepper cans.

Agatha's previous trip to Arkansas came with the realization that she was very good at being alone. But this time, after three years in a relationship—now broken up in practice yet still married on paper—the act of experiencing a new place, however bucolic and convenient, was mostly grim and sobering. Agatha poured the almonds into a small glass bowl and laid two wedding magazines on the table. She sliced the orange into eight slivers. She took one of the La Croixs, wished it was colder, and popped it open. Being alone in a new college town was kind of like watching the local news in a hotel room. With someone else it could be amusing and fun. By yourself, it was a little depressing.

Millie returned to the room with three young women behind her. "So this is Agatha," she said.

Agatha stood. "Hi. Thanks for coming."

The shortest one wore sneakers and looked to be coming or going to the gym. "Oh," she said of the cutting board. "I love that. How cute is this."

Agatha guessed they were around twenty years old. Each young woman had a thin layer of matte-finish makeup, cotton shorts like Millie's, and long, straight hair that didn't look necessarily straightened. The most compelling correlation was the fact that each of them wore an oversized T-shirt, the colors of which were faded but deep: a butter yellow, lacinato kale blue. Seeing them, Agatha was reminded of what the dog owner had yelled back in Louisiana, just before she was bitten. *Hi!* she'd said, cupping a hand to her mouth. *Don't worry. They're friendly.*

"Hah there," the blond one said. "So nice to meet you. Ah'm Casey."

There weren't many on faculty or in her classes, but accents this strong could still derail her train of thought. Agatha fought that innate instinct to mimic the songlike sounds. "Hi, Casey," she said flatly. "Nice to meet you, too."

"Hi, I'm Jenna," the tall one said. Jenna did not have a discernible southern accent, but she did have a dark and even tan that looked deliberate. Her hair was dark brown with light sweeps of chestnut highlights. Agatha said hello, thinking, Jenna, tall, tan. Casey, blond, accent.

"I'm Tyler," the last one said. "Ohmygod, I love cheese like this." She took up a piece that was impressive and big. Tyler wore a muted-blue baseball cap with a thick brown braid hanging out the back. Beneath her heather teal T-shirt she wore black biking shorts that ended a few inches above her knees. Tyler was the type of person Agatha could picture holding her phone for the entire duration of a painfully slow, high-resistance elliptical ride. There was a familiar, greedy, adolescent edge about her. It implied that she was accustomed to getting her way. Perhaps she was wrong, but pressed for time, Agatha categorized the residents like this: Jenna: tall. Casey: southern. Tyler: mean.

"So I'll be doing rounds," Millie said. "But text me if you need anything."

"Thanks so much, Millie. Ladies, are you ready?"

The three young women pulled out chairs and took a seat. Agatha pushed her hair behind her ears.

"So I'm sure Millie told you the basics, but I'm Agatha Paul. I'm a visiting professor this year and I'm teaching nonfiction as well as culture and media studies in the graduate nonfiction program. I'm also doing some research on weddings and I'm really excited to ask you a bunch of questions."

Jenna placed an apple slice in her mouth. "Is this like, for your own wedding?"

Agatha looked up and saw that her question was in earnest. "No no. My first book centered around funerals and grief. The second was about birthday celebrations. And this one will be about weddings. All of them focus on money and culture and traditions. And you're all big wedding fans, yes?"

Jenna nodded. "That's like, all we do."

"What's that?"

"We just like . . ." Casey laughed a bit. "We watch a lot of the highlight videos. Or we send each other things we find on Instagram or whatever."

"Okay, great. But let's back up. I want to make sure we start properly."

Agatha took out her phone, switched the setting to airplane mode, and then began to record. Next, she retrieved her small, black tape recorder, pressed the recording buttons, and placed the device between the cutting board and the young women. "As I said in the email, your names and your likenesses won't appear anywhere in the book. So speak freely and honestly. There are no right answers."

Casey folded her arms on the table and said, "Why did Ah just get nervous?"

"I know, me too," Tyler said.

"There's no need to be nervous, I promise."

"Actually?" Jenna stood up. "Can I grab my sweatshirt? My room is like . . . right there."

"Oh, of course."

Jenna left and silence took the room. This moment was familiar: the sudden dread that it would be a struggle to pass the next forty-five minutes, let alone with something inspiring. But after hundreds of interviews in the last ten years, Agatha's brief apprehension was eclipsed with the firsthand knowledge that, for the most part, people liked talking about themselves.

Casey pointed at a La Croix. "Do you mind if Ah take one?"

Agatha said, "No, please. Help yourself."

Casey opened the can with both hands. "May Ah ask what type of stone that is?"

Agatha looked down at her ring. "Oh, sure. It's called a sunstone." She thought twice about it, then slipped the ring off her finger. She reached and handed it to Casey.

Casey held the ring up to her line of sight. "A sunstone," she said. "That's so neat."

Tyler leaned into Casey. "I love that. It kind of matches your hair."

"Huh," Agatha said. "You're right. I guess it does."

Casey carefully handed the ring back. "It's real pretty," she said.

Agatha said, "Thank you," and slipped it back onto her hand. When she looked back up, she found that Tyler's brown eyes had centered on Agatha's neck and chest.

"So this is a weird thing to say?" Tyler said. "But you dress how I want to dress when I'm older."

Agatha wished she could fight the impulse, but her face pouted at Tyler's words. She looked down at her outfit with a "This old thing?" expression. Light blue chino pants. A white boatneck top. Gold bar necklace. A chambray vest that went past her knees.

Agatha leaned forward and pulled up on the waistband of her pants. "That's very nice, Tyler. Thank you."

"Mm-hmm," Casey agreed. "Ah see what you mean. Mah goal is to have really solid pieces that all kind of go together."

"Exactly, same," Tyler said. "Okay, also? I have a random question. Do you get to write about whatever you want?"

"For the most part."

"That's so neat. So you're like, a journalist?"

"I am."

"Ohh," Casey said. "Ah didn't realize. That's so neat."

Jenna came back into the room, but this time with a large adornment. A gray knitted throw blanket was wrapped around her shoulders.

Tyler snorted. "Jenna, what are you *doing*?"

"I couldn't find my sweatshirt," Jenna said. Holding the blanket in place, she sat back down.

As Casey laughed and said, "Ohmahlord," Tyler held up a questioning hand. "Jenna's like, 'What? I couldn't find my sweatshirt.'"

"Okay," Agatha cut in. "Ladies, are you ready?" But as it seemed, Jenna's blanket scarf was still incredibly funny.

"That actually looks kind of good," Casey said.

"I'm gonna be so mad if I lost my sweatshirt, though."

Tyler patted down a piece of the blanket so she could see Jenna's face. "Awwww, look at her. Little Mexican bebe," she said.

"I know," Jenna said. "I'm just a cute little refugee over here." She adjusted the blanket and crossed her legs. "Sorry," she said to Agatha. "Okay, I'm ready now."

Agatha blinked and closed her mouth. She experienced a warm rush of blood to the face. The residents' eyes sat ready and patient; they were waiting for her to begin. Wow, Agatha thought. Robin will absolutely lose it. But then she blinked again. Crossed her legs on the other side. For just half a second, she'd forgotten the two of them were no longer together.

"Let's start with some introductions. Just tell me your name, your age, where you grew up, and your major. Tyler, do you want to start us off?"

"Sure. I'm Tyler Hanna . . . I'm a junior and I'm twenty-one. I'm from Dallas, Texas. I'm a hospitality management major with a minor in marketing and . . . yeah. I think that's it."

"Great. Jenna?"

"I'm Jenna." She adjusted her blanket. "I'm nineteen. Do you need my last name?"

"No, that's fine."

"Okay. It's Saddler in case you do. I'm a sophomore. I'm from Waco, Texas. My major is exercise science, and . . . I'm nineteen. I said that already. Sorry."

In her lap Agatha took pointless notes. *Waco. 19.* "Alright, Casey?"

"Okay. Hah there." Casey bent toward the recorder. She introduced herself as if she were leaving a voice mail. "Ah'm Casey. Ah'm a senior at the University of Arkansas. Ah grew up in Clarke County, Alabama. Mah major is birth through kinder, and Ah'll be twenty-one this Saturday."

"Happy early birthday."

"Ohthankyousomuch."

"So," Agatha said, hands in her lap. "Who here wants to have a wedding?"

The girls, all of them, raised their hands in a similar way. They weakly held their arms up next to their shoulders, all their fingers slightly curved. It was as if Agatha had asked three children how old they were, and they were shyly answering "Four."

"Do you have friends who don't want a wedding?"

"Ah don't think so . . ."

"Me neither," Tyler said.

Jenna placed a handful of almonds into the pouch that she'd made with the bottom of her shirt. "We have friends who want to travel," she said, "and be more independent before they settle down. And I'm kind of the same way. I went to Amsterdam and Italy last summer and it was so fun. So yeah, I want to get married but I'd do it late. Like . . . thirty-one, thirty-two."

Tyler smiled. "Ohmygod. No thank you."

"Tyler, why isn't that ideal for you?" Agatha asked.

Tyler stretched her forearms out on the table; they were slightly freckled with a surprising amount of brown hair. "I'd just rather travel with someone," she said. "And I think it's hard to have a good wedding later. Because then some people have kids and things, or they don't know how to have fun anymore when they're all old and thirty-eight or whatever. You know what I mean?"

Casey said, "Ah know what you mean."

Agatha pressed her lips into a smile. In her lap, on her legal pad, she wrote, *all old and thirty-eight or whatever.* This was the age she would be in a little less than a month.

"Let's talk about paying for a wedding."

Jenna did a sharp intake. "Ohmygod. So expensive. It's crazy."

"What do you think of the tradition of brides' families bearing the cost?"

"My parents expect it," Jenna said. "But also, they have certain expectations. Like, I get an allowance from them that comes with them expecting me to save up. So if I was getting married, and there was something insane that I wanted, they'd be like, 'Okay. You're gonna pay at least half.'"

"My mom is the same," Tyler said. "And even though my mom will pay, there's an understanding that I'm not gonna be all, 'Oh, I want this ten-thousand-dollar dress' or whatever."

"I see," Agatha said. "Casey, what about you?"

"The short answer is yes, mah parents will pay. But sometimes it depends on mah mom's moods. Like when mah sister got married mah mom was like, 'You need to pay for your shoes,' out of nowhere. And mah sister was like, 'Ummm okay?' But yeah. They know that we know that they saved for our weddings, but if something was too much, or if Ah wasn't pullin' the grades they expect me to, they'd definitely be like, 'Hay. You need to calm down.'"

Agatha looked down at her next question, which touched on dream wedding locations. But she was stuck on Tyler saying that she wouldn't ask for a ten-thousand-dollar dress. Now she was wondering if five thousand was too much, if three was a better number. She reached up and, with a pen in hand, she gently touched the back of her neck. "Can I ask what your parents do for a living?" she said.

Jenna swiveled an aluminum can between her hands. "My mom manages the Airbnb for this little add-on to our property during Baylor's football season. And my dad is an orthodontist. Technically, I work for him."

"What's that?"

"So, me and my brothers get our allowance from his payroll. Even though we don't do anything, obviously. But that's how I save for things. So I can be more independent later. He made it so it's like a practice paycheck."

Agatha scribbled *practice paycheck* into her notebook. As she did, she thought, Hmm. That sounds a lot like fraud but sure.

"But I also have a job," Jenna corrected. "Ohmygod, sorry. I'm talking so much. But yeah, I work in the alumni services office twice a week. And that's like . . . my fun money."

Agatha thought, Hm, and, That's cute. She wrote *Fun Money* in cursive script.

"Alright, Casey?"

"So mah mom is a title guarantee claims attorney. And mah dad is the payroll director for a medical supply factory back in Mobile."

"And Tyler?"

"My mom is the office manager at this sandblasting and powder-coating place. Annndddd my dad is currently incarcerated so his job is just like . . . being in prison."

Tyler's delivery, the way she rolled her eyes, and the fact that she'd clearly made this joke before, it all made Agatha flattered and embarrassed.

"And no, I do not visit him," Tyler laughed. "People always ask me that. And my mom and me are still close with his parents. But yeah, that's why I'm here."

"What's that? That's why you're here?"

"Oh, yeah," Tyler said. "There's a housing scholarship thing that we have." Her thumb went back and forth between herself and Casey. "This is like, the scholarship and transfer student dorm."

"Yeah, we don't live here on purpose," Casey said.

"Jenna has a scholarship, too," Tyler explained. "But not housing. It's tuition."

"So you have a scholarship because of your father?"

"Yeah. Casey's scholarship is the only real one. She actually gets good grades."

"Jenna, can I ask what your scholarship is for?"

Jenna had picked up a piece of her hair and she was inspecting the ends. "Mine is an ethnic/diversity scholarship, but I'm here because my parents just think dorms are more safe."

Agatha looked up, took Jenna in, her straight hair, her tan that looked intentional. She said, "Okay," and looked back to her notes. Slid the clasp of her necklace behind her neck.

There was something thrilling about the young women. The sensation they gave her was one of intrigue and revulsion, and it reminded her of Robin. Robin coming into Agatha's office to say, I'm watching the worst movie and I need you to see it. Or Robin putting her nose to sweaty clothes from rehearsal. Oh God, she'd say. You have to smell this. Or she'd use the bathroom while Agatha brushed her teeth. I'm so dehydrated, look at my pee. Agatha would say, That's disgusting, and she'd spit into the sink. But then she'd come over and say, Don't flush. Lemme see.

"So what's the worst wedding you've ever been to?" Agatha asked.

"You know what's funny?" Tyler said. "I feel like I haven't been to that many."

"Me neither," Jenna said. "Except for family friends, but those don't count."

"Well, we did go to Tessa's last summer," Casey said.

"Oh yeah," Jenna said. "That was fun."

"Meh. It was fine," Tyler said.

"Say more on that, Tyler. Why was it just fine?"

Tyler looked at the others. "Am I wrong? I feel like it was just kind of tacky."

"No, I see that," Jenna said.

"What does 'tacky' mean in terms of a wedding?"

Tyler wavered her head back and forth. "Well, it was in this big old rope factory, which would have been really pretty. But there was more than one venue inside of it. And there was another event right next door. And I just feel like it would have been better if they'd rented out the entire thing, because if you went out in the hallway or something, you'd be like, umm . . . who are these people?"

Agatha said, "I see." She wrote down the word *Tacky*. It was something her late mother would have said about someone using a gift card at a lunch they'd invited you to. There was something about this word and Tyler's example that made Agatha sit up in her seat. She was coming to understand two very important things. The first was that she didn't really care about weddings, not enough to write a book about them. The second was that she was completely enraptured by these young women, their relationship to money, what they said, and how they said it. For now, it seemed, she could ask them about money as much as she wanted. As long as the proposition was framed around weddings.

"So what's the opposite of a tacky wedding?"

"The opposite of tacky is classy," Jenna said.

"Mm-hmm. Ah agree."

"What does 'classy' mean to you?"

"Oh, Ah love that question," Casey said. "Classy is when you're bein' respectful, not just of others but of yourself. And to have a classy wedding . . . it doesn't have to do with how much anything costs. It's about the whole experience bein' intentional and fun."

"Well?" Tyler's eyes went up to the corner of the room. "Okay, I agree, but at the same time . . . I don't know. You do have to accommodate your guests and like, sorry but that costs money."

"Can you give me an example of that? What's a way of not accommodating your guests?" In her journal Agatha wrote down *Sorry but that costs money.*

"Actually yes. And this is a hot take but I don't care. You cannot not have an open bar."

"Ohhh," Jenna said. "I agree with that."

"I'm sorry but at a certain point it's just rude. Like, I just flew to your wedding and got a dress and hotel, and you're gonna give me a drink ticket? No, you need to grow up."

Casey said, "Tah-ler."

"I'm sorry but it's true!"

Jenna looked up from a new piece of hair. "Remember when Amber said she wanted a *Soul Train* line at her wedding?"

"No, she did not," Tyler said.

When Jenna confirmed with a look that Amber in fact did, Tyler shook her head. "Why would you want that? So friggin' ghetto."

Agatha placed the top of her pen at her chin. "Is 'ghetto' a word you use often?"

Jenna snorted and said, "Yes."

"What does that word mean to you?"

Casey smiled. "Mah mom is always askin' me things like this. Ah'll say somethin' and she'll be like, 'Casey, what does that *mean*?' And Ah have to be like, 'Uhh, wait a minute . . .'"

"Actually? No, here's an example of what's ghetto," Jenna said. "So the glass on my phone is all smashed, but I can't get another one till my upgrade. So whenever I can't click on something, I'll be like, 'Ugh, my phone is so ghetto right now.'"

"Exactly," Tyler said. "Jenna, that's really good."

Agatha scribbled in her notebook. "So what would a ghetto wedding look like?"

For a moment, the girls said nothing.

"That's like . . ." Tyler proceeded to move her hands in a circle. "That's when it stops being fun-wedding-dancing, and it's more like, 'Oh hey, I'm at spring break' or whatever."

"But also?" Jenna said. "Just to be super clear? Being 'ghetto' or whatever isn't necessarily bad. It just depends on the person."

"Can you say more on that?"

"It's hard to explain. You could be totally normal but maybe it's how you walk or how you sound . . ."

"That's interesting," Agatha said. She looked at her watch. Twenty minutes left. "So what does being ghetto sound like?"

Casey held her hands up and said, "Ah'm not even gonna try."

"I know. Me neither," Jenna laughed.

"Okay, actually . . ." Tyler touched Jenna's arm. Her voice went down as she pointed toward the door. "You know Millie? The RA?"

Agatha sat up. Carefully, she said, "Sure."

"Okay, sometimes—just being honest—Millie can be . . . a little ghetto." On the word *little*, Tyler held two fingers an inch apart.

"Nooo. Don't say that. Ah love Millie."

"But I'm not saying it like it's a bad thing."

"No, I see what you mean," Jenna said. "Sometimes she'll be all like . . ." She pushed her hair behind her ears. She looked as if it were her turn in a game of charades and she was considering how well she knew the reference. "Ohmygod, I can't even do it," she laughed. "Okay, if we're being too loud or something? She'll be like, 'Gurl, you know iss quiet hours!'" Then she poked her lips out. She put a hand on her hip and she shifted her head from side to side.

"Ohmahlord, yes," Casey laughed.

Tyler agreed. "Yes. That was good."

Jenna sat back, satisfied. She placed a piece of cheese in her mouth. "Ohmygod, ugh," she said of the cutting board. "Get this thing away from me."

One of the more frequent arguments that Agatha and Robin partook in, especially near the end, was what Agatha considered an unfair assertion: that Agatha didn't like anything. And sure, there were many things that she did not enjoy. Like zoos. And musicals. And photo booths at weddings. Burlesque was another one. Any type of parade. She hated Little Free Libraries in wealthy neighborhoods. (Just use your public library? Which is also free because that's the point?) She hated when restaurants and stores offered human food to dogs. "I'm going to scream," she once told Robin, watching a dog receive a puppuccino. Of course there were things that she did enjoy, like reading, but that didn't mean she found it easy to find the right things to read. Once, Agatha said that she'd hated the last four books she'd read. Robin responded, rather cruelly, "Well. Maybe you just don't like books."

Agatha actively rejected the claim that she didn't like things, partially because it came from a person who owned thirty pairs of high-end leggings and subsisted on iced coffee, but she mostly rejected it because of moments like this: sitting inside a dormitory in Arkansas, feeling wildly inspired and obsessed. There was something about Tyler, Jenna, and Casey. She didn't want to be friends with them, but she liked listening to them. She *liked* sitting there. Even when they were at their worst, she liked letting their vernacular wash over her. Weddings had seemed like such a natural next subject, but did *she* like weddings? Not particularly, no. Now that she considered it, the weddings she'd

been to had all felt relatively the same. This conversation, however. This felt like something. Agatha crossed her legs at the
sensation. How can I use this?

With fifteen minutes left, Agatha bent down into her bag.
She stood up and handed out three sheets of paper. It suddenly
felt like she was a child playing school. "I'm going to ask you a
few more wedding questions . . . but I want to go off on something Jenna said. I want you to write down what you spend your
fun money on? And try to be specific."

Casey accepted her sheet of paper. "Ah love things like this,"
she said.

"Guys, I'm so sore." Tyler massaged her right hip. "I need to
get one of those butt pads."

"My grandma has like, four of those," Jenna said.

"Y'all," Casey said. "She's still recording this."

Tyler exhaled into the back of her hand. "Whoops," she said.
"Can you take that part out?" Before Agatha could answer, Tyler
looked up and took her in. "Ohmygoodness," she said. "Wow,
you're really tall."

WHEN THE SESSION ended, Agatha gave each resident a
white envelope with a ten-dollar bill inside. Tyler began to clap
with the envelope in her hands. "Fro-yo. Fro-yo."

Casey said yes but it had to be quick because she had to
study; she was serious this time. As they pushed in their chairs
and said their goodbyes, Millie appeared at the door. The phone
was still in Millie's waistband and her lanyard keys made a lot of
noise. She told Agatha that she could walk her out. A minute
later they were in the elevator; a recycling bin filled with aluminum cans and glass bottles sat in the space between them.

"Oh—" Agatha reached to her purse. "This is for you."

"Oh, thank you. I—"

The elevator opened. "Sorry, I'm not following you," Millie said. "I just have to take this out."

Agatha said, "Yes, of course."

She signed out at the front desk. Outside, the sky was dark with delicate pinpoints of stars. Millie walked the wheelchair ramp. She dumped her recycling into an even bigger receptacle.

"Do you need help with that?" Agatha asked.

"No no, don't touch it. It's gross."

Millie brushed one hand on her shorts. She carried the bin back to the sidewalk.

"Here you go," Agatha said.

Once again, Millie hesitated. "Are you sure? I just made a sign-up. It only took two seconds."

"Don't be silly. It's a huge help."

Millie took the envelope in her hands. "So this is your job? Interviewing people?"

"That and reading and writing. And teaching, of course."

"That's cool."

"Do you write, too? What's your major?"

"I write papers when I have to. I'm a hospitality management major. And I minor in Spanish."

"That's interesting. Good for you."

"Yeah, no. I'm definitely not a writer." Millie set the recycling bin down, and curiously, she crossed her arms. "I'm probably just like . . . way too ghetto for that?" she said.

A small part formed between Agatha's lips.

Millie laughed. She reached out with one hand. "Ohmygod, I'm sorry. I had to! And I wasn't spying, I swear. But I keep my door open and my room is right there. Ohmygod, your face. I'm so sorry."

Agatha let out a surprised little cough, feeling complicit and relieved. "Well, now I'm dying to know what you thought of that comment."

Millie lifted her shoulders and lips. "I mean, I don't think I talk like that. But even if I did it wouldn't . . . I don't know. And I know why Tyler said that and it's so dumb. The other day I was trying to get paper towels from this storage closet? And she was right there and I had the wrong key. And I think I said like . . . I don't even know. I said, 'That's not the right one,' or something like that. And then she was like, Ha ha ha, Millie's all, '*Girl*, this ain't the right one.' And yeah . . . I did *not* say it like that."

Agatha nodded. There was that feeling again. Oh, that's interesting. How can I use this?

"But whatever." Millie waved a hand. "People hear what they wanna hear. Also, I feel like that was really mean what I just did."

"No no no. That was very funny." Agatha could feel it—her face was still terrifically red. "I'm just curious. Do most students speak that way?"

"My friends don't. And I definitely don't think most students have practice paychecks . . ."

Agatha smiled and said, "Right."

"Which, by the way"—Millie held up a finger—"Jenna's job definitely does not cover her 'fun money.' She works at the alumni office, which pays like nine dollars an hour and the shifts are like, three hours long. *But*, she also has a weekly appointment to get her nails done at this place that does the fancy artwork? It's like, sixty dollars for a set. And . . . ohmygod. It's so dumb that I know this. She does balayage hair? Do you know what that is?"

Agatha reached for the pen in her bag. "Balayage?"

"Yeah. It's like, super expensive Christian girl hair."

In her journal, Agatha spelled the word as best she could.

"And I've also heard her say that she gets seven hundred dollars a month from her parents. So yeah," Millie said. "Her job does not cover her like . . . fun, spending money."

Agatha considered this number out loud. "Seven hundred dollars?" she asked.

"I know. Which . . ." Millie squinted. "Sorry . . . yeah. It's just funny to hear her take."

Agatha looked back at the dormitory door. The residents would be exiting soon, if they were still getting fro-yo.

"And she . . . she mentioned a diversity scholarship?"

Millie smiled. "It's the same as mine. Her grandma is from Mexico."

Agatha turned her head. "Is it a lot of money?"

"It is for me. Six thousand dollars a year."

Agatha made a face of baffled intrigue.

Millie said, "I know."

Agatha laughed and said, "Okay."

A group of residents came from the front door carrying buckets, poster boards, and folded towels. Agatha and Millie looked back to each other. They started to speak at the same time.

"Well, thank you again—" "But yeah, you have my number."

Millie picked up the recycling bin with her fingers under the ledge. "Sorry . . ." she said. "I don't know why I just told you all that." She shook her head, laughing at herself.

Agatha found this admission strangely charming and adult. "No no, that's okay," she said. "It was nice meeting you. Thanks again." She walked up the hill toward her home. She listened to the sound of Millie's lanyard tapping gently against her chest.

2.

MILLIE COUSINS WAS BORN IN JOPLIN, MIS-
souri, in 1993. Her father, Richard, was six foot and fair
with hair that had turned gray in his forties. Her
mother, Glory, was a foot shorter with sharp cheekbones, and
she came from a Black farming family near Albany, Georgia.
Glory had short hair that was curly, black, and gray. She only
wore makeup for celebratory dinners, when she used blush,
tinted ChapStick, and a tasseled pashmina draped over whatever she was wearing. For Richard and Glory, a child wasn't
necessary or a dream, but when the opportunity presented itself
at their joint age of forty-two, the thought of it was quite nice.
The three of them went camping several times a year, mostly in
the Ozarks, where Millie's penchant for Fayetteville began.

Millie's father was an international and political affairs professor at Missouri Southern State University. Glory was the
manager of the Papyrus stationery and greeting card store located in Northpark Mall. She had a monthly book club meetup
as well as a bunco night. She loyally helped her friend Myrna
with her soap and candle booth every Saturday at the Empire
farmers market. Millie's parents pushed her to do lots of activities as well, in service of being a flexible person, an excellent

sharer of her things. She later understood this as overcompensation, a correction of her status as an only child. But very quickly, the things she was pushed to do as a child became the activities she liked to organize as an adult.

Millie did Girl Scouts, volleyball, and camping club, for which she was voted president two years in a row. In high school she was on the yearbook committee, prom committee, and student council, where she served as vice president in her senior year. She was the stage manager for two musicals, dressed in all black with a headset backstage. After high school she took a gap year. She worked at a bed-and-breakfast and a coffee shop in Fayetteville. She saved a good amount of money and earned in-state tuition status.

Halfway through her sophomore year at UA, Millie became an RA. This was something Aimee Pearson, the housing director, said she'd never allowed before, but Millie happily replaced a student who'd had a bedbug scare and subsequent mental breakdown, and she transitioned into RA status with ease. She worked as a camp counselor in the summers. She volunteered to be at the dorms for January term. She house-sat for Aimee and took care of her dog. When Glory told her friends what Millie was up to at the moment, she often ended with "Oh yeah. You know her. Exactly. Always likes to be in charge."

FOURTEEN MONTHS BEFORE her second senior year, Millie was finishing her junior year at the University of Arkansas. Her mother was driving home from work when the pressure in her eyes became so severe that she had to open the driver's-side door and throw up. In the parking lot of an Anytime Fitness and

Firehouse Subs, Glory dialed 911. The police came and sat with her. Glory said she didn't need an ambulance, but the officer kept shaking her head, saying, "I think it's best we get some help." Millie's father arrived as the ambulance did in all its unnecessary splendor. Glory collected her things and got into Richard's car. "If I don't get in, they can't charge me."

Glaucoma was a word that had been said often in the Cousins-Arnold household. It was one of the few reminders that Millie's parents were older than most of her friends' parents. She didn't sleep for two nights after her mother's episode in the car. The idea of it happening again or Glory vomiting inside the vehicle, Millie couldn't abide by it, at least not while living in another state. Before confirming with her parents that leaving was a good idea, she went to Aimee's office.

"Hey, girly," Aimee said. But then Millie sniffed and Aimee turned around completely. What proceeded was a lot of moving chairs, offering tissues, and holding up a small waste bin. Aimee was as kind as she was unflappable. "Hey. Listen to me. I know this sucks," she said. "But you are not the first to take a year off. And you won't be the last."

Millie didn't remember saying that explicitly. A year seemed extremely long. But who was to say what her mom's eyes would be doing in the fall, especially if she had surgery. Yes, Millie thought. She was taking a year off. One year off and then she'd come back.

For the next two weeks, Millie completed assignments that the rest of her classmates had not yet been assigned. She did made-up tasks meant to substitute for group activities, and she set up her fellow RAs to take on her residents. A few times, Millie was back in Aimee's office as Aimee helped her tie up loose ends. "Your professor's not responding? Who is it? I'll take care of it. My husband taught with him in Little Rock. We see them at tailgates."

Three weeks before the end of the academic year, Millie moved back to Joplin and Glory wasn't pleased. "I'm fine," she'd said, on the phone and through texts. When Millie pulled up in front of the house, Glory said it again. "See? Look at me. I told you I'm fine." Millie completed her final exams and papers by emailing two and completing two more online. She got her high school job back at the Starbucks inside the Barnes & Noble at Northpark Mall, which she was not allowed to call Starbucks; she had to say Barnes & Noble Café. Her RA friends—there'd been two she was close to—went intermittent and then quiet on their once-active group text. In the fall Millie took three online classes. She drove her mother to and from work.

DOCTORS AND THE internet insisted that glaucoma couldn't be cured but it could be controlled. Millie and Glory googled remedies, vitamins, lists of foods to avoid, and holistic approaches that internet forums cited and swore by. Glory gave up coffee completely, as it could increase her intraocular pressure and lead to more optic nerve damage. Millie wasn't about to give up coffee, especially when she got a shift drink for free, but when it came to meals, she became an active participant. Together, she and Glory transformed the contents of their refrigerator and the colors on their plates.

The leftover Tupperware that Millie took to work became filled with grilled asparagus, Brussels sprouts, cold-water fish, and strips of eggplant. At home, she and her mother snacked on goji berries and black currants, watermelon and grapefruit, sometimes with mint and salt. There were so many eggs being cooked that Richard purchased an egg storage keeper and drawer. "Look at this," he said. "This is really slick." Millie propped her computer on the counter next to the stovetop and watched YouTube tutorials: poached, shirred, omelet soufflés, a béarnaise sauce that tasted better on a second try. It was these protein-heavy meals, the absence of sugary cocktails and beer, and the family gym membership her dad added her to that resulted in the first of three significant things that happened back in Joplin. Over the course of the year, and without meaning to, Millie lost eleven pounds.

The fact that she was losing weight became less important than where she was losing it from. New negative space was seemingly being forged solely around her midline and waist. She didn't have much boob to lose, but her small breasts didn't seem so small when she stood in the shower and pressed her hands into her sides. Millie had returned to Joplin as a practiced size ten. By Christmas there were size-eight pants under the tree. "See?" Glory said. "See what happens when you don't eat all that candy?" Millie didn't reveal that her kale-and-bean-based meals had no bearing on her consumption of sweet and sour gelatin-based snacks. Haribo Peaches were her favorite. Sometimes she had Cola Bottles, too. But she tried to go to the gym more often because she liked the way she looked. She felt as if her body had gotten its braces off. Like she'd reentered her room after a deep clean.

The second significant thing that happened back in Joplin was that Millie and her mom started microdosing marijuana. Glory had purchased two large pairs of sunglasses from Target to protect her eyes. She wore the bigger pair on the day that Millie drove her to apply for a medical marijuana card.

Millie laughed as Glory got in the car, holding her purse in two nervy, flat hands.

"If I get this thing"—Glory shut her door—"you can *never* tell Myrna."

Millie put the car in reverse. "Why would I tell Myrna literally anything?"

"Not just Myrna. We can't tell nobody."

Millie pulled out onto the street. "Well, you're in luck because I have no friends."

"Mill, don't say that."

"Mom, it's fine."

Glory didn't want to do brownies because of her new gluten-free diet, so Millie found a recipe for caramel edibles. She purchased a candy thermometer and a silicone pan from a confectionery shop in the mall. They added pecans that Glory put in a Ziploc bag; she smashed them to pieces with the bottom of a mug. Glory had tried smoking in her early twenties and she remembered it making her nauseated and paranoid. But now, after a caramel square in the evenings, her stare became soft and steady. It didn't take such a pointed effort to read an email or a recipe. She said it felt like she was getting her eyes ready for bed.

Millie partaking in Glory's medical marijuana hadn't been discussed prior. But she'd tasted the samples and said when she felt it, so the idea of creating rules around her not having it seemed a bit belated. Sometimes she'd take half a caramel before her shift at work. Activities like washing her dog or sectioning and detangling her hair became moments where she could be clever and inspired. Being tepidly high, in addition to her recently pulled waist, made Millie feel creative and not so alone. But this sensation had much less to do with the edibles than it had to do with her mom. This was the third thing to happen back in Joplin. Millie and Glory became terribly close.

They watched a lot of HGTV, betting on which house the couple would choose. They watched *Scandal* from the very beginning, and when Richard entered the room, Glory would shush him and Millie would scream, "Daduhh!" They went to movies on weekends and timed their caramel intake, sitting toward the back for Glory's eyes. Glory quizzed her every morning over breakfast the week of Millie's final in Intermediate Spanish. They listened to podcasts while Millie took care of her plants, redoing the soil to get rid of gnats.

By spring, so much of their conversations were in their own shorthand. Once, at breakfast, Glory said, "Mill. Guess who finally got married."

"Who?"

"The bad guy we like from that show. The one with the name."

Millie made a face. "To that woman with the mouth?"

"Yes, girl."

"Yeesh. Well, good for them."

"That's what I said."

Richard placed his spoon onto his plate. "You two can't be serious."

Millie thought her dad was being dramatic, but there were other times when she saw his point. Once, while she was on a walk, Glory phoned her cell. "Hi, I'm in line. So I gotta be quick. Mill, do I like the salad or the bowl?"

Millie sighed. "You like the bowl."

"And do I want the thing on it?"

Millie was alone, save for her dog. Still, she felt mortified to answer the question, and to know what question was being asked. "Yes," she said. "But you want it on the side."

Millie needed to go back to school. But with the absence of friends and four-dollar coffees, and with her B&N shifts and occasional house-sitting, Millie started saving more money than she ever had before. Coming off of so many summers living in dorms and cabins and rooms that weren't hers, and after becoming mildly addicted to TV shows featuring tiny houses and youngish owners, the idea of owning a home came down on her like a dream. With six thousand dollars in her bank account, Millie allowed herself to entertain the idea that maybe, if she was very, very good about it, she could make a down payment in two years. This fantasy home would not be in Joplin, it would be in Fayetteville. But then in April, Millie was offered a shift manager position at the café, and she found herself tempted to stay one more year.

"No," Glory said. "Absolutely not."

"Okay okay, hang on," Millie said. Yes, she missed Fayetteville, but Joplin wasn't terrible. And there was a big difference between the $9.12 she was currently making and the $11 an hour she could be making full-time. "You're acting like I'm not going to graduate. I'm just thinking that if I took one more—"

Glory held up her hands. "This? This was a mistake."

Millie knew that Glory wasn't referring to Millie's year off of school. The mistake was letting her in as something other than a boundaried, limited, and professional daughter. For Millie's entire childhood, Glory's approach to parenting had been almost clinical. The way she punished, the way she encouraged, and the way she loved. Everything from Glory, whether she said it or not, came with the same admonition: I'm not your friend, I'm your mom. Sometimes Millie felt that the approval that she wanted from adults or superiors in general was in response to the way her mother tried to establish this partition. But after her year in Joplin, she also felt certain that she just liked being around her mother. Glory was fun to be around.

"You are going to go back to Arkansas and you're going to have a real senior year."

"Okay, but just hear me out for two sec—"

"Millicent? You don't need a house."

"Well, of course I don't *need* it—"

"You're a kid and you need to be doing kid things with other kids. And if you want more money? Fine. This is what you're gonna do. You're gonna tell Starbucks yes—"

"Barnes & Noble Café."

"*Ma'am.* You're gonna say yes and take that position. And then in August you're gonna say, 'Oops,' and you're gonna go back to school."

"Okay, first of all, I'm not a kid. I'm twenty-three."

"Then go be twenty-three in Arkansas."

"Can you relax? And that's so not cool to take a promotion and then quit three months later. They would never take me back again."

At this, Glory staggered back and reached her hands into the air. She blinked as if she'd seen a vision, and she uttered an emphatic "Well, *good*!"

For the next few months Glory pointedly brought up minor logistics regarding Millie's return to Fayetteville. Yes, she'd signed up for classes. And yes, she'd talked to Aimee. Everything was fine for her to return as an RA.

"We're all good to go," Aimee had said over the phone. "But—don't be mad at me—I have to put you back in Belgrade." Millie had been in Belgrade for her junior year, a fact made fine because her friends had been there, too. But the transfer/upper-classmen/scholarship dorm was not great, affectionately nick-named Smell-grade and Cell-grade. "I know," Aimee said. "But Josh is an RD now and I need to put him with someone who's been there before."

"Josh from accounts payable? He's an RD?"

"Yes, he's great. He won't be at orientation—grandma died, poor thing—but don't you worry. He'll be there for move-in."

Millie blew through her lips. Welp, she thought. It had been her decision to leave. Now she was coming back to the bad dorm with the new RD. And this time she'd be friendless and old.

"Hey, Aimee?" Millie said. "While I have you . . ." She went into the backyard so Glory couldn't hear. Millie told Aimee she was looking for a house to buy after graduation, something small, for just one person. If Aimee had any leads, she would love to know. Aimee said, "Hoo boy. You're growing up. Okay."

That summer, Millie worked full-time. She went to the gym twice a week. Instead of social media apps, she was always on Zillow. Sometimes she couldn't help herself; she used some of her tips to purchase Haribo Peaches after work. But mostly, Millie took the cash and stuck it in the right foot of a pair of rain boots; what she came to think of as her "down payment shoe." Every other week, she delivered its contents to a new savings account. That summer, she turned twenty-four, and she saved twenty-three hundred dollars.

Two weeks before she moved back to Fayetteville, Millie sat in her RAV4 in the Barnes & Noble parking lot. She psyched herself up, memorizing the speech she'd written in her phone. She asked her boss if she had a second to talk. In response to her prepared lines, Millie's boss clapped and said, "Oh! Well, that's a bummer for us, but good for you! Would you be open to training Samantha? I have to ask, but I think she wants the hours."

———

BELGRADE DORMITORY HOUSED one hundred and twenty residents on its third and fourth floors. On the first floor was a lobby, a mail room, a common room with a small TV, and a parking garage, where Millie parked her car. The second floor held an expansive, dusty gym that had a weight rack, treadmills, and some old medicine balls. The other half of the second floor was a large common space with a Ping-Pong table, an air hockey machine, and four battered beanbags. Two weeks before she met Agatha Paul, Millie entered this room with a duffel bag, a rolling carry-on, a backpack, and a hat. It was August nineteenth, staff move-in day, and three of the four beanbags were already in use.

"Oh, hi," she said. "Am I late?"

"No, you're good. Millie, right?"

"Yeah, hi."

"Joanie," the girl said, a hand to her chest.

"Cool, yeah. Nice to meet you."

That morning, after two and a half days of RA orientation (eighty students, policy trivia games, campus scavenger hunts, and reminders to drink water), Millie received her dorm assignment letter. The letter told her something she already knew—Belgrade—and it listed three other names that she didn't know at all. Millie set her things next to a few other suitcases. She sat down with her back against the last beanbag. It felt like the moment was naturally bending toward the other two staff members introducing themselves, but Ryland—Millie guessed his name

35

from the staff list—placed the bottoms of his feet together. With his elbows he gently pressed down on his knees. The other RA reached to plug a charger into an outlet. Lying on her left side, she connected her phone and began to scroll. Millie crisscrossed her legs beneath her and held on to each of her ankles. From the dorm assignment letter, she knew this person must be Colette.

Joanie bent forward. "Aimee said you lived here before?"

Millie said, "Yeah, I have."

"How was it?"

"It's . . . about what you'd expect."

"Ha," Joanie said. "Right on. I like the honesty."

Millie smiled. A brutal silence settled in. Colette stayed on her phone. Ryland stretched his triceps. "Yeah," Millie said, "it's not that bad," immediately wishing that she hadn't.

"Hey, guys!" Josh's voice came with a mechanical squeal of the metal door. He approached the beanbag circle and knelt, placing folders, keys, and documents on the floor. "Thanks for being so on time. I have snacks for us so hang tight, but go ahead and take the folder with your name on it. I'll be right back and we'll get started."

Just as quickly as he'd arrived, he was gone. Millie exhaled and thought, Ohmygod.

Ryland was seemingly having the same thought. He turned to Colette, placed a hand to his chest, and coughed. "Okay, he did not look like that last year."

"Right?" Joanie said. "He really bulked up. I see him in the weight room all the time. Ryland, if you're looking to put on some—"

"No." Colette stopped her. She took up the folder with her name on it. "No, he's good, but thanks anyway," she said.

Millie reached for her folder and opened it. The first document was labeled *Residence Life: Policies and Procedures.* There were phone numbers and an academic calendar. On top was the floor breakdown. It read *Third Floor: Joanie Madsen and Ryland Pentecost. Fourth Floor: Millie Cousins and Colette Whistler.*

"Alright!" Josh was back. In his arms were pretzels, veggie sticks, and a mason jar filled with M&M's. "So we're gonna do a little icebreaker. Take a few, but don't eat any. Hey, Millie! Welcome back."

Josh bent into a squat and handed her the jar. Millie accepted it and said, "Hi, thanks." Once again she thought, Oh my God.

Millie had known Josh, barely, as the thin and smiley graduate student in the Residence Life office who collected and reconciled program receipts. She recalled an email from him that she'd ignored, a mass e-vite to watch a cultish horror movie, something like *Gremlins* or *Pet Sematary II.* Millie ignored invites all the time, but she'd felt slightly guilty for not attending. Not just because Josh was so friendly, but because he was the only other Black person on staff aside from her, her friend Dani, Victoria the security guard, and a receptionist who'd been there sixteen years. Millie partially chided herself for finding him so attractive, as if, from her, it was doubly expected, but she was still a young woman with a body and eyes, coming off a year of living with her parents.

Josh had a dark brown complexion, large and friendly teeth, tortoiseshell glasses with boxy frames, and thick black hair in a short-all-over cut. His chest had grown at least half an inch; his thighs seemed bigger, too. His arms made him look like the ideal person to find and ask to open a jar of anything. Josh—and this had been true since Millie first met him—had the spirit and attire of someone meeting their girlfriend's parents for the first time. Stiff khakis, staff polo, firm handshake, nice smile. If Millie had had friends to discuss this with, she'd say that yes, he'd gotten hotter, but it had less to do with the muscles and more to do with the new glasses.

Josh grabbed a chair from against the wall and sat on it, backward, in between Millie and Ryland. "So hey! Welcome to Belgrade. Sorry to not be at orientation but I'm happy to be here now. Most of you know me as the accounts payable guy, but I'm really excited to be a resident director this year. I'm really looking forward to learning a thing or two from you all and hopefully vice versa. So let's do it. Does everyone have a few M&M's?"

Millie opened her hand to reveal her picks. Joanie shuffled hers like dice.

"Okay, great. So just in case you guys don't know each other yet . . . however many M&M's you took? That's how many things you'll say about yourself."

Joanie smiled and rolled her shoulders back. She did a humiliating "Oohh man."

"And since I'm making you play"—Josh held up a yellow chocolate—"I'll break the ice and go first. I'm Josh Wyeth. I'm from Oxford, Mississippi. I have two sisters, both older. I'm very into films. Recent favorite is *The Revenant*. Definitely watch it if you haven't. Aaanndd this summer I started making my own trail mix. I had no idea you were supposed to put it in the oven? Complete game changer. Okay. That's me. Who is next?"

Joanie raised her hand with an athletic zeal, and Josh gave her the floor.

"Hey, guys. I'm Joanie"—she waved a flat hand—"and let's see . . . I'm a senior. The rec center is usually where I'm at. Started weight lifting about two years ago? And I feel like I'm a pretty decent teacher, just in case anyone wants to learn some new techniques. Other than that . . . I'm in the Sustainability Club. Love finding new ways to keep things green. Umm, I'm half Irish and half Danish. Maybe that's obvious but still pretty cool. But yeah, I'm from Jonesboro. Majoring in food science. I was in Hawthorne last year so I'm definitely excited to be with upper-classmen. And my big goal this year is to do a seven-minute mile. So yeah. Wish me luck."

Joanie had a long, neat blondish-brown ponytail held back by a cotton headband, the kind from Walgreens that comes in sets of three. She had a big round face, athletic legs, and porcelain skin that was very smooth and probably burned fast. Just before she ate them, Millie peeked at the number of M&M's balanced on Joanie's knee. Despite learning so much about her, there had only been four. Millie felt bummed out by Joanie's personality and justified in her initial aversion. She experienced a sharp fear of running into her at the gym. Joanie saying something like Oh hey! Good for you!

Josh tapped his thighs and said, "Awesome, thanks, Joanie. Colette, you wanna take it away?"

Next to Joanie, the dark-haired young woman reached for the two chocolates on her leg. "Hey," she said. "I'm Colette and I'm a senior."

Joanie did a little laugh and looked at Millie. Millie refused to return her stare. Ryland cupped his hands around his mouth. He blurred his voice as he said, "Booo."

"How about one more?" Josh said. "Your name doesn't count, let's do one more."

"Okay," she said. "Ummm, my blood type is O negative. Universal donor, which is cool. But I'm also Rh negative, which means if I get pregnant, I'll have to get a special shot so my immune system won't attack my baby."

Josh gripped the back of his chair. "Okay, great!" he said. "Very very cool."

Colette sat on the floor in a sporty, summer-camp, after-school activities position: ankles crossed in front, arms circling her knees. She had fine brown hair that ended at her shoulder blades, and she had the slim frame of someone who did a New England activity, like equestrianism or crew. She had brown eyes, freckles on her nose and cheeks. She was wearing a white T-shirt, athletic shorts, checkered slip-on Vans with white tube socks. After delivering three facts about herself, Colette stretched her legs and leaned back on her elbows, another position that looked relaxed and cool, like a leather jacket or a lit cigarette. Millie was all at once highly anxious and intrigued. Colette, her lean, and her refusal to play the game sat at the axis of glamorous and rude.

Ryland raised a hand. "Is it my turn?"

"Absolutely, go for it," Josh said.

Ryland sat up and Millie heard the swish of about thirty M&M's. They rustled together in the hammock he'd created in the bottom of his tank top. Josh must have heard the noise, too. He lifted his head and said, "Oh wow, look at that."

"So I'm Ryland. I'm a junior. I'm from Lake Charles, Louisiana. I'm an art education major. I love the Sacramento Kings. I'm on Accutane right now so, you know, be nice to me. When I was born my mom wasn't conscious—she's fine now—but she obviously couldn't pick a name. So my birth certificate and my social security card both said Baby Boy Pentecost."

Ryland still looked like a baby boy. His face was youthful and blushed and his forehead was dotted with a few pimples at various stages. His blond hair looked destined for an elementary picture day, and his knees, crossed beneath excellent posture, looked too big for his legs. What stood out more than Ryland's energy and diction—there was always at least one RA who could project—was the fact that Ryland had Colette's complete attention. Hands under her chin, Colette looked his way. She nodded at every new fun fact.

"I own the complete box set of *Dr. Quinn, Medicine Woman*," he said. "My mom's first name is Trish. This summer I made Rice Krispies treats and you know what? They were just okay."

"That's cool," Colette said. "It was your first time."

"You're right. I'm so hard on myself. Anyway, my moon is in Aquarius . . ."

Joanie said, "Alright . . ."

"My mom? When I was little, she used to do this thing at the movie theater where she would ask for an extra cup for water, but then she would fill it with butter from that li'l pump thing instead. And then when we got to the middle of the popcorn bag, we'd pour it in, and it was like a li'l butter refresher midway through. And now I'm like, wow, that is so disgusting. But honestly, at the time it was so good. I don't think they even do the pump anymore. But anyway . . . I'm five foot four. I only like mac and cheese if it's baked with government cheese. My favorite color is probably clear. I also like it when—"

"So how about . . ." Josh cut in. "How about one more and then we're all set?"

"One more? Okay." Ryland took a deep breath. "If I were going to be murdered in any state, it would be . . . this is so hard." He tapped his finger to his lips. "Okay. New Mexi— No. No . . . I take it back. Okay. Final answer . . . Michigan."

Josh blinked three specific times. Then he clapped with "Okay, great!" Ryland pulled out a plastic Ziploc from his shorts pocket. He began transferring the candy into the bag.

"Millie?" Josh said. "Wanna finish us off?"

In an attempt to sit up, Millie sank deeper into the beanbag. She tried again, using her arms, all the while thinking, Wow, I wanna die. "Okay, yeah, hi. I'm Millie Cousins," she said. "I'm from Joplin, MO. I worked as a barista all summer. I . . . can cook an egg ten different ways. I'm a hospitality management major with a Spanish minor. And this year, I'm a senior . . . again." She sighed.

And then a few memorable things occurred, at least for Millie. Joanie gave a big unwarranted "Ha!" which made Millie cringe. Josh said, "We're glad to have you all the same," sending her heart into a spiral. And then Colette nodded twice. "Yes," she said. "Take that victory lap." Millie found herself flushed with relief. Okay, she thought. Okay, that's good.

"Wait, Millie?" Ryland leaned forward. "Are you . . . okay, you're not related to . . ."

Colette looked at him. "Don't ask her that."

"Shh, lemme talk. Do you know Boogie Cousins? Is he maybe . . . your cousin?" Ryland asked.

"No, sorry," Millie said. "Well, technically." She smiled. "All Cousins are Cousins, so."

Ryland stared at her. "What?"

Mortified, she said, "Hmm?"

"Drinks!" Josh said. "I'm forgetting everything today. I have waters and lemonade. I'll be right back." Josh jogged out the door and into the stairwell. Once again, silence settled in.

Ryland went to work, placing pretzels and veggie sticks into his Ziploc. Colette watched him. "So this is just who you are now?" she asked.

"Girl, I told you," Ryland said. "I'm not paying for shit this year."

Colette slumped and slid back onto the floor. She reached and detached her phone from the charger on the wall.

"Hey, Colette? Are you done using that?" Joanie pointed to the outlet.

Colette looked at her as if she were lost.

"So this is crazy," Joanie said, "but chargers actually still use a bit of electricity even when your phone isn't plugged in. So when you're done, it's a good idea to just pop them right on out."

There was a chemical shift in Colette's gaze, something turning both off and on. She took Joanie in and sighed deeply and looked down at her phone. "Joanie . . ." she said. "Is electricity your dad? No? Oh, okay. Then maybe chill the fuck out."

Joanie's eyebrows went up into her head. "Geez," she said. "Just trying to help."

One last time, Joanie looked at Millie for affirmation. But Millie turned her face to her lap. She reached down to her sandal and tightened the velcro strap.

———

MILLIE AND COLETTE took the elevator to the fourth floor. By noon the next day, the hallways would be chaos and clutter, filled with the belongings of sixty young women. The floor beneath them would be the same, with the exception of guys on Ryland's side. But for now, everything was hollow in a way that felt fun and scary. At each end of the hall there were two rooms that were slightly larger than the others. Stepping out of the elevator, Millie asked, "Do you care which one you take?"

Colette said that she didn't.

Millie picked the room facing the east, hoping for more sun for her plants. She made her bed and then she unpacked her RA supplies: bulletin decorations, door decs, info cards, and lots of Sharpies. She brought them into the study lounge, where Colette was already seated. Colette's phone was in her hand. Her shoes on the window ledge.

"So I'm flexible with a theme for this month." Millie was standing as she spoke. "I did a pool party theme and I did like, a cactus/succulent one, too . . ." She opened a folder to the work she'd done: palm trees, sunglasses, and pink inner tubes. In another paper clip were hand-drawn saguaros and succulents in little brown pots. "But if you wanna do August," Millie said, "we can totally use yours." Colette eyed her things, touched one with her hand. Then she sat back and did a slow nod.

"K, so I actually didn't make any of these?" she said. "So let's use yours for August and September. I'll just do October, if that's cool."

Millie nodded. She wondered what Colette had been doing during the three-hour decoration session the day prior. "Okay," she said. "Are you sure?"

"Yeah, I'm sure. And I don't mean this in a bad way, but I can tell that you're way more into this than I am. So just tell me what you want and I'll just do it. I'm good at math. I have nice handwriting. I'm a good sous chef so just like, put me to work."

Millie scratched the space beneath her shoulder blade. "Okay. Well, if I get too bossy, just let me know."

"You won't. It's cool. Should I put names on these?"

"Yeah, sure."

Millie pulled out a chair. She began cutting out little cards that would go on the desk of each resident: green slips of paper with the RA on duty phone number, a crisis hotline, the dorm address, and so on. Colette got to work on the residents' door decs. Millie wished she'd observed Colette's handwriting before she'd given up this task. But when she looked up she was promptly relieved. Colette had written the name *Morgan* on a pink inner tube, and her handwriting really was quite nice. It was as if she were good at doing an accent; the letters' curves were feminine and round.

Millie crossed her ankles. "So where were you last year?"

"South Gate. It was such ass. We hated it."

"You and Ryland?"

"Yeah. I'm hoping this will be a lot more chill."

"It will be. Students here already have friends. Or they're on that housing scholarship. Or they're in a sorority, which sounds annoying but it's not because they're always out."

Colette placed sunglasses reading *Kira* to the side, holding the edges so the ink wouldn't smudge. "I don't mind that. I'll be good as long as there's no freshmen. And if I don't have to communicate with Joanie."

Millie laughed through her nose. "Was Joanie in South Gate with you?"

"No, she wasn't. Thank God," Colette said. "But we both worked at Clubhaus Fitness last summer. And she was annoying for obvious reasons. But then, okay, so when the minimum wage changed from eight to eight-fifty? I made this presentation on how I should be getting nine-fifty because I was killing it over there. I got like, four old people to start taking Pilates. Probably added years to their lives. And they loved me. But whatever. Anyway, the management ate it up. They were all like, 'Ooo PowerPoint, look at this *initiative*.' And they gave me nine-sixteen an hour, which was dumb but I was like, 'Fine.' But then Joanie was like, 'How is that fair? I've worked here longer than you, blah blah blah.' And I was like, 'K, you've worked here for like, four months longer, but if you want a raise, then go ask, loser.'

And she was like, 'That's not the point. That's disrespectful . . .'" At this, Colette looked up. With a Sharpie in hand, she did that quick, listless motion for someone jerking off. "And she was just a huge dick to me all summer. She'd be like, 'Hey, Colette? The spa water needs ice.' Like, ooh, cool. Thanks for telling me."

Millie smiled. "That's really dumb," she said.

"I know. She's such a pill. She also got pissed because this one time—I don't even remember what I said—but I had always assumed she was gay because . . ." Colette lifted her shoulders. "Like, fucking duh. And I said something about it and she was like, 'What? Why would you say that?' And I was like, 'Whoa, my bad, but I'm gay so chill out.' But yeah. When I saw her name on the dorm list I was like, wow. I'm going to jail this year. But then I asked Aimee who I was paired with and I was like, okay fine. She seems normal."

At this, Millie experienced what she knew was a surplus of flattery, and what felt like an adolescent intrigue at learning that Colette was gay. In order to not draw attention to Colette's gayness—something she hadn't considered one way or the other—Millie picked up another sheet of cards.

"Do you still work at Clubhaus?"

"Barely. I do a shift on Sundays and I close. I have too many labs this year."

"What's your major?"

"Chemistry. What's yours?"

"Hospitality management."

"Oh right, you said that." Colette shook out her hand. "Can I ask an annoying follow-up question? Do you know what you're doing next year?"

Millie dipped her head side to side. "Kind of. I took a gap year before my freshman year and I worked as like, an innkeeper at this bed-and-breakfast. They told me they'd have me back as like, a weekend manager. But I'll probably apply to a few other event spaces, too."

"You lived in a hotel for a year?"

"Yeah. So I could get in-state tuition. And I worked at Onyx, too. But it's not like, a hotel hotel. It's just a really big house with lots of rooms."

Colette considered this. "Onyx is weird," she said.

"Yeah. But tips are good there."

"I can see that."

"Do you know what you're doing next year?"

Colette finished writing the name *Kennedy*. "No. And it's starting to stress me out. I want to get something with health care so I can emancipate myself from my parents. Which I can't do yet because they think I'm living in an apartment but I'm just taking their money."

Millie stopped cutting. "Wait, seriously?"

"Yeah. I told them I was renting a guesthouse from an old lady who only takes cash. And they think Arkansas is super hick so they were like, 'Oh yeah, that makes perfect sense. Here you go.'"

"That's amazing. Where are you from?"

"Atlanta, or, Peachtree. It's weird. But yeah, I'll probably do grad school later but I just want like, a couple years off and a really chill job. Nothing I care about. Just like, go to work, do the thing, come home, be a person."

"Yeah, I can see that." Millie knew, as the words were leaving her mouth, that the phrase "I can see that" was not something she typically said. Evidently, she'd liked the way it sounded moments ago, when it was coming from Colette.

Colette finished writing the name *Hayley* and brought her

knee up to her chest. "How was working at a bed-and-breakfast? Should I do something like that?"

"It's basically being an RA. They were really old-school and I had to like, write down credit card numbers all the time. But mostly it was just prepping rooms and ordering cars. Well, a weird amount of people got sick?" Millie raised her hand. "From long drives, I guess. I don't know. But I'd just like, sit with them and get them ginger ale or whatever. That was a weirdly big part of my job."

"That sounds awful."

"Nah, I kind of loved it."

"Hmm," Colette said. "So you're like, nice nice."

Millie completed her last card but kept the scissors in her hand. "Yeah," she said. "Yeah, kind of."

Colette raised her eyebrows in a way that was not unkind. "Okay. That's cool. Should I do these now? I can get some scissors."

Millie, feeling abruptly endeared, set her scissors on the table. "You can just take these," she said.

3.

ILLIE'S LANYARD SWUNG OUT AND BACK IN.
"Hi. I'm Millie," she said. "Welcome to Belgrade."
On the other side of a folding table was a student
with pockmarked cheeks and a mother with two oversized IKEA
bags. "Good morning!" the mother said. "Thank you so much."

Josh put his coffee down and placed his hands on his hips.
"Congrats on being the first ones here."

"Ohmygod," the student said. "I *told* you."

The mother looked at her and said, "Beth Ann?"

Ryland rolled up with a move-in cart and said, "Y'all look
like you need a buggy."

The mother and daughter began to fill the cart with suitcases
and bags. Millie assembled the resident's welcome packet, the
dorm keys and fobs, a UA drawstring backpack. As she checked
the girl's name off a list, Josh caught her eye. Very cutely, he
mouthed, *Oops.*

Millie smiled. "Good job," she said.

Josh adjusted an invisible tie around his neck. "Alright, easy.
It's my first day."

Millie liked wearing matching polos with her team, watching parents hug their children goodbye, beg them to please eat

real food at some point. Her time as an RA had given her a mental game of bingo where she stamped off inflections and phrases she'd heard many times before. Parents asking siblings to get off their phones. Residents telling their moms that they could definitely go now. And some iteration of a sweating mother catching her breath. "Good *lord*, Maddie, how much stuff you got?"

As Millie helped move her residents in, she glanced at newly purchased journals and planners, knowing most of them would become warped and unused. Many of her residents would develop horrific dust bunnies behind their doors, and girls who Millie had assumed were smart would do very dumb things like own a miniature turtle, or flush tea bags down the toilet. But Millie let herself give in to the promise of Residence Life Move-In Day, the potential of the new year. There were residents to meet and greet. There were twin XL beds to be made. Even when she was dusting off her shorts, or clicking a closet door back on its hinges, Millie kept catching herself alight on the same dreamy phrase: This is my last first day.

Ryland and Colette did not feel the same. Around noon, they were starting to break.

"I *hate* move-in day," Ryland said, repeatedly stabbing the elevator button.

"I know," Colette said into her phone. "It looks like a fucking war hospital in here."

Millie tried to participate. "Yeah. I'm sweating pretty bad."

"Oh. Hi there." A voice came up from behind. "Is one of y'all my RA?"

Millie turned to see a resident in a tank top and shorts. Ryland and Colette said nothing. Millie said, "Yes, hi."

"Can I talk to you in private?" she asked. "Sorry . . . that sounds so serious."

"Oh, for sure," Millie said. "What's your name?"

"I'm Tyler. I'm in one of the suites."

BELGRADE WAS A giant rectangle. The two elevators opened up in the middle of the third and fourth floors, which were identically laid out. Each floor had a singular hallway that wrapped the perimeter, displaying doors to single rooms. At one end of the floor was a communal kitchen. The other end held bathrooms and a laundry room, four coin-operated machines inside. And at the four corners of the floors were apartment-style lodgings that were referred to as the *suites*.

Residents who applied close to or after the deadline ended up with the contentious suites: a larger setup meant for three residents that came with a bathroom, a tiny kitchen, and a "dining room" to be shared. Every year, upon arrival, the suite-assigned residents would enter their new home, prepared to share a room with two others. But to their surprise they'd find not one but two bedrooms. "Oh wait. There's a single in here," they'd say. "Well . . . hmm. That's good, at least."

But then there came the question of which two residents would live together in the larger room, and which lucky resident would receive the luxury of a single. Typically, the first to arrive would place their belongings in the single, and the first-come, first-served-ness was difficult to argue with. But Millie had seen residents make a deal to switch rooms at the end of the semester, and then, in January, one of them would refuse. Millie had even seen one group of suitemates grow to despise each other so much that one moved all her belongings into the dining room and kitchen. When Millie had entered their space, the door stopped short on a dresser. "Christina . . ." she sighed. "Do I even need to tell you that this is a fire hazard?" The resident, cozied up for bed next to the refrigerator, had replied, "Do I need to tell you that I don't care?" It was in Millie's best interest to make all the suites harmonious, for the sake of her residents but also herself. Millie's junior year at Belgrade had been shaped by the sound of the suitemates on the other side of her wall. Playing Ariana Grande on loop. Performing a soft, nasal snore. This year, Tyler's suite shared a wall with Millie's room.

Clipboard in hand, Millie walked to the suite door. She raised and tapped her middle finger just beneath the peephole. On the door, paper flip-flops read *Peyton*, an inner tube said *Tyler*, and across a palm tree was *Kennedy*.

"Hey there, it's Millie. Mind if I come in?"

A pull from the other side met Millie's knock. A resident appeared and said, "Hi."

"Hey there. I'm one of your RAs. What's your name?"

The resident stepped back. "I'm Kennedy . . . but I'm not done yet or anything."

"No, that's perfect. That's why I'm here."

Kennedy was cute and nervous-looking. Her hair was platinum blondish gray. She had large eyes that were a Nordic blue beneath multiple layers of mascara. Her entire vibe was all a bit overkill for move-in day. Yellow polo dress, French tips, loose sausage curls. But Millie wasn't worried. Kennedy would learn. By fall, she'd be a bit more natural, opening the door in T-shirts and Birks.

Another voice said, "Oh, hi." Millie heard the cracking of someone hopping off a bed. Tyler made her way out of the double room and into the kitchen. "I'm Tyler," she said. "Nice to meet you."

This wasn't the first time Millie had conspired with a resident, made a plan to pretend they hadn't just discussed the issue at hand. Tyler was a pro, she didn't overdo it. At Millie's arrival, she looked almost bored. Tyler was about five feet tall with thick brown hair that was loosely braided down her shoulder. She wore a blue baseball cap, denim shorts, and a white tank that said *Fayettechill*. She had relatively thick calves that looked firm but not athletic, and she had some sunspots on her shoulders and chest. Tyler wasn't gorgeous, but she had something else. A social ease. One layer of brown mascara. A thin rose gold bracelet wrapped around her wrist.

"Cool, nice to meet you, too," Millie said. "And we're missing Peyton?"

A deep voice said, "I'm here."

Peyton emerged from the single bedroom. She was wearing a sweatshirt with *Seminoles* on the front; it looked old and worn and loved. On bottom were black athletic shorts that were a strange length; not long and sporty but also not cute and short. Peyton was boxy, a fact not helped by what looked to be an ill-fitting bra beneath her sweatshirt. Her dark brown hair was in a ponytail. It lay on her hood like a paintbrush that needed to be soaked. Peyton had wide-set eyes and a small gap in her teeth. Her complexion was almost exactly that of Millie's.

Millie had two distinct thoughts. The first was, How are you not hot in a sweatshirt? The second was, Wait a second, this is Peyton? Millie was in no position to hold it against her, but Peyton was a very white name.

Not five minutes prior, Millie and Tyler had whispered and schemed in the fourth-floor kitchen. "So right now," Tyler had explained, "Peyton is in the single and Kennedy and I are in the double. And listen, I'm fine in the double, but Kennedy just has too much stuff."

Millie had folded her arms in thought. "The only problem is that your other roommate—Peyton? Yeah, if she got the single fair and square, it's not right to have her move."

"No no no. I've already talked to Peyton. And she was expecting a roommate, too. But . . . sorry, this is so awkward. We just don't want to hurt Kennedy's feelings, and I was hoping you could help."

Millie had said of course. They made a plan to pretend they hadn't spoken. Millie would arrive and take it from there. But now, standing in front of Peyton, Millie blinked and sidestepped.

"Hi," Peyton said. "Should I get my student ID?"

"What's that? Oh. No no, you're good. I'm just here because we're actually in charge of who lives where in the suites."

Millie looked at Peyton for a sign. Anything to confirm that she was cool with the situation. But Peyton stared at her with a gaze so flat and breathless that Millie was almost offended. "So yeah," Millie said. "Do you guys mind if I look around?"

Tyler stepped aside. "Not at all, go for it."

Millie lightly pushed the door to the double room, but it caught and dragged something behind it. She said, "Oops," and inched herself in the rest of the way. Upon entering, she thought, Oh man.

Millie knew it was Kennedy's side of the room, not just because Tyler had warned her, but because of two large pillows, monogrammed with letter Ks. Kennedy's space was an overwhelming embankment of recently purchased items in neutral yet feminine shades. A faux sheepskin rug. White wicker baskets. A stack of velvet hangers. Throw blankets wrapped with matching ties. There were four boxes of string lights, an unopened box holding a "mini chandelier." There were lawless piles of leggings, jeans, and sweatshirts. Wide-neck tops meant to function off the shoulder. In the middle of the room was a wooden kitchen cart filled with coffee paraphernalia. A boxed Keurig. A bowl of the Nestlé half-and-halfs. A mini trash can. A placard said *Rise and Grind*. The mess of newness went past Kennedy's bed and spilled onto the dorm-provided desk. A porcelain unicorn for hanging jewelry. A DVD box set of *Friends*. Corkboard. Shower caddy. An empty picture frame. There were also a ton of statement necklaces and canvas art to be hung. The one Millie could see had petals and flowers. Beneath marigolds, it said *Bloom Where You Are Planted*.

"So my mom is out getting lunch?" Kennedy said. "But she's really good at organizing. We just dumped everything to start."

"No, I get it," Millie said. "Don't worry. Everyone's room looks like this right now."

No one's room looked like this, nor had they in Millie's time as an RA. The way everything was piled was somehow violent, and Millie almost expected to see streaks of blood. Back at the door, Tyler leaned against the wall. She looked at Millie and her face said, *I told you.*

On the other side of the room were Tyler's things. Above her bed was a canvas-colored tapestry that read in black letters *Wild and Free*. In the closet Millie spied two Patagonia jackets, one olive and one gray. An over-the-door compartment hung on her opened closet door. Flat iron, sandals, travel-sized bottles of dry shampoo. On her desk sat a white-noise machine. A dream catcher waiting to be hung. A few books were on the desk. *Bossypants. Me Before You.* Virginia Woolf's *A Room of One's*

Own. There were two bookends that hadn't been set up yet. One read *Be Still* and the other said *And Know.* On the bed was a comforter that looked plump but not new, the refreshing blue of an Easter egg. Near Tyler's side of the window were two milk crates; the first was full of food. Snyder's pretzels. Amy's organic soup. Red Vines and Kind bars. The other milk crate held miscellaneous items: a Polaroid camera, neoprene weights, a baseball glove. There was a picture frame holding a photo of Tyler next to a yellow Lab. It sat next to a white mug that said *Nap Queen* on the side.

"Okay, cool." Millie smiled. "Peyton, can we take a peek in the single?"

The group migrated to the other room. In the single, a Glade plug-in had been administered, extending a scent of Hawaiian Breeze. The bed was made in a purple-and-green duvet, two colors that Millie would have never put together. Peyton's closet held seven more sweatshirts, two phantom fists in the long pocket of each. Beneath her sweatshirts was a plastic shelving unit with labeled drawers: *Toiletries, Medication,* and *Cleaning Supplies.* Lined up on the hutch like Russian dolls were colorful Tums, a bottle of vitamin B_{12}, and a jar of quarters labeled *LAUNDRY.* There was a lined Post-it that read *Before I Go,* and beneath was written *keys, wallet, phone, epi-pen.* There was also a framed photo of what looked to be Peyton and her parents. They were standing in snowsuits in front of a glacier. Peyton's mother had silk press hair in a bob. Her dad was bald and smiley. Peyton was standing with her hands in her pockets. A closed-mouth, yearbook smile.

And because she had so few items in comparison to Tyler and Kennedy, what truly took center stage was an industrial-sized jar of Lubriderm Daily Moisture Lotion. It was on the window ledge and the way it sat in the sunlight made it appear like a freshly landed spacecraft. Millie smiled. Had she been alone, she would have taken a picture. The tub of Lubriderm seemed like something Colette would enjoy, and they now had each other's numbers.

"Okay." Millie smiled. "Do you guys wanna have a seat in the kitchen real quick?"

The suitemates walked over to the table and sat down. There was Tyler with her side braid and milk crates of toys, her chic collegiate indifference. There was Kennedy with her blue eyes and her *stuff*, all of which appeared chemically treated. And then there was the overly clothed and parented Peyton—potentially the only other Black student in Belgrade. At the table, Peyton sat like she was in a baseball dugout, patiently waiting for her turn. Millie wished she could pull her aside, so quickly, and just make sure this was what she wanted, too. But if Millie was going to do this, she needed to move before parents returned. She decided to trust her gut, which meant trusting Tyler, and get Kennedy and her stuff safely inside the single.

"Okay, so unfortunately, Kennedy, it looks like the amount of stuff you have might be a fire hazard, so obviously we can't have that."

"Oh," Kennedy said. "I didn't know . . . I can just call my mom—"

"No, let's talk first," Millie said. "It's great to get some of these roommate things settled anyways. So let's start here . . . what always helps with the suites is making a list of priorities. It's just like with class schedules or anything else; you can't always get everything you want, but we'll try to get everyone the most important thing. So, I want y'all to think of the most important thing you need to have a good living situation. Can you do that?"

Tyler, Peyton, and Kennedy stared back blankly.

"I can go as an example," Millie said. "Mine would be my plants. I need space for my plants, my plants need light, it's super important to me . . ." Millie laughed as if this were a dorky hobby; she knew that it wasn't. "So if I was in a suite, plants would be on top of my list. Tyler, do you wanna try? What's super important to you?"

"Ummm . . ." Tyler partially closed one eye. "Well, the most important thing to me are my dogs but they aren't here . . . so other than that? I would say sleeping."

"Perfect." On her clipboard Millie wrote down Tyler's name and *sleeping*. "So you need a good night's sleep every night?"

"Yeah. And I'm a big napper, too. And I've had lots of room-mates before so it doesn't need to be silent or anything."

"Awesome. Peyton, how about you?"

Peyton sat up. "So I'm Peyton, I'm a junior. And my biggest priority is cooking."

"Oh, awesome." Millie looked at Kennedy. "You guys may have lucked out—"

"I also like," Peyton cut in, "to have a sanitary kitchen, and to have everything put away for the next day."

"Uh-oh . . ." Tyler smiled. "You need it super clean?"

Peyton nodded.

Tyler held up her hands. "No, I'll be good, I swear! Don't worry. I only have like . . . baby carrots and string cheese."

Millie thought, Of course you do. She wrote down *Peyton, cooking*. "Awesome. Kennedy? What about you?"

"Ummm . . . sorry." Kennedy peeked inside the double room. "I'm just thinking about it, and I think that I can put a lot of stuff under my bed."

"No no, it's still good for you guys to talk about this."

"Okay . . ." She played with a key chain in her hands. "Sorry," she said. "That's so hard."

Millie looked back to the double room. "You've got like, a nice color palette going on in there. Are aesthetics important to you?"

"I'm not really sure . . ."

Peyton bent slightly, her elbow on her knee. "Well," she said. "You must *really* like coffee."

Tyler smiled from one side of her face. Then she hid it with a closed fist.

"Kennedy, what do you think?" Millie asked. "Is coffee important? Do you make it every day?"

"Yeah, I do."

"Okay, great. So maybe coffee and aesthetics . . ."

"Well, I also write, so . . ."

Millie's pen hung in the air. "Oh cool. Are you an English major?"

"Well, kind of. But technically yes."

"Okay. Do you need it to be quiet when you write?"

"Oh, no. I can write anywhere."

"Okay, well that's good."

Millie looked at her clipboard and thought, Girl, you are killing me here. The thought of Peyton's mother walking in— that silk press, the deep side part and bang—it shocked her back into motion. "So I'll put coffee and writing down for now, but being flexible is great. And lastly, will you guys tell me what time your first classes are?"

"Can I go get mine?" Peyton asked.

"What's that?"

"I have my schedule written down. Can I go get it?"

"Oh sure. Tyler, let's start with you."

"So Monday-Wednesday I have a nine thirty," Tyler said. "And Tuesday-Thursday I have a ten a.m."

"Great. Kennedy?"

"I have class at eight on Monday, Wednesday, Friday. And not till two on Tuesday and Thursday."

"Ohmygod," Tyler said. "Eight a.m. I'd die."

Peyton reappeared and handed Millie a small laminated card. At the top was *Peyton Nicole Shephard*, and below that was *University of Arkansas*. Then it read *Emergency Contacts. Mother: Jerilyn Shephard. Father: Wallace Shephard.* Both of Peyton's parents had cell and work numbers. Also listed were Peyton's allergies: penicillin, shellfish, and bees. Wow, Millie thought. Your parents' names are Jerilyn and Wallace, and they laminated this card for you. Millie forced herself to focus on the times of Peyton's earliest classes. She handed the card back, and as she did, she caught text in bold. At the bottom it said *EpiPen located in yellow case.*

Peyton returned to the kitchen table and took a seat. "So," Millie said. She took a deep breath. "Here is my diagnosis. I feel like it makes more sense for Peyton and Tyler to take the double and for Kennedy to take the single. That way, a few things happen. Kennedy doesn't have to get rid of anything. Her alarm won't wake anyone up. Tyler can take the bed farthest from the hall so she can enjoy her naps. And Kennedy, what do you think about keeping your coffee cart in your room so Peyton has more space in the kitchen? Is that fair?"

"Oh. Yeah, sure," Kennedy said. "I'm . . . yeah, that's fine."

She didn't seem upset. She didn't seem fine either. But more importantly, Millie just wanted to confirm . . .

"Okay, great. But Peyton?" Millie said. "I don't want to take the single away from you if you were really stoked to have it."

"That's okay," Peyton said. "I don't mind."

"Okay. Are you sure?"

Peyton sat back in her chair. She gently flapped her knees in and out. "Yeah," she said. "I already said to Tyler that I thought I'd have a roommate anyway because—"

"So you're fine with it," Millie cut her off. "Okay, cool. Just making sure."

"Yeah, that's fine."

Tyler's eyes went down with relief.

"And . . ." Peyton smiled. She put her hands together at her chest. "Now . . ." she said. "The kitchen is *mine*. Muahahaha!"

The silence that followed Peyton's joke, Millie could feel it behind her eyes.

Amazingly, Tyler came to Peyton's rescue. She exhaled with "Girl, you are crazy," and stretched her arms above her head.

"And we're gonna . . ." Millie tried, "just to be clear, the kitchen is for everyone."

"I know," Peyton said. "I was just kidding around."

Millie texted Ryland—she had his number now, too—and he came to help with the switch. In the double room, Millie did her best to tuck the sheets as Peyton's mother had before. It was common knowledge that when purchasing a duvet cover, you should get a full, not a twin. But Peyton's purple-and-lime-green comforter was perfectly twin XL and therefore, it was too small. Millie pulled it farther down on the exposed side; tried to make it look like everyone else's.

Before she left the suite, Millie peeked into the single room. "Kennedy? You all good?"

Within the confines of the single, Kennedy's belongings

appeared to have doubled in size. She, herself, looked a little smaller. "No, yeah," she said. "I'm all good."

Millie said, "Great," and left the room.

AN HOUR LATER, with nearly all her residents moved in, Millie sat on the toilet and scrolled on her phone. She flushed and washed her hands, and as she dried them under a hot blast, Tyler appeared in the open door.

"Hi. Oh wait. This is actually perfect," Tyler said. She came in and leaned her hip against the sink. "So I just wanted to say . . . the biggest thank-you." Through the open bathroom door, a resident passed by. "Don't worry. She's gone," Tyler said. "She went somewhere with her mom."

Millie lightly shook her head. "No, yeah. I'm glad everything worked out."

"I really appreciate it. I'm very into what an environment feels like and I just think it will be way better this way."

Millie nodded. "That's great. Me too."

Then Tyler glanced down into the sink. "Am I insane?" she asked. "Or was that a gnarly amount of stuff?"

Millie lightly arched her back. "You know what? It happens every year."

"Really? I imagine it happens with freshmen. But yeah. Anyway." Tyler dug into her back pocket. "My mom said to give you this. She was like, 'Don't ask her for nothin' else this year!'" With a two-finger hold, she extended a twenty-dollar bill. It had been folded into an origami square.

"Oh, no," Millie said. "I'm happy to help. It's my job."

"No, it's not even mine. My mom was so relieved. She'll just pay me back."

"That's . . . you know what?" Millie lowered her voice. "I'm not even sure that's super allowed, so it's fine."

"Oh, I won't say anything. And you deserve it. You should have some fun."

"Thank you, but—"

"Whoops!" Tyler slipped the bill into Millie's front pocket. Then she left the bathroom with a closemouthed smile, as if they'd just shared a secret or a cigarette.

Millie went back to her room, where she reapplied deodorant. Standing in the mirror, she reached for the bill. The corners and folds were tucked so neatly that Millie didn't want to unwrap it. She opened her closet door and dropped the money inside her boot. Then she bent and felt around. She took out a nonfolded twenty, placed it in her pocket, and considered what she should get.

She looked once more in the mirror, and then she grabbed her keys. When she opened her door, Aimee was on the other side.

"Oh!" Millie laughed. "I was just coming back."

Aimee laughed with her. "I'm just dropping by. You have a second?"

"Yeah, of course."

Aimee held up two fingers. "Two things. And one is not for me. Can you email"—she dug in her pocket—"Agatha Paul? She's a professor and wants to interview some students about weddings. You can just put a sign-up on your bulletin board. Does that make sense? She'll give you twenty bucks."

Millie looked down at the Post-it Aimee was extending. Another twenty dollars. "Oh sure. I can do that."

"Okay, great. And there's one more thing . . ." Aimee studied Millie's face. "Let's you and me . . . take a little ride."

4.

ENNEDY TEXTED HER MOM TO WAIT FOR HER in the car. She grabbed her brand-new lanyard and her dorm keys and took the elevator down. Nichelle texted back with question marks, that she'd picked up breakfast sandwiches; it was lunchtime but she thought it would be fun. But Kennedy had already made it to the sidewalk. She texted that she was almost there.

She got into the passenger seat of her mother's Nissan Rogue. Nichelle waited in the driver's seat with an expression that said, *Okay, now let's hear it.* Kennedy felt moved to put her seat belt on. But then she remembered that they weren't going anywhere, that Fayetteville was her new home. So she explained what had just transpired with the RA and the room switch. That all of her stuff was in the single now, and that, she supposed, that was where she'd be, too.

"Huh," Nichelle said. "Well, you guys were busy in there."

Kennedy couldn't help herself. She pinched her nose like she might sneeze. And then the rest of her face fell, too. She put a hand over her right eyebrow and started to cry in little bursts.

Nichelle hitched her knee up onto the console. "Kennedy. Sis, look at me. This is *good*. Do you know how special that is?

To have your own little sanctuary? You can come back after school and just breathe and relax and write . . ."

Kennedy used her pinky fingers to dab the insides of her eyes. "It just felt like— I don't know. It seemed like Tyler . . . not that she and Peyton are friends or anything . . . but I don't know. It was just really weird."

Nichelle moved her sunglasses to the top of her head. She had a short, light brown, asymmetrical cut, and with her sunglasses pushed back, the front fanned out like feathers. "Kennedy. Look at me. Remember what we talked about? You're doin' it right now, sister. But guess what? Everything that happens is not related to what happened before. This is just plain ol' life stuff. That's it."

Kennedy flipped the mirror flap down. She tapped the space around her eyes. "I know."

"You gotta start thinking it's okay if *good* things happen to you, too. And this? This is a very good thing. Ohmygoodness"— Nichelle gasped—"Remember that adorable sign we saw? Well, guess what? Now we can get it, 'cause you got your own space and you can do whatever you want. Should we go over there now? Actually, you know what . . . here. Eat this right quick. I'm gonna call and see if they can hold it for us. Okay? Sis, look at me. You're gonna be fine."

Kennedy took the foil package in her hands. Her mother turned the key and pumped the AC. Kennedy soon felt childish at how much better she felt with something in her stomach. Nichelle hung up the phone—they still had the cute sign—and she put her sunglasses back down over her eyes. "Ken, you know what?" she said. "You might just see Miss Agatha Paul walkin' around."

Kennedy rolled her eyes. "Mom, no. Probably not."

They went back to the little shop called Crimson and Clover.

They picked up the sign as well as faux eucalyptus garland and a cute little piggy bank that was actually a Razorback. The room switch had occurred because of the amount of stuff Kennedy brought, but the fact that she now had a single somehow legitimized acquiring more. Kennedy just let her mom do her thing. She trusted her and she didn't feel like making any decisions. And the door sign that they went back for was actually really cute. It was cream and mauve and it said *This Must Be the Place.*

Kennedy's mom had a lot of short adages and aphorisms. One of her favorites was: "Clean means everything has a home." After everything that had happened that morning, and everything that happened back in Iowa, Kennedy found comfort in watching her mother assign a home to all the new items in her room. Above her bed, Nichelle made a collage with the frames and artwork they'd collected that summer. She made a "little vanity set" by attaching a mirror behind her desk, securing tap lights to the underside of the hutch. After six children—Kennedy was the youngest—Nichelle never got overwhelmed looking at a giant mess. "It's just like the tangles in your hair," she said. "You start from the bottom and just work your way up."

By dinnertime, her bedroom was quite nice. The throw pillows, now staggered, behaved on her bed. The coffee cart was snug behind the door. Over the summer they'd purchased a poster-sized graphic that said *For Like Ever.* They paired it with a frame from a thrift store, and now it hung nicely above her desk. Something else Nichelle always said was how curtains do wonders. Kennedy's were bone-white with a beige pom-pom trim. Nichelle had gotten Dollar Tree brooms, removed the heads and handles, and spray-painted them gold in the backyard. She slid them through the curtains while Kennedy gave direction. Nichelle said they weren't perfect, but they "got the job done."

They went to a barbecue restaurant for dinner called Penguin Ed's with checkered tablecloths underneath panels of plexiglass. Each booth had a landline telephone attached to the wall. When you were ready to order, you picked up the phone, and someone answered it from the kitchen. "Ohmygoodness," Nichelle laughed. "Okay, well hello." She ordered pulled pork for herself and a chicken sandwich for Kennedy. Corn on the cob and baked beans to share. When the order was done she hung up the phone. "Come on," she said. "Now, how cute is that."

It was kind of cute, but Kennedy knew that the end of this dinner would be the part where she'd say goodbye. Then she'd officially be living in a new state, not knowing anyone aside from her roommates, two people who couldn't be more different, except they didn't want her in their room. When they finished eating, Nichelle and Kennedy walked through the parking lot, which was oddly pretty and private; an asphalt plane with thick trees on three sides. "Okay," Nichelle said. "I'm gonna hug you now, and when we go back you're gonna go up to your room like it's no big deal."

Kennedy did cry. Nichelle rocked her side to side. "You're not gonna want to come home. Just watch." At the dorm Kennedy pretended like she would see her mom tomorrow. She said, "Bye, I love you," and Nichelle said, "Okay, sis, see you soon."

Peyton was cooking when Kennedy walked into the suite, something that looked like ground beef, but it could have been something else. The bathroom door was closed and the light was on inside. Kennedy smiled at Peyton and put her leftovers into the fridge.

Tyler came out of the bathroom in a towel and wet hair. "Hey," she said. She pointed to the new sign on Kennedy's door. "That's so cute. I love that song."

Kennedy swallowed and told herself to be normal, but she didn't get what Tyler was saying. She had pointed at Kennedy's door. But she'd said, *I love that song*. But that couldn't have been what she said? She must have said, *I love that sign*.

"Oh, thanks," Kennedy said. "I just got it today."

Tyler lifted one of her feet off the floor. "Is . . . are you a Talking Heads fan?"

Kennedy giggled. "Talking who?"

Tyler let out a strange half smile. "No, never mind, sorry," she said. "I thought that you said something else." She walked to her room, leaving tiny dots of water in the place she'd been standing.

At eight p.m., Kennedy, Peyton, and Tyler went to the fourth-floor Belgrade Welcome Meeting. Sixty young women sat and stood in the hallway just outside the elevator doors. Millie led the meeting and talked about rules and quiet hours. She made everyone put the RA on-call cell number into their phones. Then she did an icebreaker. Everyone had to say their name, where they grew up, and their favorite breakfast food. Kennedy thought there would be more people like her, transfer students who didn't know anyone, but she was dismayed to see how many people said, "I'm from NWA," or, "I'm from here." A few of them said, "I was here last year." More than half the residents were from Arkansas or Texas. When it was Peyton's turn, she cleared her throat and said, "I'm Peyton. I'm from Florida. And I like quiche."

Tyler sat next to two other girls, who Kennedy learned were named Jenna and Casey. Jenna said it was boring but she loved

Cheerios, and Casey said she liked "anything that came in a skillet." Tyler said she was from Texas and that she liked sweet potato pancakes. Kennedy had planned on saying pancakes, too. But she didn't want to copy Tyler, so she said waffles instead. As soon as she'd said it she couldn't remember the last time she'd actually had one.

When it was over, Kennedy, Peyton, and Tyler went back to their suite. Jenna and Casey came, too. They introduced themselves, but then they went and sat on Tyler's bed. Kennedy went to her bedroom. Her goal was to make one friend. One person she could go to coffee or watch a movie with. But the transfer dorm made it appear, even on the first day, that all of the friendships had already been assigned.

Around nine p.m., Tyler told Casey and Jenna to leave. "Get out, I'm serious," she said. "I need to get this room together." The suite quickly turned quiet. Kennedy laid out her things for school. She went to the bathroom and washed her face. Peyton was doing something weird on her bed; it looked like she was putting white tape on her heels. Tyler was standing out of sight, but Kennedy could hear her move. A zip of luggage. The jingle of plastic hangers. Kennedy closed the door to pee. When she finished, Tyler was visible again. She knelt on her bed as she reached up. She attached Polaroid photos to mini clothespins that hung on a stretch of twine.

Kennedy felt confident that Tyler and Peyton's new proximity would not be the start of a friendship. People like Tyler did not hang out with people like Peyton. If anything, Peyton would be a funny story: the roommate who was obsessed with cooking, who wore sweatshirts in the summer. For maybe the fourth time, Kennedy told herself that the room switch was customary and that she wouldn't be missing out. But then, as she closed her bedroom door, Kennedy heard Tyler's voice through the separating wall.

"Peyton. Are you an oatmeal person? Okay, good. Because my mom bought me this."

Kennedy heard Peyton say, "Whoa."

"I know. You can have some whenever. You don't need to ask."

A few seconds later, Peyton said, "Thanks."

Kennedy sat on her bed. She reached for her teeth-grinding guard and popped it in. As it settled into her bite, she pulled the cord to her nightstand lamp. Then she heard another exchange.

"How many of those do you have?" Peyton asked.

Tyler laughed. "My sleep masks? Umm . . . a lot."

"My aunt Ivy gave me one. But I haven't used it yet."

"Oh, you should. It's the only way I sleep."

Kennedy pulled back her covers. She lay down and tucked herself in.

"Why do you have a necklace that says 'Dixie'?" Peyton asked.

"That's my old dog's name," Tyler said. "She's in the picture right there."

"Did she die?"

"Yeah, two summers ago. I'm gonna get another one next year when I move into an apartment. Or." Tyler paused. "Unless you're cool with me hiding one in here . . ."

Kennedy heard nothing. Then she heard Tyler snort. "Peyton," she laughed. "Ohmygod. I'm *kidding.*"

Kennedy turned to her bedside caddy. Inside were two of her favorite books—*The Alchemist* by Paulo Coelho and *Rising Strong* by Brené Brown. But these two were mostly just shielding the book underneath, the one that had ultimately brought her to

Fayetteville. The title was *Satellite Grief: The Science and Second-ary Response from Inciting Accidental Death*. It was part memoir, part study, written by Agatha Paul, PhD. Before she fell asleep, Kennedy flipped through the paperback copy, rereading things she'd highlighted and underlined. It had been gifted to her only eight months ago, and yet the pages were impressively worn.

5.

A GATHA MET ROBIN AT THE HOUSEWARMING party of a woman named Maureen who, like her, worked as an associate professor at DePaul University. It was 2014, Agatha was thirty-five, and it was the kind of event she would have never gone to on her own had she been at home before it started. She didn't know Maureen well (Maureen was a media and cinema studies instructor), but there had been a department-wide meeting on campus. The Friday night spirit and the group pressure of her colleagues was enough to make her slide into an Uber. In the backseat, she thought, Why not? I'll stay for an hour.

For the grand presentation of her three-bedroom apartment, Maureen hired a bartender and catered very good hors d'oeuvres. Discussing work matters with colleagues off campus was mildly cathartic, and it made one hour slip into two. Agatha was on her second drink, something with elderflower, when she saw Robin come through the front door. Agatha quickly clocked her as the second-tallest woman in the room, Agatha being the tallest. Robin was followed by two other young women who, like her, were remarkably long and leggy. They immediately stood out, as they were all in formfitting Lycra with cigarette jeans or dark athletic joggers. They also had what appeared to be selective remnants of stage makeup—a bright-red lip, a tired pair of falsies. But aside from the aerodynamic clothing and glitz, Robin stood out on her own. She had very dark skin that looked finished in matte, and a short, boxy haircut razored close on all sides. Robin was holding a feathery fuchsine jacket. When Maureen reached to take it, Robin handed it to her with an apologetic lift. Maureen said something that Agatha couldn't hear. Robin tossed her head back and laughed, revealing an extraordinary gap between her teeth.

An hour later, Robin and Agatha ended up in the same chatting group, five people gathered at the end of a sofa. Agatha and her friend/colleague Jean sat on the couch's arm. Robin stood on the other side of Jean. A couple—a man and a woman—stood as they explained what led them to believe that their recently purchased home was haunted. "There are a bunch of little things, but two big things," the woman said. "Our plants were looking amazing. I said, 'You're doing great with the plants,' and he says, 'What do you mean? I haven't touched them.'"

The man lifted his shoulders and dropped them back down. "Don't think I've watered a plant in my life."

"Just wait," his wife said. "So the next day one blooms. Full-out *blooms*. So I did a little two-finger test to check the dirt. The soil sticks to my fingers. It's *that* wet."

Agatha watched Robin place a hand at her cheek.

"So that was the big one. But the other thing was a missing cantaloupe. It was huge and then it was just gone. So we're pretty positive we have a hungry ghost, but at least they have a green thumb."

Just as Robin said, "I guess it could be worse," Jean softly asked, "Are you sure it's not . . . a person?"

"What do you mean?" The woman pointed at her husband. "He doesn't even like cantaloupe."

"No. By any chance do you have an attic? Or a crawl space you don't use?"

Agatha swatted Jean's arm. "Oh God. I read that thing. Don't tell her that."

As the woman said, "Tell me what?" Robin looked up with "What did you read?"

Agatha explained that there was this article a few weeks back in either *The Atlantic* or *The Cut*, she couldn't remember, but it detailed how burglars sometimes hide so as not to be caught, or just come upon a quiet place and stay. "They make a little nest in a crawl space or whatnot, and sneak out at night to get food. There was a very disturbing video from a guy who set up surveillance because his food kept going missing . . . but, but you know what?" Agatha smiled. She was in that rare but nice drunk place. She was chatty but in control. She looked at the woman, grinned, and said, "I'm certain that's not the case with you."

The five of them laughed politely as the woman placed her hand at her throat. "I . . . we have to be going now," she joked.

Later, during a lull in the conversation, Agatha asked Robin how she knew Maureen.

"Oh, I don't really," Robin said. "She was being nice. We live down the hall." Then she got pulled away by one of the bony women she'd entered with. Agatha didn't see her again for the rest of the night.

The next day, a Saturday evening, Agatha was making pupusas with curtido. Her phone dinged with an email. The subject line read *From Robin*. She tapped the phone's screen with her pinky and read the rest. *Hi—I hope it's okay that I asked Maureen for your email. I could barely sleep thinking of the poor burglars sneak-*

ing food and building nests. Any chance you can send the article to me? Loved meeting you, Robin. P.S. That guy threw the cantaloupe away, yes?

Agatha thought, Huh, and went back to her bowl.

She barely thought of herself in terms of attraction, and when she did, Agatha considered her body too tall for most and her face just fine for some. She was six-one, had been that way since she was sixteen, and she looked like any of the redheaded celebrities when their names were put into search engines with *grocery store* or *no makeup.* It had little to do with her opinion of herself, but when she read Robin's email, the first thing she thought was Oh. Okay. This woman thinks I'm straight.

There were moments, like this one, where Agatha accepted the obligation to make sure that women didn't feel embarrassed when they assumed she was straight ("So, do you have a boyfriend?"). It wasn't that Agatha felt like the responsibility was hers, but sometimes, sitting under the arbor of straight women's mortification, or assuring them that no, she hadn't been offended, she found herself wishing she had just let it slide. ("No, I'm actually single right now.")

When she was faced with straight women doing things that would have been, in other circumstances, flirtatious—like this email—Agatha felt the need to be formal, factual, and platonic to a severe degree. Perhaps this stemmed from her experience as a tall person, but it was even more grounded in something one of her roommates had said when she was twenty-three years old. Agatha was attending graduate school at Northwestern and lived in an apartment with three other women. One of them was an MBA student named Emily from Irvine, who was very into Trader Joe's and foods that contained "seven whole grains." One day, Agatha's roommate Naomi pulled Agatha aside and told her this: "So I said to Emily, 'You can lock the top lock. Agatha's at her girlfriend's.' And she goes, 'Wait, what? That's interesting . . . Maybe I shouldn't be walking around in a sports bra all the time.'"

Agatha had never really liked Emily, so this wasn't a huge loss. She thought Emily was spoiled for a number of reasons, one being that she refused to pump air into her tires when it was cold ("My dad told me how and I was like, no," she once said. "I just give an auto mechanic twenty bucks"). Agatha had heard worse things about her sexuality (she had an aunt who said Agatha was seeking attention, then later, that her gayness was *because* she was so tall), and more than anything, what Emily had said became a funny thing between Naomi and Agatha, Emily gleaning that if Agatha was gay, then she must be gay for Emily and her sports bras. But nevertheless, Agatha thought of it often, that someone saw her as a person with predatory ambitions. And it was this experience, plus the painful memories of straight women assaulting her with apologies, that made Agatha sit at her computer and draft a quick, sexless reply.

Hi Robin, she wrote. *Here you go. Don't watch too close to bedtime.* Then, because she felt it could be flirtatious to mention Robin's bedtime, she added: *And yes. He 100% threw it away. And I think their wet soil situation could be a mold issue but I didn't want to mention it. Nice meeting you as well. Agatha.*

The next night, Agatha was returning home from seeing a late movie with Jean when she checked her phone in the elevator and saw this response: *I watched three times. Absolutely chilling. And I'd like to think a ghost is watering their plants but that's fair . . . I guess you're not a fan of the two-finger test?* Then there was a semicolon and close parenthesis. A face winking below the text.

Agatha practically choked. In her apartment, she changed from pants to sweats. She sat on her toilet, read it two more times. On her bed, she pulled out her computer. In the search bar she typed three separate phrases. *Burglars don't leave. Robbers stay. Burglars stay in house steal food.* Each time the *Atlantic* article came up first, making it clear that Robin could have found it on her own. Agatha experienced a stirring transition. Oh shit, she thought. She knows I'm gay. Still on her bed, she phoned Jean.

"Hi," Jean said. "Are you okay?"

"Yes, sorry. I'm home now."

"Okay good. I'm still walking. I decided that I hated that movie."

"I think I did, too. But I have a question. Was I being weird at Maureen's?"

Agatha heard Jean's shoes clip against the sidewalk. "No, why?" Jean asked. "Was I being weird?"

"No no no. I usually don't drink that much."

"I'm pretty sure I had more than you. But why are you asking?"

Agatha made her way through the correspondence. "Hmm . . ." Jean said. "Interesting. Mold . . . Uh-huh . . . wait, no. Read that last part again? . . . *Agatha.*"

"I *know.*"

"That woman was very attractive."

"She was. I'm nervous that I did something embarrassing."

"If you did, then it worked."

"But how do I respond?"

Jean made a light *pff* sound. "I'm flattered by you asking me this because I've been with the same person for eleven years, but . . . yeah, I have no idea. Wait. Hang on. She's gonna be at that thing next week. That children's fine-art higher-learning thing with River North."

"Is that where she works?"

"I remember her saying that, yes."

Agatha seized her computer. She typed *Robin River North*.

"Why am *I* nervous right now?" Jean said. "Okay, honestly, though? Sorry . . . I'm just making sure Adam isn't outside. Okay. So when people are that good-looking? It makes me uncomfortable. It's like they're not real. Do you know what I mean?"

Agatha clicked on an image of Robin in a bodysuit the color of a dusty-blue agave plant. Her leg was extended in front of her body, her nose close to her knee. "I know exactly what you mean," she said.

"Okay, good. This reminds me of the other day when I was googling 'young Richard Gere' for like, five whole minutes. It was so pathetic. And I was just like, fuck. You are *so* good-looking. But if I met him? And he asked me out or something? I'd be like, no. Get away. You're fake."

Agatha was listening but she was also scrolling. Robin's last name was Silva.

"Wait," Jean said. "Is that mean? It's completely unsurprising that she liked you."

"You're not being mean." Agatha looked at the email one more time. "I don't do anything tonight, though, yes?"

"No way. Don't do anything. Just let it sit and cook for a bit."

Agatha agreed. She'd let it sit. But the next night she found a picture of Robin at rehearsal, sitting in pike position, wearing thick leg warmers. The response she'd considered writing suddenly seemed like way too much, so she went another night. Without fanfare or meaning to, Agatha let the email sit for eight whole days. Each passing evening, she came closer to under-standing Jean's hypothetical response to young Richard Gere. No. Get away. You're fake. But on the night of the "children's fine-art higher-learning thing," Agatha showered and combed her hair. She put on lipstick the shade of a fig baked in honey. She wore a black blouse with a square neck and billowy sleeves. She did a French tuck into pants from J.Crew that were com-pletely overpriced but had a track of leather down the sides. Ag-atha took a cab. She met Jean outside. She had a plan and she had a line. The plan was to approach Robin when she was alone. The line was Hi. I think I owe you an email.

The event took place at a high school near campus. In a blue gymnasium, four basketball hoops were raised. Like Maureen's housewarming party, it was the type of thing Agatha would never normally attend. The chair of her department was there and pleased to see her. She sat next to Jean through two boring speeches. Two groups of children did two dances, which were very repetitive but fine. Then members of River North did a short performance, but Robin was not included. After the per-formances, Maureen came over and said hello. She didn't bring up the fact that she'd passed Agatha's email to Robin, which made Agatha feel as though she couldn't bring it up either. This was a shame, as Agatha was desperate to know if Robin had asked for her by name. Or if Robin had described what she looked like, and how.

Then there were light drinks and mingling. Children from the performance received roses from parents that grew heavy in their arms. Agatha feared that Robin was backstage. Jean was also cruising the room to no avail. She looked at Agatha with a face that said, *Weird.* Agatha said, "I'm going to use the bath-room and then we can go."

At the sink in the ladies' room, there she was. Robin stood in a pear-green dress that was very modern in that it looked backward. High neck in front, plunging V down the back. She had a line of clean, white liner at her lids, and she was wearing heels, putting her in direct eye line. Agatha stopped walking and held her breath. Robin looked up. A toilet flushed inside a stall.

"Oh, hello." Robin smiled. On the counter in front of her was a laughably small purse. She was digging into it with two fingers.

Just say it, Agatha thought. Just say the line. But Robin was so stunning and her purse was so small. A woman stepped out of a stall. She pumped the soap dispenser six loud times.

"You know . . ." Robin retrieved a Band-Aid. "I think you might be ignoring me."

Agatha watched Robin stand on one high-heeled foot, slide a strap down, and apply the Band-Aid to her heel. "Okay," she said. "I might be doing that."

Robin leaned past her, threw white scraps into the trash. "That's fair," she said. "Did I scare you off?"

"No."

She turned the faucet on with her elbow. "Are you sure?"

"Yes."

"Okay. Then what's up?"

Agatha crossed her arms loosely and laughed. The other woman finished and Agatha moved so she could pass. "What's up?" Agatha repeated. "Is—is that a real question?" She hoped she was conveying a number of rhetorical questions. Have you seen you? Have you seen me? Do you think I'm an idiot? What are you trying to pull?

Robin kept Agatha's gaze as she ripped a paper towel from

the wall. "Oh, alright," she laughed. "Well, don't be like that, then."

"Right, okay."

"Do you have to pee or what?"

"Not anymore."

Robin laughed again. She took up her highly impractical little purse, which, under her arm, looked like a political statement. "Well, good," she said. "Then let's go somewhere."

Robin was twenty-nine years old. She'd graduated from Fordham University and she'd been dancing since she was three. She was from Chicago, where her mother, her brother, his wife, and their child also lived. They all convened every other Sunday in the house where she grew up. She was funny and direct. She owned approximately thirteen small duffel bags, each filled with clothes, half soles, Tiger Balm, and tape. Robin expressed the same distaste Agatha did when friends or strangers commented on their height, or referred to them as a power couple. She'd say, "Ha. That's funny," and bend into Agatha's ear. "Those are the most uninspired words to have ever been strung together."

Agatha hadn't anticipated how sublime it would be to date an artist who was actually good at what they did. Sitting in a packed theater, ripped comp ticket in her pocket, Agatha found herself completely moved and, once or twice, close to tears. Whatever the opposite of ego was, that was the place from which Robin danced. Night after night, she accessed a midpoint between the hunger of an artist and the diligence of an artisan. Four weeks into their relationship, an ad went up at the Washington/Wells stop featuring Robin and two other Black women in tulle. Agatha found herself looking at it every time she passed. I am dating that person, she'd think. That person and me are dating.

Agatha got to be naked in front of her, too. She could say, "No, I don't like that," and, "Yes, that's better," as Robin appreciated choreography in many forms. They liked cooking together and taking long walks and sending each other disturbing articles (*Doctor finds fourteen contact lenses behind woman's eye. Man has live roach in his ear*). Agatha's second book came out. It was titled *Birthday Money*. It was about rituals, traditions, and the cross-cultural obsession with coming of age. The book did very well. Robin went to her readings in Philadelphia and New York. They stayed in fancy hotel rooms that they didn't need to pay for.

They were officially together when Agatha decided to donate more than half of her wardrobe and stick to a strict number and color palette (fifty items in cream, chambray, navy, and black). Robin came to her apartment with a bottle of champagne. "This is everything I own," Agatha said. She showed off the fourteen piles of clothing and her four pairs of shoes. There were three pieces of jewelry total: a necklace, stud earrings, and her giant sunstone ring. Robin walked around the soft little stacks. "I am very attracted to this," she said. "I would absolutely never do it, but I think it's really great." In the weeks that followed, Robin took to assessing Agatha's outfits whenever she entered a room. "Oh, okay. She's got class pants on today." "Uh-oh, jumpsuit. Watch out, she think she cute." Agatha would say, "Alright" or, "Be nice," but it made her laugh every time.

The months grew into a year and more and Agatha fell into Robin's family with ease. Robin's mother, Celeste, had a Fitbit that often beeped at her to move. No matter what they were doing—eating dinner, playing a game—she'd hop up and step in place, continuing the conversation as if nothing had changed. Her twin brother, Rashad, was a Genius at the Apple Genius Bar, and his wife, Toni, worked part-time at a Blick art supply store while finishing a teacher's certification at night. Their daughter, Ruby, was five years old, and upon meeting her for the first time, Ruby pointed at Agatha's large blue purse. "Do you . . . is there anything in there for me?" she asked.

"Ohmygoodness, *Ruby*," her mother said.

Ruby was undeterred. She said, "Please?"

Agatha bent to riffle through her bag. "Maybe . . . ?"

"Don't you fall for that, Agatha," Celeste said.

But Agatha produced a lanyard from a recent conference she'd attended. It had a long blue strap and said *DePaul University*. She also found a Sharpie. She slid the white card out and put it to her knee. "How do you spell your name?" she asked.

Touching two twists in her hair, Ruby took an exceptionally long time. "Arrreeee. Youuuuu. Beeeeee. Whyyyyy."

The next time Agatha came for dinner, Ruby had the lanyard on when she arrived. Toni looked at Agatha and pointed at the top of her daughter's head. "Every night," Toni whispered. "'Mom, where's my necklace? I need my necklace.'"

"Miss Agatha?" Ruby said. "Um, do you remember that you gave this to me?"

Under the table, Robin's hand was in hers. Agatha nodded and said, "Yes, I do."

THAT AGATHA HAD always picked up the check was neither disregarded nor ignored. She was happy to do it, she was met with gracious thank-yous, and it felt nice to spend money on someone who she loved. Robin made a small and inconsistent amount of money, partially due to a rehearsal schedule that was limiting and grueling. She often came home at one in the morning, rehearsals the next day at eight a.m. Sometimes parents canceled on her an hour before a private lesson with their children, without an offer to pay in part. Most significantly, Agatha had plenty of financial stability that made picking up tabs mostly a joy and hardly a sacrifice. But whether she'd been conscious of it or not, Agatha had privately hoped or assumed that if Robin did ever get paid properly, that her lifestyle—*their* lifestyle together—would shift into a more equitable place. In 2015, that very thing happened. With one signature, everything changed and stayed the same.

Robin signed what Agatha learned was a "big contract" as a principal dancer at River North: twelve hundred dollars a week plus health care. She moved into a studio apartment. She got rid of the students she didn't like, and she raised her rate for the students that she did. There were several celebratory dinners—Agatha gifted her a blender—but aside from the number on her paycheck and her new home in a high-rise on Grand Avenue, Robin's financial situation and all her corresponding limitations remained exactly as they'd been.

Robin was constantly throwing down her card at bars and restaurants, surrounded by dancer friends who were "so happy for her" and making significantly less. She was always breaking down boxes from purchasing neon athleisure wear, items with purposes that were laughably bespoke. ("I needed a pair with pockets on both sides," she'd say. "It's a jacket for after class. The studio can get really cold.") It wasn't that she was doing anything wrong, but it was irritating and it stressed Agatha out. If Agatha asked if she wanted to go away for the weekend or get a massage, Robin would say she could *next* Friday, which began to sound like *I could . . . if you're paying.* Even with her new paycheck, Robin attended events and parties just for the dinner or hors d'oeuvres provided. This was a habit Agatha now credited to the way they'd first met.

Robin also continued to organize parts of her health care through deals she found on Groupon. One day, returning from an optometrist appointment, she inspected her dilated eyes. "It's probably fine," she said. "I just feel like they went really fast." The argument started with concern—"Robin, don't do that again"—but very quickly, it became heated on both sides.

"I've done this for years. Why do you care now?"

"I just don't understand why you can't go to a real doctor."

"What are you talking about? She was a real doctor."

"A real doctor doesn't need to be on Groupon!"

Robin's new salary solidified her as someone who enjoyed nice things. But she vehemently rejected the planning necessary to be someone who paid for them. She'd drunkenly retrieve her credit card with a "Why not?" And when she didn't have enough, it was "Meh, who cares?" It was like she'd been broke for so long that she couldn't understand how her spending habits affected anyone but her. Sometimes, when she made the "Meh, who cares?" face, Agatha wanted to say, Me. I do. I am affected by this, too. Please stop living like a broke club kid. Get a grip. You are thirty years old.

Once, Robin forgot to book a hotel for a wedding weekend. Agatha had left her credit card number with her, but because Robin had forgotten, the group block was now full. Rooms were $402 a night. Agatha could feel herself waiting for Robin to apologize, but instead, Robin began to text someone on her phone.

"We can stay with Terrence," Robin said. "He has two beds. He says it's fine."

Agatha placed her hands in her lap. This was such a hallmark

Robin response. She and her dancer friends were always in the process of changing clothes, lying on the floor, and sleeping in each other's beds. Agatha had met Terrence twice. One of those times he stretched his foot above his head. At a baby shower.

"I don't want to stay with Terrence," Agatha said.

Robin laughed. "Well, you can't be mad about the money and mad at my solution."

Agatha neatly tucked her hair behind both ears. Evenly, ready for a fight, she said, "I can absolutely be mad at both those things." As predicted and self-prescribed, a significant fight ensued. In the end, Agatha paid $804 for two nights in San Jose, just as she and Robin knew she would.

Agatha's two books were the reason she owned an apartment. With Robin, she bitterly understood that when you made a large amount of money, you forfeit saying normal couple things, like, Okay, since you forgot, can you please cover the difference? And when it came to Robin specifically, Robin with her big teeth and talent, this seemed inconveniently true even without the money. Robin, in so many ways, was completely wonderful. It always felt hard and stupid for Agatha to say no. But Robin was also like a teenager in a movie, left alone with the house for a weekend. Regardless of whether she'd been left with fifty dollars or five hundred, she would always cash out at zero by Sunday night.

In the second year of their relationship, Robin moved in. Her studio had ants, the landlord was a dick, and Agatha simply wanted her to. Out loud, Agatha assured Robin that the apartment was just as much Robin's as it was hers. Privately, she hoped the fact that Robin would no longer be paying rent would smooth over the money issues on both sides: Robin would have

more income with no rent to pay, and Agatha would have less
guilt saying no. Robin's money did even out, but with their new
proximity, it seemed they had become bereft of a once-reliable
mutual interest.

Once, sitting at her computer, Agatha said, "Did you know
that when a pregnant woman has an autopsy, they ask the family
what to do with the baby?"

Standing in pajamas, Robin said, "Say what?"

"The options are putting it back inside the mom, or they can
put it in the mother's arms."

"Agatha? It's eight in the morning . . . like, fuck."

Robin once came home with Lululemon bags on both arms.
Agatha said, "Isn't Lululemon being investigated for . . . what
was it, their factory workers are being beaten?"

Robin blew through her lips. "I'm not sure. But thank you.
I'll definitely look into that."

And once, on a Sunday afternoon, Agatha asked Robin if
she'd heard of corpse wax. "It's this soapy film that forms on a
dead person's body when they're left in the—"

"I'm going to stop you right there. Agatha? This is important. I don't like knowing things like that."

It all seemed unfair. Robin used to like knowing things like
that. Agatha only knew about the corpse wax and the autopsy
details because she was writing a piece for *National Geographic*
on new burial traditions and morticians. By saying she didn't
like knowing things like that, Robin was saying, *Don't talk to me
about your work.* That was an unreasonable request. And it was
so confusing. They used to share disturbing information all the
time.

Their arguments ended in three distinct ways: Robin saying

she'd do better, Agatha saying she was sorry, or Agatha snatching up a receipt. But when arguments combined Agatha's sundry knowledge with Robin's precarious funds, it was as if they had no end. Those disagreements lingered. They moped and plodded around the house. The Knife Fight specifically was emblematic of this dynamic, and it refused to go away.

Robin was a relatively healthy yet strange eater. A meal consisted of an entire avocado, some cashews, and some pickles. Or a bowl of hummus and a champagne mango, eaten standing, bending over the sink. Robin loved tomatoes, big orange heirloom ones. One of her favorite dinners was an entire tomato, a chunk of mozzarella, olive oil, and basil leaves. The problem was the way she ate it, which was cut and eat, cut and eat. Slowly. Over the course of an hour. Every cut made with Agatha's knives.

The knives had been an expensive purchase that Agatha gifted herself when her second book went into its third printing. It was a Wüsthof seven-piece set and it came in a beautiful walnut block. So there was the Money part—the set was three hundred dollars—and there was the Things Agatha Knew part—that cutting on a plate dulls a knife, that tomato juice strips a blade. This resulted in the Knife Fight, which was performed more times than Agatha could count on two hands.

"Robin, can you please use a cutting board?"

"But I don't know how much I want."

"You do realize tomato juice wrecks the blade, yes?"

"I realize you've told me that."

"Hey, can you please just wash the knife really quickly?"

"I'll wash everything. Girl, I just sat down."

"How about I make you a nice little plate that's all sliced up?"

"Did you seriously just ask me that?"

"Robin, those knives were expensive, and the tomato acid—"

"Agatha, look at me. Ain't nobody else live this way."

"Do you not believe me? Or do you just not care?"

"Should I buy my own knives? If it's that important, then I will."

And that was where the argument stalled and limped to the side of the road. Agatha's money and the things she spent it on became a place where Robin pushed her to the edge. Oh, yeah? That's how you feel? Okay fine, then prove it. If you don't want to spend your money, then let's stay with my loud friend Terrence. If you don't want me using your fancy knives, then just tell me to buy my own. But Agatha would never tell Robin to buy her own knives. She didn't want to live in a home where she used a good set and Robin used one she'd probably purchase secondhand. The way Robin looked at her in these arguments was devastating. *Look at me*, her face said. *Aren't I worth ruining your knives?* Of course she was worth it, but Agatha wanted to say, Wait. How about you look at me? Can't I just have nice knives?

It was all a huge deal until it very quickly wasn't. The Knife Fight was abandoned altogether when Robin abruptly lost her job. In 2016, River North Dance completely folded, abruptly, unceremoniously, and in the middle of several dancers' contracts. The following week, Robin was in and out of tears, existing in the same pair of joggers. She answered phone calls with "Hey . . . yeah, it is what it is."

Agatha felt terrible. She offered condolences and gestures that she truly hoped were helpful. ("Hey, my grocery list is there." "Hey, I'm doing laundry, let me know if you want something thrown in.") But as the days went on, as the phone calls ceased, and as Robin—sans rehearsals and performances—

started going to bed at nine p.m., Agatha couldn't help but wonder if there was a small part of Robin that was taking this termination with a bit of relief. Robin's body was struggling to keep up like it used to. Even before the end of River North, she'd grown perpetually tired. She fell asleep in the first fifteen minutes of any film, even the ones she'd picked out, and she was constantly going to the bathroom with an upset stomach. She'd come out and say, "Phew. That was close." The premature ending of River North presented an opportunity to reevaluate what her life could look like as a thirty-one-year-old dancer. Robin talked about finding a better situation, a company that met her body on its terms. But then the offer from the University of Arkansas came into Agatha's inbox. One academic year, 2:1 schedule, lots of time to research and write. To Agatha's absolute delight, Robin's enthusiasm surpassed her own. "Is it weird that I want to go?" Robin asked. It was a bit sentimental but nonetheless, Arkansas began to feel like something they'd leave saying, It was exactly what we needed.

And for a moment—a long moment, about four months—things were very nice again. The 2016 election was more important than nice knives and hotel rooms. Agatha's agent retired and she was assigned a new one, a twenty-seven-year-old named Charlotte. Charlotte wrote emails with no less than four exclamation points, and she believed Agatha should have an "online presence." Agatha read Charlotte's emails out loud in a monotone yet peppy voice that always made Robin laugh. She read Charlotte's suggestions that Agatha go on a reality star's podcast, invitations to do essays for *Better Homes & Gardens* ("I think this will be a good fit!"). Agatha also dictated her responses out loud; they were clear and cold nos, which Robin also enjoyed. Making Robin laugh became a responsibility and comfort that made Agatha very sad.

Robin got a part-time gig doing administrative work at a ballet studio. She subbed friends' classes and she scrambled to book doctors' appointments while she was still covered. Agatha resumed paying for the bulk of their expenses, but this time, either tired, humbled, or both, Robin reciprocated with her best behavior. She picked up dry cleaning. She took better care of the knives, and in return, Agatha cared less.

One night, Robin said, "I don't know what I would do without you right now."

Agatha turned to her. Rested her arms on her shoulders. "Hey," she said. "You're sure you want to live in Arkansas with me?"

Robin held on to Agatha's elbows. "Oh, I'm so sure," she said. "I am so ready to not do a winter."

SEVEN WEEKS BEFORE their moving date, Robin called and said this: "I need you to go to dinner with me and this woman Keisha. She's with Giordano. She's inviting her husband, too."

Through a friend of a friend, Robin had met Keisha, a principal dancer with Giordano, and more importantly, the close friend of Hubbard Street's artistic director. Agatha didn't want to go to dinner. She wanted to be at home, on her phone, partially watching something calming, like a nature show or *Top Chef.* She was sick of conversations where friends and acquaintances said, *"Arkansas?* Wait, you're *still* going?" And she didn't see how a friend of an artistic director could have that much pull when Robin would return in a year. But Robin rarely asked for her presence or participation, and so, she said, "Sure. That's fine."

Five minutes after seven, seated on an outdoor bench, Agatha heard a voice call, "Hello."

Robin stood and Agatha followed suit, but her response was half a second delayed. To her surprise, Keisha, the woman Robin was bending down to hug, was very short and very white. Keisha had thin, flat-ironed hair and pretty green eyes that looked a little drunk. She didn't look like Robin's other dancer friends (angular faces, hyperextended knees). She was small and extremely compact: the body of a woman who was a gymnast as a child.

Agatha shook Keisha's hand. She said, "Nice to meet you," and Keisha said, "Likewise." The fact that she was white didn't matter, but the fact that Robin didn't mention it did. The Robin she knew, the Robin she'd been dating for nearly three years, would've said, I met a white woman named Keisha today.

Keisha introduced her husband, Ryan. "Sorry," she laughed. "We just got married a month ago and saying 'husband' still sounds so weird."

Ryan had blue eyes and fluffy brown hair and he looked like a Ryan. He wore a light blue button-down and he had the complexion of a person who loves "being out on the lake." Together, Keisha and Ryan looked like a couple on *House Hunters* in somewhere like Asheville or Baton Rouge. Robin told Ryan that she'd heard he'd been working long hours. Ryan scratched the back of his neck. "Yeah, it's been a crazy few weeks."

Agatha held the door for everyone to go inside. Their table had two chairs on one side and a long booth on the other. Keisha said, "Ryan, let them pick, since they're so tall."

"Oh, thank you," Robin said. "This side is fine. I love a booth."

Keisha accepted a menu from the hostess. Then she looked

across the table. "Ohmygod," she said. "You guys look like a photograph. Such a power couple. I love it."

Agatha looked up at Keisha's and Ryan's Christmas-card faces. She felt certain that they had taken engagement photos holding hands in front of the Bean.

"Ha, thank you." Robin crossed her legs, touching Agatha's knee briefly. The touch said, You need to be nice. Agatha opened her menu.

The restaurant was a dark little place that was more expensive inside than it had appeared from the outside bench. There were cloth napkins and candles in glass; the bartender had sideburns and suspenders. This, Agatha thought, is the kind of place you think is neat when you're twenty-six and you make money for the first time. Keisha ordered a Tequila Mockingbird, which somehow proved her point. Agatha asked Ryan what he did for a living and the answer was so boring that she instantly forgot. They discussed River North closing; Keisha nodded gravely. "No, I would be so upset," she said. The waiter came back with their drinks. She took their orders and left again.

"So Arkansas, yeah?" Keisha said.

Agatha was still recovering from seconds before, when Keisha prompted the group to do a big "Cheers!" She touched her lips to her glass and nodded. "Arkansas. Yes," she said.

"That's a big move," Ryan said.

"It is, but the change of pace will be nice."

"That's amazing," Keisha said. "Robin, when are you going down to visit?"

In a miserable glitch, they answered at the same time.

"Oh, I'll be down there a lot—" "No, Robin's coming with me."

"Oh," Keisha said. "I didn't realize that."

Agatha refolded her napkin on her lap. Robin placed her elbow on the table; two big bracelets fell down her arm.

"I'll actually head down there with her in August," Robin said. "They're giving her this huge three-bedroom house and everything. And yeah, I'll be a frequenter but obviously based here."

"Gotchyou," Keisha said. "Well, that'll be nice."

"Planning on hitting up a few Razorback games?" Ryan asked.

"You know," Robin said, "I didn't go to a single game in college, so I feel like—"

"I'm sorry." Agatha touched Ryan's arm. "Do you mind if I slip out and use the restroom?"

"Oh, for sure."

In the bathroom stall she remained standing, staring at the checkered tile floor. Confusion shifted into anger, hurt gave way to mortification. She imagined Robin telling her friends she couldn't leave just yet, that she wasn't paying rent. She also pictured Robin standing on one foot, placing a Band-Aid on the back of her ankle. Agatha felt sick then, like she'd built something on sand. Hands on her hips, she tilted her face upward and stared at the middle of a water stain.

When she returned to the table, Keisha was saying, "Exactly. You get what you pay for."

Agatha said, "Sorry about that," and Keisha said, "Oh, you're fine. Actually . . . that reminds me. The craziest thing happened today."

Robin asked what happened, and Keisha gripped her husband's biceps. "Ohmygod, poor Ryan," she said. "He's heard this like six times now. But yeah, this morning . . . I had an appointment at this new gyno. Wait, Robin, do you know Fatima? From Joffrey? Okay, yeah, she recommended it . . ."

Agatha squeezed the tops of her thighs. She wanted to go home and she wanted to have a fight. She wanted to scream, I fucking knew it, but she also wanted to stay annoyingly calm. She wanted to act as if she saw it coming. I have nothing to say to you, she'd say.

"I go in," Keisha went on, "and immediately, bad vibes. No one is friendly, no one says hi."

Agatha hated stories like this—Getting-There Stories. It was like someone talking about their dreams. They were only interesting to the person they'd happened to. Robin nodded thoughtfully. Agatha exhaled through a circle in her lips. If you're not coming to Arkansas, she thought, then I shouldn't have to listen to this fucking story.

"Then," Keisha went on. "They can't find me in the computer, and the receptionist asks how to spell my last name *four* times. My last name is Hendricks. Not that difficult. And if you're a receptionist, I feel like names are your one big job?"

Agatha glanced down at the table. Upon seeing the small lit candle in the center, she had the desire to pick it up like a fruit tart and stick the entire thing into her mouth. She wanted Ryan to watch her. She wanted to wipe the wax by dabbing a napkin at her lips. And she wanted to say something hackneyed and dumb (I like it because it's sweet? But not too sweet).

"So then," Keisha said, "I wait fifty minutes. And they finally call me back. And I shit you not, I wait fifteen more minutes. And listen. Things happen. But I'm the kind of person that . . . if I'm late? I'm like, 'Hey, I am *so* sorry.' But this woman? Nothing. She walks in like, 'Keisha? How's it going?' Uhhh, not well? I've been here like, all day? And, if you can believe it, this is when it got really bad."

Robin said, "Oh no."

"So right off the bat, I say I'm a dancer. She goes, 'Okay, do you do any other work for supplemental income?'" Keisha mushed her lips together in offense. "Um, do *you* have any other work for supplemental income? Like, I'm twenty-seven. Mommy and Daddy aren't helping me out, but thanks."

Agatha rested her chin on her hand. She was angry but also felt protective of Robin and her annoying dancer friends, all of whom had nothing but supplemental sources of income. Tutoring, yoga instructing, nannying, waitressing. Half of them were uninsured. Agatha looked at Keisha and thought, There is absolutely no way your cell phone isn't on your parents' plan.

"So then, she's like, 'Are you sexually active?' Um yes, I'm here to have a baby, but way to admit you didn't read the forms. Then she asks if I'm married. I say yes. And then she goes, 'Great. What does your husband do for a living?'"

Ryan lifted his hands and set them back down. "I know," he said. "Crazy, right?"

Keisha folded her body practically in two. "At that point, I was *done*. I said, 'Ma'am? My income, the income of my partner, that's absolutely none of your business. And implying that it has any bearing on my sexual health or the health of our future child? That's honestly disgusting.' She tried to apologize, and I was like, 'Not necessary,' and I asked her to leave the room so I could change and get out."

"Whoa," Robin said. "I did not see a dramatic ending coming."

"I've never done anything like that in my life. But come on.

You're a doctor. You can't just ask what my partner does for a living."

Agatha sipped her cocktail. You've never called him your partner till this moment but sure.

"You know what," Robin said. "If you're not comfortable just talking to someone, they definitely shouldn't be your gyno. Good for you."

Agatha looked over at her then. Robin vehemently refused to look back.

"Thank you," Keisha said. "I decided I should storm out of places more often."

"You should!" Robin said.

Agatha wanted to do another "Cheers," but this time, she wanted to lob her drink like a shot put, deeply lacerate her hand. Instead, she folded her arms on the table with a brutal resolve. She could feel it now: she was going to ruin this evening before entrées had arrived.

"So I'm fairly certain," Agatha started, "that doctors ask about partners' lines of work because some work conditions can contribute to passing on a number of infections. So if your partner worked as something like a construction worker, they could digitally spread lead poisoning or asbestos, particularly if hygiene was an issue or there was an open cut. And there's that staph infection called MRSA—I'm not going to remember what that stands for—but it's high-risk for people in correctional facilities, veterinary clinics . . . oh, and wastewater workers. They're at risk, too. And you know, this is a wild example, but there was an outbreak of HIV among sex workers in Togo, I think. Which didn't make a lot of sense because they were using protection. Come to find out that through open sores and bloody gums, they were contracting the virus during oral sex. Isn't that interesting? So anyway. All of that is to say that it sounds like your doctor should have been clearer. But ultimately, it is in your best interest for her to know what your partner does for a living."

Robin stiffened. Ryan looked at his wife. Keisha's green eyes were suspended in time. A ruthless silence settled over the table and Agatha took a bath in it.

Keisha came out of her stupor and took Agatha in with a strange, old-fashioned, mother-of-the-bride displeasure. She did a cute little shake of her head and said, "Well, that is very interesting."

"Yeah . . ." Robin said. "That's a lot of information."

"I'd just hate for you to think she was being inappropriate," Agatha said.

Keisha nodded like she was in a lecture hall, theatrically pretending to take notes. "No, I appreciate that. And that's all super interesting, but I think—and I'm sure Robin can back me up on this—I think it was more about her challenging me professionally. So many people think that what we do isn't work. And after dancing for so long, it's easy to tell when someone doesn't take you seriously. And when it comes to a doctor, especially when it comes to having a child, I just . . . it's so important that we're on the same page."

"I completely understand," Agatha said. "That's a very emotional process and you're absolutely right."

Two servers arrived and one said, "I have hot plates." The way Robin reached for her fork, Agatha knew she was livid. But the degree to which Agatha didn't care was almost unhealthy. Her resentment felt round and hard, a tender cyst under the skin.

"Keisha," Agatha said. "Can I ask where you got your name?"

"Oh, ha. Of course. I wish it was a better story. My mom wanted either Alicia or Keisha, and my dad picked Keisha. But yeah, so many people ask me that. And—well, wait." She grinned. "Have you seen *Mean Girls*?"

Agatha said, "I have."

"Okay, yeah. So whenever people ask me about my name, I'll be like, 'Ummm . . . you can't just ask people why they're white.'"

Ryan tapped the back of a bottle of ketchup. Everyone smiled. No one laughed.

"Ha." Agatha cut into her salmon. "That's really funny." She wanted to bend down and kiss Keisha on the top of her head.

The cab ride was silent. The elevator was worse. Agatha violently changed her clothes while Robin went into the second bedroom. Agatha wasn't planning on saying anything. She was an only child; she could entertain herself for days. But on her way to the bathroom, she accidentally locked eyes with Robin. From a cross-legged position on the floor, Robin took her line.

"I have nothing to say to you."

Agatha's face recoiled. "You have nothing to say to me? Robin . . . clearly!"

"Agatha? You know what? A world does exist where we could have gone to dinner and thought they were annoying and came home and said ha ha ha."

"In this world would you have told me that we were having dinner with children?"

"See? You know what?" Robin laughed. "Agatha, why are you dating me?"

Agatha flinched and said, "What?"

"You don't like people younger than you. Did you know that? Especially if they're having a good time."

"Right, Robin. That's the issue here. I'll start to process that.

But, in the meantime, how about you let me know when you'd like to visit me in Arkansas."

"Agatha?" Robin leaned back on both her hands. "Tell me when I said I was quitting dance."

"I knew you would do this."

"Are you kidding me right now? I told you who her friend was. I'm sorry if I didn't spell it out more than that, but I got up at five thirty for an MRI today and I worked ten hours, for what, a hundred bucks? And I can barely think straight and I'm exhausted. But that doesn't even matter. This is my life. You're supposed to support me and have my—"

"Oh right. I do nothing to support you, Robin. I just take and take and take."

Robin closed her mouth. "I ask you to do one thing for me, one thing that has nothing to do with money—"

"But that's the thing, you *didn't* ask me. You didn't tell me anything."

"We've been together three years. I shouldn't fucking have to."

Agatha stretched her arms up above her head; she held on to the doorframe.

Robin smiled and shook her head. "I don't even know what to do with this because—it's not like you have low self-esteem. You were very pleased with yourself tonight. But I don't understand why you can never just chill out and believe we're together. It's exhausting."

"So no matter what, you're going," Agatha clarified. "No matter what audition or callback you get, you're still going to Arkansas."

"Are you telling me that you wouldn't be happy for me if I got a callback right now?"

"Why aren't you answering the question?"

Robin let her head fall back. "I can't do this," she said to the ceiling. "I'm so, *so* tired."

Agatha blew through her lips. "Well, great," she said. "What else is new?"

Robin brought her head back and violently clicked her tongue. She looked not as if she'd been slapped, but as if Agatha had tried and missed. She laughed and hopped to her feet. She went to the closet and retrieved a yoga mat. "Well, I have a doctor's appointment in Evanston at eight a.m., so I'm going to go to bed."

"Don't do that," Agatha said. "At least take the couch."

Robin pulled a blanket down as well. "The mat is better for my back, but thanks."

The next day, while Agatha was walking from the train to her office, Robin phoned her cell. Her voice was echoing, she was crying. Her images had come back showing Crohn's disease, that she'd probably had it for some time.

"I'm so mad right now," she said. "I'm so mad at that other doctor."

On an intensely upright bench next to a historical marker, Agatha sat and she cried, too.

Two days later, Robin said, calmly and definitively, that she would not be going to Arkansas. She'd found a doctor she trusted; she wanted to get better in a familiar place. "I can stay at my brother's in August," she said, "or with my mom if it needs to be earlier."

Agatha sat in her armchair. It was one p.m. on a Friday. Her apartment had turned so formal and strange. Good lord, she thought. Are we breaking up?

"You can stay here," she said. "You can stay here until I get back next year."

Robin twisted her lips. "That's a nice offer, but why don't you think about it?"

"I don't need to do that. Just take care of things. It's fine."

The next few days were punctuated by Agatha entering rooms and whispering, "Are you on the phone?" Robin spent hours on hold with her insurance company, a supplement company, a temp-work agency, and on the HealthCare.gov website. The cheapest health plan available to her was $336 a month with a $6,550 deductible. At one point, Agatha heard Robin ask, "Would Toni let me be Ruby's nanny?" Via speakerphone, Rashad replied, "And what makes you think we have nanny money?"

Agatha called another formal meeting in the living room. She sat down with her elbows to her knees. "I'm still fine with you staying here while I'm gone," she said. "And I think it might be helpful if you and I got domestically partnered. So you have coverage for the year."

Robin dipped her chin.

"We can just get rid of it when I come back," Agatha said. "And I think I get a tax break, so . . . it's fine."

Briefly, Robin looked like she'd swallowed incorrectly. Then she dropped her head and cried.

That evening, in Jean's kitchen, Agatha sat at the kitchen island with Jean's youngest son in her arms. Jean was on her computer, pulling up facts about Arkansas: that diamonds were the state gem, that it was the twenty-fifth state.

Agatha told her what she was doing for Robin. Hands on the counter, Jean took a breath. "I get it," she said. "But you're nicer than I am." She turned the computer around, where a video was playing. Thousands of people in a football stadium raised their hands. They shook their fingers in the sky. The crowd called out,

"Woooooo Pig Sooie!" "Pay attention," Jean said. "You need to learn this dance."

But then, Agatha felt stupid for offering, for thinking that Arkansas recognized domestic partnerships, that Illinois did, too. Only six states honored domestic partnerships to the degree that health insurance could be shared, and Agatha would be living in none of them. But she'd been the one to offer, she had a "Why not" spirit of her own, and on August 1, 2017, Agatha and Robin were married at city hall. Robin wore a sequined shift dress. Agatha wore her cream-colored jumpsuit. She waited for Robin to introduce her outfit like she used to. Uh-oh, it's fun Agatha, or, Watch out, jumpsuit. But instead, Robin said, "Thank you." Agatha said, "Of course." Agatha never imagined that two days before moving south to write about weddings, she'd be having one of her own. Jean and Terrence stood as witnesses. Afterward they had drinks at a bar nearby.

Agatha's fifty items fit in two large suitcases. She made a terrible joke of saying a final goodbye to all her plants. Then she got into the rental car. Robin waved from the curb.

She could have made it in a day—Fayetteville was eleven hours south—but five hours into her drive, she saw an exit for St. Louis. She checked into a room at a place called the Moonrise Hotel. She lay on the bed and looked at the internet for an hour. She watched a TV show called *Naked and Afraid*. She called room service and ordered an entire rotisserie chicken. She fell asleep in her clothes.

On August fourth, she arrived in Fayetteville. The first person she spoke to was the director of the master's program. He showed her to her office; they'd gifted her a plant. The second person she met was a woman named Aimee, standing behind her in the Ozark Natural Foods Co-Op line. Aimee looked like a PE teacher and Agatha trusted her immediately. When each of them had asked if she was alone ("Isn't your husband here?" "Did your family come down, too?"), Agatha didn't blanch. "No, he actually decided not to," she said. "No no. It's just me for now."

6.

AIMEE SETTLED HER FOOT ON THE GAS. "OKAY, so here's the deal," she said. "My uncle's wife—not my aunt—we get on but she's a piece of work. Her name is Kimber and she grew up in Little Rock. Her dad is from here, but he passed last May."

Millie zoomed down a tree-lined path in the passenger seat of Aimee's golf cart. Move-in day had come to a close, and she didn't understand why Kimber's father mattered, but it felt appropriate to say, "Oh no. I'm sorry."

Aimee waved her condolences away. "I only met the guy once. Kimber is responsible for his house, but she's a 'boat stewardess.'" She rolled her eyes. "She's in Boca Raton for a year. My uncle is meeting her there. Beach house and everything. Per diem. Must be nice. Anyway, they need someone to look after the house till they get back. Nothing big. Just turning on a light. They'll pay fifty dollars a month. What do you think?"

Millie reached up and held the roof of the golf cart. Ohmygod, she thought. All this money, for doing nothing. Immediately, she was performing simple arithmetic in her head. Of course some would go into her savings, but with an extra fifty dollars a month, she could get the big conditioner, the one that came with the pump. A fifty-four-ounce jar of coconut oil also popped into her mind. Technically, she mused, she could get HBO. She was dying to watch *Big Little Lies*. And then Millie thought, Ohmygoodness. She gripped the railing as the cart took a turn. With an extra fifty dollars a month, she could get a nice haircut.

"Yes. Totally. I can definitely do that for them."

"Great. They'll do Venmo. If she ever forgets to pay you, just let me know. But here's the other thing."

Aimee parked at the edge of the sidewalk, underneath the street sign for Douglas and Taylor. "They wanna sell it," she said. "When she comes back to town in May." She eyed Millie over her glasses.

Millie bent to see around the brim of Aimee's visor. She gasped and said, "No."

"Ah ah ah!" Aimee held a finger up. "Do not get excited. We'll take a look—it won't take long—and then we'll have a chat."

On the street corner a tiny yellow house was surrounded by overgrown grass and neglect. The front door was fairy-taled right in the center. Two windows on each side, a smaller one up above. The house looked to have once been painted a canary yellow, but now it was the shade of a lemon rind left in a glass. The roof came together in a darling point that Millie had an urge to cup in her hand.

They walked through the grass. Aimee fiddled with a set of keys. Millie waited behind her. A rush of heat and hope. Entrance required a shoulder, a shove, and a bit of lift-and-push. The house opened with a suck, like it was coming up for air. There was a small living room, a bigger kitchen, a bulky set of stairs separating the two. There was a lamp on the floor, a wood-fire stove that Millie assumed was defunct, and one lonely piece of furniture: a dilapidated denim armchair. It was dark and dusty and it smelled like potting soil, but Millie promptly experienced a magnetic surge. Ohmygod, she thought. It's perfect. I love it. How much.

Millie's Tevas and Aimee's sneakers began a concert of cupping and slapping on what looked to be real hardwood floors. A flatter sound was produced on the tile in the kitchen; four stove burners, cabinets in need of paint, a window above the sink that faced train tracks and a dry stream. There was a teeny room hanging off the kitchen. A washer, dryer, and water pump for a sink. Along the baseboards, in a holiday dusting of borax, were several brown bugs, bone-dry and legs in the air.

The last year of her life had equipped her with what she knew was a pointless skill, but nonetheless, Millie knew that this house was six hundred square feet. She took the stairs to the top of the landing: a bedroom door, a long, thin closet. There was an alcove beneath a window. I'm supposed to put a desk there, she thought. But I'm going to do a twin bed. She'd keep it neat, lots of pillows. No, Mom, you take the big bed. Yes, I'm good right here. She peeked inside the bedroom. Space for a full. Maybe a queen. Through the window she could see down to the golf cart on the street below.

Millie pressed her lips into a taut line of longing.

"Don't you dare," Aimee said. "There are a lot of 'buts,' which I will explain."

"Is one of them the bathroom?"

Aimee stepped back into the kitchen. "It's real funky, don't fall in."

Next to the refrigerator was a half-sized door that Millie must have missed the first time around. It opened to two steps and an L-shaped wood-panel bathroom. Millie pulled a beaded, rusted cord. A ghostly underwater glow revealed a sink, a shower, and a toilet with a foot flush. Above the toilet was a circular window covered in a milky spiderweb. Three sleepy brown legs removed themselves so slowly that Millie almost felt as though she should have knocked. She crawled up and out of the bathroom. "I'm kind of freaking out."

Aimee shook her head. "As soon as you said you wanted a house I thought, Oh lord. Turn that light out. Let me show you the backyard."

The backyard took up more space than the house. A long patch of wild green ending in a sunken fence. Spokes tied in brush and ivy. There was a dried raised garden and a patch of gravel around the side where Millie knew her car would fit. She squinted at the sun and shielded her forehead. "I mean, I love it. Where do I sign?"

Aimee said, "Hoo boy. Let's back up. First of all, I'm not sure about the price. I know she doesn't want to be bothered with it, and she doesn't think anyone will want it because of the train. And it ticks me off because she should really just give it to you, but she's not that kind of person so it is what it is. Lemme tell them that you'll house-sit. I'll poke around about the price."

"Okay."

"But I just want to be clear that this is an as-is kind of deal. I know they're gonna fix the stairs and do a deep clean, but other than that, what you see is what you get."

"I understand."

"There's one more thing . . ." Aimee shifted her weight. Millie held her abdomen in one hand. "I know I just got you all excited . . . but if I told you that someone died in there—nothing funny, just old—would that change your mind?"

Millie took what she hoped was a respectful breath. "No, ma'am. It would not."

"Are you sure? It's fine if you wanna sit with that. I do think he was in there a few days."

Millie tried not to smile. "I'm more concerned about the price."

Aimee said, "Alright, then. Good girl."

Two days later, Millie received a set of keys and a number: one hundred and two thousand dollars. Aimee said the lowest Kimber would go was ten percent down, but she still wanted to mull the whole thing over. The first time Millie went back on her own, she stood in each room, imagining what she would put where. She texted Aimee and asked if Kimber would be weirded out if she cleaned up a bit. *God no*, Aimee wrote back. *But don't do anything worth more than what she's paying.*

On what became a Friday tradition, Millie completed her last class, grabbed a yogurt and banana, and took a bucket of tools from the Belgrade custodial closet over to the tiny yellow house. A dead mouse underneath the armchair made her shriek. There were large bugs that she disposed of at arm's length. In a drawer, she found a small slip of paper: a grocery list written with an intense right-lean. *Today*, it said. *Butter. Soup. Olives. Ch.* She taped the unfinished list onto the refrigerator door. She guessed the last part was meant to be chocolate or cheese.

Two weeks into the school year, Glory came to visit. She brought a Tupperware of chili, some ibuprofen, tampons, teas, and a glass container of caramels. When Millie opened the door to the yellow house, Glory said, "What is this mess?" But then, in the kitchen, she said, "Oh, Millie. This is cute." She liked the old Craftsman tiles along the sink in the bathroom. She told Millie what a transom window was, as there were two on the first floor. "This wouldn't take us that long," Glory said of the cracked backsplash above the stove. They went down to Home Depot, then carefully recaulked the backsplash where the countertop met the wall. In the weeks following, Glory sent Millie links to sinks she found on Craigslist that could go in the back room. Millie texted her questions about cleaning products. Pictures of vintage cabinet pulls.

As she settled into her senior year, Millie found herself either at the yellow house, in fairly easy classes, or with Ryland and Colette. When one of them was on duty, they talked in Millie's room. They hung out on weekends, too, doing things that weren't extraordinary but seemed special at the time. They drove to farms and looked at cows; the cows came up to the fence when they turned the radio up loud. Millie liked to do homework on Colette's unmade bed. Colette sat next to her and looked at the internet. Her favorite was YouTube; old clips of *To Catch a Predator* and *Rescue 911*. She also loved videos of Mormon teens opening their mission call letters. "Look," she'd say. "He's so mad. He does *not* want to learn Spanish. Ohmygod, his mom is pissed." The three of them hung out at Walgreens and Walmart. Ryland knew of lots of places that gave free samples if you asked. Ryland also loved getting ice cream bars from certain gas stations. Millie usually drove; they always ate standing. Colette once brought Millie a packet of Haribo Peaches, to which Millie gasped and asked if she liked them, too. Colette made a face and said, "Eww, no. I just saw the bag in your trash."

The yellow house remained Millie's alone. Sometimes she did lunges in the grass, or she practiced her Spanish words out loud. On Friday afternoons, after cleaning the stove and stairs, Millie brought her Nalgene and snacks out to the back porch.

She ate with her earbuds in and the sun on her legs. She buried her container of caramels in the dirt under the porch. There was something emotional about the backyard, and the wax around her edibles. She didn't want to share them just yet. They felt like something she had to earn.

7.

WHEN SHE WAS BACK HOME IN IOWA, Kennedy was either at practice, in class, or at a game-day-related event. If her life and her time had been a bedroom, they would have been Nichelle's definition of clean. But Fayetteville was different, and Kennedy was never sure about what she should be doing, how she should do it, or exactly when. On Tuesdays and Thursdays she struggled to pass the day before attending her two p.m. class. On Monday, Wednesday, and Friday she was done by eleven a.m., when it seemed like everyone else was just waking up. There were always little programs and events, dodgeball games and fellowship nights. Kennedy wanted to go but never did. Once, there was a sign-up on Millie's bulletin board to talk to a journalist about weddings. Kennedy decided that she should write her name down, that it could be interesting and fun, but when she went to sign up, the three slots were already filled with Tyler's, Jenna's, and Casey's names.

It always seemed like while she'd been deciding what to do with her time, she'd somehow completely wasted it. After a never-ending afternoon, it would somehow be seven fifty p.m., with an event starting at eight. (A taco night. An improv show.

A tie-dye thing where you just had to bring a shirt.) But even if it was happening in her dorm, just an elevator ride away, Kennedy never felt like she had enough time. And she couldn't tell what would be worse, showing up to see that she was one of two attendees, or arriving to a bigger group of already acquainted people. And then there was what she'd wear or what kind of shoes she should bring. Ten minutes was never enough time to figure out how to be a person.

So instead of spending her first weeks in Arkansas making friends, Kennedy found herself passing the time with intimate activities that she knew were kind of gross. A popular go-to consisted of shutting her bedroom door, taking off her pants, and searching for ingrown hairs on her legs and bikini line. When she got bored doing homework, she'd clean out the dust particles between the keys on her laptop, pulling up impressive clusters of lint. She inspected the pores on the side of her nose. She used the flashlight on her phone to shine light into her mouth. She took the side of her nail and picked at the plaque behind her teeth. She knew she should put music on, but she also preferred the quiet. She thought about getting a job.

She'd babysat before. Maybe she could hostess somewhere. But Nichelle said she shouldn't, that *school* was her job. And did she need money for something? If that was the case, they could talk. But Kennedy didn't need money for anything. She received three hundred and fifty dollars a month; she had all throughout college. Kennedy had a little over five thousand dollars in savings, and she didn't know what to do with it. Back in Iowa she used it for gas money and frozen yogurt, or maybe concert tickets once in a while with some friends. But here, she didn't really go anywhere, the only money she spent was on food, and her mom put money in her bursar account, so that was kind of free. Tyler had a job. She worked three times a week at this music library on campus. Her mom only gave her money for gas. On Fridays Tyler went to the bank to cash her checks. This chore, for some reason, seemed like fun, something that Kennedy would have loved to do.

Tyler was true to her word. She was obsessed with dogs and took lots of naps. She took one every day around three p.m. Sometimes, after a dinner of hummus and baby carrots, she'd sleep again for twenty-five minutes. Then Jenna and Casey would come over. Kennedy kept her bedroom door open and she did normal activities, like fold her clothes or eat a bowl of cereal. But they never invited her to hang out or go out, and after they left, she found herself watching a movie on her laptop, or going back to the weird ways she liked to pass the time. Kennedy could not picture Tyler partaking in any of these activities. Tyler was never gross. The bathroom smelled amazing after she took a shower. When Tyler ate cheese and vegetables and tzatziki, she didn't use a plate. Instead she stood at the kitchen counter on her phone or reading a book, and she ate them out of the bag.

Kennedy started to feel insecure about things she'd never thought twice about. Food was definitely one of them. There was this dessert she and her mom liked to make, and it looked insane but it was so good. You put a banana, skin and all, in the oven for fifteen minutes. Then you partially peel it, add peanut butter and chocolate chips, and put it back in the oven real quick. Kennedy didn't like the idea of Tyler seeing a blackened banana peel ready to be enjoyed and not thrown promptly in the trash. The thought of this made Kennedy wait to make it until Tyler was in class or out for the night with friends. And it wasn't just food, it was other things, too. There was space in the bathroom for Kennedy's pads and tampons, but she kept them in her room. Kennedy wasn't sure why, but Tyler seemed like the type of person who needed one tiny tampon to last her for hours. Oh, that's so interesting, Kennedy could hear her say. I guess I just don't really bleed at night.

Another thing Kennedy felt insecure about was her room. Several residents kept their doors open, and she could peek inside as she passed. Many of the rooms were cute and curated; Etsy art and banners and colorful rugs near their beds. But none of the other residents had headboards, dust ruffles. A chandelier. A butcher block. Kennedy felt like her room made her look dumb. The transfer dorm was very different than the dorm-tour videos she'd watched the summer prior. Once, Jenna peeked in Kennedy's room and promptly flinched. "Whoa," she said. "Sorry, hi. It's like . . . a little store in there."

ONE NIGHT, AS August dropped into September, Kennedy turned her window AC unit down to low. She stood at the window and looked down on manicured grass, and through the air vents she heard the voices of three others. In between the horizontal slats, she could hear the RAs talking in Millie's room. It was Millie, Ryland, and Colette. They were laughing about something. They went on for an hour, and with nothing better to do, Kennedy, unintentionally, listened the whole time.

The next night, they did it again. They talked about their residents and their RD named Josh, and sometimes they went off on things that she didn't understand. One of them would have the dorm phone on hand. When it rang, they'd say, "Belgrade RA on duty." After a few "Uh-huhs" or, "Nope, just recycle it," they'd hang up and say, "Ohmygod. What an idiot." Kennedy wished she could listen to them from her bed, but they weren't as discernible through the wall. So she set her phone up on top of the AC unit and pressed play on an arm workout video. She picked up her three-pound hand weights. She kept the volume set to mute. Kennedy knew she didn't need the pretense of working out to hide her eavesdropping. No one had ever just come in her room; why would they now? But listening to the RAs gossip while toning her biceps—just in case—became something that she looked forward to. The RAs were a TV show she didn't want to miss.

One evening, Kennedy heard Colette say this: "Okay, which one of you has a resident named Dixie?" Kennedy had been doing an overhead triceps press, watching her top half in the window's reflection. At Colette's comment, her mouth dropped open so cartoonishly that the naturalness of the gesture made her laugh.

"Oh. Ha," Millie said. "Okay, so me. Her name is Tyler but Dixie is her dog. And she lives next door so shh."

Colette said, "Wow. Why don't you just wear a necklace that says 'antebellum'?"

"See, I'd prefer that," Ryland said. "Context aside, 'antebellum' is beautiful."

Kennedy began doing plié squats with a biceps curl, pausing with her knees bent so she wouldn't miss a word.

"What's her name? Tyler?" Colette sounded disgusted and pleased. "Of course it is. Girls with boy names think they're so interesting."

"Okay," Ryland said. "You know who else I'm getting sick of? People with *glasses*."

"Oh, I completely agree. But wait, Millie. Is she psychotic or no? Wearing 'Dixie' on a necklace is . . . a choice."

Kennedy smiled into another plié. She didn't trust her own feelings toward so many things, like whether she seemed weird or if she'd taken too long to speak. Or if someone seemed cool because they were, or if she was just a lonely freak loser. But Millie, so cheery and responsible, and seemingly older than the other RAs, was an excellent person to gauge the important matter of whether Tyler was psychotic or no.

"She's fine," Millie said, her voice just loud enough to hear. "But she's in the suite and she leaves the door open. And she's constantly talking about dogs. Every day. It's kind of nuts."

Kennedy found herself practically tearing up. Yes! she thought. She *does* do that! When Tyler wasn't napping or at class or with her friends, she was on the phone with her sister, discussing dogs, specifically Labs. She spent a lot of time looking at different breeders, sending links and saying, "This one looks legit." Once, she said, "Am I a brat for wanting the AKC full? This lady charges fifteen hundred." Kennedy learned that AKC meant American Kennel Club. Kennedy couldn't tell if Tyler thought that fifteen hundred was really expensive or not that bad. Tyler wanted a dog when she moved out of the dorms. She made it clear that her mom wasn't helping her out. But from the way she spent her money, she seemed to have no plans of saving up in order to get one. One time she said to Casey, "You can't think that way. The money will always come." It was one of Kennedy's lower moments, catching herself with the thought that she could offer to pay for Tyler's future dog. She did have the money, and Tyler could just pay her back. Ohmygod Kennedy *no*, Kennedy thought. That's so weird to even *think* like that.

Ryland snorted. "How much is there to say about dogs?"

"You have no idea," Millie said. "She wants a Lab. But it has to be red or blond. And if it's blond, it has to have the angel wings on its back."

Ryland said, "Angel wings? The hell is that?"

"It's like, white marks on their backs? It's so dumb that I know this. Anyway, she wants it from a super-fancy breeder. And she's gonna name it . . . you're not ready."

Ryland said, "Oh lord," and Colette said, "Tell me immediately."

"Boy or girl . . ." Millie taunted, "she's going to name it Navy."

Ryland said, "No," and Colette said, "Stop it."

Tell them! Kennedy thought. Tell them how she'll spell it.

"And if it's a girl," Millie added, "with an *ie* instead of *y*."

Ryland threw something and said, "I'm leaving."

"Wow, I hate that," Colette said. "Millie, don't you have a dog?"

There was a palpable pause. Then Ryland said, "Millie . . ."

"So I just want to say . . ." Millie prefaced, "that I was twelve when we got her. And at the time . . . ugh, whatever. Her name is Fajita, okay?"

"Fajita?" Colette clarified. "That's a great name."

"Yeah," Ryland said. "Why were you embarrassed? 'Fajita' is *beautiful.*"

Wait, no, Kennedy thought. Go back to Tyler. She bent forward and tilted her head as if she could adjust an antenna.

"I have to do rounds." Millie sounded like she was standing.

"Wow. I can't believe you actually *do* the rounds," Colette said. "I just keep the phone on silent and chill."

"Colette. You *what?*"

"The ringer is so annoying."

"But what if there's an emergency?"

Colette was walking around now, too. "Listen," she said. "If someone is calling the RA phone, then it is not an emergency."

"Y'all, wait," Ryland said. "When are health and safety checks again?"

"Tuesday at eight a.m.," Millie said.

Kennedy blinked at this information. Tuesday at eight a.m.

Millie's door opened and their voices went down the hall. Then they were completely gone. Kennedy placed her weights in a caddy underneath her bed. Face-to-face with herself in her vanity, she expressed a closemouthed grin.

Tyler wasn't actively cruel to Kennedy, but she definitely wasn't all that nice. The small "Hey" she gave when Kennedy opened the door stung with the truce of roommate civility. Perhaps it felt more hostile in comparison to the way she greeted Peyton. She'd go, "Oh hello, roomie," or, "Pey-pey's home." And then Peyton would say, "Okaayyy. Hiii." But suddenly, amazingly, thanks to the RAs, Tyler's dogs and the name she picked and the way she left the suite door open . . . it all wasn't as cute as she must have thought it was. The fact that Kennedy would have been friends with her in an instant didn't detract from the pleasure of knowing that Tyler wasn't universally adored.

Now, with the RAs gone, Kennedy could hear multiple voices just outside her door. It was eight p.m. on a Thursday night, and Jenna, Casey, and Tyler were getting ready to go out. Kennedy needed to make her dinner, and typically she'd wait until they'd left. But this time, she changed into pajamas. She removed her makeup with a wipe. She walked out to the kitchen because this was her dorm, too. For once, it wasn't so terrifying, entering a room with a secret.

Peyton stood at the kitchen counter cutting cilantro. A bowl of some kind of stew was steaming next to her. Tyler stood in the bathroom with her blow-dryer on. She bent and worked a round-barrel brush through her hair. "Mitch just said he's getting there around nine," Jenna said. From the double room, Casey said, "Psh. Nuh-uh. There is no way."

Thursdays in Fayetteville had a going-out tenor to them. Not that it mattered. No one ever asked Kennedy to join. Once, she'd been asked by a resident in the elevator, "Are you going out tonight?" When she said no, she felt pressured to use her eight a.m. class as an excuse. She wanted to say, Well, not unless you invite me, because then yes, I'd love to. But admitting she had no opportunities other than the one standing in front of her, well, that would probably cancel the appeal of inviting her at all. Tonight, she actually did kind of have plans. Kennedy and Nichelle had a "date" to watch a movie "together" by pressing play on *27 Dresses* at exactly the same time.

As she walked to the refrigerator and bent down to see her shelf, Jenna came out of the double room. "Tyler," she said. "Do you have any food?"

"I have pretzels in my crate, but don't eat them all," Tyler said.

Casey came out of the double room and held her arms out wide. "So Ah need everyone to be honest right now. Tell me for real, is this cute?" She was wearing a strappy romper in a muted shade of red, the homey color of a plunger head. She had Tory Burch sandals on and white shadow at the corners of her eyes. Her blond hair was done in flat-ironed curls that kind of looked like pasta. She looked incredibly cute.

"I like it," Tyler said. "I like it a lot."

Jenna reappeared, the bag of pretzels in hand. She wore a loose white T-shirt and black denim shorts with pockets hanging below the hem. "Yeah, it's super cute," she said.

"Okay, but Ah kinda feel like Ah look like a giant baby."

Kennedy had thought exactly this. The one-piece looked like the kind a toddler wore. But Casey did look very nice regardless. And it wasn't like she was looking for Kennedy's opinion.

"Kennedy," Casey said. "What do you think? Yes or no?"

Or maybe she was. A La Croix in one hand, Kennedy turned around. "No, yeah, I agree. It looks really cute."

"Okay, good. Peyton? You gotta weigh in, too, sister."

Peyton looked up from her bowl. "I think that it looks fine."

From the refrigerator Kennedy retrieved basil, pepperoni, mushrooms, and a small container of wet olives. She bent for Peyton's cutting board, the one she said Tyler and Kennedy were welcome to use. Casey said, "Alright, then," as she turned to the kitchen table. She took up an Aquafina water bottle, poured two fingers into an amber-tinted glass. Then she reached for a bottle of club soda. Jenna said, "Can you make me one, too?"

Tyler, Casey, and Jenna had done this a few times before, dip into a water bottle with a clear liquid inside. Kennedy knew she'd get in trouble if anyone found out, but Peyton and her passivity had come to dictate Kennedy's reactions, too. Peyton never seemed to care that the suite door was open, so Kennedy didn't say anything either. And if Peyton, of all people, didn't mind getting in trouble, well then Kennedy definitely couldn't care either.

"Can I dip a few of these in your peanut butter?" Jenna asked.

Tyler stepped out of the bathroom with mascara in hand. "Ohmygod. Yes, Jenna. Just a few."

With a loud skid, Peyton pushed her chair back and stood up. She came over to the sink to wash her bowl. She was always doing this—cooking super-elaborate meals and taking all of five minutes to eat them. And she never said it, but she definitely didn't like other people using the kitchen (she'd come in and say, "Ummm . . . never mind," and then go and wait in her room). "Are you . . ." Kennedy looked up. She just knew that Peyton was going to comment on the cutting board. If there was a wrong way to use one, Peyton would know. But as Peyton rinsed her bowl, she said, quite nicely, "Do you want a better knife?"

Kennedy stopped her hand midcut.

These were such small keepsakes. Casey saying, "What do you think?" Peyton asking if she wanted a better knife. But Kennedy stopped and held them as if they were expensive and old. "Yeah, sure," she said. "That would be great."

Peyton handed Kennedy a knife with a short silver blade. In their handoff, Kennedy accidentally knocked her phone off the counter. She saw it fall and she reached behind her back. She caught it between two fingers.

"Whoa," Peyton said. "You're really good at catching things."

Carefully, Kennedy said, "Oh. Yeah, thanks."

"Tahler," Casey said. "Your room is so clean!"

Tyler stepped out of the bathroom and grinned. "Okay, this is so weird?" she said. "But I love to clean my room before I go out. And then when I come back I'm just like, ugh, look at this sweet bed that's been waiting for me all night long."

Kennedy tried not to stare, but man. Tyler looked really cute. She wore white lace shorts and a mint-colored tank top. On her chest was her *Dixie* necklace in gold.

"Mine looks like the opposite of this," Jenna said. "Don't we have health and safety checks next week?"

Tyler said, "Yeah," and Jenna crumpled up the bag of pretzels—it looked like four of them remained. "What does that even mean? How does it work?" Jenna asked.

"Oh, it's nothin'," Casey said. "The RAs peek in your room

and just make sure it's tidy and that there's no fire hazards or anything."

"Uh-oh," Jenna said. "My room is literally a fire hazard. When is it?"

"Next week," Tyler said. "But they don't tell you when."

Kennedy continued to slice her basil. It's Tuesday, she thought. It's Tuesday at eight a.m.

Jenna moaned and rolled her head in an orbit of irritation. Then she went over to the suite door and pushed it shut. "That's so stupid," she said. "I hate stuff like that so much."

"It's really not a big deal," Casey said. "The RAs come and they go, 'Okay, you're fine.' Or if it's a real big mess they go get the director person. Ah think ours is a guy and if he is who Ah think he is, he's kinda cute."

"Exactly," Tyler said. "Jenna, it takes like ten seconds. Ohmygod, do you know what I just remembered?" Tyler beamed as she went up onto her toes. This was something Kennedy noticed that she did often, laughing before she got her story out. It was childlike and odd but it seemed natural on her part. Whenever Kennedy was present for it, she thought, Okay. I see why people like you.

"Okay, so when I was at Hawthorne my freshman year?" Tyler said. "The girls next to me did such a good prank. They found out when health and safeties were before they happened? And then they completely trashed their room. It was so gross. Stuff was everywhere. And we all knew it was happening; it was so funny. And then the RAs were like, 'Okay, we have to bring in our director to take a look.' But then they cleaned it up by the time the RD came. And then they were like, 'Sorry, what? Is there a problem?' It was honestly so funny."

"Ohmahgoodness," Casey said.

"I love that," Jenna said.

"It was hilarious. I would so do it if I knew when they were."

Kennedy looked up at her reflection in the black microwave.

"See," Casey said, "Ah feel like no one would do that here. Everyone is so *serious*. People barely sayin' 'Hah.'"

"I know, I hate it," Tyler said. "This dorm is so boring this year—"

"It's Tuesday," Kennedy said. "It's Tuesday at eight a.m."

Casey let out a little gasp. Jenna looked up from her phone. Tyler placed her hands on the back of the chair. "How do you know that?" she asked.

"Oh," Kennedy said. "I just heard the RAs talking about it . . . and yeah, that's what they said."

Tyler stared at her for a moment. Then she turned back to her friends. In a cartoonish move, she tapped her fingers on her chin. "Hmmm," she said. "Interesting."

"Tahler, you're so bad."

"It's actually perfect because I don't have class till ten."

"Wait, you're sure?" Jenna was on her phone. "This Tuesday at eight a.m.?"

"Yeah."

Casey crossed her arms. "You heard them say that from your room? Oh lord"—she touched her lips—"Can they hear me right now?"

Tyler began to make herself a drink. "No, because there's music on. Kennedy and them share a wall. Ohmygod, but wait. I so wanna do it now."

"But won't it be Millie?" Casey asked. "Nooo. She's so nice."

"No, exactly. That's why it's fun," Tyler said. "She'll think it's funny, too. Ohmy*god*." Tyler bent then. She gripped the edge of the table. "Do you know what would be hysterical? What if it was just on Peyton's side of the room?"

Casey gasped and Jenna said, *"Yes."*

"They would never expect Peyton. That would be *so* good."

Peyton was at the counter, oiling down a cast-iron skillet. She looked up and said, "I am not getting in trouble."

"No no no, that's the whole point!" Tyler said. "You wouldn't get in trouble. Ohmygod Peyton, *please.* I'd take care of the whole thing."

Peyton placed her skillet in a bottom cabinet, a move that came with lots of noise. She said, "That sounds weird," and headed into her room.

"Peyton, wait." Tyler followed.

"Ohmahlord. *Tah*ler."

Kennedy looked over her shoulder to see Tyler tiptoe up to Peyton's bed. "You wouldn't have to do a thing."

Peyton said an even "No."

"But what if I pay you? And I'll clean everything up."

Peyton made a sound, like she was trying to find the right pitch. Then, in a softer tone, she said, "Well . . . okay, how much?"

This sent Tyler, Casey, and Jenna into a fit of laughter. Tyler pressed her hands on Peyton's knees and bounced. "That's my girl," she said. "This is gonna be so fun."

Watching Tyler touch Peyton was so strange, almost as odd as it was watching Peyton not care. The whole thing was so confusing, but it was annoying, too. I don't understand, Kennedy thought. Why can't you be like that with me?

Tyler stepped back out into the common space. A tiny crossbody bag was on her shoulder.

"Kayla said they just got there," Jenna said.

"Okay, yeah. Let's go," Tyler said.

Peyton came back into the kitchen. She took up her electric teakettle and began to fill it from the tap. Then she looked at the cutting board. "What are you making?" she asked.

"Oh. Just pizza," Kennedy said.

Peyton turned the kettle on. "What are you using for the dough?"

"Oh. No, it's . . ." Kennedy didn't want to explain. She went into the freezer and pulled a frozen cheese pizza out from underneath Peyton's wrapped cuts of meat. Years ago, Nichelle had accidentally taken a gluten-free pizza from the frozen-food aisle. It was called Against the Grain and it was so good. That past summer, they got them all the time. They'd add their own toppings, or as Nichelle would say, they'd "doctor it up."

"Ohhhh," Peyton said. "Okay. I get it."

"Yeah, it's gluten-free but it's actually really good."

Peyton paused. "Are you gluten-free?"

"Oh. No, I'm not."

Peyton looked at her face.

"But wait," Kennedy said. "Did you . . . do you want some?"

"No, thank you. I'm full," Peyton said. "Sorry, I thought you were making real pizza, but this is different so never mind."

Standing at the table, Tyler snorted at this response. "Ha. Peyton's like, 'Um hi, I'm a chef.'"

Kennedy smiled and went back to adding her toppings, all the while trying not to cry. She carefully slid the pie into the oven. In her room, she sat on her bed. So it's September, she thought. I've been here almost a month. At what point do I consider like, killing myself?

The group migrated to the door. "Bye, Peyton, have a good night," Jenna said.

Tyler popped her head into Kennedy's bedroom doorway. "Hey," she said. "You're positive? Health and safeties are Tuesday at eight?"

"That's what they said."

Tyler tapped the wall as if she were passing a piano.

"Let's go," Jenna said. "Sara said she's walking from Phi Mu."

Tyler said, "Okay, I'm coming." She gathered the cups on the kitchen table. She ran them under water, did a fast wipe-down of each. Once again, Jenna said, "Let's *gooo*." Tyler jogged to the door. The echo of sandals came and went.

Kennedy's pizza turned melty and warm. She cut the pieces with her pizza wheel, placing half in a Tupperware. She took her plate and her cup into her room. Via phone, she and Nichelle talked for a bit. Then, at the same time, they pressed play and hung up to watch the film.

At the part where Katherine Heigl's sari gets stuck in the cab door, Kennedy walked her dishes to the sink. Ten minutes after that, when Katherine Heigl gets flowers from James Marsden— she doesn't know they're from him—there was a knock on Kennedy's door.

She sat up in her bed. "Yeah?" she called.

Peyton slowly opened the door. She had changed into what Kennedy understood as her sleeping sweatshirt and shorts. The sweatshirt was black and the shorts were like her other ones, but this pair was royal purple and a bit pilled on the sides. On Peyton's head was this thing she wore at night; it was black and shiny and it looked like a bonnet. She stood there as if Kennedy had called her in. When she failed to speak, Kennedy said, "What's up?"

Peyton looked at Kennedy, then glanced at the kitchen sink. "Sooo are you done cooking for the night?"

Kennedy expelled a flip laugh. "Um, yes?"

"Okay. Just make sure to do your dishes before you go to bed."

Kennedy looked past her. The cutting board and knife.

After washing it, Kennedy placed the cutting board on the drying rack. She washed the knife and then, carefully, dried it with a paper towel. She placed it with Peyton's other knives, closed the drawer, and tiptoed back to her room. But ten minutes later—Katherine Heigl was stress-cleaning her apartment—Peyton knocked on her door again.

This time, Kennedy said, "What?"

"Hi," Peyton said. She opened the door. "You're going to do the rest of them, right?"

"Your knife is in your drawer. I washed it and put it back."

"Yeah, I know. But you're going to do your dishes, too, right?"

Kennedy tipped her head to the left. "Yes? Peyton, I'll always do my dishes. I don't like . . . expect anyone to do them for me."

"Well, sometimes you forget, and we agreed that the kitchen would be clean for whoever in the morning . . ."

Kennedy sighed. By *whoever*, Peyton meant herself.

"Peyton, it's not even that late. It's nine fifty. I'll do them."

Peyton swiveled in her white socks. "Okay . . . well, I'm going to go to bed."

Kennedy laughed. "Okay, that's great. Good night."

Peyton closed the door. Ohmygod, Kennedy thought. She'd kind of sounded like Tyler just then.

When the movie finished, she went to the bathroom to brush her teeth. She picked at her hairline, rubbed some lotion on her legs. She looked at Tyler's belongings on her shelf. She yawned into her hand. And then Kennedy crawled under the covers, completely forgetting about her dishes. She inserted her night guard. She turned her pillow to the cool side. She reached to the bottom of her bedside caddy. She opened her copy of *Satellite Grief* and fell asleep with the book in her bed.

8.

"OH, GOOD. PERFECT," JOSH SAID. "I'LL BE right with you guys. Two seconds."

Millie brightened and smiled around the plastic straw in her cheek.

Josh's office was a windowless room with a desk, three chairs, and an industrial shelving unit. The shelves were so big that everyone had to enter single file. On the morning of health and safeties, Millie leaned against the side of it. Colette and Ryland sat in front of Josh's desk. Joanie stood against the wall. She wore windbreaker track shorts, and they rustled aggressively every time she moved.

It felt mean, the fact that Millie held an icy plastic cup in her hand. That Ryland held the same with the addition of caramel and cream. That Colette's black coffee sat next to her chair, in a cardboard zarf that read *Arsaga's*. This had happened a few times before, and Millie felt bad about it then, too. When she, Ryland, and Colette came to staff meetings as one, a bit buzzed on ice cream, smelling like sunscreen and grass. What Millie could have done was text Joanie, something like, Hey, let me know if you want anything from Arsaga's. But she hadn't, and the to-go cups felt cliquish and catty.

Josh returned holding documents of varying sizes. "Okay! Health and safeties, yes?"

Millie said, "Yep," and Ryland said, "Sure."

Josh proceeded to finger through his documents—the inspection checklists, warning slips, violation tags. "This is probably overkill," he said, "but you know what . . . that's fine."

"Hey, Josh," Joanie said. She put her phone down and stood up straight. "So I actually ended up watching both of those movies you mentioned."

Josh looked up. "Oh yeah? That's great!"

"Yeah, I was on duty so it was actually perfect. And after *The Revenant* I was like, man, Leonardo DiCaprio is *good*. So I was pumped to watch *Django*. And then I was like, holding my breath? It is so freaking good!"

Millie watched the back of Colette's head rise with a delicious, honeyed pace.

Josh glanced down at his forms. "Yes, he is good in that."

"Yeah," Joanie said. "And then I actually googled it. Did you know that in the scene at the end that he actually cut his hand on the glass? Like, that was real blood and he just kept filming. And for *The Revenant* he ate raw bison organ. Which is actually really good for you, but still. So nuts."

At this, Ryland met Colette's gaze with the longest blink Millie had ever seen. Josh—still bent at the waist—looked up with wide eyes. "Totally," he said. "Very cool he went that hard. I'm glad you enjoyed them, Joanie. You know what?" He trailed off. "This isn't the right key. I'll be right back, guys. Two secs."

The moment Josh was out of sight, Ryland swiveled to face Colette. "Coco," he whispered loudly. "Did I tell you about my new diet?"

"No," she said. "Tell me everything."

"Okay, so basically I don't eat anything until three p.m."

"Mhm."

"And then, if I go to the gym, I just do like, violence the whole time."

"Right."

"And for dinner, I print out a picture of a baked potato, and then I rip it all up and it's lights-out for me."

Joanie's jaw shifted right and left; the bottom half of her face looked pained and sore. Ryland had taken to completing full turns in his chair, using Colette's eyes as a spot.

"Okay, first of all?" Colette said. "That is . . . so smart."

"Thank you."

"No, seriously? I love that for you."

Joanie looked at her phone and expelled a bitter laugh. "Yeah, guys. Keep going," she said. "Eating disorders are hilarious. Really cool."

"Joanie," Ryland said. "I have a serious allergy? So it's actually not that funny."

"Oh really?"

"Yes, really."

"What is it?"

Ryland pressed his chin to his shoulder. "I can only eat items . . . purchased by someone else."

Millie smiled into her hand.

"Ryland, can I be real with you?" Joanie placed her shoe against the wall. "You have serious definition in your arms. You could be really strong if you wanted to."

Ryland rolled around to face her. "Pretty sure I'm already strong. And I'm the happiest I've ever been. Ask anybody."

"No, Ryland. I'm serious."

"So am I." He stood.

Josh came back into the room. "Ready, folks?"

Millie straightened and said, "Yes."

THE ELEVATOR DOORS opened onto the fourth floor. One of the bright-orange flyers tacked to the bulletin boards bobbed up and down as Millie and Colette passed. Millie readied her clipboard, checklist, and pen. "Okay," she said. "Do you wanna do your side first?"

Colette swallowed and made a strained sound. She lifted a shoulder in tepid approval.

The first door on her side of the floor read *Holly* on Millie's cactus door dec. Millie leaned against the wall next to it, her clipboard pressed into her side. Colette raised her fist and held it inches from the door, but then she dropped it back down. "Millie," she whispered. "Will you just do all of them? Please?"

Millie let her head fall back; the wall gently met her curls. "Why? Are you okay?"

Colette rubbed her palms against her thighs. "I went to bed at four a.m. And health and safeties just creep me out. I'll buy you a drink tomorrow. Can you just do them all?"

Millie gave Colette's shoulder two little pats. "Yes, but you have to stay with me."

"Yes, I'll do whatever you want."

Millie raised her fist and did four loud raps on the door. "Good morning! Health and safeties!"

Colette flinched and exhaled.

"Why did you go to bed at four a.m.?" Millie whispered.

"I honestly don't know."

A sleepy-looking resident appeared and a retainer bobbed in

front of her teeth. She said she didn't have a bra on, but they could still come in.

Most of the dorm rooms smelled the same: a mixture of dryer sheets, bodies, plastic, and perfume. The less clean ones held the breath of wet laundry, a load left in the washer and discovered the next day. Millie and Colette made their way through the single rooms, leaving the four suites for last. Before Millie left, she told them they did a good job. Sometimes she'd whisper, "Okay. Go back to sleep." They made it to Millie's side of the hall, and two rooms in, she knocked to no avail. "Good morning . . ." she went on. "Health and safeties. I'm keying in . . ."

"Don't," Colette said, holding her face. "I feel like it's a crime scene in there."

"Well, if it is, we should probably find out. Health and safeties . . . coming in . . ."

The bedroom was pristine. There was a Post-it on the edge of the desk. *Hi Millie! Sorry to have missed you! Hope my room is okay! xo Lindsey.*

"See? She's fine," Millie said.

Colette looked around the room. "I don't buy it," she said. "Something is weird about today."

"I think you just need to get some sleep."

They arrived at one of the two suites on Millie's side. Millie grinned. "You'll like this one," she said.

Kennedy answered the door in much less makeup than the first day. She stood in a big T-shirt with a pink ombre effect. At the sight of her Millie thought, Oh hey. Good for you.

At the kitchen table, Peyton had just taken a bite of a toasted English muffin. Tyler, in denim shortalls, was standing in the bathroom, completing a fishtail braid. When Millie said, "Hi, ladies," Peyton covered her mouth and waved. Tyler peeked out of the bathroom. Hair in her hands, she said, "Hey."

They started with Kennedy's room. Millie went inside. Standing under the mini chandelier, she heard a zip of air pass through Colette's teeth. It was overwhelming to say the least. The tulle canopy, the coffee cart, the art collages on the walls. Maybe one of these elements would have been fine, but together like this, it was severe. As Millie went through the checklist, she saw that the problem with Kennedy's room was that it looked like it was done by something corporate and removed. It was as if someone had hired a team to make the room look and feel like "home." Colette pointed at one of the paintings, the one that said *Bloom Where You Are Planted*. She pursed her lips, covered one side of her face, looked at Millie, and mouthed, *Racist*.

The kitchen was incredibly clean. There was an electric teakettle, a mixer, and one of those wire holders for tacos to sit upright.

"Why are you looking under the sink?" Peyton asked.

"To make sure there's no leak," Millie said. "Everything here looks good. I'll just check out the double and then you're all set."

She paced to the double room, but upon entering she stopped short. She caught herself with a hand on the wall. Her vision began to swim. Rocking back onto her heels, Millie took in Peyton's side of the room.

There was food, papers, and trash—literal trash—pooling up and around Peyton's desk. Candy wrappers. Loose-leaf pages. Opened bags of potato chips. A piece of string cheese with a bite out of it—out of the *side* of it—was sitting directly on Peyton's chair. The bed was unmade, covered in strange blankets and cans of La Croix. More garbage overflowed in and around the trash can. Next to a pizza box was a knot of extension cords tied together like some kind of threat. Millie recalled that first day, the sweet and sad sight of Peyton's shoes. New Balance sneakers, Old Navy flip-flops, dorky tassel loafers in black. Now there were at least ten pairs of sneakers, just strewn around the floor. The drawers of her IKEA shelving unit were pulled out at odd, feverish lengths. And in one corner was . . . Millie had to bend to see. That's, okay wow, she thought. That's just a pile of straight-up dirt.

Tyler's side was as it had been on that first day, dormified and cute, now more lived in. Her bed was loosely made. A denim jacket hung on her chair. A collage was forming on a bulletin board above her desk. Ticket stubs, Polaroids, a dowel stick and cardboard crown. All of Tyler's items were behaving nicely in her milk crates. Colette stopped walking when she saw the dream catcher on her wall. Once again, she pursed her lips, looked at Millie, and mouthed, *Racist.*

Millie said a quick "Shh" and walked back out and into the kitchen.

"Hey, Peyton?" she said. "Is this your side?"

Peyton said, "Umm," and looked at Tyler. Then she looked at Millie and said, "Yes."

Millie felt sick. She didn't want to embarrass her. "Is this how you've been keeping it? Or have you just been kind of busy?"

Peyton said nothing. Tyler stepped out from the bathroom. "That's pretty much how it always is," Tyler said.

Millie wanted to bend into a squat and think. Peyton was different than the other residents, but it would have been wrong to treat her that way. "Okay," Millie said. "So unfortunately there are a few concerns that we need to take care of? So don't move. We're gonna finish the suites. And then we're gonna grab the RD? He'll come check things out with you. He's great, so don't worry. He's actually super nice."

Peyton looked at Tyler again. She seemed to have said, Did you tell on me? Millie thought, No, but she should have. Back to Millie, Peyton said, "Okay."

The last suite held three roommates with matching bedding and a room that was very healthy and safe. Millie and Colette walked down to the elevators. Colette waited till the doors were closed.

"Okay, the messy room was a lot," she said. "But it scared me less than the other one."

Millie leaned back against the railing.

"Did you see her eyes?" Colette went on. "That girl is *medicated.*"

Millie reached up and touched her neck. "I honestly feel sick. I had no idea her room was like that. And she's super weird and not friendly but I don't want her to get in trouble."

"She won't get in trouble. She'll have a whole day to clean it up."

"I know but . . . that just sucks."

Colette nodded. Millie could feel her taking it in. Colette had these moments of genuine concern, like when she asked Ryland if he was sad, or if he needed a hug. Most nights Colette literally tucked Ryland into bed, which seemed, like everything they did, a joke, but also like something they both enjoyed. "Josh is nice," she said. "He's not gonna be a dick."

Millie nodded, eyes to the floor. She thought of the picture on Peyton's desk, the one with her parents and the large block of ice.

Colette lightly kicked the side of Millie's Teva. "Millie, you care too much. She'll be fine."

"I know."

"And she has more Lubriderm than anyone could ever dream!"

Back in his office, Josh pushed his chair away from his desk. "Hey there. What's the damage?" he said.

Colette delivered her checklist. "All good on mine."

"I need you to check one room in a suite," Millie said.

"Uh-oh. How bad is it?"

Millie knew Colette was right. Josh was nice, and Peyton would be fine. But still, the image of Peyton's EpiPen above the refrigerator did something sour to her stomach. "It's pretty bad," she said.

"Okay. No biggie. I've heard there's always one." Josh stood, placed his hands on his hips. "Let's do it. Colette, you lead the way."

Inside the elevator, Colette's right foot squirmed beneath her. She bent down, removed her shoe, and shook out whatever was inside. As Colette bent down, Millie looked at Josh. She took a breath; tsked her lips.

"You say something?" Josh asked.

She shook one hand. "No, sorry." She placed one hand behind her back.

Colette was right. If anyone was good at these situations, it was definitely Josh. But standing there, Millie understood that if she and Josh had been alone, she would have said something else. She would have whispered, Hey, or, Just so you know. She's the only Black student on my floor.

The suite door was open but Josh knocked twice. "Hi there. Josh here. Resident director. Is it okay if we come in?"

Kennedy came to the threshold of her room. Peyton was washing dishes at the sink. Tyler was still in the bathroom. "Yeah, hi," she said. "Good morning."

"Good morning. I'm Josh. Nice to meet you. Mind if I take a look at the double?"

"Not at all."

Josh walked over to the bedroom, and, to Millie's surprise, he stepped right in.

Millie squinted. Something was off. She could hear his lace-up shoes moving freely about the room. Next to her, Colette made the smallest hum. Millie paced to the room and touched the doorframe with her fingers. Colette came up at her right side and there was the zip through her teeth.

The bedroom glittered with move-in newness. All the trash was gone, the garbage filled with fresh lining. Peyton's bed was made, two flat pillows on top. The floor looked shiny like the tile inside a mall. The food and the shoes and the cords and dirt had vanished. Standing between the two lofted beds, Josh looked around and hummed. "I'll just look in the closets really quickly . . ." he said. They were perfect because of course they were. Colette slipped past Millie and stood at the windows. Millie gripped her clipboard in both hands, cursing herself for not snapping a photo. She glanced over her shoulder and saw Peyton in the kitchen. She was drinking orange juice from a small glass cup.

Tyler turned off the bathroom light and came to the bedroom door. "Y'all mind if I grab my backpack?"

Colette's nostrils formed two circles. Josh said, "Not at all."

When she left, Josh took his voice down. "Millie, this actually looks pretty good to me. Was there anything that you were concerned about?"

Colette rubbed her nose, did the tiniest shake of her head.

"No," Millie said. "No, just wanted a second opinion."

Josh did an adorable *Welp!* with his hands. He walked back

out through the main room. "Okay, ladies. Sorry about that. Keep it up. Best of luck this semester."

They walked down to the elevators. Inside, the doors sealed shut and Josh turned around. Then he let out a laugh that made Millie want to die. "Someone want to tell me what that was all about?"

Millie's mouth dropped open. Josh was smiling but he looked mad. "It's . . . Guys. Listen." He looked to the floor. "If that's supposed to be funny, it's not. Please don't put me in the position of going into young ladies' rooms. Especially if I don't need to be."

A rush came over Millie like she was overheating. She felt that Josh would have said this differently, too, had they happened to be alone.

Colette raised her hands. "No no no. Josh, you don't understand. That room was completely trashed. They just swiped the whole thing. I swear to God, that was a PSYOP, insider-dealing, conspiracy situation. I honestly don't feel safe right now."

Josh's eyes went from Millie to Colette. "They just pranked you two? Is that what just happened? Why would they do that? Whose residents are those?"

"It's—they're mine," Millie said. She watched Josh come upon her humiliation.

The elevator dinged as it reached the first floor. "Okay," Josh said. "Colette, you're all good to go. Millie, let's go to my office."

Millie said, "Okay." In the lobby, she and Colette parted ways. Before Millie took the corner, Colette turned around. "That?" she whispered. "That was all Dixie." She pointed to the space on her chest where the charm of necklace would be.

Millie said nothing. She went and sat in Josh's office. Knees together, feelings hurt. Josh returned. Behind her shoulder he said, "Millie, here." She accepted a travel pack of tissues.

He went behind his desk. "Do you need a minute? I'm happy to give you one."

"No no. I'm just—" She wiped her nose. "Sorry, I'm just confused."

Josh pulled his chair up to his desk. There was a black binder clip that he began to hold in his hands. "First of all, if I came off a little harsh, I apologize. I'm new here and just trying to do my best."

"I know."

"But listen. It's probably a good idea to try and find out why that happened. But . . ." He held a hand up. "It's a dorm. People play pranks. And that was . . . I mean, it sounds like they really got you."

Millie dropped her head with a sound somewhere between a cough and a cry. "I could kick myself for not taking a photo," she said.

"Right, you gotta be fast. Documentation is key."

"Well, I'm also just an idiot. Like—the same person who keeps her kitchen that clean doesn't sleep next to a pile of dirt."

"A pile of dirt? Damn, Millie," he laughed. "Yeah, she played you. I'm so sorry."

At Josh's reaction, his overarticulation, Millie experienced a giddy ascent in her heart. She clutched the tissue. Recrossed her legs. Oh my God, she thought. You are literally so cute.

"I also just . . ." She looked at a stapler on his desk. Her hands were folded between her knees. "This isn't a big deal, but Peyton is the only other Black resident on my floor. And when I saw her room, I was like, shoot. She's been having a hard time. So I guess it's a relief but I was just . . . yeah."

Josh's chair bobbed up and down in agreement. "That's totally valid. I felt the same way about Black students coming through accounts payable. And now I'm obnoxious. I'll just wave at any Black person I see. I'm turning into my dad. I need to stop. But anyway . . . you're doing great. Your floor and your bulletin boards look awesome. Your programs are well-attended. No one is mad at you. Well, that girl might be mad at you. But aside from that, you're doing great."

"Okay. Thank you." Millie stood. "My reports are right there. And . . . okay. Sorry I cried."

Josh shook his head, dismissing her apology. He jiggled the mouse on his computer, waking up the screen. "When, or if, you RD here next year, I'm sure you'll return the favor at some point."

Millie placed a hand on the back of the chair. She lifted her chin and said, "Wait, what?"

Josh froze. He pushed his glasses up his nose.

"What did you . . ." Millie said. "When I'm here next year?"

"Nope. I didn't—you didn't hear that."

"Wait, no."

"*No*"—hands to his head—"I thought you knew! I thought Aimee . . . Millie, I thought you knew."

Millie sat back down, gripped the sides of the chair. "But if I was RD . . . where would you be?"

"I would be . . ." He closed his eyes. "Assistant director? For residential education. And a new role they're creating. For diversity and inclusion . . ."

"Wait wait wait. Sergio's leaving?"

Josh said nothing.

"Does . . . does he know he's leaving?"

Josh closed his eyes again.

"You are *kidding*."

"You could destroy me with this. I messed up, but Millie, please don't—"

"No no, I would never. I want this to work out, too. But wait . . ." Then she whispered, "Congratulations."

Josh sighed and mouthed an embarrassed *Thank you.* "I'm just trying to lay low and get through the year with no hiccups. But I feel terrible about this. I'm sure Aimee had something planned for how she wanted to ask you—"

"No, don't be sorry. I need to figure out next year. It's nice to hear that I might have an option."

"Well, of course. You'd be . . . yes."

Millie inhaled. Ohmygod. I'd be what?

"And so far"—he took his voice down—"not a bad workload. You do have to live within a mile of the dorm, which can be tricky but not impossible."

Millie swallowed, an incredible lift in her frame. "I think I could make that work."

———

THE NEXT DAY, Millie pushed her closet door closed and appeared in her full-length, over-the-door mirror. As she tucked in her tank top, she picked up the count of Tyler's laugh. Tyler was speaking to someone on the phone. Millie didn't know why, but she thought Tyler's laugh was pretty. It sounded dreamy, like a flashlight bouncing through a country wood. "You are nuts," Tyler said. "Okay, perfect, I'm coming down." There was a "Bye, Peyton" and a silence that probably held a wave.

For the past twenty-four hours, Millie had been possessed by the potential of a house and a job. Through lunch in the student union and Spanish class and showering, Millie had a recurring fantasy of walking into her new home, wearing a cardinal polo with *Resident Director* embroidered in white. She'd enter with a phone between her ear and shoulder. A jingle of keys. The tug of a cord. Hello? Oh, hi. No no, I'm free, she'd say. Yeah, exactly. I just got home from work. But the house wasn't hers yet, even though it felt that way. And Aimee hadn't offered her the job; perhaps she was still considering. If this was true, or even if it wasn't, Millie knew that she had to fix things with Peyton.

There was a quick inventory of items (phone, wallet, and keys), all of which went into a black fanny pack. Millie tightened her ponytail, applied deodorant, and locked her door. She walked a few steps to where she could see the suite door. As always, it was left open. At the small dining table, Peyton's head was down.

Millie tapped on the door. "Hey, Peyton?"

Peyton's face rose. She was wearing reading glasses. "Yeah?" she said.

"Hey, can I come in for a sec?"

Peyton made eyes at the table, as if someone else were there. Finally, she said, "Um . . . suurre."

Millie hadn't had many interactions with Peyton since move-in day, but the few she did have recently resurfaced in her mind. One day, Millie had been in the lobby when Peyton received a box in the mail. The side of it said *Harry & David*. She lifted the lid, revealed six peaches sitting inside. They were perfectly ripe, tucked in straw; some had little green leaves and stems. Victoria at reception watched Peyton sign for it. "Someone got a crush on you?" she asked. Peyton resealed the lid with mild offense. "Um no. It's from my grandparents."

Millie once saw Peyton walking with bedding in plastic

wrap. It was folded and pressed in a professional way. Another time, Millie had been in line behind Peyton at a pricey corner store on Dickson. The cashier rang up sixty dollars' worth of simple syrups, teas, granola, and produce. Then Peyton said, "So actually—my parents set up an account for me." The cashier said, "Oh, right. I remember you." There were a few more clicks and then she said, "Shephard, right? Okay, yeah. You're good to go." Peyton took up her bag and left. She definitely saw Millie but she did not say hi.

Peyton closed her textbook on top of a notebook. Millie shut the suite door. She wanted to report back to Josh that she'd smoothed things over, but if Peyton did have a soft spot somewhere, Millie wanted to find it. That first day, after seeing Peyton's info card, Millie had googled *how to epi-pen*, just in case. A brief YouTube video said you could practice on an orange. Be sure to hear the click, it said. Blue to the sky, orange to the thigh.

Millie, about to sit, said, "If it's not a good time, that's okay."

"Well . . ." Peyton looked down at a watch with lots of buttons. "I do have choir in an hour and ten minutes."

"I . . . okay. This won't take that long." Millie sat down, but then she stood back up. She shimmied slightly as she readjusted her fanny pack. "Sorry," she said, hating herself. She sat down once again. "So, I just wanted to check in and make sure . . . that we don't need to talk about anything."

Peyton kept her gaze, but it was a hollow return. "What— or—how do you mean?" she asked. She tried to tuck a thick piece of hair behind her ear, but half of it popped back out.

Millie tried not to look at Peyton's edges, which were in desperate need of retouching. She could picture Peyton's mom doing Google searches for *Black hair salons in Fayetteville*. She'd make a few calls; schedule a Saturday appointment. Peyton would probably take a Lyft. Once finished, with the hair of a little girl (middle part, bump at the ends), she would approach the front desk. Right, they'd say. I remember. Shephard, right? Okay, yeah. You're good to go. But until then, Peyton's hair would look like this. The uneven thickness left Millie distracted and racked with guilt. She wanted to take Peyton, a hot comb, and a chair down to the kitchen. This felt terribly mean. Millie didn't press her own hair, but she did help her mother with hers. But that was her own mother, and Peyton wasn't asking. Millie scratched the space behind her ankle. You need to chill out, she thought. Stop trying to fix her.

"Well, first of all"—Millie smiled—"it's not a big deal. People play pranks. But I just wanted to make sure that yesterday was just a prank and nothing more."

Peyton raised her index finger. "Okay, so I'm actually not allowed to get in trouble about that?" She pulled down at the hem of her shorts.

"No, no one is in trouble. I just wanted to make sure you weren't mad about something."

Peyton placed a hyperextended hand to her chest. "*I* said I didn't want to help out. Which I didn't. You can ask."

Millie's hands went to her thighs. Colette had been right. She usually was.

"Okay. Yeah, no. I believe you," Millie said. "And . . . sorry. Did Tyler just want to have some fun?"

Peyton glanced at her watch. "But I'm not getting in trouble about this, right?"

"Of course not, no."

Peyton rolled her eyes to the floor. "She just said that someone at Hawthorne did it and that she wanted to do it, too. So then Kennedy told her when the health and safety checks were and . . . that was kind of it."

Millie crossed her legs. "Can I ask how Kennedy knew?"

"She just like, heard you guys through the wall," she said. Then Peyton yawned, turning her head, and something shifted in the lenses of her glasses. Millie's mind was moving so quickly—she was horrified that Kennedy could hear her, and she couldn't wait to tell Colette—but in that moment, what seemed most important was the fact that Peyton was wearing Transitions lenses.

"Did Jenna and Casey help out, too?"

"It was mostly Tyler, but they were just like, being part of it. And I probably wouldn't have agreed to it if I knew they were going to have food in my sleep area. But they did clean it up, and Tyler . . . well, that's basically it."

"Okay . . . no, I get it," Millie said. "Sorry. Just one more thing. Why didn't Tyler mess up her own side of the room?"

"Oh," Peyton said. Her face looked as if the thought had never crossed her mind. "They just like . . . they said it would be funnier if it was mine."

Millie uncrossed her legs, abruptly sad and out of place. "Okay," she said. "I appreciate you telling me. And obviously this is between you and me, but yeah, Peyton . . . it's super important that no one, is like . . . taking advantage of you and your space."

Peyton did another side-eye at the invisible person at the table. "Umm . . . okay?" she said. She made a strained noise in her throat. "How would they take advantage of me? I'm pretty sure we're all friends."

Millie nodded. "Okay, great! So you're good, then? And you're fine being in the double?"

"Oh. Yeah," Peyton said. "That was fine with me. I was in a single back in Tallahassee, which we decided was not good for me in terms of time management and personal boundaries. But this is fine so far. I used to wake up sometimes when the elevator would go off at night. But my dad got me these earplugs that are like, clear gel. Olympic swimmers use them. They're really weird. And I got a vibrating alarm watch. So now it's fine."

"Okay. Well, that's great. And I appreciate you chatting with me. Let me know if you need anything, and I'll—"

Peyton raised her hand. "Actually? I do have a question. If we said in the roommate agreement that we wouldn't leave dirty dishes overnight, and if Kennedy keeps doing that, what exactly do I do?"

"Have you talked to her about it?"

"Yes."

"Well, if you don't want her using your dishes, you can totally tell her that."

"No, it's not my dishes. They're hers."

Millie bit her lip.

"She keeps saying she'll do it and then she always forgets," Peyton explained.

Millie touched her hairline. Oooh, I get it, she thought. She tapped the space below her mouth. "Well." She stood. "Ha. Actually. I had a resident who was bad about doing her dishes, too. So her roommates started putting her dishes on her bed. Which is . . . I'm not *telling* you to do that." She grinned. "But . . . yeah. I don't know. It worked for them."

Peyton was so visibly nonplussed by this story that Millie's feelings were almost hurt. She reopened her textbook—*Business Statistics and Analysis in Practice*—and said, by way of dismissal, "Okaayy."

"Alright. Good luck. Lemme know how it goes."

Millie turned to leave and glanced into the double room. Peyton's side was just how it had been—overly parented and uncool. But her desk was gently coated in brilliant, yellow light. A rainbowed refraction bent around the jar filled with quarters. It was marked *LAUNDRY* on one side. Millie wondered why Peyton had quarters if she just sent everything out to be cleaned. But she promptly stopped caring when she saw inside the jar. There was the outline of a twenty-dollar bill. It was sitting vertically on top of the silver quarters, leaning on the edge of the glass. The bill had been folded and neatly tucked into an origami square.

———

COLETTE PULLED HER shoe up to the stool. "Okay, so I was right?"

Millie said thank you to a bartender who delivered a glass of water. "Yeah," she said. "Tyler literally paid her to let her trash her side of the room."

"But why?" Ryland said. "Why wouldn't she just trash her own side?"

Millie removed her fanny pack. "Evidently," she said, "Tyler thought it would be funnier if it was Peyton's side."

Ryland hummed.

Colette squinted. "That feels racist to me," she said.

Millie slapped the bar. "Me too!"

Maxine's Tap Room was a windowless stretch with a brick-lined wall, tight little booths, and stools without backs secured to the floor. At five p.m., at the center of the bar, sun came in through a single skylight and completely charmed the three seats beneath it. This was where Millie had met Colette and

Ryland every Wednesday since the school year began. Sometimes she feared that by being there, they were ruining it, spoiling the place with their volume and youth. But it was so fun. They had popcorn and mint juleps. Millie had never been to New Orleans, but she imagined it felt like this.

Millie hopped up on the stool and said, "Do you know what's almost worse, though? Kennedy, the one with the room and the eyes? She heard us talking in my room. That's how Tyler knew."

Colette said, "Gross. Get a life."

The bartender returned. "Hi, sweetie. What can I get you?"

"Sorry. Hi. Can I have the Bee's Knees?"

Ryland looked at Colette. "Did I not say she'd order that?"

"No," Colette said. "Millie, get something better. Remember? I'm paying."

Millie gasped. "Sorry, can I actually have"—a glance at the menu—"the KC Bootlegger?"

The bartender said, "You got it," as Ryland asked if he could have a sip when it came. That Ryland knew what she'd order, that Colette told her to get something better, it all made Millie feel terrifically young and included.

Colette retied the laces of her shoe on the stool. "I'm mad now. What a dark triad little shit."

"Okay, we're lucky that's all they heard," Millie said. "We can't talk about residents in my room anymore."

Ryland pouted. "That's no fun."

"How much did Tyler pay her?" Colette asked.

For having received a similar fee, Millie felt a wave of guilt. "Twenty bucks," she said.

Colette set her gimlet down. She rubbed her thighs and looked at the mirror behind the bar. "We are going to knock that girl out."

"Colette, no. We need to be cool."

"Who is this person?" Ryland asked. "Is she cute?"

"She's cute," Millie said.

Colette made a face. "Millie's being generous. She's missing-person-on-*Dateline* cute."

"Oh, I know exactly who she is."

The bartender delivered Millie's drink, honey still in motion at the bottom. She said thank you and on further inspection she squealed. A piece of candied ginger floated on the surface.

"Millie, pay attention," Colette said. "Tell me everything you know about her."

"Yes!" Ryland said. "Let's do a home invasion. Can I have my sip?"

Millie handed him the drink. "I don't know anything about her."

"Psh. Do not lie," Colette said. "I've seen your reports. 'Lindsay aced her test! Jennie is homesick . . .'"

Ryland's eyes went wide above the rim. "Oh, this is so good."

Colette snapped her fingers. "Hey, focus. Who is Tyler?"

Millie carefully retrieved her drink. "I don't know. She's a junior. I think she's from Texas . . . Colette, this is so boring."

Ryland shook his head. "Millie, I feel like you don't understand the ask. Is she pregnant? Is she on probation? When she listens to hip-hop, does she . . . sing along?"

"I have no idea. She likes some guy named Kyle. Oh, actually. Her dad is in jail. She has that children-of-inmates scholarship thing."

Ryland balked. "You get a scholarship if your dad is in jail? Wow. Nepotism at its finest."

"Ohmygod, actually?" Millie felt herself being loud. "I heard her call me ghetto once."

Colette raised both hands and said, *"What?"*

"I know. But she was like, 'Not in a bad way. I like Millie.'"

"Okay, yeah. We're gonna mess this girl up."

"Colette, no we're not."

"Tell me what else."

"That's honestly all I know. She's planning her sorority's Halloween lawn decoration thing. She picked the theme and I've heard her explain it at least six times."

"Ohmygod," Ryland said. "I *hate* that thing. Like, oohh a graveyard theme? For Halloween? Amazing, Kailey. Keep it up."

"Did you know they win money for that thing?" Millie said. "The house gets five hundred dollars and so does the decorator."

"Okay, Millie?" Colette said. "You need to close your door."

"I agree," Ryland said. "Wait, what's Tyler's theme?"

"Instead of Woo Pig, it's Boo Pig," Millie said. "She's getting all of these vintage Razorback pictures and she's adding little costumes with like, glitter and felt."

Colette sighed. "Maybe we just do a home invasion."

Ryland bent forward onto the bar. "So I know this isn't about me," he said. "But guess what theme *I'm* doing for October? I'll give you a hint . . . it's basketball."

"I love that," Millie said. "What door decs?"

Over one shoulder, Ryland said, "Li'l hoops."

"So Joanie's doing Halloween week?"

Ryland blinked and said, "Who?"

"Wait." Colette gripped the bar's edge with both hands. "When is October?"

Millie looked at her. "October is on Sunday."

Colette's shoulders dropped. Her chest rounded and hollowed. She put two fingers on the bar and walked them over toward Millie's cocktail. "Millie . . ."

"No. No way. I did August and September. It's your turn."

"This isn't fair. I can't draw and I hate themes."

"Yes, you can. And October is easy. You love creepy things."

Colette gathered her hair and dropped it down on her back. "I could do a blood spatter? Can blood be my theme?"

Millie winced.

"I can also make pretty good circles."

"You want the theme to be circles?"

"Don't make me feel dumb!"

The bartender delivered a bowl of popcorn. Ryland seized it with "Oh, thank God."

Colette tsked. "Ryland, make me a theme."

"Oo, okay. Outer space!"

"That's cute," Millie said.

"No. Space freaks me out. I can't."

Popcorn in his mouth, Ryland said, "How about . . . bodies?"

Millie blanched. "How—I don't know what that means, but no. How about you post something on your bulletin board and ask what theme residents would want?"

"Fuck no." Colette reached for popcorn. "Millie thinks she's Martin Luther posting all this shit. Why can't you just put me to work? I know you have like six themes ready to go."

Millie said, "That's not true," even though it certainly was. If it had been up to her, she'd do root vegetables for October— little carrots and turnips as door decs. She didn't share this idea; she didn't want to look like a pushover. But she did want her floor to look great, just in case Aimee came by.

"Okay okay, I'll do October."

"*Yes.*"

"But you have to do Halloween week. I'm serious. And November."

"Oh thank God. Okay, so I have three weeks."

"Yes, but then you have November, too."

"I got it, geez."

Ryland itched his throat, put his hands between his knees. "Coco," he said. "I have a theme for Halloween."

Millie looked over at him and said, "Okay?"

He tucked a long, invisible strand of hair behind his ear. "Well, instead of Woo Pig, it's Boo Pig? And it's like, a bunch of vintage Razorbacks with li'l costumes and glitter on top."

Colette made a choking noise. She flung her right arm over her mouth.

Millie looked at her. "Colette? You can't."

Into her arm, she said, "Holy shit."

"Colette."

"I'm doing it."

"You can't."

"It's done. My blood is on cocaine right now. Ryland, why are you so smart?"

"It's called God's plan," he said. "Look it up."

"Colette, *no*," Millie said. "She will have a heart attack."

"Fucking good. She started it."

"Ooh, you know what?" Ryland plucked popcorn from his hand. "You could make a cape and goggles for one? Li'l superhero? That'd be cute."

"Excellent idea. You are hired."

"You *guys*." Millie's hands were curled in supplication on her thighs. "We can't mess with residents like that. She'll know."

Colette snorted. "Yeah, that's kind of the entire point. Millie, you are so cucked by Residence Life. Did you murder someone? What does Aimee have on you?"

"We live there. I just don't want to—"

"*Millie.*" Colette pressed her hands into the side of the bar. "This is not a deep-state operation. We're not stealing the Ark of the Covenant. It's a dumb Halloween theme. And it's mine now, okay? Residence Life isn't your dad."

Millie placed her elbows on the bar. "Please just do circles. I'd honestly prefer circles."

"Millie Cousins." Colette shook Millie's knees as if she were trying to wake her up. "You're a senior! Again! Why do you care? Look at me. You're never going to work in Residence Life again. You're free now. They can't hurt you anymore."

Millie's mouth hung open to say something more. She gently bit the side of her nail.

Colette stood up in the space between their stools. "Okay, come here," she said. "Let me hold you."

"What? No."

But Colette's arms were already around her, her chin atop Millie's shoulder like a bird. Ryland contributed a hand to Millie's knee. He shushed her, saying, "It's okay."

"Oh, Millie." Colette rocked her. Ryland swayed in kind. "My sweet little angel normie baby. Listen to me. You will not get in trouble. You don't have to help—"

"I'm not helping at *all.*"

"That's fine. You're fine. Everything's fine. And do you know who else will be fine? Tyler. She's gonna be real mad. And she's gonna call her mom, but then guess what? She will be perfectly fine. And then one day"—Colette's cheek to Millie's hair—"she'll buy her stupid yellow Lab. And she'll graduate with a major in like . . . petroleum."

"She's the same major as me—"

"Doesn't matter. And then she's gonna take graduation pictures, and be like, 'One degree hotter! Ha ha ha.' And then she'll take some unpaid internship in D.C. at like, Capital One Think Tank Design Labs."

"Mhm. So true," Ryland purred.

"And every day for lunch, she's gonna go to Sweetgreen."

"Yes," Ryland said. "Build Your Own or Harvest Bowl."

"And one night she's gonna take a pasta-making class. And she'll give her dad's HBO password to all her friends . . ."

"The password is like, MaritimeLaw4000," Ryland said. "And she's like, 'Ugh, Dad! So embarrassing!'"

"And then?" Colette went on. "She'll get a job or she'll clerk at some law firm. And she'll be like, 'No, I'm different! I wanna *help* people! This is just for now!' But then she'll sit at her laptop and be all, 'Beep, boop, beep . . . How much does . . . one body cost . . .'"

"Colette, please get off—"

"And then she's gonna go home and order Seamless, and she'll be like, 'Ohmygod, the delivery guy loves me ha ha ha,' and she'll sit on her bed and watch *The Handmaid's Tale*. And she'll put on one of those stupid headbands for when you wash your face. And she'll fall into a deep sleep under a little wooden sign that says like . . . I don't know. 'Live, laugh, police.'"

"Mmm," Ryland said. "I've seen those before."

"The moral of the story is that when you see us making glittery little Razorbacks, it's okay if you wanna have fun, too."

"I don't want to have fun. And you're not allowed to use glitter in the dorms."

Colette hugged Millie even tighter, and promised not to use glitter in the dorms.

At the back of Maxine's in a dimly lit bathroom, Millie stood at the sink. For her second drink of the evening, she ordered the Bee's Knees. She felt the teeniest bit out of control, as if she were a video with the audio a second behind. She washed her hands with lots of soap and precision, just to prove that she could. Standing beneath the twilight of two cocktails, the threat of Tyler wasn't such a big deal.

She opened the bathroom door and held it open for another woman. The taproom had become quite busy and dark. She maneuvered past a band setting up amps and instruments. She passed a dog on a leash; a woman saying, "Can I pet him?" And then she realized she was passing red hair; a hand holding a pen above a small stack of papers. Before she truly decided to, Millie said, "Oh, Agatha. Hi."

Her hair was down as it had been the night they met. Two gold bobby pins formed a delicate X above her ear. She wore a beige button-down, slim dark jeans, and tiny gold studs that caught the light. A cell phone was on the bar top next to her stack of papers, facedown in a case of blond wood. It sat next to a glass tumbler with an inch of cider or beer at the base.

Millie saw that Agatha recognized her but didn't immediately recall her name. Then Agatha pointed her pen with certainty. "Millie. Hi. How are you?"

Millie teetered on the edge of wishing she hadn't said hello. She reached up and righted her waves, feeling more drunk and more sober than she had in the bathroom. She was messy but methodical and aware. More than anything, she was filled with an impulse to conjure intelligence and charm. "I'm good," she said. "How's your research going?"

Agatha clicked the top of her pen. "Well, at the moment, it's not going anywhere because these are student papers."

Millie glanced down as Agatha unfolded a front page. The

heading read *Professor Paul* and the date. Around the text were lots of comments and strike-throughs in red. One said *Redundant.* Another said *What does this add?*

"But research is . . ." Agatha wavered her head. "Well, it's going somewhere. I'm actually glad I ran into you. The night at your dorm shifted my focus quite a bit."

"Shifted in a bad way?"

"No, just further away from weddings. The girls were very inspiring, to say the least. Not in an aspirational sense," she clarified. "But they were very blunt and . . . well, yes. I don't have to explain that to you."

"Oh. Right," Millie said. "And just so you know, I wasn't listening to the whole thing."

Agatha shook her head. "No, I know. And it would be fine if you did."

"Well, I did hear Tyler say that people don't know how to have fun when they're 'old and thirty-eight or whatever.'"

"Ha. Right. Which is actually very funny because I turn thirty-eight this Friday."

"Oh, no way. Happy birthday," Millie said. "I guess you better go crazy till then."

"What's that? Oh, right." Agatha smiled. "No more fun after that."

As she spoke, Agatha bent and dropped her pen into her purse. Millie thought, I should go; she wants to leave. But then Agatha opened her mouth, a question at the corner of her lips. She placed her chin on her hand. "You know, I thought about you," she said. "When I relistened to that night. And I hope this isn't too forward . . . but that can't be easy to deal with. Especially when they live so close."

The way Agatha looked at Millie then, it made her feel special. There was no pity or emotion. Her assessment seemed scientific. Her head on her hand and her voice low and hushed. It felt important, like a doctor checking your reflexes. Pull against my fingers? Push back against me? Good. Millie looked down at one of her hands. Her cheeks felt very full and warm.

"Oh. Well, I'm from a really white town," she said. "And no one is ever like, outright mean to me. And most of it is in response to the fact that Belgrade isn't the greatest place to live. Which brings out a lot of interesting views. And as an RA you just kind of end up fielding a lot of comments about— Wait, sorry." Millie laughed. "You're like, working right now. I'll leave you alone."

Agatha was tipping back the last bit of her drink. She made an *Mmm* sound and placed the glass on the bar. "No no no, that's interesting. Why do you think your dorm brings that out?"

Millie arched her back. "Well, no one wants to live in dorms in general. And since it's not very cute, people will . . . complain about it in a certain way. And this is my second year living there, so I've heard a lot of like, 'Ugh, this is so ghetto. We live in the poor-people dorm.' Stuff like that. This one time the air-conditioning broke and these girls were like, 'Ohmygod. We live in the projects . . .' And it's not my job to be like, 'Well, actually, Melissa, we do not live in a housing project' or whatever. So yeah. Usually I'm just like, hokay, moving on."

"Right," Agatha said. "That's interesting. Especially since it's a scholarship dorm?"

"Kind of. It's for transfers, upperclassmen, and scholarship housing. So basically older students who don't want to live in a dorm."

Agatha smiled. "I get it. Are you there because of the diversity scholarship you mentioned?"

"No, I'm there because I'm an RA. I do have three scholarships but not a housing one. I have one because my dad is a vet and one that's academic, but it's small. And then I have the diversity one. But all of those don't cover my whole tuition . . ." Once again, Millie felt like she was talking too much, but she didn't know how to stop. "There's like, two thousand dollars a year left," she said. "So my parents pay for that, and I pay for like . . . my life here. Which is fine because I could have gone to school for way less. My dad teaches at Missouri Southern. But my parents couldn't pay for the whole thing here, so they were like, 'Well, you've gotta make it work.' So I just applied to every financial aid thing. But yeah. Sorry. That's why I'm an RA . . ." Millie knew as she was saying it that that was not the question originally asked.

The bartender arrived and removed Agatha's empty glass. He asked, "Would you like another?" and she said, "Just the check."

Back to Millie, Agatha smiled and said, "Millie, keep going. What were you saying?"

Millie looked at the freckles underneath her eyes. Okay, she thought. Why am I obsessed with you? "No, sorry. That was it." She laughed once and touched her neck. "I'm not drunk but I feel like I'm talking a lot."

The bartender returned with a shot glass holding a pen and receipt. Agatha smiled and reached for her tab. "You don't seem drunk to me," she said. "And this is actually where my research is heading. How students navigate money. I actually contacted the honors program and a few sororities to see if I could sit and observe. But none of them got back to me."

"Ooh, yeah, no. They'll never let you do that."

Agatha made a little click in the right side of her mouth. "Well, that's a bummer. I'll have to figure something out."

"Well, would you want to come back to Belgrade?" Millie pushed her bra strap up. "I can do another sign-up, or if you just want to sit and observe . . . yeah, you could always come and just like, hang out."

Agatha said, "That's an interesting idea." Her thoughtful expression made Millie feel certain that she'd definitely been to Europe. Maybe once to visit a friend.

"Well, I'm on duty every Thursday," Millie said. "And for one weekend every month. And you could honestly come and just sit in that little room. And Thursday is a big going-out night. Lots of money talk. You'd be . . . inspired."

"Would you need to get that approved?"

"No, I'm allowed to have guests. And you wouldn't even need to sign in. No one cares. Okay—actually? I'm on duty this weekend. You should come on Saturday because it's Blues, Bikes, and Barbecue."

Agatha reached into her purse. She came back up with a small black journal with a leather loop and a tiny brass pen. "Blues, Bikes, and Barbecue? Is that what it sounds like?"

"Yes. It'll be kind of rowdy. You're welcome to stop by."

Agatha looked up. Her hand stayed in the fold of her journal. "Well first of all, this is very generous. I'm definitely interested, but . . . hmm."

The heat of her thoughtfulness made Millie reach up. Hands in back pockets, tongue against her teeth.

"Well, how about this? I'm going to text you tomorrow to make sure this still sounds good. And if you completely ignore me, I will not be offended."

"I'm not gonna ignore you. Do you still have my number?"

"Write it down just in case."

Millie wrote her name and number down a few lines beneath

Blues, Bikes, and Barbecue. Agatha gathered her papers and slid them into her bag. Millie handed the journal back, consumed with excitement and regret. She was so nervous. She couldn't wait for her to come. She was also very certain now. She should not have said hi.

Agatha stood. "Well, I'm glad I ran into you." She set her purse on the stool. Millie was struck by the beauty of it. Lightly pebbled leather in a romantic navy blue. "Are you here with friends?" Agatha asked.

"I am. They're down there."

"I think I see them. They . . . I believe they want you back."

Millie turned. Down at the other end of the bar, Ryland tapped his left wrist. Colette held up a limp hand. Her lips said, *The fuck is this?*

"Yeah, sorry." Millie turned back around. She found Agatha leaning onto the bar.

"Let me cover your first round," she said. In one of her hands a long, flat wallet had appeared.

"Oh, no. You don't have to do that."

"No, I insist. It was nice of you to chat. Hi, can I cover her first round? And her friends' as well?"

The bartender said, "Sure thing," and tapped the register's screen. "You're with Ryland, right?"

Millie said she was. "That's really nice of you."

Agatha shook her head. Then her chin went an inch to the right. She pressed her lips together and placed her fist next to her mouth. "Millie. I'm so sorry. You are twenty-one, yes?"

Millie could barely speak. "Oh. Yeah, no. I'm twenty-four."

Agatha wiped imaginary sweat from her brow. "Okay," she said. "I figured."

The bartender delivered a new tab and pen. Millie watched her sign her name. "Thank you again."

Agatha dropped the pen in the glass. "Did you say twenty-four? Did you take a gap year?"

"Oh, yeah. And then—it's complicated . . ."

Agatha raised a hand, implying, *It's none of my business.* "I'm going to duck in the ladies' room. Thanks again."

Millie walked back down to the other end.

As Colette said, "About time," Ryland announced he hadn't eaten in fifty-two minutes.

Millie grabbed her fanny pack. "Sorry. I'm ready now."

Colette asked for the check.

"Was that a professor?" Ryland asked.

"She's a professor, not mine. I helped her out with something. Aimee knows her."

Ryland rolled his eyes. "Aimee knows everyone in this town. Oh, I've decided who Aimee looks like. She's a therapist . . . in a *Far Side* cartoon."

Colette looked up and said, "That is correct."

A flash of red hair made Millie go stiff. Agatha passed by in the space behind her. "Bye, Millie. Take care."

Millie waved.

Ryland's eyebrows went up into his hair.

"Hey," Colette said, a pen in one hand. "This is weird. Why is this so cheap?"

"Oh. Because, yeah." Millie slipped her fanny pack over her chest. "She actually paid for our first round."

In a strange, monotone voice, Ryland gasped and said, "Daddy."

Colette said, "What?" Her eyes went to the front door.

For a second, before she left, Agatha turned profile. Millie watched Colette watch this, too. Colette turned back around. She pointed behind her with the bottom of the pen. "That very tall lesbian just paid for our drinks?"

"I—yes." Millie swallowed. Something felt buoyed inside her brain.

"Interesting . . ." Colette wrote in the tip. "If I'd known, I would have worn my tennis whites."

"She's ugly hot," Ryland said.

Colette dropped the pen in the glass. "That's exactly right. I love ugly hot. No makeup, bad attitude, goes to therapy, academia top."

Millie was suddenly very flustered and embarrassed. "Colette, you don't know that," she said.

"I don't know what?"

"That she's gay."

"Millie . . ." Colette retrieved her backpack. "I'm gonna have to hug you again."

"Okay, but why do you think that?"

"Do you mean why do I know that?"

"Don't make me feel dumb!"

Colette held her backpack with both hands. "Okay, fine. How do I know that woman is gay? First off, because I have eyes. And second, if she was straight, then she would have dyed her eyebrows."

9.

ERHAPS SHE COULDN'T HAVE FUN ANYMORE AT
age thirty-eight, but for the past seven weeks, there were
many instances where Agatha found herself sunburned
and soothed by two phrases. The first was this: No one knows
where I am right now. She thought this on hikes, while driving,
at the butcher counter in the grocery store. And the second one
was this: I can do whatever I want. She thought the latter all the
time.

It was like she'd been left at home for the first time with a
fresh license in hand. She sat on her porch during lightning
storms. She watched with wet feet as the tornado siren wailed.
Every Friday, she drove twenty minutes to a decent sushi place
for takeout. She ate the rolls while sitting on her bed, watching
Survivor on Hulu. She found herself gasping out loud at immu-
nity idols and blindsides. The reasons she left the house became
bookish and wild: to check how high the stream was after rain,
to see if a gorgeous gray fox had returned. One afternoon, she
slipped four singles under the glass at the Wilson Park public
pool. The woman behind the glass leaned in. "Honey, are yew
sure?" she asked. "The pew's gon' close in twenty-fahv minutes."
Agatha said that she was sure. She jumped off the diving board,

floated around for fifteen minutes, and then she went home. Via FaceTime, Jean was always delighted and surprised to see her state. "You're so tan," she'd say. "Your hair is wet from a *pool?*"

There were some moments where Agatha found herself in a bad made-for-TV movie, cast in the role of City Woman in the Country. Most of these were amusing, like when she asked for small bills at the bank. "Alright. Ah'll try," the teller said. "But the government usually only gives me the one size." But some of these moments were embarrassing, like when she forgot that alcohol wasn't sold on Sundays. A young person behind a cash register took up her bottles from the conveyor. He reminded her of the rules and placed the bottles out of sight.

But Fayetteville wasn't country, not hardly. It was very much a state school town, and therefore, many of the stores and restaurants were preoccupied with trying to resemble Williamsburg circa 2010. Exposed brick. Snake plants and succulents. Thin, geometric wall decals and tattoos. Two specific extremes dominated: highbrow and hip, and lowbrow and comfy. A macaron store. Waffle House. Lululemon. A bar called Shotz. At a pricey coffeehouse called Puritan, a latte came in a beaker and it was delivered on a notched slab of wood. Across the street, you could order a ladle of chili in a Cheetos bag, served with a plastic fork on top. The city was powered by young people. They were walking to class and ordering lavender iced coffees. They were opening laptops covered in stickers at cafés and asking strangers to watch their stuff. Standing between Agatha and her new freedom to do as she pleased were young people, seemingly working their first or second jobs. Her interest in campus culture grew. She felt inspired, guilty, and strange.

Three days after her interview at Belgrade, Agatha transcribed the recording. When she reheard Jenna comparing herself to a refugee, Agatha wrote out the words, and she placed the quote into a separate document. She meant to show it to Jean later as she knew her friend would laugh and be appalled. But Jenna had so many worthy pull quotes. The practice paychecks. How she technically worked for her dad. Agatha also liked when she couldn't stop eating the cheese ("Ohmygod, get this away from me," she'd said). To give Jean full context, Agatha created a breakdown at the top of the page: Jenna's age, major, hometown, and the occupations of her parents. Agatha continued to move Jenna's best quotes into a separate document. She added some of the questions that she'd asked as if she were interviewing Jenna alone.

Jean enjoyed it very much. Over FaceTime she asked, "This was the first interview you did?"

"It was."

"I think you can just quit now," Jean said. "I love how she can't stop eating the cheese. Call me crazy . . . but is this something on its own?"

Agatha rested her elbows in front of her keyboard. "I hadn't considered that."

"Send it to your little baby agent. See what she thinks."

"That's not a bad idea."

Agatha went to class, and then she walked home. She sat at her computer and read the interview once more, the one she'd pieced together for Jean. There was a large bookshelf in her living room with dozens of paperbacks, all incredibly old and used. She perused the titles and landed on *Justine, or The Misfortunes of Virtue*. Agatha did a find and replace, and changed Jenna's name to Justine. She sent the interview to her agent, Charlotte, feeling charitable and sportsmanlike. The subject read, *Is this something?*

They didn't communicate often, but when they did, Charlotte

had this habit of replying by using a different mode of communication than the original method, which was exactly what she did. Agatha emailed her the profile. Charlotte texted, *Is this real?* Agatha texted that it was. Then Charlotte called her cell. "I love this," she said. "You know who would love this, too? Natasha over at *The Cut.*"

"Oh, that's interesting," Agatha said.

"Let me send it to her. Ohmygod, I'm so excited. And I like the title. *Fun Money.* That's so cute."

An hour later, Charlotte emailed, asking if Agatha could hop on the phone. "Okay," she said. "Don't be mad at me, but I haven't sent it to Natasha and here's why. You know how Refinery29 is doing that *Money Diaries* thing? *Teen Vogue* wants a money thing, too. And there's a woman over there who loved *Birthday Money.* She went to Georgetown, too, but she was after me. Anyway, she's super smart and she's a big fan of yours. So I sent it to her, not officially, but she loved it and she said she would do seventy-five cents a word. Which is really good right now. Not that you need it." According to Charlotte, *Teen Vogue* was very up-to-date since the election. Her excitement made it clear that Charlotte still did not fully understand Agatha's interests as a writer. But somehow, in Fayetteville, that was okay. "They get a lot of hits," Charlotte said. "And they'd want more. Can you do more?"

Agatha looked up at the bookshelf full of paperbacks. She said she didn't see why not.

The editor at *Teen Vogue* couldn't have been older than twenty-seven. She, and seemingly everyone else on their staff, had chic first names like Ana and Lise. The editor asked if Agatha could have "Justine" answer a few more questions: how many roommates she had, her savings, and what she made from her job and parents. Agatha didn't seek Jenna out again, but she filled in the answers as if she had. Jenna did not have a roommate—of this she was certain. She called the alumni office where Jenna said she worked. She said she was doing a story on wages, and could they tell her what the pay was for students.

A young man said, "I'm not sure I'm supposed to say . . . but I get nine an hour."

"And how long are your shifts?"

"Only three hours. It's awesome."

"Okay, great. Thanks so much."

Agatha entered these numbers beneath Jenna's parents' occupations. *Work-study job: $54 weekly before taxes*, she wrote. She also included *$700 monthly from parents* because Millie seemed like a reliable source. The question of Jenna's savings was the only one she really didn't know. But the idea of reaching out to her for this seemed wrong, and Agatha didn't want to tell her that this was actually for *Teen Vogue*. So Jenna's savings became the one prompt that Agatha truly ad-libbed. *Yes*, she wrote, as if she were her. *I have one but I'm not sure how much.* Filling in this blank herself was liberating, and it strangely left room for Agatha to add something she felt the piece was missing. So she wrote the prompt—*Something I splurge on*—and then she wrote the answer—*Balayage*. When the magazine sent back proofs for how the article would look, the word *balayage* linked to another article: "Fallyage Hair Trends and How to Fake Them." The interview section was done in a traditional typeface. The short answers were in a handwriting font, as if Jenna, or Justine, had completed them herself.

Agatha had an online following of around four thousand made up of academics, journalists, and readers. When the profile went live, it was featured on the magazine's home page, and

Agatha gained another five hundred. The comment section beneath the interview was incredibly active; Agatha's eyes hurt
from scrolling. She knew the enjoyment of the interview was not
just in Jenna's vernacular, but in the formality of her own. She'd
made herself sound hyperserious, academic to a fault. An old
classmate from graduate school had shared the article and written: *Agatha, I didn't know you were so funny.* People loved and
hated Justine. Seven hundred dollars? A *month*? They couldn't
believe it. They bet she went to Auburn or Duke. Agatha didn't
give the name of the school. These were dispatches from, simply,
Southern U.

That the answers were not all genuinely acquired was not lost
on her. Agatha would have done the math this way: Jenna,
ninety-two percent. Herself, eight. But Jenna *had* signed a release. Her real name wasn't used. And Agatha felt strongly that
most of the fabrications, Jenna wouldn't have remembered if
she'd divulged them or not. The hair and allowance parts felt
different, as they had come from Millie. But the speed of the
publication, the length and lightness of the piece, it all felt fun
and harmless. It was something to do alone in the South, in a
post-breakup season. Agatha wished she didn't feel this way, but
she liked publishing something that Robin could come upon,
something her teenage clients or dancer friends might read.
Robin would have thought the publication too lowbrow for Agatha. In any other circumstance, she would have been right.

With the success of her first profile, *Teen Vogue* upped the
deadline for a second piece and Agatha obliged. She put up a
sign-up sheet on the English department bulletin board, and
she interviewed four young women. Each of them said nothing
of interest, and two of them said, unprompted, that family
meant everything to them. But then she ran into Millie, chatty

and a little drunk, who had offered up her residence hall again. Agatha felt an elfin shame at texting a twenty-four-year-old, but once again, the quickness of it made the whole thing feel harmless (*Yes!* Millie had replied. *Just text me when you get here*).

In the parking lot of Ozark Natural Foods, Agatha responded to a happy birthday text from her dad. She started her car (a twelve-year-old Camry she'd recently purchased) and drove back to her home at Wilson Park. Her plan was to go on a long run, order sushi, and then watch *Survivor*. It was a pitiful effort on her part, she knew this, but nonetheless, she'd saved a season finale for her birthday.

Agatha went for her run after an early lunch. The sun's placement in the sky felt redemptive, as if she were paying penance for all the television, sushi, and paraphrasing she'd been doing. But it didn't take long for the pain to turn peaceful. Nothing was playing from her recently purchased AirPods. Around mile three she decided to push herself to a degree she knew she'd regret. She ran to the edge of Lake Fayetteville. Once there, she sat in a patch of dirt, her face up and toward the sun. Before she left, she placed her hands into the water. No one knows where I am, she thought. I can do whatever I want.

Sunburned and almost home, Agatha slowed and rested her wrists on her head. The trail emptied out into an unshaded stretch with thick trees on one side and train tracks on the other. There was a slightly quicker way home but Agatha took this route routinely, as this was where she saw that thin gray fox drink from a stream. But the fox was gone and the stream was dry. Agatha stopped to switch from one podcast to another. Beneath the theme music, she heard the closing of a door.

Across the train tracks, on the porch of a yellow house, was a large bun of curls and a bucket of cleaning supplies. Agatha said, "Millie?"

"Oh, hey," Millie said. "That's so funny. Two times in one week."

Agatha hoped she wasn't alarmingly red, but Millie looked pretty sweaty herself. She was in an oversized white T-shirt and little red shorts. A black-and-white bandana hung loosely at her neck. Between them was asphalt, train track, grass, and dirt. They were too far to speak normally but still too close to yell. Agatha stepped off the trail and shielded her eyes. "I guess it'll be three times, if you're still good with tomorrow."

"Oh yeah, for sure. It'll be a big going-out night. I can tell."

Millie stepped into the grass as she spoke. She pressed a button on a fob. A parked car made a noise. Agatha thought, Wow, that's exactly the car you would have. It was a nail-polish purple, two-door RAV4. It looked very used and like a large children's shoe.

"So yeah." Millie shut her door with her hip. "Just text me and I'll come down."

"Sounds good. Thanks again."

Agatha knew she should leave, but Millie's bucket of supplies pulled her back. "Is this . . ." She removed an earbud. "Do you live here?"

"Oh. No . . . or not yet."

"Not yet?"

Millie crossed her ankles. "It's . . . okay, you know Aimee, right?"

Agatha raised one finger and then she stepped closer. She did a little leap over the stream.

Millie explained the situation, talking with her hands. If all went well, she'd own it in the spring. "It's dumb but . . . I wanna work on it so when they come back, they're like, 'Oh wow, she's done so much, we should definitely let her buy it.' But I also just like projects. And sometimes I just sit and study. And there's . . . well wait. Do you want to see it?"

Agatha lowered her hand to her hip. "Yes," she said. "I'd love to." She followed Millie up through the grass.

"It's not . . ." Millie paused. "Keep your expectations low."

Agatha wiped her shoes as she said she understood.

Inside was an adorable mess of a house. The front room was shockingly dark, the wood floors impressively uneven. There was a clunky set of stairs that took up way too much space. The air smelled like cleaning supplies, a toolshed, and a grandparent's house. A place with trinkets and nonperishable food. And yet, everything about the space was immediately special. The house felt like a preserved homestead. It looked like the home of some artist or poet who spent their last days writing letters, eating only bread and honey.

Millie walked into the kitchen, which was sunnier and hot. "I'll obviously get more lights but I'm just trying to get everything clean."

Agatha peeked in the bathroom but she didn't go in for fear of getting stuck. The sound of the creaking door rang out pretty under her hand. "This is very charming," she said.

"Yeah, I hope it works out. And sorry, it probably smells like chemicals in here."

Agatha peeked in the farmhouse sink: flecks of copper and black around the sides. "You do open the windows when you clean in here, right?"

"Oh yeah, no," Millie said. "I open all the windows and doors. And I put this over my face." She touched the bandana at her neck. Then she removed it and held it in her hands.

"I love stuff like this. I hope you get it."

"Me too. I don't have the whole down payment just yet, but I'm on a strict budget and I think I'll be okay."

"Can I ask what they're asking for it?"

"Oh sure. They want one-oh-two and ten percent down."

"One-oh-two?" she clarified. Then she said, "Oh, wow."

It felt cheap to think of Robin then, but her mind went and stayed there notwithstanding. Millie, at twenty-four years old, must have had at least seven or eight thousand dollars if she was going to make her down payment by spring. She had a long-term goal, she was on a budget, and the thing she wanted required work, which she was already putting in on a Friday afternoon. Agatha couldn't tell if she was overly impressed with Millie or readjusting to a relationship with money that wasn't shaped by Robin. Robin, who loved hotels, who said Airbnbs creeped her out. Robin, who paid six months of a subscription to Birchbox before realizing that she'd never received one box. Robin, who once made sixty thousand dollars—as a dancer! As she should have, of course, but come *on*—who, despite the fact that she didn't pay rent, was often left with less than two hundred dollars the evening before payday. But here was an undergrad with lots of ambition and foresight, working hard for a house with little light and square footage. Agatha recognized this triumph as a shallow one, but—much like purchasing Air-Pods or doing pieces for *Teen Vogue*—it felt like a win to do things that Robin would have never seen coming. Agatha knew it was petty, but it was also just nice. Standing in a house that Robin would have hated and could never afford.

"Haha, yeah." Millie shifted her weight to the other hip. "I don't know. I like it, so . . . we'll see."

Panic rose in Agatha then. While she'd been thinking of

Robin, something had moved in Millie's face. Agatha saw that her reaction to the price, her mindless "Oh, wow," had meant something different for Millie. That Millie had potentially heard *Oh, that's nothing* was bad enough; but if she'd heard *Oh, that's much more than it's worth*, that was somehow even worse. Millie shifted again in her Tevas. Her nervous "Haha" broke Agatha's heart.

"Oh. No," Agatha corrected. "The price makes sense. I'm just impressed you can save up that much in college. I'm not sure I could have."

"Oh. Yeah, I was at home working part-time last year. And I worked full-time this summer."

Agatha wanted to ask where, but sweat was dripping down the backsides of her arms. "That's great. Good for you. I don't want to keep you."

Millie followed her outside. She turned and shut the door. "Were you out for a run?"

"I was," Agatha said.

"Wow. It's so hot. I could never— Oh wait. Isn't it your . . ."

Agatha turned around in the grass. The roof of Millie's dream house shaded her left eye.

"What's that?" she asked.

Millie shook her head. "No, sorry." She smiled. "I was thinking of something else."

———

AT SEVEN FIFTY P.M., blocks before she saw a bike, the rip of hundreds of engines met Agatha on her porch. With her legal pad and recorder tucked into her purse, she walked down West Avenue through a thin layer of smoke. Hundreds of motorcycles swept down Dickson Street at a leisurely shared pace. The sidewalk overflowed in leather and denim. Faded tattoos, graphic tees, stars and bars.

At the Belgrade entrance Agatha pulled out her phone, but then she looked up and saw there was no need. Millie stood inside the entryway, lips moving, facing the reception desk. She glanced over and came to the door. "Hey," she said. "Perfect timing."

The same security guard as before was sitting behind the glass. Agatha smiled at her. "It's kind of crazy out there."

"Yeah, it's a big weekend. Oh"—Millie turned—"Can you hold that?"

The elevator had opened and dinged. Millie stepped in and held the door with one arm. Agatha followed, holding her bag to her side. Once inside, Millie said, "So there's a little problem . . . but it's totally fine."

Agatha crossed her arms. "Uh-oh, what's up?"

Millie checked the screen on her phone. "So the AC in the study room was making noises and leaking and now there's a guy fixing it. And I'm not sure how long he'll take but it's totally fine, because you can just sit in my room."

Agatha tried to soften the movement happening around her eyes. The light above the elevator door signaled that they were passing the third floor. She suddenly felt nervous about the fact that she hadn't signed in at reception. She knew she'd put too much pressure on this evening; the promise of a second piece in three days. But Agatha found herself saying the things she knew she should. "Is that . . . that sounds inconvenient for you. If we need to reschedule—"

"No no, not at all. It might even be better for you this way because"—the elevator opened—"well . . . lemme just show you."

The word Millie had used back at Maxine's presented itself in audible form. The floor was rowdy. Several doors left open. A trace of dry shampoo in the air. Voices of young women tapered over music playing from laptop speakers. The pool-themed nameplates on the doors had been replaced with potted cacti and succulents. Agatha followed Millie down the hall, and she read names on doors both opened and closed. (*Tierney, Natalia, Jenna, Annie.*) They passed the study room she'd been in before. A man in jeans knelt near a toolbox. Millie stopped at a door with her own name on a cactus. With a wash of unease, Agatha watched her insert a key.

Just inside Millie's room was a narrow corridor. On one side, a thermostat. On the other, a closet door. At the end of the tiny entryway hung a thick navy curtain secured on a rod squeezed between the walls. Millie pushed it back with one hand. It gathered on the floor in theatrical little folds.

"So I can't sleep unless it's dark"—she held the curtain in her hand—"and the hallway lights are always on. But this also makes it feel kind of private, which is nice. And we can leave my door cracked open. That way, you'll hear plenty. But yeah, we can keep this shut"—she touched the curtain again—"so you can have some privacy. Well, I'll be here. I have to do Spanish. But you can make yourself at home and take my desk if you want." Millie motioned for Agatha to step farther inside. Once she did, Millie pulled the curtain closed. The dorm room became a perfect square.

It hadn't clicked properly in the elevator, when Millie had said the words *my room.* But now that she was standing in it, Agatha thought, Ah. You meant your *bed*room. Several amenities would have put her at ease: a sink, a stovetop, an IKEA table for two. But this was very much a bedroom: a bed, dresser, and desk. There were personal belongings and a thoughtful color scheme. But if the situation was at all inappropriate, Millie showed no signs of thinking so. She stood bright-eyed in her red RA polo with the posture of a zookeeper who feeds sea lions for a crowd. Agatha touched her thumbnail to her mouth as Millie itched her ankle with the top of her other shoe. She's fine, Agatha told herself. It's just one night. "Okay," she said. "As long as I'm not putting you out."

"No. Not at all."

"You can carry on like normal?"

"Oh yeah. I've lived in a dorm for a long time."

In the hallway, someone yelled, "Does anyone have rose gold bronzer?"

"Wow." Agatha blinked. "The noise really does carry."

"It does."

Agatha lowered her bag and took a breath. She looked at the room, admiringly, and said, "Well, alright."

Millie said she had to do rounds and then she'd just be doing Spanish. And did Agatha need her desk? She worked on her bed all the time. Agatha said no, that she was quite comfortable on the floor. She settled in with her back against the wall, her left side lightly touching the curtain.

Before Millie left, Agatha said, "Millie." She asked what she should do if someone knocked.

"Oh, they won't," she said. "I put a sign on my door. It says that I'll be right back." Millie took up an impressive amount of items (Nalgene, clipboard, lanyard, and phone). "Okay. See you soon," she said. She pulled the curtain closed. She left the door open one inch.

In Millie's absence, the room's colors and textures began to materialize with context and currency. Agatha looked up and took in the window. It was draped with tiny lights on copper twine. The sill held several potted plants: aloe, jake, cacti, English ivy. The bed sat beneath it and was covered by a comforter with swirls of leopards in white, peach, and kelly green. A black mini fridge served as a nightstand. Marble contact paper had been added on top. There was a pink glowing orb of light—a lamp meant to resemble a block of Himalayan salt. A few pieces hung on the walls. A white macramé rainbow. Two French medicinal posters featuring plants and their names. Agatha took a breath and crossed her legs. *No one knows where I am right now.*

There were two shelves above a dresser. One held more plants and a small television. On the other were storage bins. One was filled with snacks (dried apricots, peanut butter, white cheddar popcorn, a spotted banana). The other was for toiletries (Aveeno bodywash, Tom's deodorant, a tube of toothpaste, a wide-toothed comb). A small bin of makeup and dried flowers in a terrazzo vase sat on the dresser top. There were four hardcover books in a neat stack. *Americanah. Sweetbitter. The Omnivore's Dilemma. The Girl on the Train.*

A few inches from the bottom of Agatha's clogs was the left side of Millie's desk. From the floor, she could see a textbook that read *Aula Internacional 4.* A bright-red planner read *2017.* Taped to the wall were several documents. A class schedule. A calendar. A list of conjugated verbs. There was a picture of a black cat. A very old-looking dog. A few grainy Polaroids featured the friends from Maxine's. A Post-it—in what Agatha felt wasn't Millie's handwriting—read *A Millie A Millie* some dozen times. Another Post-it in a more formal script said this: *Millie will pay $20 when a. She realizes Colette is right about JonBenét Ramsey, b. The truth comes out, or c. Whichever happens first.* Agatha looked up at the documents above Millie's desk and tried to see a last name. But as she tilted her neck she heard a sigh and a twang. From the next room over, she heard Casey speak.

"Ah don't remember it bein' this loud last year," she said.

"I'm gonna have my noise machine like, all the way up," Tyler said.

Agatha knew their voices immediately. She'd listened to their first interview three times over. Now, just one room over, they came through eerily close. Agatha reached for her device and began to record.

"Did y'all hear Bailey?" Casey said. "She was like, 'Where do they go once they drive down Dickson?' Ah was like, 'Girl, they turn around and do it again.'"

Jenna laughed. "She thought they were going somewhere? That's so funny. Like—no. This is it."

"Hey, Peyton?" Tyler called. "Can I have a bite of this?"

A new voice said, "Yes, but use a fork."

Effortlessly, as if she were watching television, Agatha thought, Ooh, who's that? The recorder wobbled between her knees. She picked it up, reached between the wall and curtain, and gently set it down on the other side.

Casey gasped. "Wait a freaking minute. Did Kahl ask Raelyn to Hayride?"

There was a pause, and then Tyler let out a two-syllable "Yep."

Jenna gasped low. "*Kyle* Kyle? Lemme see."

"No. Tahler. Why didn't you *say?*"

"Honestly? Because I'm over it and I just couldn't be bothered."

"Ohmygod," Jenna said. "She's so annoying." Something in her voice implied she was looking at a phone.

"No, honestly?" Tyler went on. "I'm glad he's shown his true colors. If that's what you think of as a good time? Going apple picking with someone who *vapes*?"

"No," Casey said. "She does not. Good lord."

"Exactly. If that's what you want, then be my guest."

There was movement on the other side of the curtain. Agatha pulled her legs to her chest as Millie appeared and whispered, "It's just me." Millie pulled the curtain closed and set her Nalgene on her desk. She hung her clipboard on a tack and pulled out her chair. Next door, Jenna asked if something was too short. Tyler said, "Turn around . . . no, it's fine."

Millie opened her textbook on her desk and Agatha felt a surge of indiscretion. She pushed it down with No, it's fine. Next door Jenna said, "What's that?" Then she asked if she could have a bite. Please, Agatha thought. Please let this turn into something good. She imagined a breezy beginning with these quick captures of campus money in *Teen Vogue*. But then, maybe a manuscript, something longer and more honest. Intriguing in-depth profiles of monied college women. She'd sit in on their classes and meet their families, too. Agatha imagined Millie as well, three or four years ahead, browsing in Barnes & Noble with a friend. Oh hey, she'd say. I know her. She wrote some of this in my dorm room. Millie's friend, slightly uninterested, would say, She sat in your room? Millie would consider how this sounded. Yeah, she's a journalist, she'd say. It sounds weird but it wasn't.

From the other room was a sigh. "Oh, Kahl," Casey said. "We were all rootin' for him."

"I know," Tyler said. "Did y'all know he's a twin?"

"Who? Kahl?"

"His brother goes to UT Austin."

"Really? That's so weird," Jenna said. "But he is kind of an idiot so I guess that makes sense."

Agatha looked at her knees. There was a pause in the other room.

Tyler asked, "What makes sense?"

"That he's a twin," Jenna said.

Millie's pen paused above her desk.

Tyler laughed. "Wait, why would that make sense?"

"Um, because he's dumb? He's failing stats," Jenna said.

Casey made a series of audible guffaws. "Jenna, what does that *mean?*"

"Yeah," Tyler said. "What are you saying? Twins aren't dumb."

"My mom is a twin," the newer voice said.

"Yeah," Tyler said. "And Peyton's mom is smart. She went to Vanderbilt."

"Well, obviously not *all* twins. Guys, it's not . . ." Jenna swallowed. "It's not my personal opinion. It's just like, basic science."

Millie winced around a smile.

"Excuse me?" Casey said. "What science says that twins are dumb?"

"Ohmygod. I never said that. If you have parents who give a shit about you, or if you just wanna be successful, then yeah, you can be smart. But it's basic science that twins come from one little egg meant for one little brain, and then the cells split and that's why they have to share."

Agatha recoiled as if she'd watched someone take a bad fall in the snow.

Casey gasped and said, "Jenna, *no.*"

"K, I don't know how it happens," Tyler laughed, "but I know it's definitely not that."

"So Ah *do* know how it happens? 'Cause this is literally mah major? And twins do *not* split a brain."

"Not—okay. I'm right about this," Jenna said. "It's why twins always end up in the NICU. Because their cells—"

"Okay, honestly? Ah'm gonna leave the room."

Tyler was still laughing, and her laugh was strangely melodic. "Ohmygod," she said. "Casey's like, 'Um, hi. I'm a doctor.'"

Over the course of the next hour, Tyler, Casey, and Jenna proceeded to get ready for a night out. There was lots of telling each other that they looked great, borrowing things, asking each other to stand a certain way. Agatha found herself putting things they mentioned into a search bar on her phone. Microblading. A trip to the Maldives. Evidently, Crocs were back in style. And then, once again, without meaning her to, Millie became part of the equation.

"Did y'all see Demarcus today?" Tyler said. "Eric went to sit at his table and Demarcus was like, 'No narps allowed!' And then Eric goes, 'That's discrimination, bro!'"

"Ohmygod," Jenna said. "That's so funny. I love him."

Agatha leaned forward. "Millie," she whispered. "Are they saying *narp*?"

Millie smiled. "Yeah. It's . . . hang on." She took up a Post-it, wrote something down. Then she stuck it to the side of her desk. Agatha read it with her lips moving. *Non Athletic Regular Person.*

"Seriously?"

Millie nodded.

Agatha smiled and wrote it down. "So am I a narp?"

"Yes."

"Are you a narp?"

Millie laughed. She looked down at her body, in reference to it. "Are you serious? I mean . . . *yes.*"

Agatha smiled, heartsick and endeared.

Later, Casey said she needed to call her mom to put some money on her Razorbuck$. Agatha asked Millie what Razorbuck$ were. Millie explained that it was a bursar account in the form of a campus debit card. She held hers up and her lanyard made lots of noise.

"I see, okay." Agatha wrote it down. Hesitantly, she said, "Can I ask who puts money on yours?"

Pen in hand, eyes on her notebook, Millie did a long, performative blink. "Whoooo do you think puts money on mine?"

Agatha laughed and said, "Good for you."

Around nine forty-five, the group said goodbye to Peyton, and they marched past Millie's room to the elevators. Agatha retrieved her recorder. At the base of her right hand was the pinch of a cramp. She stood and retrieved two twenty-dollar bills from her purse. She slid the bills underneath the corner of Millie's desk lamp.

"So that was great," she said.

"Oh. Are you sure? I feel like that's too much."

"No no. Don't be silly. And . . . just one more thing." Agatha readjusted her bag. She's an adult, she thought. She's twenty-four. Just ask. "Do you mind if I close your door?"

"Oh sure."

Agatha stepped past the curtain and shut the door. Millie brought her legs to the side of her chair. "So I'd love to come back if you'll have me," Agatha said.

"Oh, no problem," Millie said. "Any Thursday works for me."

"That sounds great. But I just want to be clear . . . if I were doing this properly, there would be a couple avenues that I'd need to go down first. I'd have residents sign release forms. I might need IRB approval. And it may come to that, but so far I haven't. And . . ." Agatha stalled. "I'm still figuring out what my angle is." She couldn't bring herself to say *Teen Vogue*.

A text appeared on Millie's phone. She reached for the device and turned it over.

"If any of that makes you uncomfortable, I'd completely understand," Agatha said.

Millie pushed her knees together. "Are you saying you need me to sign something?"

Agatha did a vague gesture with her mouth. "No. I guess I'm saying the opposite."

Millie tipped her head. "Ohh. I get it. Okay. Yeah, no. I don't care that it's not official."

"Are you sure? I don't want to put you in a bad position. Especially since you do work here."

Millie shook her head. "No, I really don't mind. Especially if it's just you like . . . exposing Tyler and those girls."

This delighted Agatha. She crossed her arms. "Are they troublemakers for you?"

Millie rolled her eyes. "They . . . this is so stupid. They played a prank on me and my friend; she's an RA, too. And it's fine but it just made me look dumb. So yeah. Expose them. You have my full support." She raised her foot and placed it under her thigh.

Millie was saying all the things that Agatha wanted to hear, but there was still something unfinished. The idea of saying *Can you keep this between us?* was awful, so instead Agatha looked down at her desk. She eyed Millie's clipboard, her noisy lanyard. The little sign that said *Be back in ten!* One last time, Agatha said, "You're absolutely certain?"

Millie followed her gaze and blushed. "No, yeah, I am. I really don't care. And it'd be different if you were doing something wrong. And you're not using real names, right?"

"No no."

"See, then yeah. But even if you were. There's no moral obligation. And as far as me working here, I don't feel weird about that at all. Residence Life isn't like, my dad."

Agatha laughed. She thanked Millie again. She told her she was a great informant, that she could see herself out. Hand on the door, Agatha turned around one last time. "Millie, you know what you have to do when someone plays a prank on you, right?"

Millie exhaled and ran a hand through her hair. "I'm working on it," she said.

10.

ON TUESDAYS AND THURSDAYS, KENNEDY HAD Intro to Gender Studies in a large theater-style lecture hall from five to six fifteen. The class was taught by an energetic professor who sang and jumped around, and Kennedy therefore sat in the second-to-last row. One day, four weeks into the school year, the professor told the class to find a partner and to answer the workbook questions up on the screen. Kennedy did what she did in other classes: kept her head down and opened her workbook, making it difficult for roaming TAs to urge her to do more. But then, two rows ahead of her, a head of teak-colored hair turned around. "Hey. Do you have a partner?" she said. Kennedy shook her head. The girl said, "Cool." She stood and her seat noisily flapped closed.

Kennedy removed her backpack from the next seat over. The long-haired student sat down and crossed her legs. "I'm warning you now," she said. "I'm not very good at this stuff."

"Oh, me neither," Kennedy said. "I feel like I never know what she's talking about."

"Ohmygod, same. And I kind of wish she didn't say that the final is open-book because now I never pay attention."

"I know. Like—please lie to me so I do better."

"Exactly." She opened her textbook on her legs. "Anyway. Hi. I'm Shea."

Shea had a thick widow's peak and Adidas sneakers that she placed on the seat in front of her. She wore jean shorts and a T-shirt that said *Hogs*, but the *O* was an actual Razorback. Shea looked strong, like she had once done or maybe currently did some kind of strength training. On her upper arms, against pale skin, were little clusters of soft red dots. Once they completed the assignment, Kennedy learned that Shea was a junior, too. That she was from NWA and majoring in apparel merchandising and product development. When Kennedy asked if she lived in an apartment, Shea said, "No, I wish. I'm in the Kappa Delta house this year."

"I think I'm like—right near there. I'm in Belgrade."

"Oh, no way. I've probably seen you. How do you like Belgrade?"

"It's . . . not great," Kennedy said.

"Yeah, that's what I've heard. This girl in my sorority is from Serbia and she was like, 'Why is it called Belgrade? That's *wrong*,' and I was like, I have no idea what you're talking about, but anyway. Don't most people get a single there? See, I'm so jealous of that. I have two roommates and one gets up at six for diving and the other has sleep apnea. So I'm just like . . . oookay, do I need to go to Belgrade? Because I will."

Shea continued to sit in Kennedy's row. She was fun and nice and Kennedy made sure that she wasn't outfit-repeating for their Tuesday/Thursday class. They used the seat between them to hold their belongings, and for partner work, they placed a textbook on their bags. Shea typically received two or three texts during class. She hid her phone behind the seat whenever she typed back.

Once, in the middle of class, a guy sitting three rows ahead pulled the headphone cord from his computer. The game he'd been playing, something with lots of gunfire and yelling, came alive, and the surrounding students flinched. He quickly muted his computer and raised his hand. "Sorry, guys." Up front, the professor eyed him before she started up again.

Kennedy exhaled and looked at Shea. She whispered, "Geez. That scared me."

Shea leaned in. "Okay, not to be a prude? But if you're just going to play games the whole class, then why come?"

The way Shea leaned into her, the way she partially covered her mouth, Kennedy caught herself blushing down into her neck. Wait a second, she thought. Are we—could we be friends?

"I know." Kennedy rolled her eyes. "It's not like anyone is taking attendance."

If the class had been in the morning, if it had ended at one or two, Kennedy would have tried something like, Hey, do you have class right now? Do you want to grab a coffee? But six fifteen was so late and awkward. She didn't want to do it wrong or make it feel like a weird date. Then, miraculously, their professor announced that there would be a department-led barbecue that Saturday evening. And if that wasn't incentive enough, two points would be added to midterm exams for attendance. Kennedy's shoulders ached from forcing herself to not look directly over at Shea.

The class was dismissed. Shea stood up. "Are you going to that?" she asked.

Kennedy zipped her backpack. "I was thinking about it, but I'm not sure."

"Me too. Do you want to take my number? And if you end up going you can let me know?"

Kennedy retrieved her phone and took a breath. "Yeah, sure. That sounds good."

"Okay, cool." Shea handed Kennedy her phone. "Just type your number in. My roommate has this professor for a class she's not doing well in, so I'm guessing she'll want to go, too. And since you're in Belgrade . . . yeah, that would actually work out great. Since you would be on the way."

Kennedy typed her number and Shea said, "Cool, I'm texting you." Standing there, she received a message from a new number. The body of the text read *Shea!*

Kennedy walked back to her dorm a different person; a regular college person capable of making friends. She imagined Shea pulling her aside. This is boring, Shea would say. Do you want to grab a drink? Kennedy would say yeah, that she was thinking the same thing. She imagined saying other things, too. Not at the barbecue, but later on. Not to be weird, Kennedy would say, but I was kind of depressed before I met you. Shea would tell her she would have never known. If things went really well, then maybe Kennedy could say the whole thing. She'd go, Can I tell you something really sad? Shea would say, Ohmygod of course.

SATURDAY CAME. The barbecue started at seven. After living in such close quarters to Tyler, Kennedy knew that a text near the start time of an event was the proper way to coordinate getting there. So she busied herself with laundry and an essay. She watched a tutorial on winged eyeliner. In a wet towel, she blow-dried her hair. And after laying out outfit options, she settled on the one she'd thought of first. A fitted denim skirt. White Keds. A violet top with a print of white flowers. Delicate ruffle at the sleeves.

Hey, Shea, it's Kennedy! Let me know if you're still down for the barbecue tonight. At six fifty, she typed this into her notes app. After a few rounds of edits, she copied, pasted, and pressed send. When Shea failed to reply immediately, Kennedy told herself to get up. Shea was also a normal college person. She might take a while to respond. Kennedy needed to eat something, as she'd probably be too nervous to eat anything later on. So she took herself and her cute outfit into the kitchen. At the counter she ate a rice cake with peanut butter and salt.

Two minutes later, Peyton came through the front door holding a bin of clean bedding in plastic wrap. She said hi, Kennedy smiled at her, and then she went to the double room. Peyton bent at the knees and opened the door with her elbow. From the darkness within, there was a rustling of sheets. Tyler said, "Don't worry, Peyton. I'm awake." Kennedy checked her phone to no avail.

A minute later, Tyler emerged: low pony, lines at her cheeks, sleep mask pushed up onto her hair. There was something about the vulnerability of Tyler's face that made Kennedy feel like she was the mother of a toddler. Like Tyler was hers. Like Kennedy was supposed to say, Well hi. Look who's up. Kennedy dusted her hands over the sink and began to put her items away. Tyler stood next to the table and yawned into her arm.

"Are you going out?" she asked.

Kennedy closed a cabinet and said, "Yeah."

Tyler went up on her toes and placed her elbows above her head. "That's fun," she said. Then, to no one she said, "How am I still so sleepy?" She walked into the bathroom and closed the door.

Kennedy began to play a game called Don't Look at Your Phone Until (__). Until Tyler gets out of the bathroom. Until you make your bed. The thought did cross her mind that Shea would fail to text her back, but Kennedy struggled to envision a scenario in which she wouldn't make it okay. Hey! She pictured Shea typing around eight p.m. *So sorry, I randomly ended up seeing a movie. But do you want to meet up on Dickson? Or, even better . . . I'm so sorry!* she could say. *I took a weirdly long nap. But would you want to do brunch tomorrow?* Kennedy would have loved to.

It was seven twenty-two p.m. Kennedy organized her jewelry stand. She carefully untwisted the chains and charms. The idea of Shea not texting back was bananas—it had been her idea!—so Kennedy refused to get worked up just yet. But then Shea did text back, at seven twenty-six p.m. The message was somehow even worse than if she hadn't.

Hey! she wrote. *We just walked in. Are you here?*

Kennedy sat down on her bed. The top button of her skirt cut into her skin. *But I thought— Didn't we . . . you're already there?* A sharp cramp shot through her right side. She knew—she *knew*—she wasn't remembering incorrectly, that Shea had said that Belgrade was on the way. If that was true, then hadn't that meant . . . How had she messed this up?

Kennedy stood up to shimmy her skirt down. She could fix this. This could be okay. She could text, *On my way!* and be there in ten minutes. But then she reread Shea's text once more. *We just walked in*, she'd said. How many was *we*?

Something Tyler had previously discussed at length was her annoyance with Friends You Have to Babysit. "It drives me nuts," she said, "when girls are like, 'Don't leave me. Sit next to me.'" One Sunday morning Tyler went on about someone who was needy in this way. "I was so annoyed," she said. "I was texting Casey under the table like, 'Okay, so when can we ditch her?'" The idea of Shea feeling remotely similar, it made Kennedy's eyes sting. Hey, sorry, Shea would whisper to her roommates. I didn't think we'd be like . . . babysitting.

No, just go, Kennedy thought. She is nice, you can just go. She took up her purse and did a once-over in the mirror. She would text Shea on the way. She'd say, Almost! Be there in five. It would be nerve-racking but she'd be glad that she'd come. Kennedy moved, trying to create inertia. She spritzed the air with perfume and quickly walked through the mist.

Tyler was at the kitchen table when Kennedy emerged from her room. A phone was in her hand and a bowl of cereal was beneath her. "Have fun," she said.

"Oh. Thanks," Kennedy said. At the door she thought, Okay, that's like . . . the nicest you've ever been to me.

She started for the elevators and went to check the time. A new text from Shea sat waiting to be read. Kennedy stopped walking and clicked the screen. *There's like no food left lol*

If Kennedy had called her mom right then, Nichelle would have said, Well, okay! Kens. You're thinking too much. Just scoot on down there and hang out. But Kennedy could not just scoot on down to a girl she barely knew, to a barbecue with no food. She would not be able to live with herself if her night got worse from there. And suddenly, peculiarly, she didn't trust herself to be so sad and alone.

And so, in a strange, snowballing panic, Kennedy forced herself down the hall. She went to take the elevators but then she took the stairs. She summoned an Uber on the first floor.

A man named Greg who looked like a dad picked her up in his Durango. Once she was inside, he said, "Kennedy?"

"Yes, hi."

He clicked his phone's screen. "Target, right?"

"Yes, please."

THERE WEREN'T A lot of people there. The music playing from the speakers above sounded louder than it normally did. Kennedy picked up a red shopping basket and poked around the front section. Halloween items, autumn décor, flashy tumblers, dinnerware for girls' nights. She picked up a scented face mask. Cactus flower and green clay. She looked at it and thought, You're okay. She placed it inside her basket. It looked dumb there by itself.

Merona crewneck sweaters were two for twenty-five. There were chevron-printed maxi dresses that Nichelle would have liked. In the shoe aisle, Kennedy tried on cork wedge sandals and ballet flats. Her basket held the face mask, a lip balm, and some copper paper clips.

An Aerosmith song came on from the overhead speakers, the one where he doesn't want to miss a thing. Standing in front of the DVD section, Kennedy set her basket on the ground and proceeded to walk back and forth. She and Nichelle used to do this all the time: go to Target, get fun snacks, then pick out a DVD. She knew that DVDs were now dated and useless, but she couldn't shake the satisfaction of shopping for them, holding the cases in her hands. Her mom's favorite was when there was a two-for-one DVD situation: two complementary movies in one split-screen case. *Elf* matched with *Home Alone*. *My Sister's Keeper* and *The Fault in Our Stars*. Romantic comedies with Queen Latifah. Kennedy liked the one where she thinks she's dying but she's not.

An hour later, she purchased the three items. Then she ordered an Uber home. A woman named Clarissa picked her up. She had an accent that implied that she spoke Spanish as well. Clarissa asked if Kennedy would like a mini bottle of water. She said no thank you and the silence settled in. When she recognized where she was, Kennedy said, "Can you actually drop me here?" Clarissa said, "Are you sure?"

Her Keds tapped on the sidewalk with a round sound that made her feel like she was about to be stabbed. This was highly unlikely, she knew, as she was passing Wilson Park. The houses and their Razorback flags suggested that professors or alumni lived inside. But the cold had settled in, and it felt like something she should run from. Through the dark, leafy shadows, Kennedy clutched her elbows in her hands. She began to count her steps. She heard something skitter into a bush. Okay, she thought. I really hope I don't get robbed. She imagined a stranger popping out of the landscaping on her right. The sound she'd make, the adrenaline in her throat. But then Kennedy imagined what would come after. And maybe . . . She slowed down. Maybe that could be kind of good.

The man would be skinny with patchy facial hair. Hand it over, he'd say. Kennedy would scream. The logistics of the attack mattered less than the aftermath: Kennedy walking into the suite. She pictured herself closing the door behind her. Her shirt greened by a fall in the grass. Purple knees and a split lip. At the kitchen table, in going-out attire, Jenna, Casey, and Tyler would go hushed. Ohmygod, Jenna would say. Tyler would ask, Are you okay?

Kennedy wouldn't make eye contact. She'd walk to the bathroom; say, I'm fine. But she wouldn't be fine and they wouldn't believe her. She'd be sat down at the table with a flurry of perfume

and concern. Jenna, Casey, and Tyler would administer patch-
work advice. Don't wash your hands. DNA under your nails.
Don't fall asleep. You might have a concussion. Millie would be
summoned. She'd call the police and they'd do a report. Yes, she
was alone when it happened. No, she didn't get a good look at
his face.

At some point, either waiting for Millie or the police, Kennedy would say, Sorry. You guys don't have to stay. Tyler would
laugh. Kennedy, we're not just going to *leave* you. Casey would
say that wherever they'd been going hadn't looked fun anyway.
And then Tyler would do something for Kennedy that she could
have done herself. She'd bend down to untie her shoes, or she'd
hold a compress to her knee. From the floor, Tyler would look
up. Sorry, am I hurting you? Kennedy would shake her head.
No, you're not. That feels good.

11.

AT 10:29 A.M. ON THE SECOND TUESDAY IN October, Millie did a middle-finger knock at Josh's office door. The door was open and Josh sat at his computer. On top of a cedar-colored sweater he wore a navy fleece with sporty-looking pocket-pulls. The mere sight of these pocket-pulls left Millie girlish and heart-struck. Ohmygod, she thought. He has a vest. It was the first day of the semester to truly feel like fall.

"Ah! Hi!" Josh looked at his watch. "Ten thirty already? Shoot. Hang on." He bent down behind his desk. "Just one sec. Shut that door."

Millie did so and sat down. Her backpack was still on and squished behind her.

"Okay," Josh said. "Close your eyes."

There was a ping of plastic in the air. Millie's eyes were closed, but her eyelids fluttered still. Finally, Josh said, "Open." She did so and touched her cheeks.

On his desk was a small paper plate checkered in cardinal and white. In the center was a single cupcake. Blue liner, cream cheese frosting. Draped around it was a red-and-white lanyard, tag still on, pricing sticker removed. The lanyard had an official-looking font that read *University of Arkansas*. Near the key clip, it read *Staff*. Millie's spine pitched up and to the left. "Ohmygoodness. Wait, this is so nice."

"Congratulations. Officially this time."

"Well . . ." She slipped her backpack off. "Not *super* officially, but yeah."

That past Friday, Millie dropped off receipts at Student Housing. She'd waved at Aimee and then Aimee called her back. Aimee folded her hands under her chin. "I think you know what I'm going to say . . ." She offered Millie the RD job, in confidence. An official contract would come in the new year.

Richard and Glory took Millie to dinner, where she'd ordered a mushroom risotto with truffle oil and parmesan. It felt a little like bad luck, toasting to her first real job without legitimate documentation. But on Monday morning, as she sat in the lecture hall of her Destination Marketing and Operations class, Millie's eyes glazed over with freedom and relief. She stared up at the overhead screen filled with facts about common customs in Brunei. She took a deep breath and sat back in her seat. None of this really matters anymore.

"I went home last weekend," Millie said. "And I got to celebrate with my parents, so that was nice."

"That's great," Josh said. "Joplin, right? I haven't been there. I'll have to change that."

Millie's toes curled under his desk.

"But. Anyway. Aimee may have told you, but I'll be in Berlin for most of the summer next year. That's when I would typically train you. But if you're open to it, we can set a weekly drumbeat to start going over things now?"

"Oh, sure. That sounds great."

"Awesome. You're on duty Thursdays, right? You could come by then if that works for you."

Millie closed her mouth. A cut of shame rose at her throat. "So my duty nights are actually kind of busy, but would now work? A longer check-in on Tuesdays?"

Josh turned to his laptop and made a few clicks. "Ten thirty to eleven thirty? Works for me."

MILLIE WAS SPENDING her second senior year keeping company with Ryland and Colette, saving twice as much money as she'd planned, and nursing impossible crushes for two very different people.

Josh was what ten-year-old Millie would have liked to think would be her boyfriend someday. All he had to do was give her a high five or wear an Ole Miss sweatshirt, and her feelings for him would surge. Once, he had four little cellophane bags of trail mix on his desk, all tied with ribbons on top. "This one is for you. And can you give this one to Colette? Is she in a bad mood today? Let me know and I'll reach out."

Millie's crush on Josh reminded her of the hoydenish feelings she'd experienced as a tween. A waiter could say, "What can I get for you?" and Millie would blush into her menu. If a ticket taker said, "*Meet the Fockers* is down on your left," Millie thought, Wow. We're gonna be together. Liking Josh was akin to this. Millie imagined him saying things that were unoriginal but nevertheless and hopefully true. You're so pretty. Is this okay? I've wanted to do that for a long time.

But then Thursday night would arrive. Agatha would come

and sit and leave. Afterward, it took a long time for Millie's room to resume its natural shape. She'd wash her face and lie in bed fully awake, thinking, Why am I like, insane right now?

Millie thought of Agatha often and unprompted. She loved the way Agatha did just about everything: the way she sat, the way she listened, the way she nodded as she wrote something down. Millie also noticed the distinct way that Agatha spoke, the way she never uptalked, not once. This became something that Millie actively tried to do herself. She noticed herself talking differently on the phone, when she was called on to speak in class.

On their second night together, Millie's Thursday duty night, Agatha leaned forward and said this: "Millie, can I make a running list of questions to ask you before I leave?"

Millie said yes, that that was fine, but she could just answer in the moment, too. Most of the questions were about campus culture and sorority terms. "Was she saying GDI?" "Is she saying dorm-cest?" But sometimes Agatha's questions were about Millie. "Is that something you would go to?" "Are you in a small group, too?" One night, Agatha said, "Tell me if this is too personal, but do you identify as a believer?"

Millie was alarmed by her physical response to Agatha's attention. By means of stalling she did a little shake of her head. "Sorry . . ." she said. "Are you recording me?"

Agatha reached behind the curtain. "I don't have to." Millie heard the now-familiar click. "We can talk, just you and me. Do you want me to shut the door?"

"No," Millie said. "Or—actually, sure." She crossed her legs and thought, Okay so . . . I guess I'm kind of bi.

In the beginning, it was easy talking herself out of Agatha, especially walking out of Josh's office, eating his trail mix on her bed. She definitely wanted to make out with Josh, of that there was no question. But with Agatha, not so much, and the distinction seemed of note. But in the middle of October a very nothing-thing happened that made her completely reassess. Agatha was taking notes on her legal pad, and upon flipping to the next page, she banged her elbow against Millie's dresser. "Ouch," she said. She let out a little cry. With her elbow in her hand, she said, "Goddammit."

"Are you okay?"

Agatha laughed. "Yes, I'm fine." She inspected her arm and her hair fell over her face. "Sorry," she said. "I really clocked myself there."

Millie felt something like a stomachache in her hips.

"I have an ice pack if you need," she said.

"No no, you're sweet. I'm fine."

Millie turned back to her homework and secretly checked her pulse. Hokay, she thought. She crossed her legs. So maybe I'm just like, straight-up gay.

On October nineteenth, Millie bent toward her bottom drawer. She hung her fingers on the pull. "Do you . . ." She looked up. "I'm gonna have an edible, if that's okay. Do you . . . would you want half?"

Agatha's blond eyebrows went up into her forehead. She opened her mouth, then held a finger up. She reached around Millie's curtain. Once again, there was the click. "Do I want half an edible? Is that what you said?"

"I also don't have to if that's not—"

"No no, please do."

Agatha laughed and Millie felt herself seize. She slowly opened her desk drawer. "Do you want one?"

"I have to pass. But thank you." Agatha smiled down at her

notes. "That's just about the last thing I thought you were going to say."

Millie set the glass container on top of her Spanish workbook. That morning, she'd dug it up from her spot underneath the porch. She'd cleaned it off in service of this exchange. "I don't do it a lot." She unwrapped a cube. "It's just like, my one thing."

"Good for you," Agatha said. "Everyone needs a thing."

Millie took a bite and salt and sugar filled her molars. "Do you have a thing?" she asked.

On her legal pad, Agatha's hands went slack. "That's an interesting question," she said. Then she did something with her jaw. "I'd say coming down here was a bit of a thing. It was a decision that not a lot of people understood. Originally, I wasn't planning on doing it alone. I was with someone for a number of years and we separated . . . so this all became a bit of a thing that I wanted to do for myself. Does that make sense? Is that a thing?"

Millie felt certain that she'd later struggle to fall asleep. "No, yeah," she said. "That's a really big thing."

Frustrated by her obsessions, Millie told no one. She couldn't shake the feeling that her attraction to either Josh or Agatha should have dulled and clarified her feelings toward the other. There was also the issue of telling Ryland and Colette specifically. To tell one of them anything was to tell both of them everything. She knew it was an adolescent trepidation on her part, but the act of being attracted to the same sex felt like their thing and very much not hers. But perhaps the greatest reason Millie kept Josh and Agatha to herself was that she feared a throwaway response like, That makes sense, or, I knew you were a little gay.

Even worse was the idea of Colette dismissing her feelings altogether. No, Millie. Come on, she'd say. You want to *be* like her. There's a difference.

On Fridays, Millie had one class in the morning, and by eleven fifteen she was done for the day. She walked back to her room, retrieved her cleaning supplies and snack, and in the backyard of the little yellow house, she ate a caramel in the sun. The heat and the cleaning supplies made room for the Josh/Agatha bifurcation in her brain. Alone, done for the week, and a little high, Millie dropped into her reveries, however humiliating they were.

Millie wanted Josh the way she wanted this house: spiritually, emotionally, forever and no matter what. She wanted to be his valentine. She wanted to host a board game night for their friends. She needed to have her wisdom teeth removed, and she wanted to be dating Josh when she did it. They'd roll her into the waiting room. Aye! he'd say. Look who's here! There wasn't a single place that wouldn't be made better by his presence (the post office, the DMV, a wedding, a hotel). She wanted to take him back to Joplin. Fajita would look up, concerned, whenever he left the room. Millie wanted to be older, to look at Josh with a chemical reaction of accord. This is our dog, she's the one. This is our house, let's sign the papers. Millie knew she was going too far, but a little high and scrubbing baseboards, the idea of Josh slipping a ring onto her lanyard didn't seem quite so far-fetched.

The dreams of Agatha, however, were dire and thrilling, the context and conditions dour and expensive. Millie considered a situation where she and Agatha were trapped in her room, rationing her food, using their bodies for warmth. She wanted Agatha to touch her body with equal parts urgency, precision, and care. To look her in the eye and test her visual fields. To pop her shoulder back into place. One . . . two . . . I know, I'm sorry, you did great. Everything Millie imagined her saying was short and clipped this way. Come here. Look at me. Let me see it. Get in the car. She wanted to travel with Agatha, to have a reason to get a passport. She wanted to watch her order meals in a language that was harsh and beautiful like her name. Millie wanted to roll over in white hotel sheets, to see Agatha awake and on her phone. She wanted Agatha to have glasses, to frown in thought at something she read. Millie would arch her back in a stretch. Hi, she'd say. What time is our flight?

She wanted Josh to sing her "Happy Birthday," holding a plate and shielding a flame. But the idea of Agatha singing anything was horrific. Instead she'd say, Hey. Come here. Good morning. Happy birthday. It would never happen but Millie pictured Josh defending her honor, humbly taking a punch to the face. You should see the other guy! But the idea of Agatha being physical on her account was exquisite. Excuse me? What did you say? Don't talk to her. Fuck off.

Thursdays became so momentous that Millie almost forgot about Halloween altogether. It later became clear: had she not been consumed with Agatha and Josh, she would have tried to stop Colette from executing her revenge. The week before Halloween, Millie entered Colette's room and was dreadfully reminded of Boo Pig. Colette's room typically held bare walls and stacks of library books (*The Wretched of the Earth*, *The Dispossessed*, *The Lover*, Jane Fonda's *My Life So Far*). But the space had become a crafting station with vintage Razorback cutouts, witch hats, crowns, and pumpkins. There were big bloody letters tacked to her wall that spelled out *Boo Pig Sooie*. From the floor, Colette looked up with red eyes. "Millie," she said. "Have you ever heard of this thing called Pinterest?" Millie looked at her for a long time. Then she said, "Yes, I have."

By this point, Millie would have estimated that at least forty-five percent of her thoughts had Agatha somewhere in the foreground. She never stopped liking Josh, but those feelings relocated to a different part of her brain. Agatha was even starting to enter her Josh reveries. Millie fantasized about telling him the truth, later. That she and Agatha were still friendly, but it was over now. Josh would be kind and a good listener. Okay, cool, he'd say. Thanks for trusting me with that.

One night, Agatha arrived at Belgrade in a gorgeous blue cardigan and a beige jumpsuit. At one point she asked Millie if she could explain the concept of lampshading and Millie said, "Oh yeah, sure."

But Millie wanted to say, Okay. I know this is weird. But I like you so much it's making me kind of ill. Am I nuts or . . . could you feel similarly at all? "Lampshading," she said, "is when you wear shorts with a big shirt. I'm basically doing it right now."

At the end of the night, Agatha delivered forty dollars to the lamp stand. She told Millie that she'd see her next week. Millie said, "Sounds good," and she looked at the cash. For the first time in her adult life, she thought, This is almost not worth the money.

12.

ENNEDY SURVIVED HER NIGHT AT TARGET BY texting Shea the next morning. She said she was so sorry, that her roommate had gotten sick. Shea said, *Oh no! I hope she's okay!* They agreed to meet up another time, and they continued to sit one seat apart. But it never felt like it was the right time for Kennedy to ask or try again.

It was around this time that the RAs stopped chatting in Millie's room, at least without the barrier of music. Kennedy put her ear to the vent when she knew they were there, but it wasn't the same and it felt like a loss. She could only hear them if she sat on her bed, put her ear against the wall. But if she did that too long, a pain shot through her neck. That she couldn't sit and listen comfortably made her feel desperate and weird.

Even worse than the fact that Kennedy hadn't made a single friend was the recent development that Peyton had. Simi (pronounced *see-mee*) was a food science minor like Peyton, and she started coming over on Mondays, Wednesdays, and Fridays. Simi was short with dark, shiny hair, and she had a very round and firm face. She had a huge backpack that had lots of zippers and books inside. Kennedy couldn't quite explain it but Simi and her backpack looked alike. And it wasn't just her backpack. She looked like Peyton's backpack, too. It didn't make a lot of sense but Simi looked like a backpack. Sometimes she came over before their Culinary Nutrition Lab. Sometimes she came after, just to hang out. She and Peyton would sit on Peyton's bed with laptops balanced on their thighs. They'd go on some website called Twitch for hours and just be really annoying and loud.

"Peyton. Did you see this?"

"Yes."

"Ohmygod."

There'd be some typing and laughter, too.

"Peyton! No. Are you commenting that? Okay, you are out of control."

More dumb laughter would ensue.

Simi was friendlier to Kennedy than Jenna and Casey were, but Kennedy would have preferred her not to be. She had pepper spray on her key chain, a rape whistle she claimed to sleep with, and she was frequently rattling off safety tips for fleeing an assailant. "If someone grabs you? You want to pinch the skin underneath their biceps. No, I'm serious, try it. See? It hurts so bad." "So actually, you want to hold your keys like this. So then if you're grabbed from behind, you're still able to stab *down*." Peyton didn't seem all that interested, but that never stopped Simi. "If you see a car with its lights off? Don't flash yours. It's a gang." "If you find a zip tie on your car? Don't take it off. It's sex trafficking." Peyton would say, "That's good to know," and Kennedy would typically walk out of the room. Why are you both so weird? she thought. You guys don't even have a car!

Simi was annoying other times, too. She snorted when she laughed, which seemed purposeful, like she thought it was cute. And she began too many sentences with uptalk qualifiers. "Well, as a woman?" she'd say. "Speaking as someone who is four foot eleven?" "So as a white-passing Native person?" "Well, as some-one who comes from a family of divorce?"

In between these attributives and ways to protect yourself at night, Kennedy begrudgingly watched Simi and Peyton's friend-ship crystallize into something that she desperately wanted, too. On a Thursday night, they watched an M. Night Shyamalan movie on Peyton's laptop (as soon as it was over, Peyton said, "I have to go to bed"). One Saturday night they saw the new Lego movie (Peyton said, "My mom told me to pay for your ticket," and Simi gasped and went, "Ooooo!"). They had all these inside jokes that seemed profoundly unfunny. Simi would say in a British ac-cent, "Pardon *me*?" and Peyton would shake with laughter. They went to an improv show. They discussed Halloween costumes they could "do together." When Peyton talked with her parents on the phone, she'd say, "She's good . . . Okay, I'll tell her."

Kennedy was big enough to realize that her biggest problem with Simi was that a Simi hadn't happened to her. But as Octo-ber came to a close, she channeled her jealousy into focus. It was time to do what she'd come to Arkansas to do. Kennedy would meet her real friends in the spring, specifically in the under-graduate Advanced Creative Nonfiction Workshop facilitated by Professor Agatha Paul. Applications to the workshop required a writing sample and cover letter due by noon on Monday, Octo-ber twenty-third. Fourteen students would be admitted, and Kennedy was going to be one of them.

It was Sunday night, and with less than twenty-four hours to go, Kennedy was filled with an energy only matched by her nerves. She had a pen in one hand and a final draft in the other. She pushed her reading glasses up against her nose. "Okay, ready?" she asked.

Nichelle said, "Let's do it."

Kennedy coughed into her elbow. "My name is Kennedy Washburn, I'm twenty-one years old, and I'm a junior at the University of Arkansas."

"Perfect."

"Researcher and storyteller Brené Brown once said, 'Only when we are brave enough to explore the darkness will we discover the infinite power of our light.'"

"Oh, that's good."

"Writing has been a passion of mine ever since I was a little girl. In 2016, after experiencing a terribly difficult time, I turned to writing as a way of processing my anxiety, and I am thankful that I did."

"I love how you tied that together."

Just then, Kennedy, her bed, and her nightstand did a collective little shake. Outside her room, the suite door had been slammed shut. Oh wow, Kennedy thought. It's already past eight. Tyler was getting home from her Sunday chapter meeting. The movements of her roommates had come to mark the time.

"Not only was writing there for me," Kennedy went on, "but Professor Paul's book *Satellite Grief* was a source of encouragement as well. I connected with her experience and her writing emotionally and intellectually, and I'd love to be a part of her class."

"Nice, Kens."

Through the bottom slit in Kennedy's door, light went in and out as Tyler paced. "Hi," Kennedy heard her say. "Are you with Jenna? . . . Can you guys come to my room?" There was a pause. Then a little moan. "Casey, I'm literally going to kill someone . . . Thank you."

"Mom, can you hang on real quick?" Kennedy hopped off her bed. Not that they would ever knock on her door, but Kennedy didn't want Jenna and Casey seeing dirty dishes in her room. For her night of cover letter revision, she'd indulged herself with enchiladas from the Mexican place in the student union. She'd also made a chocolate chip cookie in a mug, which was so good but looked messy. So Kennedy took up the dishes and used her elbow to open the door. As she placed them in the sink, Peyton walked into the double room.

"Are you okay?" Peyton asked.

Tyler said, "Honestly no, but it's fine."

It sounded like she might be crying. Kennedy went back to her room. She felt proud of her refusal to see if Tyler was alright. "Sorry, Mom. You ready?" she asked.

"Yes, I'm ready. Go ahead."

"Okay, second paragraph. While my writing experience is limited, I feel that my dedication, curiosity, and wanderlust will set me up to succeed. Attached is my writing sample, which was previously published in *Earthwords*, which is the University of Iowa's oldest literary magazine."

"Oh, I didn't know that. That's great."

"I'm also happy to provide a—"

A streak of light shot underneath Kennedy's door. "Tahler? What's wrong?"

"You look so sad," Jenna said.

Tyler did a bitter, choked laugh. "Well. I'm sure you saw for yourselves."

"Ken, are you still there?"

"Yeah, sorry. Just one second."

Casey asked, "What do you mean?"

"Did you not see the decorations in the hall?"

There were footsteps and the opening of a door. "Oh, that's cute," Jenna said. "What's that say? Boo Pig." Then she let out a guttural moan of disbelief. "No freaking way," she said.

"Go look at the bulletin boards," Tyler said.

Kennedy listened to sandals jog down the hall. Even down at the elevators, Kennedy could hear Casey gasp. She trotted back and said, "Tahler . . . no they did not."

"Shut the door," Tyler sniffed. "No, I'm so mad right now? This is so incredibly mean."

And then, from behind her bed, Kennedy heard another gasp. She placed her ear to the wall. "She knows," Ryland said. "It's happening, it's happening, she knows."

Kennedy touched her mouth. "Mom, let me call you back."

Out in the kitchen, Casey said, "Tahler, don't crah!"

Tyler hiccuped in distress. "No, I've literally told so many people what I was gonna do. And they obviously heard me say it and then they freaking stole it."

Kennedy crawled to where her bed met the wall. She pressed her ear to the cold surface. Millie must have been on her bed because Kennedy heard her sigh. "I think I'm gonna be sick," she said.

"Honestly?" Colette said. "I think this is good for you."

"You know what else is good for you? Omega-3s," Ryland said.

"Tahler, hold up," Casey said from the other room. "You can still do your theme. Do not let some stupid RAs ruin it for you."

"Okay, no. I will look so stupid. Avery lives on the third floor. And there's some Tri-Delt in a suite down there, too. If they see my stuff go up they'll be like, 'Umm, isn't that what your RAs just did?' Ohmygod. I feel like I can't breathe."

"Wait," Jenna said. "Is this like, their little revenge?"

"Revenge for what?" Casey asked. "For the health and safeties thing? *No.*"

There was a little slap of flesh. "Well, that's just freaking great," Tyler said.

"Ohmahlord, but that was forever ago!"

"Do you guys mind if I shut this door?" Peyton asked.

Tyler sniffed and softened. "No, go ahead. Sorry, Peyton."

For the last four days, Kennedy had refused to let anything take her focus away from her application. But this was just too good. Her room was physically separating the two parties, but she wasn't in the middle. She was above it all.

Casey's voice took a seat. "If that's what's goin' on, that's real inappropriate. Oh lord, Ah sound just like mah mom."

"It is, though!" Tyler's voice bent and moved. "And I wanted to freaking win! And I so could have, the other house chairs don't care like I do. Five hundred dollars would be like, everything to me right now. And in my mind, this was my dog money for next year. And not to mention, *I'm* the resident, you know? If you're choosing to work here? Come on."

"Exactly," Jenna said. "If it's your job, treat it like one."

"She's gonna come in here," Millie said.

Colette blew threw her lips and said, "Fucking good."

"Tahler, wait. Ah know you're mad . . . but just sleep on it for now and then see how—"

"No. I'm supposed to start decorating tomorrow. I need them to take it down."

Kennedy pressed her hand to her face. She felt as though she had to prepare her body for this merger—belay herself onto a cable, lower a bar onto her lap. But it was already happening and there was no time. Another blast of hallway light appeared beneath her door. There was a loud, five-pronged knock in the hall. Tyler called out, "Excuse me."

The music stopped. "Who is it?" Colette asked.

"Can I please speak to the RA on duty?"

Kennedy heard Millie's door creak open. The quantum break was complete.

"Hi," Colette said. "I'm on duty. What's up?"

"Actually," Tyler said. "Is Millie here?"

"Millie isn't on duty tonight."

"I know, but is she here?"

There was an incredible pause. Then Colette's voice changed in tone. "Are you okay, Tyler? Is there someone I should call?"

Kennedy curled her legs beneath her.

Tyler let out a one-breath laugh. "Okay, first of all?" she said. "There's no need to be condescending. And second, you need to take all this Halloween stuff down. Right now. I'm not kidding."

Tyler's demand was followed by another long pause, so long that Kennedy was concerned that the newly formed portal had collapsed. Finally, Colette said, "Hmm . . . okay. Help me out here. I'm not sure what's happening."

"Okay, all this stuff? It was my idea and you know it. And maybe you're still mad because we played a harmless prank *weeks* ago, but this isn't cool and you need to take it down."

Colette let out another little hum. "I want to make sure I have this right. You're saying that you . . . invented Halloween."

"Ohmygod. You did not come up with Boo Pig. I did. And— okay, is Millie in there? I'm not dumb. I hear someone."

There was movement in Millie's room. Weight on a wooden joist. "Hiii," Ryland said. "It's just me. You look so sad!"

"Okay, guys?" Jenna said. "This isn't cool. You obviously heard her talk about Boo Pig. That's super messed up to just take it. And she's trying to win a really big thing. It's serious."

"Okay," Colette said. "Do you want to call our director and say we stole Halloween? I can give you his number right now."

There was a beat of silence. Ryland began to hum something that sounded like a gospel song.

"Okay . . ." Tyler laughed. "You know what? Forget it. You guys work here and you're supposed to care about our well-being . . ."

Colette said, "Oo . . . who told you that?"

"Right, exactly," Tyler laughed again. "You're way too good for that. Cool."

"Hey," Colette said. "Really quick. Are you Native American?"

"What?"

"I saw your dream catcher. Are you registered Native?"

"What are you . . . what does that have to do with anything?"

"I have a more important question," Ryland said. "No, stop. This is important, shh. Tyler, are you . . . on Lexapro?"

"What? No."

"Okay . . . well, do you wanna be?"

The suite door slammed shut. "I am going to lose it," Tyler said. This time she was crying for real.

With her voice so close again, Kennedy unfolded her legs. She set her cover letter on her lap and held her pen just above it.

Casey told Tyler to take a breath. "No," Tyler said. "It's *Sunday*. What am I going to do?" From the kitchen to the double room came the fuss of keys and sandals. Then the pull of a closet door.

Casey jogged out the front door. "Hang on, sister. Lemme grab mah keys."

"Do you want to go sit in my car?" Jenna asked.

The suite door slammed shut. In the hallway, Casey cried, "Ah'm comin'!" Then the elevator dinged.

Kennedy tried to pick up the RAs' voices, but they had turned the music up loud. She wanted to sit there and just stare at her hands, but this felt like a test, and she had to pass.

"Hi, sorry," she said.

"Everything okay?" Nichelle asked.

"Yeah. Can we start from the beginning?"

"Yes. I won't talk this time."

After reading her cover letter three times over, Kennedy and Nichelle discussed whether it was best to address the letter *To Whom It May Concern* or to Agatha Paul herself. In the end, Kennedy used the former. She printed out a final copy and set it on her desk.

For moments like this—when she completed an important task, when she didn't stay in her room all day but went for a walk or to the gym—Kennedy liked rewarding herself with an episode or two of *The Office* before bed. She turned on one of her favorite Christmas episodes, the one with the Moroccan theme. She was watching but she also wasn't, still high off of the night's events. Then, abruptly, there was a knock at the door. On her bed, Kennedy said, "Yeah?"

Peyton opened the door in her nighttime garb. Beneath her sleep-time bonnet, her brown eyes looked weirdly far apart. "Hi," she said. "I'm just making sure you're doing your dishes tonight."

Kennedy exhaled and thought, Come *on*. She was annoyed by Peyton coming to her this way, but she was also ticked at the fact that Peyton didn't pull this stuff with Tyler around.

"Peyton . . . they've been in the sink for an hour. You don't need to be like, on me about it."

Peyton's hands clenched in her sweatshirt pocket. "But it's not . . . it's not about when you put them in. And you do this all the time. It's hard to wash my dishes in the morning when yours are still in there."

"Peyton . . . that doesn't really make sense. I'm sorry but it's not my fault that you're anal about it."

"But it's what we all agreed to."

"Okay, well, things change. And I live here, too. We all have preferences."

Peyton looked sideways at the floor. She took a step back and said, "Okayyy."

Kennedy felt relieved, but then Peyton said, "Well, that's still what we agreed to. So if your dishes are still in the sink tomorrow, I'll just put them in your room."

Kennedy laughed. "Um, okay? Peyton, if that makes you happy, then go for it."

"Okay, then. I will."

"Okay, great. Good for you."

Kennedy leaned—she almost fell—and she swung her door shut. She was shaking slightly from the interaction. The sensation felt like another test. So she went to her desk and picked up her cover letter. She sat down and read it one more time.

13.

T HREE DAYS AFTER HALLOWEEN, MILLIE KNOCKED
on Ryland's door. He pulled it open with "Ooh, it's
green!" and he accepted Millie's tent in his arms.

The only lighting in Ryland's room came from the ones provided: a harsh ceiling light and a dim desk lamp. It was four
p.m. on a Friday afternoon and both of these lights were on.
There were no curtains, just the provided blinds. A simple black
comforter. A lonely white pillow. Placed around the room was a
scattershot of items. A box of Ritz crackers. A computer charger. Welch's Fruit Snacks in bulk. C-fold napkins. Tomato soup.
The only décor in Ryland's room was placed on the wall above
his bed: three posters featuring the Sacramento Kings. One had
the Kings' logo. Another had the season schedule. One pictured
a large and muscular person. His name, Demarcus Cousins,
went down the side. Next to Demarcus was a printed-out and
stapled essay. It read *Vice* at the top, and several passages were
highlighted in pink. One said *He can play both ugly and pretty
basketball.* Another said *The Kings stay the Kings.* The first time
Millie saw Ryland's room, she'd asked why he liked the Sacramento Kings. "Millie," Ryland said. "No one chooses to like the

Kings. It's more like you're chosen. So this?"—he referred to the wall—"This isn't what I want. But unfortunately, it's who I am."

Millie shut the door behind her. On top of Ryland's lofted bed, Colette sat with her laptop. She raised her hand and made a gesture for hello. Making eyes at Colette, Ryland said, "She's in a mood."

"Oh really?" Millie said. "How can you tell?"

"Ooh. Okay, Millie!" Ryland said. "Let's set this thing up."

Millie reached for the tent. "It's not hard. You'll be able to do it yourself."

"I'm not in a mood," Colette said. "I'm just trying to figure something out."

"That's fine. Oh, hey. You can use these, too," Millie said. "They're little blow-up sleep pad things."

"Oh, amazing. My back will thank you. That asphalt can be rough."

Millie laughed as she unfurled the tent. She bent and began to work a pole through a sleeve. "Wait, why would you be on asphalt?"

"Girl, I told you. I'm goin' to Chick-fil-A."

"What? I thought you were just like, getting Chick-fil-A on the way."

"No, ma'am. This is First One Hundred. Do you not know what that is?" Ryland dropped the tent pole. "Ohmygod," he said. "Okay. I love explaining.

"So whenever a new Chick-fil-A opens up, they do this thing called First One Hundred. The first one hundred people to get there the day before can stay overnight in the parking lot. And if you make it through the night, you get free Chick-fil-A. For an entire *year*."

"You get fifty-two meal tickets," Colette said, "that are valid for one calendar year."

"Colette is rude about this, but it's still fifty-two meals."

"But how do you . . . that sounds dangerous?" Millie said.

"No no no. It's a big, official thing. They fly in the First One Hundred corporate team. They give you a number. You get a cute li'l parking space all to yourself."

Millie laughed and said, "What?" as Colette whispered, "We live in a failed state."

"They give you cookies and milk," Ryland went on. "They do games and a movie. And there's a bunch of high-fiving and being like, 'excited,' but it's mostly not that bad and just vibing out in a parking lot."

At this point, Millie was setting the tent up on her own. "How have I never heard of this?" she asked. And then, because she'd recently heard Agatha say it, she said, "It sounds completely absurd."

"Oh, it's nuts. Oh, this is so cute!" Ryland discovered that the tent was nearly complete. He hopped inside and zipped himself out of sight. From within the green nylon, he began to move and sing. "Do you know the way to San Jose?" This was followed by several *la la la*s. Millie grinned at his voice, which was actually quite good. Then she thought, Oh. I get it. He's on Adderall right now. Millie herself had just taken an edible and the whole thing felt very mature. That Colette was in a mood, that she and Ryland were slightly loaded, and that the latter was going unsaid.

Ryland unzipped the entrance and placed his feet on the floor. "It's definitely absurd," he said. "In the morning they wake you up with a cowbell and they're like, 'Wake up! It's tahm to go!' And then they line you up in your order, which takes forever because people are dumb. And then they make you *parade* through the drive-through line. And the staff is all coked out and they're like, 'Way to go! Yew did it!' And you get a chicken nugget box with all your tickets inside. Then everyone grabs their shit and leaves, but *anyway* . . ." Ryland produced a big, southern sigh. He stood and surveyed the tent. "Ohmygod, Millie. Do you wanna come?"

"No, I can't."

"Well, that's your choice."

"But you're not going alone, are you?"

"No, I'm not."

Colette looked up. "Who's going?"

Ryland tucked his chin. "John, Matty . . . and Craig. Ugh, I know. Don't say anything. I can't talk about it."

Millie asked, "Do you like Craig?"

Ryland walked to a pile of clothing on his bed that he began to place into a duffel. "I love Craig. And he's so nice. And he looks like a big ol' baby giraffe . . . but we could never *be* together. And I pretend that we couldn't because he lives in Conway, but the bigger issue is . . . ugh." He cupped his hands around his mouth. "He has a SoundCloud page."

Colette gasped and said, "No."

"I know. He makes 'lyrics.'" Ryland winced at the thought.

Millie hitched both her elbows onto the bed behind her. "Colette, have you been?"

"No. Chick-fil-A is trash. But I support Ryland going."

Ryland threw deodorant into his bag. "Thank you. It's actually very radical that I make them pay for my meals."

Colette snorted. "Ryland thinks he's going to Stonewall."

"I am," Ryland said. "I'm literally throwing the first stone."

"It's still not a good deal," Colette said as she typed. "They don't let you pick out your meals."

"Well." Ryland took a toothbrush and toothpaste from his dresser. "That depends on the location, and . . . how cute you are.

"So the one down by the mall. They *hate* me. I walk in and they're like, 'Great. This bitch again.' And most places will let you add cheese or whatever, but at the mall they're like, 'That will be *fifteen cents*' and they're such losers and I hate them. Even when I'm nice and like, 'Here you go, I'll take the sandwich,' they're like, 'Here's your number one, fuckin' freeloader. Go eat it by the trash can, little shit.' So I obviously don't go there a lot. *But.* The one by the stadium?" Ryland grinned. "Different story. They're nasty and I love them. They'll all give me a breakfast sandwich and upgrade my fries. But Whitney? She's my lifeline. Stadium Whitney lets me do anything. Sub fruit cup. Sub milkshake. Literally whatever I want. Sometimes she'll be like, 'Honey, my manager here,' and then I just dick around in the parking lot till he leaves. And ohmygod, this one time?

"Okay, so last summer, I went in and Whitney just looked like, not okay. Red eyes, mess face. I was like, 'No. What is happening?' And she goes, 'Do you have class right now?' and I was like, 'Irrelevant.' And then she starts crying and she goes, 'I'm so embarrassed, but can you watch my daughter while I get a root canal?' I was like, 'Of course I'll watch your daughter. I'll die for you. Let's rage.' So I wait till she's off and then we got her kid from school. And then we go to the School of Dentistry—which is, ugh they hate me over there too but whatever—and Whitney was so cute with her kid. And they were whispering and holding hands, and then her daughter was like, 'Umm, hello. I'm Trinity. I'm gonna sing *Moana* for you now.' And I'm not kidding . . ."

Ryland held both arms out to the side. "For forty-five minutes I sat on the curb, and this girl sang me the entire *Moana* soundtrack. Choreography. Harmonies. Everything. And then Whitney came back she was like, '*Mom.* I sang da whole time. Did you hear me?' and Whitney was like, 'Girl, everybody heard you. You a star.'"

Something was happening at the corners of Millie's eyes. She couldn't think about it too much—she really should have left by now—but she felt certain that Whitney and her daughter were Black. She also felt certain that Whitney had told her daughter that everything was fine, but to sing as loud as she could.

"Ryland, I'm kind of emotional," Millie said.

"I have lots of emotional experiences in parking lots. I always have."

Colette let out a tiny moan. "Millie? Will you press on my back for a dollar?"

Millie hopped onto the bed. "You don't have to pay me."

"The internet is killing you, Coco."

Colette turned her back fully toward Millie. "I know, but I have a theory. You know Brianna in Windham? I saw her in the library on LinkedIn. I wanted to be like, 'Hey, are you leaving next year? 'Cause I'd take your RD spot in a second.'"

Millie's mouth went into a line. Beneath Colette's shoulder blade, she continued to press down.

Ryland folded a washcloth. "Colette, I love you? But are we sure Residence Life would be the best place for you to showcase your skill set?"

"Well, obviously not, but it would just be a few years till grad school or whatever. And it would be so easy. Just like, doing check-ins and emergencies."

"I don't know," Millie said. "I feel like Josh is working all the time."

"Yeah . . ." Colette said. "But that's his choice, you know? And I'd probably spend most of my time bodying stupid residents, which might be kind of fun. Ohmygod, did I tell you what Tyler said to me?"

Just the mention of Tyler made Millie tense. Tyler had gone through with her Boo Pig theme, but she did not win the Halloween lawn contest, or receive an honorable mention. A sorority house with the theme of "Monster Mash" had won; a blue ribbon was tacked to the brick wall below their lawn. Millie had hoped that Tyler wouldn't blame her, no matter that Ryland and Colette were in her room. But just that morning, when Millie held the elevator, Tyler's face popped up between the doorframe. She slowed down and looked at Millie and said, "Oh. Never mind."

"I thought I left my phone at reception," Colette went on. "And I asked Victoria if she'd seen it. And then Tyler comes up behind me like a snake-in-the-grass bitch loser, and she goes, 'Not fun when someone takes something that's yours, is it?'"

"Oh yeah, she gon' retaliate," Ryland said. "I saw her the other day at Blackboard. She looked at me with a li'l face that was like, 'Oh . . . mm-hmm. You gon' see.'"

Colette snorted. "I love that it's because I took her stupid Halloween theme. And honestly? For two gay people with a lot of undiagnosed mental illnesses, we made it look really good. Can I use this? Mine is dying." Colette reached for Ryland's computer.

Millie wanted to get away from the topic. "Ryland, how did you find out about hundred nights or whatever?"

"Oh, I just googled it. Every once in a while I'll google like . . . *free chicken, free hammock, free rain boot near me.* Stuff like that."

"He's being modest," Colette said into his computer. "Most of the stuff he searches is much more disturbing than 'free rain boot near me.'"

"Okay, mean. I search smart things, too," Ryland said.

"Oh really? Well, let's just take a look . . ."

"Colette, no!"

Ryland dove onto the bed, right over Millie. He made it about halfway and his white socks revealed gray bottoms. Colette turned away from him, using her knee as a shield. In her hands, on his laptop, Ryland's search history was pulled up.

"Alright, so this week we have . . . 'foil in microwave question mark.' 'Beef jerky surplus.' 'How to become a saint.' 'Saint application.' 'Burns when pees'? Ryland, go to the doctor—"

"Don't tell me what to do."

"'Free Band-Aids near me.' 'Anne Frank net worth.' 'Who snitched Anne Frank.' 'Who owns *math*'? Jesus Christ."

Millie touched Ryland's head and said, "I have Band-Aids in my room."

He leaned into her touch and said, "Thank you."

"Oh wow," Colette said. "You had a really big day on Sunday. 'NASA hoax.' 'Is NASA an op?' 'NASA CIA.' These are kind of legitimate . . . 'Yosemite Kill Zone.' 'Blake Lively old nose.' 'Lakers Kings game six fixed.' 'What is Palestine?' Wow. Okay, I'm bored."

"What does that mean?" Millie asked. "Blake Lively doesn't have an old nose."

Ryland propped himself up. "Not anymore she doesn't. Ugh! I can't lay down. I have to pack."

Millie said she had to get going, too.

"What? Millie, don't go." Colette reached out and held her wrist.

"Yeah, you can't leave," Ryland said. "We're having too much fun."

Once again, Millie felt emotional. "Sorry. I have to."

But Colette didn't release her arm; she pulled Millie back toward the bed. "Ryland, is that a new sweatshirt? It's cute."

Ryland turned to his mirror. Above jean cutoffs he wore a black hooded sweatshirt, the word *Champion* written in white. "I have a hookup with the lost-and-found lady at the good urgent care," he said. "She sent me a picture and I was like, 'Do not move. I am on my way.'"

"Bye, guys," Millie said. "I gotta get going."

"No, you don't." With one of her legs, Colette pulled her back into the bed. Millie let it happen. She didn't know how to leave.

"Ryland," Colette said. "You look really cute. And Craig likes you. He's gonna try something."

"He won't. He's too shy."

"Then you should try something. Do my move."

Millie poked Colette's leg. "Is this your move? Let me go."

"Okay, no. Get ready." Colette stood. She held out her arms and pushed the tent aside. "Millie, pay attention. This will change your life.

"So I hang out, and I'm just normal about it. And then, when it's time to go, I'm like, 'Hey . . .'" She walked toward Ryland. "And I act all confused like I just woke up. And I go, 'Hey, no, wait.' I say 'wait' like, eighteen times. And then, I take a second, and I do just, just the teeniest little peck." Her hands went to Ryland's shoulders. She didn't kiss him but she came close. "And

225

then they go, 'What?' and I go, 'Oh shoot. I'm . . . Dang it. Oops. Oh no . . .'"

Ryland was typing on his phone. "Coco, just get your SAG card already."

"But that's not even the important part. Then you have to be like, 'Oh hey, just to be clear . . . I wasn't trying to date you . . . I just thought . . . because you said . . .' Basically you just start a bunch of sentences but you never finish them. And then they'll be like, 'Oh no, it's okay. Don't worry. No, we're good.' And then, within twenty-four hours, I guarantee. 'Hey . . . can we talk?' Game over. KO."

Millie touched the side of her neck. "Colette," she said. "You do not do that."

"I do, my friend. And it works every time."

"*Every* time?"

"Well, I've done it twice but it worked both times, so yes."

"Coco?" Ryland said. "I love you and I'll support you no matter what, but just real quick and because I'm curious, is that assault?"

"I've thought about this a lot and the answer is no."

"I'm so sorry. Bye, you guys." Millie opened the door.

"What?" Ryland pouted. "But you're not even on duty."

"Yeah," Colette said. "Where are you going?"

It wasn't like they wouldn't find out, but Millie felt oddly vain at her admission.

"Oh," she said. "I'm actually getting a haircut."

Ryland clutched invisible pearls. "A haircut for *whomst?*"

14.

J UST BEFORE SHE TURNED IN HER SECOND PRO-
file, Agatha looked up at the bookshelf in her living
room. She landed on *Flowers in the Attic*, a book she'd
seen the adaptation of but had never read. She opened a page,
saw the name *Cathy*, and did a find and replace for Casey's name.

The question-and-answer section included quotes from that
first interview: Casey's parents' jobs, her age, her major, her
hometown. She included what Casey had said about how being
classy is not saying how classy you are, and the splurge item
she'd written down (a Cuisinart mixer). But everything else was
from what she'd heard from sitting in Millie's room. "If a gah
ain't pullin' out his wallet, well guess what? That's not a date."
Agatha used this one, too: "You know what mah mom would
say? She'd go, 'Casey Ann, we rock this boat too hard? One of
us gon' fall out.'"

Agatha included some of Casey's staunch views on what
places and things were for. "Speakerphone is for *groups*. If you're
just answerin' the phone that way? Nuh-uh. That is *wrong*."
"Y'all, the only time you should be singin' at the table is when
it's someone's birthday. Otherwise it's rude." And one night,
Casey said this: "Waffle House is fine after goin' out, or with

your bridal party to take cute pictures. But if you're just rollin' up to Waffle House? On a Tuesday for lunch? No, girl. That's not it. Time to look at your life, look at your choices."

It was not lost on Agatha that she was painting Millie's residents with broad and uneven strokes. But she wasn't using their names, she couldn't get over Robin, and these factors smoothed over her guilt just enough for her to keep going. What did make her feel truly guilty were the small violations that went against her own stipulated rules. Like when, in the nth hour, Casey's, or Cathy's, piece was running short. Agatha relistened to several recorded sessions, but she couldn't find anything else that fit Cathy's southern mom-ish motif. So she filled the missing space by using quotes from Jenna, specifically Jenna's imperfect understanding of the biology of twins. This did seem unfair. Casey was the one who had been most offended by the misconception. But the editor at *Teen Vogue* loved it, and so did everyone else. Once published, the comment section went remarkably long. Casey's Waffle House comments were characterized as poor-shaming. A few people said that they were a twin and could confirm this split-brain thing was true. Agatha hated that she liked the possibility of someone sending it to Robin. Robin would have said yes, that more brain had gone to Rashad.

The success of Cathy's profile gave Agatha the momentum to talk to her agent about her current project. "I know I came here to write about weddings," she said, "but I don't want to do that anymore."

"Okay, great! Don't write about weddings!" Charlotte said. "Keep doing these. They're so good. What if these girls were your next book?"

The idea had crossed her mind. Agatha was truly fascinated by how money worked on campus. And the *book* book, that was where she would right her current wrongs. That was where she'd interview college women the right way, under the umbrella of a signed release. The book was the thing she'd do properly. For now, she was laying the groundwork. She was also getting hundreds of new followers every week. The sales for *Birthday Money* had seen a nice little bump.

Sometimes when Agatha was out for a run or at the store, she cared little to none about her actions. She knew it was dishonest journalism and she just didn't care. She was hurt, but she wasn't hurting anyone. She was using real quotes but not real names. And it wasn't the *New York Times*. This was *Teen Vogue*.

Agatha's next profile was due on Friday EOD. She planned on using a masculine name for Tyler's persona, something like Charlie or Dylan. But at some point in October, Tyler became harder to pin down than the others. She became Agatha's most and least favorite of the three (while Jenna was the most objectionable, she held no power, whereas Tyler very much did). Tyler was a catty, socially muscular person who valued loyalty and had a beautiful laugh. She worked three days a week at a music library. She often repeated jokes just after they were made. The splurge item she'd written down that first night was Nike Air Force 1s, which Robin also owned. Agatha found Tyler's power and quirks compelling for reasons she couldn't fully articulate. She also found them hard to shoehorn into a fake interview centered on how Tyler managed and thought about money.

Then, one Thursday night, at ten fifteen, Agatha's angle on Tyler became clear. As she was leaving Millie's room, she made the mistake of stopping to pee. The hallway had been empty. Agatha reluctantly jogged to a single accessible bathroom; swirls of brown hair were all over the floor. On her way out, water still between her fingers, she ran into Tyler in the hall.

"Oh hi," Tyler said. "I know you."

Agatha held her breath. "Hi, nice to see you again."

Tyler asked, "Are you doing more interviews?" but then she feigned slapping her head. "Ohmygod, of course you're not. It's late. I should be in bed."

"Right," Agatha laughed. "No, I'm just finishing up. But good to see you."

"Yeah, you too." Then, over her shoulder, Tyler said, "I like your outfit again."

Hands on the door, Agatha said, "Oh, thanks."

She pulled back on Tyler's piece completely. Instead, she did what she mentally titled *Jenna Part 2*. She could feel it—in the way she searched the bookshelf for a name—that even within the periphery of her new illicit practices, that she was being lazy. She chose *Carrie*, by Stephen King. For this profile she completely made up the numbers, occupations, majors, and savings. She purposefully diversified this character from the others. (Carrie was an engineering major. Her parents worked at Goldman Sachs.) Agatha used some of Jenna's worse vernacular that she'd picked up over time, bits that she knew readers would enjoy. When she'd originally heard them, Agatha was almost impressed by the historic tragedies Jenna mentioned, the connections she made between them and her own life. "Ohmygod, no!" Jenna once screamed at Casey. "I don't want your grody smallpox blanket." "Hayride was not fun this year," Jenna said another night. "The fact that they made us walk in gravel, like no. I did not sign up for the friggin' Trail of Tears." "Living in a dorm," Jenna had said, "is basically paying ten grand to live in a Japanese internment camp." Once, Jenna had commented that she didn't take the stairs because it felt like "being in a 9/11." The article practically wrote itself.

It did feel unfair to paint the young women with a two-dimensional sheen. Yes, they said incredibly ignorant things, but they were also nineteen and twenty-one years old. Agatha knew firsthand that Tyler, Casey, and Jenna were not composed solely of pull quotes. They were quick and surprising; they seemed to like each other very much. Casey in particular was ambitious and smart. She once helped Tyler with her trigonometry homework. Agatha wrote down the problem as Casey read it aloud. She had been very good at math back in school, but she would not have been able to solve it on her own. When they finished, Tyler made a clever joke about conjugates, likening them to conjugal visits. She and Casey laughed so hard that they both started to cry.

Midway in the semester, Tyler decided to double minor in French. She sometimes shouted phrases she knew, which the girls absolutely loved. She was, of course, exaggerating for effect, but her accent was quite good. She must have taken it in high school, too. Agatha liked how decisive Tyler was. Her opinions were limited yet refreshing. "I'm not even that political," she said once, "but if a guy doesn't believe in universal health care? We can't date."

Casey shouted, "Ah agree!"

Even Jenna softened sometimes, especially when she spoke to someone named Spencer on the phone. Twice, she excused herself into the hallway and stood just outside Millie's door. "Why?" she asked. "Okay, yeah, lemme say hi. Spencer? It's JJ. No, I'm in Fayetteville, remember?" Her voice remained harsh but overlaid with compassion. "Okay, hang on. Why are you upset? Well, what if Mom does it with you? . . . Yeah, I know. Hey, let's do the thing with your nose. Where you inhale on the right and exhale on the left . . . Spencer, don't be like that . . .

Yes, you can." Agatha turned the recorder off. "I'm doing it, too," Jenna went on. "Can you hear me? Let's do one more." Then Jenna told him to put Mom back on the phone. "I think you should just let him do it," she said. "Okay . . . well, if he burns himself, then at least he'll learn." Then Jenna went back into the suite, where Casey was playing a wedding video on her phone. Jenna put something in her mouth and said, "Those dresses look like shit."

Agatha didn't feel bad, but she didn't feel good either. She missed Robin. She missed having sex. She liked having a low-stakes project that produced high-traffic reading. But her feelings notwithstanding, she had a fourth and final deadline approaching. Her editor reached out to say how happy they were, and how they also wanted something different this time. For the last piece, they wanted someone who readers could relate to.

Agatha did have permission—albeit verbal—from Millie. And in addition to being accommodating and pleasant, Millie was interesting all on her own. She received no funds from her parents. She house-sat for fifty dollars a month. When she was at home she worked at a Starbucks. She made two hundred and fifty dollars a month as an RA.

Millie always answered the dorm phone on the first ring ("Belgrade, this is Millie . . . No worries. I'll come down"). Sometimes, at the end of the night, she poked her head outside her door. "Y'all, it's quiet hours. Can you take this to your room?" She had a stash of Band-Aids and a bright-blue ice pack in her mini fridge. On her desk was a notebook, where she appeared to write down her expenses. Agatha wanted to look at it, but she didn't need to. Millie told her everything that she wanted to know.

She was also an excellent observer. She had a democratic way of explaining things, like a volunteer docent at an outdoor museum. "A small group is an intimate gathering of people who do Bible study or fellowship." "Meal Trade is when a restaurant has a special for a night, and you can use your Razorbuck$." She was incredibly diplomatic and she had a way of poking fun while respecting the decisions of others. She was also a strangely talented actress. She did very good impersonations.

"It's not so much like that," Millie explained to Agatha one night. "At least I don't think it is."

Agatha scribbled furiously in her journal. "Millie, say more on that."

"Well, obviously if you call yourself a believer . . . you're probably not gonna stab someone or rob a bank. But some things that you'd assume are off-limits—they're still done but they're just different."

"Can you give me an example?"

"Okay . . . so if you're a campus Christian person, and you're plugged in to a body of Christ . . ."

"Is that what they'd say?"

"That's what I've heard, yeah. And if you're just like, a cool, nature-y Christian person who is . . . probably white? Can I say that?"

Agatha smiled. "You can say that."

"So all that doesn't necessarily mean that you don't gossip or listen to rap music or whatever. I feel like it means that you do those things . . . *intentionally*. Like, you do it for the Lord."

"So if I wanted to gossip intentionally, how would I do that?"

Millie put her arm at the back of her chair. "You'd be like . . . well, do you just want me to do it?"

"Well, yeah."

"Okay." She grinned. "This is so funny to me . . ." Then Millie took a breath and put her hair behind her ears. "So, Agatha. Listen. Can I talk to you for a second? God's really putting Hannah on my heart this week."

Agatha flipped to a new page in her journal.

"The other day?" Millie went on. "And keep this between you and me—but the other day she did blah blah blah? And yeah, it just wasn't the sweet Hannah that we know. And I need to figure out a way to hold her accountable while I do my best to shower her with grace. But I also want to start asking important questions, like, is this a godly friendship? Is she going through a rough season? And maybe she is! And that's okay. But if that's the case, is my birthday weekend at Hilton Head the best place for her to do that?"

Agatha laughed at this last part. "You are very good at that."

Millie's regular cadence returned. "Thank you," she said. "I'm kind of impressed with myself, too."

Millie's experience as a twenty-four-year-old RA was drastically different than the residents next door. Here was a young person who operated without much complaint, whose efforts and time went laughably underpaid. Agatha was fascinated by Millie's gamesmanship. Her consistent positivity, her starry-eyed hustle, the way she enjoyed a little pot now and then. All of this—her income, her attitude, her ambitions—would be a nice tonal shift from the other profiles.

Two days after Halloween, Agatha asked Millie directly if she ever felt jealous of other students. Students who could call someone when they needed Brita filters. Young women who didn't work for room and board. Millie hummed in consideration, placed her pen to her cheek. "No?" she said. "I don't think so. But I do get frustrated when . . . well, it's hard to explain. Sometimes—and I'm not trying to be like, 'Oh, I'm so great'—

but sometimes I feel that being good at my job actually kind of hurts me. Not in big ways . . . well, this dorm is a good example. No one wants to live here and this is my second time. Which is fine because Aimee has hooked me up in different ways. But yeah. I don't know. I definitely feel that with residents sometimes."

"How do you feel that way with residents?"

"Well, my two good friends are RAs, too, but they don't care about it as much, or like, at all. Which is fine, but it means their residents come to me because they know I'll help them out. And it's not that I mind but sometimes I have to study. Or sometimes I just want to like, sit here and watch TV. And usually they're nice but sometimes girls will treat me like . . ." Millie blew through her lips. "I don't even know.

"Like, this one time two years ago, I was on duty for Thanksgiving break, which wasn't that bad because my parents came down and we made it a thing. But most of the residents were gone except for like, two girls, who were both staying here. And on Thanksgiving night, one of them starts blasting music with her door open. At midnight. It was ridiculous. So I go over and I say, 'Hey, Emma, can you turn it like, way down?' And she looks at me like I'm crazy. And then she goes, 'What does it matter? No one is even here.'"

Agatha looked up at Millie then. Millie held an opened palm next to her face.

"And it felt really not good to be like, 'Well, okay . . . I'm not no one, though, right?' And she turned it down and that was that. But it just felt like, okay, that sucked. So yeah. I don't think I feel jealous exactly, but it's frustrating to try and be like, 'Hey, I'm still a person, though, yeah? I see you all the time. I lent you my mini vac once . . . How do I like, not count?'" Millie stopped and recoiled a bit at what she'd just said. "Sorry. That sounds dramatic."

"I don't think it does."

Agatha used every word.

There were several moments where it felt like they were friends: not intimate, but the kind of bond that forms with coworkers, or with a dentist or hairstylist who you see into adulthood. They were both only children with parents employed at a college, both of which—Bennington and Missouri Southern—they had respectively chosen not to attend. Once, Agatha brought Millie a six-pack of La Croix. Another night, Millie texted her something that Jenna said. On a Saturday, Millie texted that a small group was meeting in the lounge if Agatha wanted to listen in. Agatha was planning on making a fish en papillote. But then Millie said the topic for the night was "questions to ask on a first date." Agatha quickly texted back, *Okay, yes. I'm on my way.*

Later, Agatha would consider these interactions, specifically the ones that made her feel culpable. Like the night she'd accidentally stayed too late, glued to the neighboring conversation. Or when she'd accidentally called Millie something other than her name. ("Sweetie, that's not your whole dinner, is it?" Above chips and guacamole, Millie grinned and said, "No?") Daylight saving was also to blame. On the night the clocks fell back, Agatha slept for ten hours, which felt less restorative and more like something from which she could not recover. Five days later, Millie opened the door to Belgrade. Her hair was in thick, loose waves on her shoulders, the black ends freshly trimmed. Looking back, and for no apparent reason, the following exchange felt like a rift:

"Hey," Agatha said. "That's a nice length."

"Oh yeah." Millie touched the back of her head. "I guess I haven't seen you."

THAT NIGHT, MILLIE was wearing a long-sleeved T-shirt instead of her RA polo. Her bedroom looked the same and it smelled like it often did—some type of shea cream and recently cleaned with a Swiffer. Agatha was wearing her one pair of jeans, leather flats, and a sweatshirt that she was getting too warm in. In Millie's room she removed her sweatshirt. She wore a black button-down with cap sleeves underneath.

By then, Tyler, Jenna, and Casey were young women who Agatha knew very well and not at all—a house she'd been to many times without knowing the street name or address. She was happy but not surprised to hear that Casey had done well on her midterms. When Tyler said, "Y'all, Kevin is being so funny to me right now," Agatha found herself agape.

"Kevin?" she whispered.

Millie nodded and said, "Mhm."

"Wow. What happened to Luke?"

Millie raised her finger. She made a slow swipe across her throat.

Agatha's mouth fell open. "Luke *died*?"

"Ohmygodno," Millie laughed. "She just thinks he's annoying."

"Oh, I see." Agatha laughed, too. "I'm not sure why I was so concerned about Luke."

"Well, he is single now . . ."

"Thank you." Agatha grinned. "Not really my type."

The evening went on like this. Kevin had two dogs, one named Maggie, the other Ten-Gauge. Jenna was eating marshmallows from a coffee mug, saying that she loved sweaters and the fall. Casey told a very long story about how she had a "complicated relationship with Olive Garden," because whenever her family went, she'd "start actin' out" and get her "butt tore up in the parkin' lot." This prompted Agatha to ask Millie what her favorite restaurant had been as a child.

"Red Lobster," she said. "I thought it was so great. And then once we went to Atlanta, because my mom has family there, and we went to P.F. Chang's and I was like, oh wow."

"I take it you were impressed?"

"Oh yeah. I was like, this is luxury. I am having a cultural dining experience."

The way Millie said this, the way her eyelids fluttered, Agatha did remember thinking (objectively, dispassionately), Oh, and, Interesting. Millie is wearing mascara tonight.

Tyler, Jenna, and Casey got ready for a night out. At one point, Tyler said, "Are y'all going to a movie?" A voice Agatha didn't recognize said yes; they were going to see the new *Blade Runner* movie. A few minutes later, Tyler said, "Bye, Peyton, bye, Simi . . . They're so dorky and cute. I love it." Around nine thirty-five, they packed up and Agatha did, too. Two twenty-dollar bills were placed on Millie's lamp.

"Can you believe Thanksgiving is in two weeks?" Agatha asked.

Millie put her pen down and said, "I know."

"Are you going home?"

"Yeah. For two days."

Agatha stepped into the alcove by the door. "That'll be nice. I hope your residents behave themselves. See you next week, then?"

Millie stood and said, "Mhm."

Agatha's hand was on the door. She had opened it an inch when Millie stepped in front of her. "Sorry," she said. "Can you wait?"

"Oh, sure."

Agatha looked at her and she felt certain that Millie was going to say something unfortunate. That she was having her duty nights switched, that she'd found the *Teen Vogue* profiles online. For a moment she thought that Millie was about to do something intimate but kind, like remove fuzz from her hair, retrieve an eyelash from her face. The way Millie looked at her then, Agatha almost said, Are you alright? She placed her shoe in the crack of the door.

On her life, it never occurred to her that Millie would do what she did: lean in and kiss her on the mouth. In the glow of her desk lamp and a streak of light from the hallway, Millie kissed Agatha for a two-Mississippi count. Agatha's eyes remained open. She kissed her back, but not because she'd meant to. The brief return was more akin to saying "Sorry" when someone bumps into you. Then Agatha placed a hand on Millie's collarbone. "Wait wait wait wait. *Millie*," she said. She didn't so much as push her, but she held her in place.

Millie took a step back. Her shoulder grazed a gold necklace on a hook. "Oh, sorry." A tiny shake of her head. "Was I too forward just now?"

Agatha blinked and looked at her. She pulled her foot back and shut the door.

"Sweetie, we can't . . ." She felt crazed then. In her chest was the sharp panic of a mistake. Millie's face, however, was conspicuously neutral. She suddenly looked a little high and incredibly grown up. Agatha shook her head. "That . . . that's not a good idea."

"Oh," Millie said. "Okay. I'm sorry."

"I do hope you understand."

"No no, I do." And then Millie did something strange. She covered her left eye with the back of two fingers, her face scrunched up behind her hand. It was as if she'd just woken up from a nap that she took on vacation. "I get it. I'm sorry."

Agatha felt the physical terror of trying to lift one's self out of a pool. Fix this, she told herself. Be professional. But as she prioritized her triage, she also wondered when Millie had deduced that she liked women.

"If I did something to imply otherwise . . ." Agatha said.

"No no no." Millie held the neck of her shirt. "I'm sorry. Yeah, no. I just misread things. That's my bad."

The ease with which Millie said this made something in Agatha's chest snag and rip. "Do you want to talk about it?"

Millie smiled. "Not really, no."

"Okay. Are you a little high?"

"I don't know, does it matter?"

Agatha crossed her arms. She'd never seen Millie so flip. "Okay . . . well, I've loved getting to know you better. And I know some of my questions have turned a bit personal, but I'd like to continue the relationship we have now, if that's okay."

"Oh yeah, of course. I hope you're not freaked out."

"No no. But just to clarify . . . I want to make sure you feel comfortable."

"Yes, totally." Millie raised her hands. Agatha felt unnerved at what she thought just then, that Millie, abruptly, had looked quite pretty. "I— Sorry. We can be cool," she said. "This is a sweet deal for me. I like helping out. And just to be clear, I'm not . . . I wasn't trying to like, date you. It was just . . . a fun thing maybe. But anyway. It's totally fine."

Agatha thought, What in the world? "Alright," she said. "Then we're on the same page."

"Okay, cool." Millie touched her curtain. "Sorry if I made anything weird."

"No no no. Not at all. Okay, then. I'll see you next week."

At the stairwell Agatha found herself uncertain as to whether her legs could descend. But she made it, breathing intentionally (not for the Lord so much as for her own safety). She waved at the security guard, who said, "Bye, honey, have a good night."

———

ON DECEMBER 30, 2014, one of the walls of the Chicago Morton Salt Factory collapsed. A flood of salt came down on the adjacent Acura dealership. A dozen cars were entombed in white. No one was hurt or trapped inside. Robin was at Agatha's apartment when they saw it on the news. "I kind of want to see it," Agatha said.

Robin took up her coat. "Okay. Come on, nosy. Let's go."

The salt factory was a frigid twenty-minute walk away. Robin had been spending the night more frequently, and they were in a honeymoonish phase that made everything intriguing. On the side of the factory was a large painting of the Morton Salt girl. Yellow dress, white tights, umbrella with a lavender underside. They stood across the street from the cascade of salt. It was huge and glittery and overwhelming to behold.

Robin slipped a mittened hand into Agatha's elbow. "I want to say something," she said. "I googled you."

Agatha turned to her.

"And normally I'd keep that to myself, but if you ever wanted to talk about your first book, I didn't like the idea of pretending that I don't know what it's about."

Agatha said, "I understand."

"That's all. I'm sorry if that puts you in a weird position."

"It doesn't."

They were awkward but light then. Shivering shoulders and pocketed hands. "I don't need to talk about it," Agatha said, "but do you?"

Robin hummed and said, "Maybe."

When Agatha was sixteen years old, she was driving home from track practice when she stopped at a crosswalk. A man was standing on the sidewalk with a large dog and a cell phone. He was looking down at it, confused. It was 1995 and Agatha remembered being a bit enraptured by the cell phone. No one she knew owned one. She gave him that two-finger wave for *Go ahead*. With a nod of his chin he said, *No, that's okay, you go*, and she pressed down on the gas. But the man's dog did not entertain their communication, and it lunged into the street. The leash's pull set the man off-balance. He fell in front of Agatha's car. Agatha slammed on her brakes. The tires screeched and burned. The gasp that came from her was so high-pitched, it sounded like someone exaggerating for effect.

His name was Jorge and he was retired after working at Costco corporate in Washington State for nineteen years. He was part of a group of men who met at a coffee shop once a week. They called themselves ROMEOs, Retired Old Men Eating Out. Agatha didn't hit him with her car, but he'd fallen in front of it and had a heart attack. In her book, Agatha wrote about how the dog barked in her face. It was the first time she ever used a cell phone; she removed the device from the man's hand. Twelve minutes later Jorge died inside the ambulance, just outside the hospital entrance.

"Did you go to therapy?" Robin asked. They were in a coffee shop. She was drinking a matcha latte with whipped cream.

"Yes. I went to therapy twice a week in high school and all through college. And I had the same therapist from when I finished grad school until just last year."

"So this is the first time in years that you haven't been in therapy? Right now?"

"Yes, I guess it is."

"Wow," Robin said. "This is all very exciting."

Satellite Grief was a biological analysis of grief and physical mourning, as well as interviews with other much more interesting accidental-death inciters. There was also a chapter where Agatha detailed her own experience, the shame and guilt and bereavement. She was twenty-seven years old when it came out. Her book did just okay.

"This may be a silly question. But was it a complete nightmare?" Robin asked.

"Yes. I was sixteen and it was a nightmare. But I had a lot of support and this sounds crazy, but not many people knew, even in such a small town. My parents really swooped in. His family was very kind. And the internet wasn't the internet, you know? Compared to the people I met, I had it pretty easy. I interviewed a guy in Akron who— You haven't read my book, right?"

"No."

"Okay, good. Don't," Agatha said. "It's a little embarrassing now. Well—I'm not embarrassed that I wrote it, but there's what I wrote it for and what people read it for. But anyway. What was I saying? Right. So one of the chapters is about this man who went home from a bar with this woman he just met. They'd both been drinking and having a good time. According to him, he tells her to put her seat belt on. She doesn't, she's pretty drunk, and she says, 'Come on. Just let me dance.' They get into a car accident and she flies halfway out the window. Cuts up her hands, breaks her collarbone."

"Oh damn."

"And he was completely fine. Her family sued for assault, and their lawyer found a way to position the car as a weapon. And this guy settled, owing the family three hundred thousand dollars. And he got partial time in jail. So for a year he went to his job as a bank teller in the day and then he went back to jail for evenings and weekends. He's still paying them back and, you know . . . he'll probably never own a house or go to school. Meanwhile, I'm responsible for killing someone, and I'm in group counseling. I got school accommodations. I wrote about it in all my college admission essays . . ."

"What an asshole." Robin smiled.

"Oh, you're not wrong. And it's not nothing, but all this guy did was break some woman's collarbone. I scared a guy with my car and he died. His daughter-in-law was pregnant. He wasn't even that old. And there's obviously race and status and a lot of other things at play, but to answer your question, it was a complete nightmare, but in many ways, it was not."

Robin asked her what specifically she went to therapy for.

"I didn't want to drive. I did an exposure-therapy-type deal. But the thing that followed me into grad school was this pleasure deprivation. It sounds small but if I wanted something, I wouldn't take it. I would choose the next-best thing because that's what I felt I deserved."

"Like what?"

Agatha felt embarrassed but pleased to be having this conversation. When they'd been standing in front of the tower of salt, she'd marveled at Robin's fingers in her arm.

"For a long time I would never order what I wanted at a restaurant. I'd only get my second choice. There was a period where I wouldn't get first place in races. Not that I was close that often, but if I was I'd get scared and I'd slow down. It's still with me a bit. Actually, just now when we were standing at the factory, I kind of wanted to go up closer. But then I thought, no, this is the view I deserve. I'm much better but I do catch myself doing it."

"I'm not making light of this," Robin said. "But I love how you went to therapy to learn how to just like . . . be a white woman in the world."

Agatha laughed. "I know. Poor me. Years of treatment to help me realize that if something is available then I should probably take it."

"Should I be taking offense to all of this?"

"Taking offense? What do you mean?"

"Are you exorcising your demons? Am I your second choice?"

Across the table, Robin's beauty was singular and electric. Agatha crossed her legs and said, "Robin. Please."

THE FRONT DOOR creaked as she let herself inside. Agatha stepped out of her shoes and set her bag on the dining room table, a huge oak slab with four claw feet. She couldn't decide whether she actually wanted a glass of wine or if she felt like it was expected of her, like someone in a movie, a woman sitting down at a bar. Instead, she poured a glass of water from the tap. On her elbows at the island counter, she felt as if she were being watched.

There was no point in analyzing everything previously implied or inferred, because the person who had kissed her that evening was a separate individual from the one who'd sat at her desk, completing Spanish conjugations. It was as if "Millie the RA" had been a college mascot, but she'd taken the costume's head off in a back alley. She held it carelessly at her side. She was swearing and smoking a cigarette, looking down and checking the time. How quickly Agatha had gone from thinking of Millie as a dutiful assistant and RA to knowing that Millie wanted to kiss her, and that she knew how to kiss. It was bizarre, feeling grateful for having done the right thing, all to walk home, stand in a large kitchen, and consider how nice it would have been not to.

It wasn't an option. Agatha knew that. She crawled into bed and she very much knew that. What had happened between them was inappropriate at best, and, albeit legal, it was the definition of *frowned upon*. There were so many times Agatha had breezed over articles about professors dating their students, barely finding them interesting enough to skim. But this was different because Millie wasn't Agatha's student. And, amazingly, *she'd* kissed Agatha. Without wanting to date her. A fun thing maybe. What in the world? Agatha lay back on her pillow. Once again, she felt like she was acting. A person on a soap opera who had gone into a coma.

She opened her eyes. Around the window a square of moonlight glowed blue. She found herself pondering an alternate history, the details that would have made it alright. What she kept coming back to was the night at Maxine's. Perhaps if Millie hadn't been with friends. She saw it then: a set of circumstances that could have occurred in which they'd had a drink and gone back to Agatha's house. Agatha would have hated herself for saying that she never did things "like this." She would have made a bad joke about Millie's age. (You do remember 9/11, yes? It's something you saw on the news?) Millie would have smiled and ignored the question. Do you want to see me again? Agatha would have said yes. But that was not how things had gone. Agatha had sat in Millie's room, recording young women, profiting menially off their words. And even after Millie had been in her periphery for weeks, Agatha hadn't seen the situation at all. She felt angry then, furious with Robin for how much she missed her, all the sex they'd had back then, the leggy dancers she was probably kissing now. Agatha was resentful toward Millie, too. She was already doing a bad thing. She didn't want to do another.

Agatha imagined another woman. Someone back in Chicago, someone closer to her own age. The woman was pale with a dark raven's peak and she looked like she played an instrument professionally. She and Agatha had been intimate but they were still in the dating phase. In this reverie, Agatha placed herself in a mental and geographic state where she'd returned to her proper self, her furtive year in Arkansas retroactively making sense. I was coming out of a relationship, she'd say. I was out of therapy for the first time. I was writing and teaching but I didn't get much work done at all. I ate a lot of sushi and wrote for *Teen Vogue*. I also watched nine seasons of *Survivor*. Oh, and I messed around with a student? Not my student, no no no.

The musician would be charmed. It sounds like you had a rumspringa, she'd say. Do you still talk to the student?

Barely but yes. She's married now.

Then the woman would lean closer and ask how the sushi was in Arkansas.

Agatha would return her lean and reply, Not half as bad as you'd think.

———

IT WAS IMPOSSIBLE to know if she'd slept for six hours or two, but when Agatha rolled out of bed her feet touched the floor with a clarity that roused her to the core. Millie had thoroughly altered her Fayetteville experience beyond recall. It was quite clear now: her year in Arkansas was a wash. So she started her coffee. She graded four papers. I can do whatever I want.

There were several different versions of a text she never sent. Hey, about yesterday . . . Good morning, can we talk? Agatha felt herself slipping into mania, doing *If this, then that* scenarios. If it rains again, then I'll text her. If I see that fox, I'll give her a call. If I pass that little house and she's inside, then . . . she didn't know. Agatha graded two more papers. Everyone got a B.

Around noon, she went for a run. She ran up the Frisco Trailway from West North, sweaty and focused and wired and numb. Something burned in her stomach as the yellow house came into view. The stream that ran along the railroad tracks held a clear and steady current. There was Millie's purple RAV4. Agatha stepped over the stream. She saw Millie standing in the open kitchen window, wringing a towel over the sink. A red bandana around her curls.

From outside the window, Agatha stepped up and said, "Hi."

Millie looked up. "Oh. Sorry, hi."

"How's it going in there?"

She sighed. "I mean, it's going."

Agatha felt strongly that she might break a tooth. "It looks really good. I can see a difference." We kissed last night, she thought. In your room.

"Oh good. It's hard to tell sometimes." Millie wiped her brow with her wrist.

And then, so much easier than she ever could have planned, Agatha heard herself say this: "So, I'm about done and I'm heading home. My house is just up the hill on Louise. There's a blue side door. It's 461. And if you'd like to stop by, then . . . yeah. I'll be around."

"Oh," Millie said. And very briefly, Agatha saw it. It was so quick but she'd die on this. A rift of surprise passed through Millie's jawline. A quick flick in her eyebrows couldn't believe that it had worked. Millie looked back at the kitchen and then through the window once again. "Okay, yeah. I'm pretty much done right now," she said.

"Okay, great. Then I'll see you in a few."

That Agatha had thought her home was haunted before was comical now. In her kitchen she listened to a once-creaky frame go hushed. The stillness made way for the sound of Millie's sandals outside. Grass to rocks and then the back step. Before she could knock, Agatha let her inside. Millie gripped the dryer's edge while she removed her shoes. "Hi," she said. "I'm kind of gross right now."

"Don't worry. I am, too."

Then they were staring at one another, all kneecaps and heat. Agatha linked her fingers together, rested her palms against her head. "Okay," she said. She'd laugh about this later, she was sure. She walked into the kitchen. "Would you like a drink?"

"A what?" Millie said.

"I have wine and I think—there's gin in here, yes."

Millie laughed. "Oh, no, I'm good. But if you need one, then that's fine."

Agatha released her hand from her refrigerator door. The baby hairs on Millie's forehead were curled onto her skin. She had sweat stains making half circles on a rose-colored T-shirt. On the bottom she wore tiny black shorts. Her arms and legs looked very soft.

Agatha leaned against the refrigerator door. "This," she said, "is such a bad idea."

Millie smiled and said, "Okay."

"It has to stay between you and me."

"Well, yeah. Fucking duh."

From Agatha's chest came a laugh that felt like choking. Jesus Christ, she thought. Is this who you are? "Alright," she said. "Okay then, come here."

Millie went to her. Agatha tipped her head back and kissed her on the mouth.

LATER, AFTER MILLIE left, Agatha had an email from the editor at *Teen Vogue*. Had she missed Agatha's latest piece? She needed it by EOD. Agatha looked to the bookshelf. There was a copy of *Rebecca*. She did a find and replace for Millie's name. In the end, she shortened it to Becca because Becca sounded southern.

15.

KENNEDY WASHBURN WAS BORN IN DEWITT, Iowa, in 1996. She was the youngest of six, but at that, she was very young. The sibling closest to her in age was her sister Reagan, who was seven when Kennedy was born.

The Washburns didn't have a ton of money but as Nichelle said, they "did okay." Her father was a firefighter and he worked in Camanche. Her mom stayed home and sometimes sold Mary Kay. They had a Christmas tradition where Nichelle drove them to the Dollar Tree in a blue van that felt like a second home. Each child would take turns waiting in the van while the other siblings picked out their presents. The whole thing felt wild like an amusement park, Kennedy running through the aisles, trying to catch up. Theo was into gag gifts. John shopped for himself ("Get me this. Don't forget"). When it was Kennedy's turn to be shopped for, she sat in the van, heart still racing, conscious of herself as a person in the world. On Christmas morning she unwrapped items that were far too young or too old for her. Play-Doh. A student planner. A lamp in the shape of a flamingo. A foldable fan with cherry blossoms. Reagan told her she could keep it in her purse.

In the year Kennedy turned five, she received a sparkly baton.

Her neighbor, Helene, used to twirl as a Half-Time Honey at Butler University. Helene had a folding chair on her porch, and she coached Kennedy from there. "First you watch and then you'll try," she'd say. In a butterfly-shaped money bank she'd received from her siblings, Kennedy saved for a real baton. It was nine dollars at the Toys"R"Us in Moline and she was shocked at the weight. Helene said she'd get used to it, and she did.

Around that time, Kennedy's dad, a man named Roy with a blond beard, became quickly and severely ill. Nichelle and Roy made lots of trips to the doctor and when Kennedy wasn't at school, Helene would "babysit," which meant she'd coach Kennedy from the porch. Roy Washburn had lung cancer and chronic bronchitis. A year and a half after his diagnosis, a bed was moved into the living room. Kennedy did shows for her dad, cartwheeling and twirling her baton. He died there, in the living room, the summer before her fifth-grade year. Everything was chaotic and sad. The kitchen became full of food. Then Reagan moved to Minneapolis to start cosmetology school with a friend, and with everyone gone, the living room doubled in size. One morning, Kennedy sat at the kitchen table while Nichelle made cheesy scrambled eggs. "It's so quiet," she told her mom. Nichelle smiled and said, "Yes, it is. It's just you and me for now, sis."

Nichelle got a part-time job as an immunology nurse. She did skin-prick tests at an allergy clinic and joked that her degree had come in handy after all. She attended a women's grief counseling session in the basement of a Methodist church. One night she came home with a flyer for twirling lessons. "Hey. Check this out. How cute is that."

The studio was over in Davenport and it was called the Talent Factory. Weekly lessons turned into weekend workshops and a competition team that Kennedy joined in high school. She and Nichelle drove down to St. Louis for intensives, private lessons, and solo competitions. Kennedy was the featured twirler at her high school football games and assemblies. Sometimes she was paid fifty dollars to perform at nursing homes.

Summers were spent twirling, babysitting, and taking summer school, the last of which was in service of graduating a year early—the current University of Iowa twirler's final year. One of Kennedy's audition dances was the Iowa fight song, and in the year she turned eighteen, she was christened the Golden Girl. She had a full ride for five years, and while it was frowned upon, she could use all of them: four years for undergrad and one for a master's. She learned to work with fire. The marching band felt like family. When the announcer called her name, he stretched it out like this: "Make some noise for Kennedyyy Washbuurrrn!" Kennedy ran onto the field first. Doing split leaps across the green were bright blue eyes, glitter, and pride.

IN OCTOBER OF her junior year, Kennedy gathered her things atop a bench in the locker room. Iowa had just beat Minnesota fourteen to seven, and Erin, the drum major and one of Kennedy's closest friends, announced, "We are going to a party right now."

Tory, a flutist, said, "No, we're not. I'm starving and I didn't bring party clothes."

"It doesn't matter. We're going. We can get food on the way."

"But why?" Leanne laughed. She set her trumpet in its case. "Why tonight? Do we even know where to go?"

"A girl in my bio class invited me. We're going. We are college students and we are cool and we are going."

On the bench, Kennedy's knees fell to the side. She said to Erin, "We are not cool."

Erin shoved her and said, "Yes, we are!" Erin and Kennedy had gone to high school together. Their moms had been good friends first. And now they were friends, too.

Kennedy didn't live on or close to campus the way other students did. Three nights a week, she was at home in DeWitt. For the rest of the week she was at her aunt's in Iowa City, a little guesthouse under a tree in her backyard. And so, it felt fun, like she was a real student, to walk with her girlfriends up to Clinton Street. They were in clothes they hadn't planned on wearing. Kennedy hadn't taken her makeup off. On her right cheek was a peel-and-stick tattoo: the outline of a yellow Hawkeye bird.

It was the second week of October and Iowa City was turning cold. Regardless, there were people standing on the lawn and on the porch, more people inside big windows without blinds. Kennedy had been to parties before, but this one was packed. She walked in behind Erin, holding her hand.

A guy with a beard pointed at her with his cup. "Oh shit," he said. "Even the Golden Girl is here."

Kennedy smiled and said, "Um, hi."

"Don't you get a scholarship to major in twirling?" he said.

As Kennedy said, "Oh, kind of," Erin laughed and said, "Ohmygod."

Then someone said, "Oh hey. Do a trick."

Someone else said, "The ceiling's too low."

Then a very cute guy said, "Hey. Don't you have to know how to juggle?"

Kennedy gently bit her lip.

Suddenly in her hands were two lemons and one large lime. She felt like a celebrity, juggling in the foyer of someone's house.

She was hardly ever recognized; her face on the field was too far from the stands. But here she was, at a party she hadn't planned on attending, catching a lemon behind her back.

There was a nice round of applause. The cute guy from before stepped toward her. "Hey, I'll take those." Kennedy handed him the fruit. "You're so good," he said. "How long did it take you to learn the fire stuff?"

"Oh. I guess not that long," she said.

"We're getting a drink. You okay?" Erin said.

Kennedy nodded. Ohmygod, she thought.

The guy leaned in a little farther. "So do you just go really slow at first?"

"Well, no," Kennedy said. "If you go slow the flames get bigger. But if you go fast you don't really see them."

He smiled, very slowly. "Interesting . . . that's deep."

"Oh. Maybe. I don't know."

"Have you ever dropped it?"

"Oh yeah. Lots of times. Not like, *on* me. But yeah. It happens."

"So what do you do if you drop it? What's the next move?"

"Well?" She was stalling. He was so freaking cute. "First, you make sure your coach didn't see? Then you scoop it up, you never bend over. And then you just keep on going and . . . kind of act like it never happened."

He nodded like this was also very deep. "Hey, were you in my Modern World class last year?"

"Ohmygosh, yes. I was. Sorry."

"No, it's cool. I was always asleep in there. You're Kennedy, right? Okay, cool. Nice to meet you. I'm Colton."

Colton had dark brown hair that appeared to stem from the center point of his head. He was from Evansville, Indiana, he loved basketball, and he was majoring in civil engineering. He was a bit gangly and had one of those very cute boy-laughs that was completely uninhibited and a bit embarrassing but also great. As they talked, four different people said hi to him. Two of them said it, the others clapped him on the back. For a second, Kennedy had felt like a celebrity, but Colton really was someone. People actually knew him, and he was talking to her.

"Wait, you've never heard of pizza farm?" Kennedy asked. "It's twice a month but only in the summer. Twelve dollars for unlimited pizza. On a farm."

"Holy shit," Colton said. "Those are like, my two favorite things."

"Then you have to go."

"It's a good thing I met you."

Kennedy felt something at her right leg. A dog had made its way to her knees. "Have you met Sadie?" Colton said. "She's my boy Drew's dog."

Kennedy said, "I haven't." She knew who Sadie was. And she knew who Colton's boy Drew was, too. Drew had been on homecoming court a week before. He hadn't won, but Sadie was in his nomination picture, and on the homecoming float, and on the field during crowning.

Kennedy bent as she said, "Hi, Sadie." The dog put its nose in her palm. Colton bent next to her. Their faces were very close together. He asked if she wanted to put her number in his phone.

She was a little bummed when he didn't ask her on a real, official date. She thought that it'd be cute to go to Buffalo Wild Wings' discount night, but if not that, then the nice fro-yo place after class. They did, however, begin to text regularly. Colton sent her pictures of random objects. He'd write, *Can you juggle this?* or, *How about this one?* In response to a milk carton, Kennedy replied,

Oh yeah, totally. When he texted a plant, she wrote, *I haven't done one of those in years!* The next weekend, when Kennedy traveled to Purdue, they texted for two hours while she was on the bus. Then, twelve days after they first met, Colton texted that "Drew and those guys" were having a party at the Sigma Pi house that Friday. How she should definitely come because he'd love to see her.

This time, he hugged her hello. He smelled wonderful, like deodorant and stadium seating. He introduced her to two of his friends ("Hey, this is Kennedy") and he made a big display of gently moving her whenever someone passed behind. At several points in the night, Sadie the dog found Kennedy and leaned into her side. Drew said she could give Sadie a sip of beer if she wanted. The bottle in Kennedy's hands was just for show; she wanted to have a good performance the following day. She got down on one knee and scratched behind Sadie's ears. "No, that's okay," she said.

Around midnight, Colton whispered, "If I wanted to kiss the Golden Girl, how would I go about doing that?"

Down the street, beneath his covers, he whispered to her again. "Hey. We don't have to do anything that you don't wanna do."

"No, I know," she whispered back. "This is good. I just don't want to do like, everything . . ."

"No, I hear that."

"But yeah. I'm having fun."

"Okay, cool. I am, too."

They kissed and touched each other into the morning.

"Ohmygod," Kennedy laughed. "I have to be up in three hours."

"Set two alarms," he told her. "I cannot be the guy who made the Golden Girl miss a game."

Kennedy pretended to doze off on Colton's arm. She loved

the way his bed smelled—like a rubber kickball and hotel body-wash. In the morning, a minute before her alarm, Kennedy stopped it on her phone. It was 6:49 a.m. With a thumb and index finger she lifted Colton's flannel comforter and slid her feet onto the floor.

"Hey." Colton rubbed his eyes. "Should I drive you over there?"

"No," she whispered. "I'm all good. I have my truck."

Eyes still half closed, he said, "You have a truck?" He reached for her with "You're my dream girl."

Kennedy walked in the center of the street, just because she was happy and she could. There were no drivers, just her and lawns and porches. Trees and leaves that were bright orange, red, and brown. She'd parked on Ronalds Street, just past the big frat houses and across from single-family homes. Her truck—a white Toyota Tacoma—was the kind that had full doors in front and smaller half doors in back. In the street, on the passenger side, she opened them both. She reached for her bag and did an inventory. Uniform and tights. Her batons and jazz shoes. Makeup bag and cougars. Flame retardant and hairpins. Her phone was at six percent, she'd need to charge it while she did her face. But her charger was accounted for, too. Kennedy exhaled. She could spend the night with a cute guy and still wake up as the Golden Girl.

Erin had texted five minutes prior. *Did I leave my bobby pins in your bag?* Facing the bed of her truck, Kennedy checked. Then she responded. *Got em. On my way.* And then she did something she'd done plenty of times before: a little push from her hip against the truck's half door. But on that Saturday morning, the gentle push from Kennedy's hip was promptly met with a whimper and a snap. The half door swung back out against her thigh, having not met its latch. At the sound, she turned around and caught the final moment of Sadie's collapse. The dog's body flopped down into the street, eyes open and neck bent back. Kennedy's hands went to her nose. She dropped her phone onto the asphalt. From her throat come an involuntary noise, which she stopped with a hand to her neck.

The steps Kennedy should have taken would later become very clear. She should have run back to Colton's. Wake up. It's Sadie. She should have picked Sadie up—no matter the sickening slack—and driven her to a vet. She should have banged on the door of the Sigma Pi house, or any house really, screaming, Help me, or, Please I need help. But in a haunting state of paralysis, one that would follow her to Arkansas, Kennedy found herself standing in a bizarre hyperspace. Everything around her was two-dimensional. A strange haloed effect appeared on her hands, around the truck. Between her body and Sadie's neck formed a complete ionic bond. She stood in denim shorts and a yellow Hawkeye crewneck, but Kennedy was no longer on this planet.

And it was in this state that her muscle memory kicked in with an automatic, chilling ease. Possibly worse than what Kennedy accidentally did was what she carefully did next. The street was cool and covered in fall. She looked around to make sure no one had seen. Then she scooped up her phone. Fingered for her keys and got in the truck. Kennedy just kept on going; pretended like it never happened.

It was extraordinary what a body could do while the mind operated in another domain. Kennedy gave Erin her bobby pins back. Tory joked with her in the locker room. Kennedy joked back as she got dressed. She ordered a coffee and drank it standing up. She performed for a group of donors in a parking lot next to a tented buffet. At a tailgate, she ate a walking taco. She took pictures with four little girls. At pregame she did her different handshakes with every section of the band. She ran out first as she always did, running and leaping across the field. In what would be her very last game, Kennedy made no mistakes. She smiled up at the sea of yellow and black. She pumped her fist singing, *Fight Fight Fight*.

COLTON'S FIRST TEXT to her came at noon. *Hey something crazy happened that I'll tell you about later. Let me know if you still want to hang out when you're done.* Kennedy didn't respond. She'd done the worst thing she could do, which gave little to no meaning to what she did next. Iowa lost to Wisconsin by six. Back to the locker room, Colton sent something else. *Never text me ever again*, he said. *And just so you know, Drew is going to press charges.*

Kennedy gathered all her things and drove home to DeWitt in silence. When she walked in the front door, Nichelle said, "Hey. How'd it go?" Like dominoes, Kennedy's legs and arms folded and she sank down onto the floor. It looked strangely fake and dramatic, and because of this, Nichelle laughed. "Sis," she said. "Are you that tired?"

Kennedy threw up on the carpet. A cord of saliva connected her to the floor.

IN 2013, ON an episode of *Shark Tank*, an invention called Doorbot was pitched. It was a doorbell and home security camera. It would later more widely be known as Ring, and in 2016, Shaquille O'Neal was featured in the commercials. The neighbor across the street from the Sigma Pi house was a longtime

Orlando Magic fan who purchased the device. At seven a.m. that Saturday morning, an Iowa student was going to work when she saw Sadie. The police were called. Drew cried on the lawn. The neighbor came outside and offered up his Ring footage, just in case it happened to "catch the guy that did it."

There was Kennedy Washburn. Ponytail up high and cell phone in her hand. Sadie trots behind the car, unnoticed. She walks to the opened door and sniffs the back seat. There's no sound to the recording, so when Sadie falls to the ground, it's like she's been trained. Then Kennedy sees what she's done. She begins to hyperventilate, which, on film, looks like she's sneezing. A full twenty seconds pass. Then Kennedy picks up her phone. She gets into the truck. She slowly drives away.

The fact that Sadie was outside was not important. The fact that she was eating a discarded Twix bar on the sidewalk wasn't discussed. All that mattered was that Kennedy had accidentally broken the dog's neck, and that she'd gone about her day. A recording of the video (not the video itself, but a recording of the recording) quickly circulated through the student body. At home in DeWitt, Kennedy threw up so hard that she broke blood vessels in her eye. She later skipped a menstrual period and developed Tietze syndrome. The doctor said the cartilage between her rib cage and sternum had become severely inflamed.

Drew did not press charges. It was so clearly an accident, and he hadn't put Sadie away the night before. Leanne and Tory refused to text Kennedy back. Erin did, too, which hurt a lot. *I know I messed up, but will you please talk to me?* Kennedy typed. An hour later, Erin texted back. *I don't think that's a good idea.*

Kennedy was called into her coach's office—Nichelle, too— and she was asked to step down as UI's Collegiate Featured

Twirler. In the back of her mother's van, Kennedy lay across the middle seat. She wasn't crying. She felt catatonic and dead.

Nichelle turned around in the driver's seat. "Look at me," she said. "You are not a bad person. And I know there's a lot going on, but you have to finish the semester, and then we'll figure something out."

She had two big classes where all the lectures were online. But the other two required participation as part of her grade. On campus, she wore a hat and a scarf. She felt like a bug; she walked close to the walls. One time, she heard a student say, "I know it was an accident, but I'd probably kill myself."

One of the classes she needed to attend was a creative writing workshop taught by a graduate student poet. In a mandatory office hours session, Kennedy met with her teacher to discuss her final project. They were the exact same height; her teacher was probably twenty-three years old. Without warning or meaning to, Kennedy broke down in tears.

"Holy shit, oh no," her teacher said. "Are you okay? I don't have a tissue. Do you want a receipt? Use my jacket."

"No, I'm sorry." Kennedy used her own sleeve. "I'm just . . . well, you probably already know."

"No, I don't know anything! What's up? What's going on?"

It was the second time—her mother being the first—that she'd repeated the events out loud. "So I don't know what I'm going to do," she said. "Well, I do know. I'm taking next semester off and applying to other schools. But everything is just really hard and my life just feels . . . really over right now." Kennedy hated how dramatic she sounded, but inside her was a specific skill that would never be useful ever again. The only texts she received now were from numbers she didn't know. Drew's friends sending threats and calling her names. There'd been a memorial for Sadie. Over two hundred people had gone.

"Okay, first of all?" her teacher said. "You have to write about this. It's so *rich*."

This was the last thing Kennedy had expected them to say.

"I'm not kidding," they went on. "There's a sacrilegious aspect to this? I love the way you describe the movement of your hip and feeling paralyzed . . . and I think that's hard to pull off on the page."

"Oh. Okay," Kennedy said. "Sorry, I thought we had to write a fiction piece."

"No no no, you can totally do creative nonfiction. And I'm obviously not a doctor, but I think this could be a good way for you to process everything. So yeah. Just write all your thoughts out. Total word vomit. Don't think about it. And then we can work through it together when you're done."

"Seriously?"

"Yeah!"

"Okay. Thank you." Kennedy redid her scarf and picked up her phone. "Sorry . . . I don't want you to be like, freaked out. It really was an accident."

"Ohmygod, of course not." The poet placed a hand on the desk. "If anything, I'm more jealous of your trauma."

So Kennedy wrote and wrote. Her first draft was two single-spaced pages. In it, she referred to Colton as The Boy. When she finished, she sat in this weird room at the graduate school that held three printers and a desk. "Mmm," her teacher said. "This is so good." Then they took up a red pen. "Do you mind if I go at it?" Kennedy didn't understand but she said yes. Her teacher began to reorganize it, make strike-throughs, change verb tenses.

Kennedy didn't fully comprehend what it had become until she was home. Once she applied the changes she saw what her writing could do. She liked this part: *A person filled with choreography. No steps on how to say you're sorry.* Kennedy hadn't considered it before, that to write something beautiful you just do it regular, and then you pull out a red pen.

The 2016 election took some heat away from Kennedy. Slowly, her lungs began to heal. She got an A on her creative nonfiction essay. Her teacher encouraged her to submit it to the undergraduate literary journal. The story was accepted and it came out on December ninth, Kennedy's last day as a Hawkeye. Nichelle read it and became emotional. Her teacher emailed and said, *Way to go!* Kennedy liked the formatting in the magazine, and the font they used for her name. But she knew the majority of students didn't know that there was an undergrad lit journal, that it was kind of cool to have a piece accepted. With her applications to the University of Arkansas and Oklahoma City University complete, Kennedy finished her finals and left for winter break. Her sister came home for Christmas and she dyed Kennedy's hair a platinum blond with white highlights. "It's still you?" Reagan said. "But it's a new you. It's perfect."

Nichelle was a big reader before, but she quickly doubled down. She swept up several books on shame and loss and recovery. She purchased two copies of *Rising Strong* by Brené Brown so she and Kennedy could read it together. However reluctant at first, Kennedy gobbled it up. She loved a line that talked about choosing courage over comfort. And there was a part that said *Story is literally in our DNA*, which made it seem like something else would come after this part of her life.

Nichelle and Kennedy cooked lots of new meals and desserts. They both loved *The Pioneer Woman*, and they watched it differently now, with pen and paper in hand. On Tuesdays and Thursdays, when Nichelle didn't work, they would take a list of ingredients to the store. Peanut butter bars. Nutella Rice Krispies treats. Pumpkin chili. Chinese chicken salads.

Kennedy did two classes online as she waited to hear back from Oklahoma and Arkansas. With more free time than she'd had in years, she started reading. Not for school, just for fun. *Gone Girl* by Gillian Flynn. *The Time Traveler's Wife* was sad but okay. She read the entire *Hunger Games* series. (They were so good! How had she missed this?) And she read a book her mother had picked up for her: *Satellite Grief* by Agatha Paul. Most of the chapters weren't about the elements of grief, but there was one that was. There were so many passages where Agatha Paul was just completely inside her head. It made her feel like she was not so alone, that she could one day move on. There were also all these things she didn't know before, like how the prefrontal cortex part of the brain can become dormant in grief. How this was the part that helps you make decisions. Kennedy learned how the event had imprinted on her brain, carved out pathways, locking the trauma in. It was like Agatha Paul was diagnosing her, and saying she'd be okay. According to Agatha Paul, Kennedy was not—biologically, spiritually, or emotionally—composed of the worst mistake she'd ever made.

In the spring, Kennedy took a writing workshop at her local library, where she wrote another essay. This one was about her dad. She was accepted to both Oklahoma City University and the University of Arkansas. Nichelle hung her acceptances on a corkboard in the kitchen.

Then, one night, when Kennedy was in her room, Nichelle knocked rapidly on her door. The University of Arkansas was pleased to welcome Agatha Paul as a visiting professor for the

2017–18 academic year. She'd be teaching creative nonfiction and a media studies course in the graduate program, as well as an advanced undergraduate class for creative nonfiction in the spring. Nichelle set her laptop down so Kennedy could read it for herself. "Can you even believe?" Nichelle said. "I mean, how perfect is that?"

16.

THE NUMBER OF PEOPLE MILLIE HAD SLEPT WITH was two. The first was her first real boyfriend in her senior year of high school. His name was Dominic and he was also on student council, and he was one of the fourteen Black students in the senior class, including Millie. Dominic was more charming and funny in public than he was in private. But he and Millie had all the same friends. It was nice to make out with him in her car. And it felt like a huge relief to have a date to all the dances.

In the spring, Dominic was accepted to the University of Missouri on partial scholarship; he planned on studying agroforestry. A few days after graduation, he made it clear that a long-distance relationship wasn't something he wanted to do. Millie found herself a bit brokenhearted by what she knew was a peevish blow, that she'd failed to say it first. The breakup also served as a reminder that most of her friends would be going to university, while she'd be living in a bed-and-breakfast, working at coffee shops, and taking condensed gen-ed classes at Crowder. But the sting of being preemptively dumped soon lost its edge. Millie and Dominic, however broken up, began sleeping together through June and July. Mostly on weekends and in Dominic's brother's apartment when he was at work or coaching intramural floor hockey. Sex with Dominic was a little like going to the gym: a chore at first, but halfway through, she was happy to have gone. But when Dominic left for Mizzou, Millie felt relieved. She assumed sex would be better with someone she was crazy about, when it was in a bed that was hers or theirs.

The second person Millie had sex with was a guy she met at a party while out with two RA friends. Millie was twenty years old and learning the hard way that a sugary intoxication could be difficult to stomach. When she went outside to get some air, a guy in a baseball cap said, "Oh, hello." His name was Cam and he was a shot put and discus thrower with a very broad palate, nose, and chest. Cam's voice kept going in and out, like he'd lost it screaming at a concert the night before. There in the backyard, he kissed her, and while it didn't feel great, it felt like something she should be doing.

They went back to his apartment. Cam didn't turn on the lights but Millie could sense that dried food was near. Whatever was on the bed had the texture of a sleeping bag, or something that was waterproof. Soon their clothes were off and it was all happening. Cam made a lot of noises, like someone playing tennis. The other strange thing about Cam's intonations was the fact that it seemed like he was making them for her.

Sometimes, when they changed positions, Millie thought, Am I going to throw up? No no no, you are fine. Some moments did feel quite nice, but it was mostly too loud and fast. And then, in a sound resembling the pop of a paper bag, Cam slapped her behind with a cupped hand. Okay, Millie thought. I think I'm fine with that. But then he did it again. This time he said, "Come on, big girl."

How quickly her brain and body sobered. She opened her eyes

and she thought, Wait. A bit dazed, she placed her hand against the wall, which Cam must have liked because he said, "That's it." With a lucidity that chilled her hard, Millie turned her head to the left. Okay, she thought. You're okay. She looked out the window and took a breath. What street am I on right now?

When it was over, she used the glow of her phone to find her sandals and her clothes. Cam was in the bathroom; she could hear the water running. She stepped down the thinly carpeted stairs, slipped her shoes on at the bottom. Outside, the rocks and gravel crunched underneath her feet. There was this Paramore song that was always on the radio that spring, and Millie could hear it playing inside a passing car. She knew where she was. She had her phone and keys. Okay, she thought. I'm never doing that again.

A month later she saw Cam on Dickson but he didn't see her. He was speaking to someone who looked like a coach or a small-business owner. Seeing him made her mad. You suck, she thought. Clean your room. Not to mention, we are like, the exact same size. She hadn't slept with anyone since. It was very easy to have sex in college, but it was even easier not to.

What Millie began doing with Agatha rendered her previous encounters insipid and bland. She instantly came into the understanding that Dominic and Cam—and she herself to a certain extent—had been administering their sex lives with a paint-by-numbers application, at best. For the rest of November, Millie went to Agatha's every weekend. Sometimes, she went twice. It was enlightening and ruining her equally, she could tell. She'd come home and lie down, thinking, Ohmygod.

Agatha didn't like to take her shirt off. She'd remove her bottoms and her bra but her shirt would become twisted at her sides. Her body was practical and businesslike, somehow resembling a bicycle or golf club. But what was more important was how much her body did and did not factor into her appeal. Seeing her this way made it clear that what Agatha looked like was completely immaterial. There was nothing presently or hypothetical about her form that could have been remotely disappointing. She was absolutely perfect, clothes notwithstanding, and it wouldn't have mattered if she weren't. There was something about her physical form that evoked a satisfying math problem, something symmetrical that rhymed. She was the movement of a decimal point. The finger trick for multiples of nine. Tiny arrows for cross-multiplication. I eight and eight till I was six on the four.

Agatha was attentive, careful, and rough. She was as bossy as Millie had dreamed (*Turn over. Take this off. Touch me here. Scoot up to the edge*). The gradual ascent Millie had felt in moderation with men was now intense and humiliating. Red skin. The loss of motor skills. Sometimes she physically shook. Once, Agatha stopped and said, "Hey. If you don't like something, then you need to speak up." She almost sounded angry. Her austerity made Millie blush. "I, yeah, no. Sorry," Millie said. "I'm like, shaking because I like it." When Millie offered to return her favors, Agatha pushed her hand away. She'd replace it with her own in a strangely polite gesture, as if she didn't want Millie to pay for a meal.

The first time they were together, on that Friday afternoon, Agatha put her shorts back on with this: "So I imagine our Thursday nights are done for now. And I understand."

"What? Why?" Millie asked.

"Well, the last thing I want is for you to feel used."

"Ohmygod, no," Millie said. "I don't want to stall your project. Let's keep Thursdays. I'll be cool."

And so they continued as they had before. Agatha sat on the

floor and Millie sat at her desk. Millie loved how Agatha packed up her things, her face flustered and resigned. "Alright. Do you—I'll see you this weekend, then?" A nod. Agatha would throw her hands up a bit and laugh. "Alright, then. I'll see you soon."

The moments before and after Agatha's bedroom were just as alluring for reasons Millie couldn't describe. She liked looking at the products in Agatha's bathroom. A vitamin C serum. Salt-block deodorant. Muscle relaxer and OB tampons in a drawer. Agatha told Millie she could use her washer and dryer, and sometimes Millie brought a plastic bag full of clothes. She stood at the washer, placing her clothes inside. From the kitchen, Agatha spoke. "Are you hungry? You've never tried jícama? See if you like this. Do you want to take some home?"

Once, on the island counter, there were two piles of documents. Millie tugged her sweatshirt over her head and asked what they were.

"Those are applications for an undergraduate class I'm teaching."

Millie read *Kennedy Washburn* at the top of a page. "Oh no way. This is my resident."

"Uh-oh. She's not in the good pile."

"Was her stuff really bad?"

From another counter, Agatha peeked at the application. Her hands were full and buzzing. She was grinding coffee beans for the next day. "I don't really remember," she said. "The sample may have been okay. But I think she was one of the students who wrote, 'My name is so and so,' and I just didn't read the rest."

"Ohmygod. That's brutal."

Agatha shook the grinder. "You know that, right? Never say 'My name is.'"

"No, I know. But still. That's harsh."

"Is it?" She released the lever. "It's a 300-level class."

Throughout all this, Millie's feelings for Josh remained as she'd left them, something she'd stored away. She still put on lotion and mascara for their Tuesday-morning meetings. He stayed charming as ever. He once brought chocolate popcorn in the same cellophane bags. Millie told herself that Agatha was something she was getting out of her system. She continued to imagine a future in which Josh knew and accepted her past. Do you still have feelings for her? he'd say. No no, she'd say. It wasn't like that at all. But of course it was. Millie had ample feelings for Agatha that fully eclipsed their physical affair.

Millie's nights with Agatha shifted her cosmology of the world, especially as it pertained to being an RA. She felt herself caring less about things she used to consider important. She wore headphones sometimes when she was doing rounds. She didn't knock on the doors of residents she hadn't seen in a while; told herself they were probably fine. Once, after helping a resident string lights above her bed, Millie spotted three bottles of rosé behind a mini fridge.

She sighed and stood up. "Okay, Sydney . . . come *on*."

"Ohmygod. It's not what it looks like."

"Sutter Home? Sydney, why?"

"I know, but we were doing something for Abigail because her mom might have lupus and she's so sad and she loves rosé. Please don't write me up. My dad will kill me—"

Millie said, "Just put it away."

With Agatha constantly on her mind, even the threat of Tyler retaliating became slightly dull and worn-out. Tyler had stopped making eye contact with Millie. Jenna had, too. Casey was still nice. When momentary fear of Tyler did return, it felt like some kind of penance, something that balanced out Millie's secrets, and her fun and seedy friends. And then, on a Saturday night, when Millie was leaving for Agatha's, Tyler came to the door of her room.

"Hi," she said. She touched the braid on her shoulder. "Can you actually help me out?"

"Yeah, what's up?"

"I need to change the height of my bed."

Her voice was kind, and Millie could feel it then. Tyler was holding out an olive branch. Perhaps it was just because she needed help, but Tyler was extending an offer to divorce Millie from Ryland and Colette. But at that moment, Millie had plans. She was going to Agatha's and she didn't feel like lofting a bed. It was a Saturday night. Millie wasn't even on duty. And calling her ghetto had been a bitchy thing to do.

"Oh, um?" Millie stalled. Then Joanie appeared in her red shirt, down at the other end of the hall. "Or actually," Millie said. "Hey, Joanie?"

"'Sup!"

"Can you help Tyler with her bed?"

"You bet I can!"

Tyler looked back at Joanie, who was performing a clipped jog, her arms pumping at her sides. Then she turned back to Millie with a glare of divine pique. Her face said, *Wow. You're a bitch.*

Joanie held her hand up for a high five. "Let's do this," she said. "Cool braid. What's your name?"

"It's Tyler," she said. Then she gently touched her palm to Joanie's without a sound.

Millie walked down to the elevators. She could smell her showered skin. You know what, Tyler? she thought. Just do whatever you're going to do. That night she lay across Agatha's bed, wearing only a thong and sharing a caramel. She told Agatha about how they'd pranked Tyler back, and she told it like she was part of the execution. "Ah," Agatha said, chewing. "Making her idea redundant. That's clever. Good for you."

Much in the way that she wouldn't have predicted slacking in her RA duties, Millie could not have ever foreseen her participation in Colette and Ryland's recreational activities. Colette went home to Atlanta the weekend before Thanksgiving, and she returned with a lot of cash and prescription medications. Sitting in her bedroom, Colette and Ryland went through them all along with the items she'd stolen for Ryland (bottles of Soylent. Beef jerky. A cheese knife). From Colette's bed, Millie heard the words *Ativan*, *gabapentin*, and "my dog's anxiety medication." When Ryland said, "Millie, do you want one?" she was mildly shocked to hear herself ask for half. That night she came to know the considerable joy of Ryland's favorite activity: vibing out in Walgreens and Walmart. She just felt so calm. She liked all the lights, and she loved being with Ryland and Colette. It felt like confirmation that she did very mature, adult things when she wasn't with Agatha, too.

The second time Millie tried half of Colette's dog's medication, she sat in Ryland's room for an hour, and then she said she was going to the gym. When Agatha opened the side door of her house, Millie laughed and covered her mouth. "I'm sorry I'm sorry I'm sorry," she said.

Amused, Agatha let her inside. "Okay. What is happening here?"

"My friend's dog takes Valium. And we had a little bit but I'm totally fine."

Agatha looked very pleased. "You're abusing prescription drugs now? Is this new?"

"Yes, it is."

"Okay. Well. Let me catch up, I guess."

Millie slipped off her shoes as Agatha pulled down a bottle of wine. "Oo, can I have some?" she asked.

Agatha looked at her and said, "Absolutely not?"

On December first, Colette hosted a birthday party for Ryland at a roller-skating rink called Starlight Skatium. She bought a birthday party package called Pizza Party Plus that included pizzas, glow sticks, song requests, and a table reserved for three hours. Ryland had requested a birthday party theme of "soft." Colette decorated the table with tea towels, cotton candy, and Beanie Babies, tags still on. There was an ice cream cake on which Colette placed purple and silver ribbons as well as tiny basketballs.

Before the party started, Colette summoned Ryland and Millie with three pills in her hand.

"No," Millie said. "No, I don't wanna fall."

As Ryland said, "You won't fall," Colette said, "I brought wrist guards. We can share."

"No, it's fine. I'll just get a beer."

"Honestly," Colette said, "alcohol is way worse for skating."

"Ugh. Fine. Cut me half."

"I don't have my knife." "But it's my birthday."

"Okay okay. Fine fine fine."

They pressed the pills to their mouths. Ryland swallowed and said, "Yeet."

Ryland's friend Craig came and he did in fact resemble a baby giraffe. Also in attendance were three other First 100 friends as well as Stadium Whitney. Stadium Whitney brought her daughter, Trinity, and her niece, Jayla, who looked to be about five. When Ryland saw her, he started to cry. "Whitney. No. The fact that you came . . ."

"I told you I would! Trinity, that's Ryland. Do you remember him? Oh, you shy now. Okay, that's fine."

"Wait, Whitney," Ryland whispered. "You don't know how touched I am. But I also just need to be clear that like . . . I'm fucked up right now. I'm so sorry. Is that okay?"

Whitney shook her head as if she refused to hear it. "Baby, it is your day. We just appreciate you having us." Then Colette asked if anyone needed a glow stick or hat. Trinity said that she actually needed both.

They did the limbo and there was a Cha Cha Slide moment. There was a backward-skating race in which Craig won. Whitney, Trinity, and Jayla were going very slowly near the wall. Jayla wasn't skating so much as she was walking in her skates. Millie slipped into a balmy, electric state. She and Colette held hands during the couples skate to a song by Savage Garden. The lights were dimmed and there were a few very good skaters wearing tank tops and cutoff shorts. They made their way around the rink, crossing their skates one over the other as they turned.

Colette closed her eyes for a moment as she held on to Millie. "It's so dumb," she said, "that we don't come here every day."

Millie wanted to tell her then. Hey, don't be mad at me, but I'm going to RD next year. I'm also trying to buy a house and that's where I am sometimes. And I've been messing around with the tall lesbian who bought our drinks at Maxine's. And now I'm in love with her maybe, I don't know. But Millie didn't say anything. She rolled on in her rental skates and the best haircut she'd ever had. "See, Millie?" Ryland said. He skated by with Craig. "I told you that you wouldn't fall."

———

DECEMBER SEVENTH WAS Dead Day and the last proper Thursday of the academic year. Millie woke with no classes to attend and the realization that it felt like winter. She spent the morning in her room writing a paper for her marketing and operations class. An hour into making flash cards for Spanish, Colette texted that Ryland wanted a bagel and did Millie want to come. *Yes*, she typed back. *Coming down. Do you have the duty phone for me?* Colette wrote, *Shit*, and then, *Yes. I dropped it in the toilet but it's fine.*

Millie left her room, lanyard and phone in hand, and she passed the open door of the suite. There was Peyton, marching from the kitchen toward Kennedy's room. Two hands full of dirty dishes.

"Hey," Millie laughed. "You okay?"

Peyton stopped and said, "Umm, yes." The dish in her hand held a pizza cutter, a fork and knife, and a mug with an owl on the side.

Millie said, "Okay. Just checking," and Peyton said a frigid "Thanks."

She did consider going back and asking if the dishes situation had been resolved. But the elevator came and she hopped in. Don't, she thought. They're probably fine.

17.

K ENNEDY SPENT THE FIRST HALF OF DEAD DAY in bed, where she could reach her coffeemaker and Wheat Thins. She made some flash cards for her test in art history; *The Office* played from her laptop on the bed. At three p.m. she got dressed and left her room. She summoned an Uber on her way downstairs. In her checking account was fifty dollars from Nichelle to cover a manicure and a chair massage. Nichelle had found the salon—Gloss Nails—and it was super cute. The women working there were all so nice. The person who did Kennedy's nails was named Sabrina, and she had brown lipstick and lash extensions that looked really great on her. Sabrina applied an icy-white polish to Kennedy's nails—the name was Suzi Chases Portu-geese. She asked Kennedy about her holiday plans. Kennedy was going home to Iowa. Sabrina was going home to Odessa, Texas, for a few days, but then she was going to Miami Beach for an entire week. Kennedy gasped and said she was jealous. A song she liked was playing as she placed her fingers under the dryer, the one that goes *Last Christmas, I gave you my heart*. Why, she wondered, hadn't she done this before? She wore a sky-blue vest over a sweater. Glitter-gray beanie with a puff.

There was a Whole Foods in the same shopping center as Gloss Nails. Kennedy walked inside and browsed, loving the way her nails looked on the basket handle. With three finals to study for and one essay to write, she decided to stock up on snacks. White cheddar popcorn, chocolate pretzels, red pepper hummus, salt and vinegar chips. At the checkout line she threw in a lavender-scented toner called witch hazel. She didn't know what toner was, but she thought it would be fun to try. Then she walked over to Zoës Kitchen, where she got a Mediterranean salad with falafel and feta cheese. She considered how she could do this again next semester; maybe she could go once a week. She'd come back to Sabrina at Gloss Nails; they wouldn't be friends but they'd be friendly. Kennedy would know when her birthday was. She could bring her something small. She could also bring a book with her. She'd make time to read again. Or she could work on things she was writing or reading for workshop. Essays and rough drafts written by her peers.

Rejuvenated and hands very soft, Kennedy took another Uber back to Belgrade. Kacey Musgraves's Christmas album played in her new AirPods. She found herself pretending she was a different person, an older version of herself, someone with cute nails in an apartment, coming home from a long day, casually checking her mail. She went past reception to the mail room, opened her box with her key. Inside the little door was a tea bag, a candy cane, and a ballpoint pen, wrapped all in red and white string. The attached tag read *Happy Dead Day! Love, Millie and Colette.*

Kennedy eyed the candy cane and she got the idea to make fudge or chocolate bark. She closed her mailbox and checked her phone. An email notification sat waiting on the screen. The subject line read *Your Application to the Advanced Creative Nonfiction*

Course. The puff on her beanie made a shadow on the wall. She saw *Dear Kennedy Washburn,* and she thought, This is it.

> *Thank you for your interest in the Spring 2018 Advanced Cre-*
> *ative Nonfiction course. Your application has been carefully re-*
> *viewed, and we regret to inform you that it was not selected for*
> *further consideration. Please be aware that the applications for*
> *this course were particularly strong, and we have been unable to*
> *welcome all promising candidates . . .*

In the hallway outside, the elevator opened and dinged. Someone said, "Hey. Are you not coming?" Someone else said, "No, I am. I just forgot the study guide." The first person said, "Oh, okay." Kennedy scrolled down to the bottom of the email. Agatha Paul had not sent or signed the letter.

She placed the bundled sack from her RAs into her vest pocket. She left Belgrade and walked down the street, her Whole Foods bag bumping against her knee. She headed toward Dickson and took a right and walked up into campus.

Beneath her riding boots were thousands of names of alumni etched into the sidewalk. It was called Senior Walk, and when she and Nichelle had visited, Nichelle had said, "Oh, that's cute. One day you'll be here, too." Kennedy read the names beneath her feet. In her pocket she picked at the packet of tea. Without realizing, she picked too hard at the paper, and then she picked at the food-grade plastic, too. Flakes of a ginger-peach black tea gathered underneath her nails. It felt incredibly ill-timed—her nails were so rounded and her hands were so soft. Kennedy had the desire to kneel on the ground. Scrape the skin of her palms into the names below.

18.

A GATHA WORE HER AIRPODS AS SHE SPOKE to Jean. A buttery garlic film covered her hands. "I'm going to tell you something," she said. "Well, actually, I'm going to tell you something but I'm not going to tell you all of it."

"Okay . . ."

Outside her window, the sun was starting to set. "I'm sleeping with someone."

"You're joking," Jean said. "Okay. That's great."

"But let me say the other half of it. We're not dating, and she's quite young."

"How young?"

Agatha paused. Pressed her hips against the counter. "I don't want to tell you that yet."

Jean inhaled. "*No*. But it's not . . . she isn't your student."

"No no no. Jesus. I would never."

"Right. But she's just young."

"That's correct. She can drink and vote. But yes, she's very young."

Agatha heard a turn signal ticking inside Jean's car. "Okay,"

Jean said. "You made it sound terrible for a second, but this seems pretty great. Who made the first move?"

"Who do you think?"

"Ohmy*god*. I wish I could have seen your face."

Agatha's deflection—her "Who do you think?"—was misleading. Millie's approach in the alcove of her dorm room was the last advance she would make. How swiftly a new dynamic had formed between them, where Agatha was the incendiary and Millie was the lightwood, shaky and red.

"How did you meet her?"

"I don't want to tell you that yet either."

"Okay . . ." Jean trailed on, like she was playing a game. "She's not your student. But she's young. And you won't tell me how you met. Does that mean . . . I can't picture you doing this . . . but are you paying her?"

There was a hitch in her hands then. Agatha knew what Jean meant, but something had slipped into indiscretion. That she and Millie had kept their Thursdays had surprised her and yet it didn't. On those nights, they didn't touch. She'd continued to pay Millie the same.

"Is she a sex worker? Is that what you're saying? No. She's . . . she's actually the one who set up the interviews I've been doing."

"Oh, interesting. Hang on. I'm switching you off Bluetooth." There was a shift on the line. Jean's voice came back close and clear. "I loved the last one. That poor girl. I was an RA, too."

Agatha turned the faucet on with her elbow. "Yeah, she was sweet. And thank you for reading."

"Of course. Are you going to tell me more when you're here? December fifteenth?"

"The fifteenth. And yes, I will."

"I do have it written down. Noah is so excited. He said, 'My friend Aggie is coming to see me.'"

"It's true. You haven't told me what he wants."

"All he wants," Jean lowered her voice, "is a vacuum cleaner, which we're getting for him so he's all good."

"Interesting. Can I get him a dustpan?"

"Oh, he would love that. As long as it's not red. We hate red right now. But wait a second. Agatha." Jean laughed then. Agatha felt a rush of deeply missing her friend. "What does she . . . Is she funny? What is she like?"

"Umm." Agatha reached for a towel. "She can be funny at times."

Whenever Millie reached her finish, she lost any last remnants of her resident-assistant, student-of-the-month, camper-of-the-year composure. In the beginning she kissed like she was trying to get an A. But then her face bent in a way that looked angry and confused. It was as if she were coming out of anesthesia, nurses telling her she did great. She made small jerks and bucks and she shook like she was cold. She sounded like she was on the brink of dropping an item, little *oofs* that were incredibly intimate to hear. Agatha thought of those emissions often; on her runs, while she was in class. They instantly made her feel giddy and embarrassed.

"It's not . . . we're not dating, though. It's more of a weekend thing, if that makes sense."

"No, I'm with you," Jean said. "Does she come to you or do you go to hers?"

"She comes to mine."

"Of course she does. This is so good."

"You're making me feel much better about it, so thank you."

"I have one more question but you can't laugh. Does she have a southern accent?"

"No, she doesn't. I've heard her say 'y'all' but the correct answer is no."

"Is that dumb of me to ask?"

"No. And I actually have to go in a second."

"Are you teaching?"

"No, it's Dead Day."

"Dead Day? What is that?"

"It's this one day after the last classes but before finals start. Everything is essentially dead."

"Oh, that's cute. We should have that here."

"I know. But I'm making that hasselback squash thing and I need to focus."

"Ohmygod. Everyone is making that thing. But, Agatha, really quickly . . . I'm not kidding. This was what you needed. Arkansas was the right choice."

Agatha felt guilty then. She loved that Jean read all the things that she wrote on her own. Agatha never had to ask. "Well," she said. "We'll see about that. I'll send you a picture of the squash when I'm done."

The squash turned out great, slightly browner on one side. Agatha went for a quick run, and then she returned and had a slice. It was the last Thursday of the school year and it felt acutely final. When Millie opened the front door of Belgrade, she said, "Hi. It's our last one."

Agatha's recent profile, the one of Becca, was well-received. People loved the parts where Becca imitated a gossiping believer. They were happy and sad to know she would continue working in Residence Life the following year. The comment section was filled with people enraged at how little university employees were paid, TAs and athletes, too. Agatha had not put down Millie's race, but many comments wished she had. Others theorized correctly that she was Black.

When Millie said, "It's our last one," Agatha had thought, Thank God. She had one more profile to write and then she'd never do this again. Perhaps she would still see Millie next semester, but she'd do it differently. She wouldn't be at Belgrade, and she wouldn't be sitting on the floor.

Tyler and Casey were going to a holiday party, and Agatha wished she could see what they were wearing. Tyler asked, "Where's Jenna?" and then she said, "Oh right. She's doing that essay tutor thing."

"Mhm," Casey said. "She said she'll try to be back by nine."

"If she doesn't . . . I'm okay with that," Tyler said. In a strained voice she added, "Jenna is kind of annoying me lately."

Into her legal pad, Agatha made wide eyes. It would not be akin to the way she missed Jean, but she knew, in some capacity, she'd miss Tyler, Jenna, and Casey. The feeling of being invested in their lives, it was thrilling and terrible. Feeling like she knew them, sitting next to Millie, knowing what they'd do that weekend at her house.

"Ohmahlord, Tahler," Casey said. "Shut the door, then. You're making me nervous."

Agatha blinked; her pen stopped moving. For the very first time, she heard the suite door close.

Millie looked up from a flash card. "Wow," she said. "It's the end of an era."

"Feels that way. Interesting." Agatha took up her recorder and pressed pause. "Maybe I should let you study, too."

"Oh, you don't have to. I'm super prepared this year."

"Are you?"

"Oh yeah," Millie said. "I'm basically fluent." She shut her book and arched her back into a long stretch. "Don't go yet. I'll entertain you."

"You'll entertain me?"

Millie went and sat on her bed. Part of her duvet crept up, revealing a plastic storage unit underneath. In frosted drawers, Agatha saw the outline and colors of tampons, cotton balls, and a large jar of coconut oil.

"Do you want to sit on my bed with me?" Millie asked.

Agatha laughed. "Do I want to sit on your bed with you?" She chided herself for this, answering Millie's questions by saying them back, and for doing what she was doing, behaving as if she would say no.

On her bed, Millie crossed her legs. "Yeah. Don't tell me no. It's Christmas," she said.

Agatha placed her legal pad in her purse. Then she looked at Millie, overcome with affection. Wait a second, she thought. I am going to miss you, too. She slipped off her shoes and went to the bed. Underneath her hands, it creaked on one side.

"Shouldn't we just go back to mine?"

"I can't. I'm on duty." Millie pointed at a cell phone.

"Oh right. Okay. Well, this can't be a habit."

"No, I know."

"Will you lock your door?"

Millie stood. "Yes, of course."

Millie locked the door and turned music on from her computer. Agatha lay down on the extra-long twin bed. The marble-covered mini refrigerator began to hum. The Himalayan salt lamp glittered up close.

19.

ENNEDY PASSED STUDENTS DRESSED FOR NIGHTS out, other groups walking with backpacks and books. It was almost eight thirty, she'd been out for a while, but she didn't feel like roaming around anymore. She didn't feel like doing anything. The people she passed, the security guard, the buttons in the elevator—none of it felt particularly real. Kennedy returned to her suite with a loose and informal plan of ending her life in her dorm room.

This wasn't exactly true. Kennedy hated blood and she was tired. Too tired to think of when and how she would do it. But she was completely heartbroken, of that she was sure. And she did wish that she could go into a coma of some kind.

She walked down the fourth-floor hallway and saw the suite door open. She heard Tyler and Casey inside. Similar to how it felt to pretend that she would never be friends with Tyler, Kennedy felt good imagining herself at rock bottom, ready to go into her room and do something destructive. She wanted to reach a legitimate place that someone official would be forced to report. She liked thinking of telling Shea about it later. No, she'd say. I'm not kidding. I was going to kill myself on Dead Day.

Tyler and Casey were in the kitchen, and they both stood in

booties, black and brown. Kennedy came in and Casey smiled. "Hey," Tyler said. "You've been gone like, all day."

Hey suddenly seemed like the dumbest thing a person could possibly say. Kennedy said, "Yep!" as she pulled the refrigerator door open.

"Ookay . . ." Tyler said. "Where's Jenna? Oh, right. She's doing that essay tutor thing."

"Mhm," Casey said. "She said she'll try to be back by nine."

"If she doesn't . . . I'm okay with that." Tyler placed a hand on her mouth. "Jenna is kind of annoying me lately."

Casey gave her a look. "Ohmahlord, Tahler. Shut the door, then. You're making me nervous."

Tyler went to the suite door, and for once, she closed it. "I know you agree," she said.

Casey sighed. "Ah think she's goin' through a rough season . . ."

"Okay. Everyone is."

Kennedy opened an aluminum can and sipped it facing the wall. It was fun to pretend that this was her last La Croix.

"Wait," Tyler said. "I know we have to be out on the fifteenth but when do we have to be out-out?"

"Ah think noon? Ah should know this."

"Should I go ask Millie? Ugh, no," Tyler laughed. "I can't. I hate them still."

"Okay, you know what?" Casey lowered her voice. "The other day Ah saw Millie and Colette at Walgreens? And the one who looks like a li'l boy? And they were not actin' right. Something was goin' on. They were bein' *real* weird."

"See, yeah. I thought Millie was nice but she's definitely one of them."

Kennedy put her hummus into the refrigerator. She wondered which RA would do a report. Maybe they'd be the ones to find her body. Kennedy looked down at her outfit. What she had on was pretty good. She went into her room and closed her door. At her desk, on her laptop, the contents of the email remained. Kennedy felt strange; there was a bizarre relief in knowing that she'd been rejected. She didn't have to wonder anymore. But she also felt like she wasn't assessing things correctly. She wasn't doing thoughts right at all.

Outside her door, Tyler announced that she'd call the RA phone. She asked Peyton if she had the number. Peyton said, "Yes, I do." A few seconds later, Tyler said, "They aren't answering. Wow, they are such bad RAs."

Kennedy picked at an ingrown hair on her elbow, tea leaves still beneath her nails. At the aching of her neck, she stood up. It was unfortunate that she wasn't killing herself, because then she wouldn't need to write an essay. She glanced at her laptop and felt herself well up. She had no idea how she was going to tell her mom.

"Ugh," Tyler said. "This is so annoying. What if I was having an emergency?"

"They really aren't answerin'?" Casey said. "Uh-uh. That is wrong."

Kennedy thought, Good. Maybe she would kill herself. There was music coming from Millie's room. For just a second, it sounded like someone was deep breathing. Kennedy hoped whoever was inside was asleep.

"Wow," Tyler said. "I hate them so much. I should have gotten them back."

"No, you know what? Ah was just talkin' to mah mom about this. The best kind of revenge is showin' you don't care."

Tyler was eating something then. "No, you're so right. I'm proud of myself," she said.

Then Casey announced that she needed to change her shoes. Tyler said, "I'll go with you," and the front door opened and shut.

Kennedy stood up and took in the poster above her desk. *For Like Ever*, it read. What did that even mean? What a loser she was. She backed up against her bed, wondering if she did kill herself, if she should leave a note. Then—with hands on the duvet cover—Kennedy hoisted herself into a seated position. She landed on her mattress and underneath her thighs, she felt and heard something break. She gasped. She got up and turned around. There on the bed were dishes from the night before. They were from the meal she'd used to reward herself for surviving fall semester. The mug she'd used to make a chocolate chip cookie was broken. The handle had popped right off. The wheel of her pizza cutter was spinning off tilt. The blade had drawn ribbons of orange grease on her duvet.

Kennedy marched to the double room. She pushed the door so hard that it banged against the wall. There was Peyton at her desk. Black bonnet, FSU sweatshirt, slinky purple nighttime shorts. "Umm, Peyton?" Kennedy said. "Did you put my dishes on my bed?"

Peyton placed an arm on her chair. "Yes. You said I could."

"Peyton, are you kidding me? I said you could put them in my room. My things are broken. This is so not okay."

Peyton's head went back an inch. "I didn't break anything of yours."

"Well, they're broken now, so thanks a lot."

The idea of explaining what had happened seemed like a waste of time. And it was Peyton's fault for putting the dishes there to begin with. The mug had an orange and brown owl on the side. It had been gifted to Kennedy by her sister the Christmas before.

To see for herself, Peyton got up and walked to Kennedy's room. Once inside, she surveyed the scene. "I didn't do that," she said.

Kennedy stood behind her. "But why are you even going in my room? I don't go in your room. I don't touch your things."

Peyton faced her. "Because you *said*. I asked if you leave your dishes overnight, can I put them in your room."

"And so you put them on my *bed*? You could have put them literally anywhere else."

Peyton looked around the room. "Um, not really," she said. "And we aren't allowed to put things on top of the AC. And I didn't break your stuff. You can ask Tyler. She was here when I put them down."

At Tyler's name, Kennedy reached back and braced herself against the coffee cart. She could see it then: Peyton and Tyler scheming together, while she'd been having a decent day, God forbid! Tyler saying something like, Do it, Peyton. She needs to learn. Peyton wandering around the room, saying, Okay . . . but where? Kennedy reached in her pocket for her phone. "Okay, you know what? I'm calling Millie."

"You don't— Ugh," Peyton said. "It was Millie's idea, but do whatever you want, I guess."

Who hadn't Peyton discussed her dishes with? Kennedy wanted to sit down and cry. "Peyton. This isn't fair. I *live* here," she said. "And you're so mean to me and it's like . . . this isn't fair." She was full-on crying now, her nose wrinkled in distress. Kennedy stared at her phone, unsure if the number was under *Residence Life* or *RA*. She looked up and wiped her eyes to find that Peyton's face had changed.

Peyton put her hands in her pockets. Very carefully, she said, "I don't think I'm mean to you."

Kennedy sniffed. "It doesn't matter. You need to pay for my stuff. My pizza cutter is broken and so is my mug. And the mug was a gift so I can't get it back."

"But I didn't break your stuff. I kind of feel like you did. Just so you could say that."

"What?"

"I heard a noise when you came in here. Did you sit on them?"

"Peyton, listen to yourself."

"Maybe you didn't see them there. I don't know. It just seems weird."

"You're paying for this." Kennedy picked up the mug. "You need to Venmo me or give me cash."

"Ummm . . ." Peyton crept to the door. "I don't think I have to do that."

"Yes, you do," Kennedy said. "This was a gift and this was my mom's. And it's from somewhere nice like Pottery Barn."

Very quickly, Peyton made a face, like she didn't think Pottery Barn was that nice.

"And not to mention." Kennedy raised her voice. "My comforter is freaking stained."

"Grease can come out with baking soda. And . . . well, you have to wash it."

An acute jab of shame made Kennedy shut her mouth. Washing her sheets was another thing she'd failed to do. She washed her clothes—every weekend—but when it came to the bedsheets, she'd get stressed out or she'd forget. And then there was too much time and then there wasn't enough and she didn't want to sleep in a bed her mother hadn't made. But now she was here and she would have to wash her sheets and all of this was so, so bad.

"I have baking soda," Peyton said.

Kennedy stared, hating her face.

"I also have Gorilla Glue that might fix your mug."

"No. Just forget it." Kennedy picked up the dish.

"And actually?" Peyton pointed at the blade. "That's not broken. It just came loose where the screw—"

"Can you please move?"

"I'm just saying. If you tighten this . . ." Peyton reached for the pizza wheel. "It'll be fine. It'll cut even again."

Peyton held the handle with two fingers. Kennedy tugged back on the tool. "Peyton," she said. "Please just let it go."

"Careful." Peyton's grip remained. "If you hold it like that it'll fall off."

"Can you *please* let go of my stuff?"

Peyton made wide eyes and said, "Okay."

And with no resistance from Peyton's side and a final yank from Kennedy's, the pizza cutter took on a brief trajectory. A silver asteroid in the night. The circular blade clipped the side of the plate. Then it made a thirty-five-degree descent down into Kennedy's flesh. An elegant slice was made across the underside of her wrist. Blood spooled out with theatrical excess. Somehow, after it was done, she was still holding the mug and plate.

Kennedy dropped the pizza wheel; her skin felt wet and numb. She slowly bent down to her knees, as if she were holding an infant. It wasn't what she meant, but she looked at Peyton and said, "Why did you do that?"

Peyton made a noise like someone had snuck up on her, like she was so scared she'd become seasick. As she stumbled backward, her right hand flailed. She tugged on the door for balance, partially closing it with Kennedy inside. The refrigerator sounded off, like it had moved back an inch. There was blood on the floor

now. Some on her rug. More on her knees. She hadn't remembered the plate falling, but it was on the tile, her fork near the
door. Next to her plate was her canvas caddy. The books were on
the floor—had she knocked those down, too? She was going in
and out. Her fingers felt cold. Panic registered theoretically. I
hurt myself. I am now hurt. Briefly, she wondered if she should
get an ice pack, but no because that was dumb? Especially
because . . . hmm. Well, wait, she thought.

Down on her knees, she lifted her palm to see her wrist.
Skin cupped open and she bled like chocolate ganache. Okay
no, she thought. This was very, very bad. And there, too, at the
back of her mind was this: Maybe if I just hold still.

20.

ILLIE GASPED AND HER BODY SEIZED. SHE lunged off Agatha's leg and snatched up the duty phone, the screen of which was bright blue.

"Shoot."

"You alright?"

"Ohmygod, the sound was off." On the phone were three missed calls. The last one from six minutes before.

Millie pushed her hair out of her face. "I just need to make sure everything is alright." As she took up her RA polo, Agatha asked if she should sneak out. "No no no. It's probably fine." She stepped into the hall and closed the door behind her.

The fourth floor smelled like hair spray and artificial winter spices. Millie passed two girls in "ugly" Christmas sweaters. Wait, she thought. What am I doing? She walked down the hall, practically trotting. She walked through Colette's side, looking for she didn't know what. It wasn't that someone had called the duty phone, it was the fact that it had been called three times, Agatha's fingers bent into the back of her shorts. Most likely, someone had locked themself out, but Millie quickly imagined the worst: that someone was choking, on fire, or both.

But nothing seemed out of place. Students were studying in their rooms. Someone was playing music from a musical, which Millie recognized from *Hamilton*, though she'd never seen it. Three girls were laughing around one laptop in the lounge. Millie rounded a corner and remembered something Colette had said: that if someone was calling the RA phone, then it wasn't an emergency.

Back on her side of the floor, she tried calling the number back. It went straight to voicemail and the greeting was automated. There was no voice or name. She passed the bathrooms and the laundry room. At the hallway's end was her room and the suite. She almost went to take the stairs, but a stark sound made her shoulders cave. It sounded like a refrigerator being moved. Like something or someone had fallen into it.

Millie approached the door of the suite. "Everything okay in there?"

A few moments of silence. Then dishes hitting the floor.

Millie touched her top lip, pressed her ear to the door. At first she heard nothing, but then she heard a singular wheeze. "Hey, are you guys okay?"

A bit of movement. Another wheeze.

"I'm gonna come in . . . is this open?" It was. "Peyton? I just wanna— Homygod."

Peyton was on the floor, her back against the refrigerator. The top of her head was arched against the door and her hands were reaching for her neck. Beneath her sweatshirt, Peyton's body labored in a fevered pace. The thick white socks on her feet were pointing out at ten and two.

Millie found herself repeatedly saying the word *Okay*. She rushed to Peyton's side and the door slammed shut behind her. "Are you choking? Go like this if you are."

Peyton shook her head. "I didn't mean to—" She took a breath. "I can't—I can't breathe."

"Okay, okay. Hang on. Stay calm." Above the refrigerator, Millie's hand trembled as it searched. She felt for the plastic and she pulled down the yellow case, released the EpiPen from its hard plastic sheath.

Peyton's wheezing sounded like the low register of a wind instrument. She swallowed hard, touching her neck. "She's—"

"No no, don't try to talk. You're okay." The cap shook in Millie's hand. For a moment she thought about counting down but that seemed worse. "Okay . . ." she said. "Take a deep breath." Millie swung the pen up and brought it down on Peyton's thigh, where she felt the pop of skin.

"No!" Peyton said. Her hands hovered over the pen.

Millie's hands pressed into Peyton's shorts. "Almost done. I just have to wait five seconds . . ."

Peyton shook her head as if she were refusing a forkful of food.

Millie removed the pen as quickly as she could. "Sorry sorry sorry sorry. Okay, I'm calling 911—" But then there was a thin fragment of light on the floor. The door to the single room fell open. Millie turned around to find Kennedy on her knees. There was a beanie on her head and blood down her arm. More blood was on the floor, the color of which looked black and fake. Kennedy bent down onto her elbows.

"I'm sorry but I think I need some help."

For the second time that evening, Millie inhaled with "Homygod." She gagged and scrambled to her feet.

As she made it to Kennedy, there was a tick at the front door. "Ah don't know," Casey said. "Is that the one where everybody steals?"

"No, that's white elephant," Tyler said.

"Okay, good. That other one stresses me out because— Oh no. Peyton, are you okay?" Then Tyler dropped her sweater on the floor. Casey yelped. Kennedy's lip was shaking. Thin strips of blood were in her hair.

"Holy shit," Tyler said. "Holy shit. Holy shit."

"Tyler, sit with her." Millie pointed at Peyton. To Kennedy she said, "Okay, sit back, you're okay."

This close, the blood smelled thick. Millie tried not to retch. It pooled from behind Kennedy's right hand, which was pressed against her left wrist. Millie managed to sit her back against the side of her bed. "Casey," she said. "Call 911."

"Ohmahgod, mah phone's on mah charger," Casey said. "Ah can run. Ah'm runnin'!" she screamed.

Tyler called after her. "Casey, just use mine!"

"Okay, yes, sorry." Her footsteps retreated with the sound of a door. "Ohmahgoodness, thank *God*," Casey breathed. "Please help us. We need an adult right now."

21.

AGATHA'S SHIRT AND PANTS REMAINED ON, but she'd taken off her bra and she felt silly lying there without it. She checked her watch, released her wrist. A room down the hall was playing something from a musical. Then she heard Millie. She was speaking very low. Millie was saying Peyton's name. "I just wanna make sure . . ." She trailed off. Then she said, "Homygod."

Agatha sat up on Millie's bed. A door slammed shut and Millie's voice went with it. Agatha calmed herself, swung her feet off the bed. It was probably something domestic, like a burst pipe or a mouse. The Broadway singing down the hall went on. The relative silence on her end conveyed that everything was fine. She heard Tyler and Casey coming down the hall. They were talking about holiday gifts and games. Then Casey emitted a sharp cry. Tyler said "Holy shit" three times. Agatha walked to the alcove and pressed her ear against the wall.

Millie was saying, "Okay, okay." Then she told Casey to call 911. Agatha's lungs cramped in her chest. Then Casey was running and yelling. Tyler was yelling, too, and someone was breathing hard. Agatha's breath was shorter now. If Millie was hurt, she needed to know. Without much thought, she unlocked Millie's door.

"Ohmahgoodness, thank *God*," Casey said. "Please help us. We need an adult right now."

Agatha said, "Are you alright?"

Casey was so much prettier than she had remembered. Her eyes were big and green and distressed. "Please," she said. "Ohmahgod, Ah know you! There's been an accident and we need an adult."

The suite was so much less glamorous than she'd imagined. The lighting was surgical and sour. There was a young woman deep-breathing in the kitchen; Tyler knelt next to her, holding her hand. In the doorway to the right was the back of Millie. Beads of blood were on the tile floor. A blond girl sat back against the bed. Her face was the color of dishwater in a sink.

"I need help," Millie said. She'd taken a lavender tea towel and wrapped it around the girl's wrist. But the towel was no match for the onslaught of blood, and the young woman's eyes looked like flags at half-mast.

On her knees Agatha said, "Is it her hand?"

Millie said, "It's her wrist."

Agatha understood, and she felt sick. She sensed something like a vital organ begin to pull across her back. "Hey, sweetie, look at me. Stay awake. Can you hear me?"

Millie said, "Casey, please call the police."

Casey gasped. "Tahler, your phone."

The girl's hand, the one holding the bloody wrist, was becoming tired and slack. "Okay," Agatha said. "We're just going to keep this elevated." She propped the girl's arm up against her chest. "Millie, get me something from her drawer, like a shirt." She wanted to see what she'd be putting pressure against. She gently removed the manicured nails. Two flaps of skin bloomed like an overripe summer fruit. Blood pooled and dripped onto her hands. Agatha inhaled and said, "Jesus fuck."

Millie handed her two T-shirts and then vomited into a sparkly beige trash can. Agatha wrapped both shirts around the wound, feeling she was pressing too hard and not enough. She didn't know for sure but was fairly certain the girl's name was Kennedy. Everything began to move in a syncopated pace.

"Ohmahgod, it's still ringin'," Casey said.

Millie spit into the trash can. "I'm sorry."

"It's okay," Agatha said.

"Peyton, look at me," Tyler whispered. "Did she hurt you? You can tell me."

Casey spoke into the phone as if she were leaving a voice-mail. "Hah, mah name is Casey Ann Napolitano and Ah'm a student at the University of Arkansas? We are in our dorm right now and there's been an attempted murder-suicide."

Head in the trash can, Millie said, "Casey, give me the phone."

"There's two people who need help," Casey went on. "One is breathin' real bad and the other is bleedin' all over."

Tyler told Casey to say that one of them was in shock.

"Belgrade Dormitory," Casey said. "Tahler, what's our address?"

Millie delivered the address and Casey said it into the phone.

Agatha scooted up closer to the girl. "I'm just gonna lift this a little higher, okay?" She was mostly talking to herself, feeling she needed to announce her next moves. The girl's eyes were going up and to the left. "Hey. Stay awake, okay?"

"It's comin' from her wrist, ma'am," Casey said into the phone.

Jenna's voice materialized at the front door. "What the— Why is Peyton on the floor?"

"Jenna?" Tyler said. "We can't talk right now, okay?"

"Wait, are you guys dressed? Were you not gonna wait?"

"Jenna," Millie said. "Go to your room."

"Go to my room? Wow." Jenna balked. "So this is just a con-centration camp now?"

"Are y'all puttin' pressure on the wound?" Casey asked.

"Wound?" Jenna said. "What the heck?"

Millie yelled, "Jenna, go to your room!"

"We are putting pressure on the wound. We need them here now," Agatha called.

"Okay. Ma'am, they're doin' it. And we really need y'all to come quick."

Jenna peeked into Kennedy's room. "Ohmygod," she said. "No way."

Agatha's nipples brushed, unforgivably, against the fabric of her shirt. "Millie, do you— What's her name?" she asked.

Millie wiped her mouth and said, "It's Kennedy."

"Kennedy? Hey. Can you try to open your eyes?"

And then, amazingly, she did. Kennedy opened both her eyes and they were an electric blue. She looked confused and annoyed. Then she took Agatha in. "Wait, no . . ." she whis-pered. "Why are you here?"

Agatha instantly felt cold. Kennedy closed her eyes and her other hand slid down to her side. Agatha reached to take her hand, to protect the girl's belongings, but she was too late and Kennedy's arm fell. Agatha lifted Kennedy's hand from a paper-back book, where splotches of red were left behind. There, on the back cover, she saw her own face.

22.

I JUST WANT TO MAKE SURE I HAVE THIS RIGHT."

Josh was standing behind his desk. He was wearing his RA polo and workout shorts, but clearly not planning on working out tonight. His shorts were a sweatpants material and kind of tight. Millie felt inappropriate just looking at him.

"So," he said. "Millie, you were on duty."

"I—yes."

"And a resident called the duty phone, but the phone went unanswered. Is that correct?"

Ryland sniffed and whispered, "Did somebody retch in here?"

Millie pushed her hair back. "Yes, that's correct."

Colette uncrossed her legs and crossed them on the other side.

Josh looked down at Millie. "So you went looking for her?"

"Yes."

"And you found a student having what you thought was an allergic reaction."

"She said she couldn't breathe."

"So you gave her an EpiPen shot that she did not need, and then you discovered another resident who'd just tried to take her own life."

"I'm so sorry," Agatha said. "I'm not sure I should be here. Should I leave a contact number?"

Josh pointed at her face. "You stay right there." Seemingly shocked at his own tone, he quickly corrected. "Just one moment." In his shorts pocket, his cell phone began to buzz. "This is Aimee. Everyone stay here."

When the paramedics had arrived, Millie stood in the hall. With the phone to her ear, blood on her clothes, she called Josh and told him that he needed to come right away. Men placed Kennedy onto a stretcher. Millie told residents to go back to their rooms. All the while her ears buzzed and her throat burned with gastric liquid. She hated herself for so many reasons. Peyton and Kennedy were the first, but she also hated herself for the infatuation she'd entertained, the one that came between her and the most important phone call of her life.

She sat in one of the chairs in Josh's office. Colette sat in the other. Ryland leaned against the wall and Agatha stood behind them. Missing was Joanie; Millie hoped she was out of town.

Out in the lobby a resident said, "Oh geez. I wonder what happened."

"Keep it moving, ladies," Victoria said. The elevator bell rang.

Ryland sniffed again. His eyes went small. "Did she slit her wrist *and* throw up?"

"Ohmygod. It's me. I'm sorry," Millie said. She turned the collar of her shirt inside out.

In the hallway, Josh was saying, "I have the number. Not a problem."

Colette turned to Millie. "Were you in there when she did it?"

"No."

"You just like . . . found her after?"

"Yeah."

Colette sat back. "Why are you being weird?"

Millie looked up. Colette's hair was creased on one side. Her eyes were a tired shade of red.

"What?" Millie asked. "What are you— No, I'm not."

"You kind of are."

"I'm a bit stressed out."

Colette looked at her, unsatisfied. She placed her shoe against the desk and said, "Hmm."

Out in the hallway Josh said, "Absolutely. I can let them in first thing in the morning."

"Alright, girls," Victoria said outside. "That's enough. Get to your rooms."

Colette sat up and checked her watch. She put her arm on the back of the chair like she had somewhere else to be. Millie felt annoyed and jealous of her ability to at least appear inconvenienced and bored. But then, with a dreamy pace, Colette turned back around.

"Okay, Millie?" Colette said. She made what sounded like a fake cough. Then she placed her thumb over her shoulder. "Why isn't your teacher-friend wearing a bra?"

Ryland gasped. Put his fingers to his mouth. Underneath them, he said, "Nuh-uh."

Millie dropped her eyes and they landed on Josh's desk, on the small container of paper clips next to his keys. She could feel her neck color. She felt she might be sick again. Behind her was the smallest sound, like Agatha was rubbing her arms.

"Wow," Colette said. She pouted in confirmation. She crossed her arms, her knees bobbed in and out. "Beam me into the fucking sun," she said.

Millie turned to her. "Colette—"

"Okay." Josh returned. "Aimee is almost here. Where—who has the duty phone?"

Millie sighed. "I do."

"Great. So here's what's happening. Colette, you're on call for the night. Ryland? You're going to grab your shirt, and when Tyler has her things you're going to escort her to"—a glance at his phone—"the Chancellor Hotel."

Ryland choked. "She gets to stay at the *Chancellor*?"

"Is your shirt clean? If it's not, we have an extra. Okay, Agatha, was it?"

"Yes, that's right. Hi."

"And you're a professor here? Can you write your contact info for me?"

Agatha walked past Millie and bent at Josh's desk. Millie puffed her cheeks with air and slowly let them out.

"Okay, then," Josh said. "Okay, great. We'll be in touch."

"Yes, of course. Okay, thanks." She left without saying goodbye.

Josh told Colette to go, to make sure the residents stayed in their rooms. Ryland was instructed to go retrieve his shirt. Millie wasn't given a task, but she wasn't told to leave. Josh went back to his phone. He typed something and said, "Alright."

Millie's lanyard folded in the space between her stomach and her groin. "Josh, I don't . . ." She bent and touched her shin. "I can't tell you how badly I—"

"Millie, give me two seconds. Joanie needs a list of allergies."

Millie sat back. She watched Josh go into a file cabinet, finger through folders with names of girls on the fourth floor. He retrieved a folder and opened it across his keyboard. Then he held his phone up above a document. Once again, Millie hated herself for what had crossed her mind. The moment Josh had said the word *allergies*, she'd pined, I should be at the hospital. Not Joanie.

"Hi, guys. Everyone okay?" Aimee appeared at the door. Upon seeing Millie's shirt, she made a face like she was whistling. "Hoo boy. We can get you another one."

Aimee wore what she always wore: a UA zip-up fleece and shorts. It was late, almost ten thirty, but her visor remained. She placed a hand on Millie's knee. "Okay. First things first. Are you alright?"

"I'm fine."

"Good. That could not have been easy. And of course we'll make sure you have all the support you need. But . . ." She scooted up, retrieved a Post-it from her pocket. "Right now, we do need to sort out a few things. Just while it's fresh in your mind. Both of these were your residents, yeah?" She consulted the Post-it. "Kennedy Washburn and Peyton Shephard?"

"Yes. I—sorry. Are they okay?"

"They're both down at Washington. Kennedy's mom is taking the first flight out tomorrow, which— Did you know she was having a hard time?"

Millie shook her head. She experienced a falling, panicky sensation, like she should do something preemptive, like ask for a lawyer. "No," she said. "Or—she didn't seem like she was." With the question in the air, Millie couldn't recall the last time she saw her. But she had seen Peyton. Dirty dishes in her hands. Once again, she felt physically ill.

"Alright," Aimee said. "It sounds like she's had a rough go at college in general. So understandably, her mom wants to keep everything hush-hush. If anyone asks, just say it's private. They can go to CAPS for counseling if they want to chat."

"Okay. Is Peyton alright?"

Aimee looked at her Post-it again. "Yes. Her blood pressure went way up so they're gonna keep her overnight. Her parents will be here in the morning—they're understandably concerned—but don't think about that. She's okay."

Millie pressed her fingers into her eyes. Right before she'd bent down with the EpiPen, she'd pictured Jerilyn and Wallace Shephard. They were thanking her, repeatedly, so grateful she'd been there at the time. She'd imagined Jerilyn asking if it was alright to give her a hug.

"Aimee, I really thought . . ." Millie couldn't find her words. Josh's perennial standing was making her uneasy, and she wished he would just sit down. "She really looked like she was having a reaction, and she wasn't speaking and I—"

"Don't worry about that now. You did the best you could do and you're gonna tell me all about it when we make a report. But I do want to talk about"—the Post-it again—"Tyler?"

Millie tilted her head.

"She's the other resident in the suite, yes? Okay. She's a bit frantic right now, but she's saying a few things that we need to get cleared up. So. There's no easy way to ask you this . . ." Aimee laughed, a hand on her seated hip. "But at any point, did Tyler give you some kind of payment to help her switch bedrooms?"

Millie placed a hand between her thighs. "Sorry, what?"

Aimee looked to the ceiling, made a vague gesture for Tyler's tall tale. "She's saying she knew Kennedy was unstable from the beginning and that she paid you to help her switch rooms? And listen. She's probably talking out her behind, but she's saying she wants to go to the dean and get a refund . . . which doesn't make a lot of sense because I think she's on scholarship. But she's also saying she'll go to the press and news stations, and of course that's not something we want."

Millie looked down at her knees. "I—wow. That's not . . . that's not how the situation happened at all."

"Was there a situation?" Josh asked.

"It wasn't—no. She just—"

Millie's heart bottomed out. Josh remained standing while Aimee waited for her to speak. Homygod, Millie thought. I'm gonna lose this job, too. "It wasn't a situation. On the first day, Tyler came to me, but it was not about that. She was concerned that Kennedy had too much stuff. So I did mediate, but *not* for money. That was never a thing that was discussed. I just helped Kennedy move, but it wasn't—I told Tyler no. I told her I was happy to help. But she just like, shoved money in my pocket—"

Josh lifted his head.

"To be clear," Millie said, "I told her that it wasn't—"

"No no, I see. Okay," Aimee said. Her abrupt decision to end this conversation was brutal and very nice. "It sounds like a miscommunication," she said. "And she may see the whole thing very differently in the morning. So, how about this . . . Josh, can we use your office? Mill, this is about to be the incident report of the century. Go wash your face. Throw that shirt away. And then meet me back down here so we can tackle this together."

Then there was an awkward negotiation concerning who would leave the office first. Aimee said, "Let him scoot out." Josh did so. Millie pushed her hair out of her face.

"So Agatha was helping out, too?" Aimee asked. "That's so funny that she was here."

Millie touched her fingertips to the wall. "Yeah, she was doing her research thing. And then everything kind of blew up."

"I didn't realize you were still working with her."

"No, it was just the one time," Millie said. "Or—yeah. I guess, the second time. She had more questions about Fayetteville. I was just helping out."

And then it was so quiet for a moment that Millie wondered if she'd imagined the inquisition. Aimee squinted with one side of her face. "Wasn't she researching weddings?" she asked.

"Yeah, no," Millie said. "No, that's—"

Aimee shook her head. "Go grab a new shirt. I'll see you soon."

THE INCIDENT REPORT was six pages long, single-spaced. As was protocol, Millie referred to herself in the third person; she called the residents and Agatha by their last names. When they finished, Aimee left. Millie walked into the lobby. The ambulance lights were no longer blinking outside.

Victoria stood at the glass door. So accustomed to only seeing her seated, Millie was surprised to see how short the woman was. Victoria turned around and raised her eyebrows at Millie's appearance. "You alright?" she asked.

Millie said she was fine.

Victoria pointed past her head. "They told me to tell you that they're waiting outside."

The back of Belgrade emptied out into staggered squares of manicured grass. It was where students in nearby graduate housing often took their dogs in the morning and at night. Beyond the squares was the double-laned Frisco Trailway, and across from it a wooded ravine. Colette and Ryland were standing in the grass, shoulders touching, looking down at a screen.

Millie stopped walking. "Where's the duty phone?" she asked.

Colette looked up at Millie with a strange, curt amusement. "It's right here. Chill out," she said. The phone sat in the mulch beneath a sapling. Colette tapped it with her shoe.

Millie came closer. "Is the sound on?"

"You have fingers, Millie. You can't put that on me."

"I'm not . . . Colette, come *on*." Millie tightened her bun. "Does the phone even work? Someone tried to kill themself. It's kind of a big deal."

"Okay, it wasn't even in the toilet that long. And yeah. Sure. That was very gross and sad. But like . . ." Colette laughed a bit. "I don't know. We don't even know her, right?"

"That whole thing was also . . . debatable," Ryland said.

"What are you— Ryland. I saw it."

"I dunno," Ryland sang. "If you mean it, you go *down* the road. Not across the street . . ."

Millie crossed her ankles and shivered in the cold. "K, she could have died. I feel like y'all aren't getting that."

"I do get that," Colette said. "It is very sad, okay? But I kind of feel like we have more important things to talk about. Like this thing. Are you Becca?" She held up her phone's screen. "I don't know why I'm asking. This is clearly you."

"For the record, *Millie*"—Ryland held up a hand—"I *do* care about Residence Life. Just last weekend I made a kickball program. And I actually *went*. I brought orange slices. So yeah. That wasn't nice."

Millie wrinkled her nose. She didn't know who Becca was. She didn't remember saying that Ryland didn't care. She felt remarkably left out. "What are you . . . I don't understand what's going on."

Colette looked up, annoyed at Millie's delay. "The thing you let your predator girlfriend write about you and your . . . money."

The air around Millie's eyes was suddenly textured and hot. She desperately wanted her face to convey that she wasn't learning this in real time. Her phone was in her back pocket, and there, it began to burn. If Millie and Colette had been on better terms, she would have asked her what thing, and to send her the link.

Colette was scrolling with both thumbs. "I hope you got something out of this because it feels unethical to me. This font is stupid, too."

Ryland peered over her shoulder. "They're trying to be *Money Diaries*."

Without looking up, Colette said, "That's correct."

Millie couldn't help herself. She reached back for her cell. She typed *Agatha Paul* in quotes, and then she typed *Becca* by itself. An article came up from *Teen Vogue*, and there was Millie's financial situation laid out in a handwritten font. Her savings account total. The two-fifty she made as an RA. The fifty dollars she made for her secret tiny house. Her major and minor, her scholarships, and her parents' occupations. It said Millie's mom worked at Hallmark, not Papyrus, and this, for some reason, felt mean and cheap. There were interview questions listed as if she and Agatha had sat down to talk.

"If she's a professor," Ryland said, "why is she writing for *Teen Vogue*?"

"Excellent question," Colette said. "Millie, I hope you didn't agree to this."

"Of course I agreed to it," Millie said. She had agreed, and yet she hadn't. Her nights with Agatha were so fluid that it was hard to know when she was helping or just talking. Millie scrolled down. There was Becca explaining the campus credit card, saying, *Who do you think puts money on mine?* Farther down was this: *It felt really not good to be like, "Well . . . I'm not no one, though, right?"* Millie wanted to throw up at her own words. Also present was the time when Agatha asked if she was a narp. Becca's answer was slightly different than Millie had remembered. *Am I a narp? Are you serious?* Becca said. *I mean . . . look at me. Yes.*

Colette dropped her lanyard down into the grass. "Did she pay you for this? If she didn't, that's messed up. And what house is she talking about?" Colette whispered this to herself. "Wait a second," she said. "Are you RDing next year?"

Ryland gasped. He gripped the phone to see what she'd read. Colette looked up, took in Millie's face. "Ha," she said. "Wow. Of course you are."

Millie rested her hands next to her neck.

"I am annoyed," Ryland announced.

"Yeah, I am, too," Colette said. "Was this all happening that night at Maxine's?"

"No. It wasn't till like . . . a little after Halloween."

"*Halloween?* Woowwww." Colette looked at Ryland. "Am I . . ." She laughed. "Am I homophobic?"

Ryland examined the underside of his elbow. "Girl, don't ask me. I know I am." Their voices were comfortable, like they were alone.

Then Colette did a gesture that was very unlike her. Phone in her hand, she tucked her hair behind both ears. "I can't believe I'm saying this . . ." A shake of her head. "But did I like, hurt your feelings? Did I do something wrong?"

This was such an unexpected and sound response that Millie didn't know what to do. Colette's curiosity made Millie feel childish, like she'd been caught sneaking in.

"It wasn't—it's not like I told a bunch of people," Millie said. "And being private about it had nothing to do with you."

"So do you see how that's the problem?" Colette's voice was still calm. She spoke like she was giving directions, pointing out landmarks that were easy to find. "I dunno. We hang out every day? I know what you eat and I've checked your moles to see if they're cancer. I thought we had a good thing going where you tell me what to do and then I do it, but yeah, I guess it had nothing to do with me so that's fine. Actually?" She pointed at Ryland's face. "I *knew* something was going on. Because that one night, when he was going to Chick-fil-A. And you were being chill and asking questions, but then you were sneaking out and getting a secret haircut. And I said to myself, 'That's fucking weird.' But now I know I'm not crazy. You've just had a secret teacher friend this whole time and you're actually not always 'going to the gym.'"

As Millie said, "I do go to the gym," Ryland said, "Mm, I knew that was a front."

"No no, it's cool. You were super busy . . ."

"Colette . . ."

"Skipping around, getting RD jobs, taking my drugs without offering to pay. And then, evidently, running off to be a little princess bottom for *Teen Vogue*."

Millie's mouth was fully open. She *did* go to the gym. And she'd always thought the drugs were fair game. She also thought Agatha had said she was writing an actual book, but maybe she hadn't. But they were sleeping together, no? This was all for *Teen Vogue*?

"Colette, is this real? I *do* go to the gym. And if you—why wouldn't you just say about the pills? Ryland doesn't pay you. I don't understand what's happening right now."

"Ryland," Colette said, "is basically from a giant Superfund site, located right next to Cancer Alley. And he coughs up black stuff every morning and half of his neighbors have respiratory disease. And his mom is in a wheelchair because she has MS, and the lift for their stairs is broken so she's just been living on the first floor of her home for six months. And that's why Ryland sends all of his checks to her so they can save up and get it fixed. So yes, you're technically right. Ryland's prescription drug abuse does get subsidized. Is that okay with you? Is that fair and square?"

Hands cupped over her shoulders, Millie looked at Ryland. "I'm sorry," she said. "That's . . . I didn't know."

"Ugh, Colette!" Ryland stomped with a little grunt. "Don't make me your little trauma gay. I barely even do that anymore. And not that it matters, but her bedroom and the kitchen are both on the first floor. It's not weird. It's fine."

Millie shook her head. Through the fabric of her clean shirt, the smell of vomit lingered on her skin. "I didn't know that. I'm sorry, Ryland. I mean it. But, Colette . . ." Millie crossed her arms. "It just happened."

"It seems like it just happened a lot."

"Colette, come on."

"You come on. Halloween was a long time ago."

"Okay, but it's not . . . I don't know . . ." Millie laughed. "Do we have to tell each other everything?"

Ryland's bottom lip tensed at the corners.

Colette blinked like she'd witnessed a camera flash. "Well," she said. "Sure, okay. But we need to tell each other *some* things, right?" She smiled to herself. "Wow, this is so dumb," she said. "Millie, you know you're not gay, right?"

"Oop." Ryland's left shoulder went to his ear. "Coco, my love. You can't say that."

"No, I'm serious. Millie? I'm not saying this to be a dick. You don't like her because you're gay. You like her because *she's* gay. And because you have a thing for like, mid-tier management and authority, which you should honestly seek treatment for."

"Alright . . ." Millie looked at her hands. "You don't really know me like that."

"I don't have to. Millie, to be clear? You're a smart person and you have lots of patience and everyone likes you and that's great. But when it comes to you liking other people? You're kind of a dumbass. And if you wanna have secret jobs and houses, that kind of hurts me but okay. But you didn't know about this *Teen Vogue* thing, did you?"

"Of course I knew about it. It was a job. I was being paid."

"Okay, but she was also getting paid. You see what I mean? And whatever she was paying you was not enough. Like, Millie . . ." Colette looked up into the night. Above her head alates hovered beneath a streetlamp. "I think that sometimes . . . you love jobs and rules and saving money so much that you don't see when you're being used. Residence Life is one thing. Like, you're convinced some resident's mental breakdown is your fault. But this is another level. This is yikes. You saying you feel invisible sometimes? That's really, really sad. No one should be paying you to say that. Do you see what I'm saying? The government should be paying for you to tell that to a therapist."

"Colette . . ." Millie sighed. "You weren't there. It was a job. My parents aren't giving me five hundred dollars a month."

Colette threw her hands up. "Okay, well. I'm annoyed for other reasons, but I'm mostly angry at you for not seeing the difference. Millie, if you wanna sell your feelings like that, fine. But Agatha? Is that her name? She's definitely not supposed to sleep with you after you do."

"Why did you let her call you Becca?" Ryland asked. "Becca feels like she thinks you're dumb."

Millie exhaled through her nose. That had been the first thing that she had thought, too.

Colette was back on her phone. "Thank God she used a different name. And if my residents go to you for things? Please tell them to just call the police. What the—" Colette stopped speaking. She looked up at Millie and read from her phone. "'Residence Life isn't my dad'?"

Millie wanted to throw herself down into the ravine.

Ryland gently toed the grass. "She should have at least let you pick your name."

Colette clicked her phone to dark and said, "Ryland, drop it."

"I'm just saying," he went on. "And it's weird that she's all, Oh, I'm at Southern U. Like, babygirl . . . this is Fayetteville."

"I'm gonna go to bed," Millie said.

"Wait. Can I ask . . ." Ryland trailed off. "Wait, sorry. Are you really RDing? What dorm?"

Millie opened the door. "I'll be here," she said.

"So Josh is moving up? Ohhhh, okay okay." Then Ryland looked to Colette. "See, yeah. That makes more sense."

Millie's hand fell from her lanyard to her side. "What makes more sense?"

Ryland said, "Hmm?"

"Why would you—why wouldn't it make sense before?"

"No no no! Not that I care! It's a good thing. I just knew he was on a committee for like, I don't know. Diverse hiring? But that's—I was just asking. And it makes sense. That's really great."

Millie looked to see Colette's eyes. Colette looked like she had something more to say. But Millie didn't want to give her the chance to assess the situation, to say the word *racist*. So she pushed against the door lever and went back inside.

23.

GATHA STOOD NEAR A HOSTESS STAND AS
Robin surveyed the restaurant. She said, "There's two
of us," to a young man as Robin wandered over to a
shelf.

"This is so cute," Robin said of a mug.

A hostess led them to a table. A tiny glass vase held white
wildflowers and greens. Robin said thank you and removed her
feathery coat. "It's cuter here than I imagined," she whispered.
"But it's more expensive, too."

The evening prior, Agatha went home with soiled clothes
and an elevated heartbeat. Her hands shook when she opened
her door. The dried blood on her arms smelled like rusted coins.
She'd thought to call Jean, but on her phone was a text from
Robin. *Don't know if I told you. I'm out of town. Neighbor collecting
mail.* Agatha clicked on Robin's name and she answered on the
second ring.

"A student did what? Slow down. Are you alone?"

Agatha was walking laps around the island counter. "I feel
like I can't catch my breath right."

"Wait a second," Robin said. "Let me google. Don't hang up.
I'm in Dallas. I'm renting a car and I'll come now."

"No no no, don't do that. I'm fine."

"No, I used miles. And I'm just with Terrence. What's your address?"

Agatha gave it to her, grateful for a task. Robin said to put her head between her knees. Agatha did so. She closed her eyes. A flap of skin. Why are you here?

Perhaps if she hadn't been so rattled by the evening's events she would have recognized this as a signature Robin move: a grand, romantic, impulsive gesture made for endings of movies meant to be watched on Christmas or on a plane. There was no acknowledgment of the fact that they hadn't spoken for more than five minutes in months, that their texts and calls had been siloed to house-sitting logistics and health insurance protocols. But here was Robin, in Arkansas, knocking in the dark at five a.m. She held a McDonald's bag in her hand, a teal duffel on her arm. The previous night's makeup was still on her face. Robin smelled like French fries and herself. They were touching each other in bursts, not quite hugging but partially embraced.

"You didn't have to come."

"Of course I did. Hi."

"Yes, but it's fine. I'm fine. I'm always fine."

"Did you see her do it?"

"No no no." Agatha's voice broke. Her lips went back against her face. Then Robin did something that was very Robin. She placed her arms on Agatha's neck and laughed.

"Ohmygod. But she's okay, yeah? Oh no . . . you're so sad."

Agatha covered her face, embarrassed to be comforted by this.

"You're so sad," Robin said. "And you're so tan! Look at these freckles. Don't be sad."

Agatha told Robin that she must be exhausted and did she need to sleep. Robin said no, she used to pull all-nighters all the time. At Arsaga's, Robin ate Nutella toast, a side of avocado, and a side of kimchi made in-house. She ordered something called a Hummingbird, a sparkling lavender lemonade. She'd given up caffeine; of this she was very proud. She was thrilled about her treatments. Her body and mind were showing improvements. She was still at the reception job, which was boring, but she took class for free. She wanted to know everything about the night before. Agatha explained, but left out names and histories. Previously, she'd been careful to refer to the residents as young women, but speaking over yogurt and berries, she unintentionally called them *girls*.

"It was mayhem. Girls were screaming. The girl who cut herself was fading out. And then, get this. I try to prop her arm up. I look down, and there's a copy of my book."

"Which one?"

"*Satellite Grief.*"

"Huh. So that's why she did it. Now we know."

Agatha grinned. "Be nice," she said.

"How creepy. She probably knows who you are."

Agatha said she wasn't sure. The girl's name was Kennedy Washburn. When Agatha googled her name, a picture came up where she was on a football field. She wore a sparkling one-piece uniform and geriatric-looking shoes. Two flaming batons were in her hands.

Sitting across from Robin, Agatha's temperament changed by the minute. It was wonderful to have Robin here, at the top of her energy, less than twelve hours after she'd called. But then she thought, No. This is a mistake. Robin was here? She'd rented a car? Agatha wanted to know how much this reunion was costing her. But no, that wasn't important. Robin was *here*. Agatha had sobbed, something she hadn't done in years, and the person she'd loved had rented a car and just come. The anything-is-possibleness of Robin was weakening the power of the evening she'd endured. Agatha still had a life somewhere. She could also drive through the night. Eat French fries to stay awake.

When they finished eating, Agatha went to use the restroom. She came back out to find Robin at the merchandise shelf again.

"I love this," she said of a bag.

A woman entered the restaurant and dramatically took them in. "Oh. My goodness!" She put a hand to her heart. "You two are both very tall."

THEY WALKED BACK to Wilson Park. In front of Agatha's home was a Cadillac SUV. She hadn't noticed it before. Walking through her front door, Agatha said, "Is that your car?"

In the living room Robin knelt down by her bag. "Terrence's mom has miles and the guy upgraded me."

Agatha closed the door. "It's very fancy," she said.

"You can drive it if you want. Technically, we could add your name." Sweatpants in hand, Robin sat into a straddle. "Doesn't that count? We are married."

Agatha looked up at her. She leaned back and felt the doorknob at her side. "This is all . . . very weird."

"I know."

"Robin, I'm glad you're here . . . but what are we doing?"

"No no no no." Robin stood. "Don't do that. I just got here."

"Robin."

"Let's take a nap," Robin said, pulling Agatha toward the stairs.

Agatha let herself be pulled. As she went up the stairs, she said, "Let's take a *nap?*" as if she didn't know what that was.

24.

ON FRIDAY MORNING, MILLIE TURNED IN A FI-
nal paper for her dietetic management class. Her
teacher handed out bite-sized Kit Kat bars as the
students completed class evaluations, and then everyone was
dismissed. Millie went back to her room, changed her clothes,
and drove to a florist on College Avenue. She purchased two cards
and two bouquets with ranunculus, roses, and ferns. The total
came to fifty-six dollars, which felt like a lot of money. She'd
never been to Washington Regional Hospital before. She wore
jeans and a ribbed mock-neck top, her hair in a low, respectful
bun. In her front seat she filled out the cards. Peyton's had flowers. Kennedy's had birds.

It was eleven a.m. and Millie knew that Peyton's parents
would be arriving soon. Much like that first move-in day, she
wanted to use their absence as an opportunity to speak freely. But
in the seventh-floor hallway, Millie heard formal voices around
the bend up ahead. She slowed and stopped her steps, kraft paper
at her chest. "This Jell-O," Peyton said, "is not very good."

Millie held still. She heard a woman's voice respond.

"Your grandmother would keel over if she saw you eat that
thing."

Peyton said she just wanted to try. A man's voice said, "You'll make the real kind with Aunt Ivy soon."

"I know."

"Or maybe panna cotta this time!"

"Panna cotta?" Mrs. Shephard laughed. "We'll just have to see about that."

Peyton had sounded like she was lying down. She also sounded like herself: judgmental and a little bored. This was a relief; Peyton was okay. But Millie had arrived too late. The status in Peyton's parents' voices was clear and severe. Millie couldn't see them, but she could sense that they were wearing something appropriate for a baby shower or church. Mr. Shephard sounded older than she'd guessed. Mrs. Shephard sounded younger, but just as sharp. Millie didn't know what to do or how to enter. There were two chairs outside the door. She went to one and took a seat.

"Sweetheart," Mr. Shephard said. "Did you sense she was unstable?"

Peyton said, "What do you mean?"

"Was she depressed or . . . did she express any thoughts of self-harm?"

There was a long pause. Peyton said a hesitant "No."

"Nothing at all, bunny?" her mother asked. "Did she have friends? Did she seem upset?"

"Well. She wasn't the cleanest. Her stuff looked clean but she never washed her sheets."

Mrs. Shephard made a sound of exhaustion and disgust.

"Boy," Mr. Shephard said. "I hate that you were there for that, kiddo."

Peyton took a long time to answer. Finally, she said, "It's okay."

Millie gathered herself; the chair creaked under her thighs. This was not what she had planned but it was certainly what she deserved. She would apologize to the Shephard family, and it would be awful, but it was the first stop on her apology tour. She stood and went to the door as Mrs. Shephard reclaimed the room.

"Now, Peyton? Hear me out," she said. "I know what you're going to say, but on top of other very good reasons, this is why I want you to think about doing AKA."

As Peyton said, "I don't want to do that," her dad said, "Jer, let's give her some time."

"Till when?" she asked. "Till she gets stabbed with something worse? This would never happen at AKA. I don't have to tell you that."

"Alright."

"There would be a den mother in charge. Not some trigger-happy RA."

"Jer."

"So wait," Peyton said. "She . . . I'm not getting in trouble about this, right?"

Mrs. Shephard said, "Of course not, bunny." Mr. Shephard said it wasn't her fault.

"Okay . . ." Peyton said. "Well, do I still have to take my finals?"

Mr. Shephard made a series of lighthearted exhalations. "Well, sweetheart. I imagine that you do."

Millie's arms and heart ached. Trigger-happy? Peyton said she couldn't breathe! She backed up from the door, grazed the chair with the backs of her knees. Then Millie saw her. Tyler Hanna. At the end of the hall Tyler pushed the door open with her back; her eyes were down and focused on a beverage holder in her hands. Millie shot up and walked around the corner to get out of sight.

"Hiii," she heard Tyler say. "Okay, one black coffee . . ."

"Tyler, thank you so much."

"Oh, not at all. One coffee with cream . . ."

"Thank you, young lady."

"And, Peyton, do you want this now? Should I set it right here? Okay, perfect. Anyone need anything else? All good?"

Millie was filled with profound hatred. That morning, when she couldn't sleep, she'd considered what she should have done with Tyler's cash. She could have slipped it under Tyler's door. Placed it in her mailbox. Turned it in to Josh. But she hadn't. She'd dropped it into her down-payment shoe. She had taken a less-special twenty to Walmart, where she'd purchased a few things. Burt's Bees moisturizer. A three-pack of thongs. Chocolate-covered cranberries that she mixed with nuts and seeds. She ambled back to the door of Peyton's room, sat back down in the uncomfortable chair.

"Tyler," Mrs. Shephard said. "I hope we're not pulling you from studying."

"Not at all. My first final isn't till three o'clock and it's easy."

"And what are you studying, young lady?"

"I'm majoring in hospitality management."

Mrs. Shephard said, "That sounds like fun," and Mr. Shephard said, "Very interesting."

"Yeah, it's interesting for sure. I'm on the events committee for my sorority this semester, so I feel like I'm getting to put some things to use."

Peyton's mom gasped. "What chapter?"

"Pi Beta Phi."

"And you didn't want to live in the house?"

"I did last year. And it honestly was a good experience, but then I got a housing scholarship at Belgrade for a year. My mom was like, 'Um, you're taking that.'"

"I don't blame her." "Oh, that's excellent."

"Oh, thank you. But yeah," Tyler went on. "Living in the house was fine but the dorm was close by. And I was like, 'Oh, this will be good,' which is hilarious now. I remember when I moved in I saw we were living next to the RA, and I was like, 'Gotta be on my best behavior.' Ha ha ha."

Mrs. Shephard patted something like a thigh. "They're right next door? You're joking."

"I told you that a long time ago," Peyton said.

"But that's ridiculous. Wally, right next door. No one sees this girl is struggling?"

"Oh, I knew," Tyler laughed. "I was always like, 'That girl ain't right.'" For this impersonation, Tyler donned a strange accent. It appeared she had been briefly influenced by Mrs. Shephard's speech: southern and academic. But then, very quickly, Tyler righted her tone. "I didn't think it would end up like this."

Millie felt as if she were waiting outside of a principal's office, like she'd been called down on the PA. One of the thorns on the flowers had broken through the paper. It was hooked and a grayish-green. Two nurses came toward Millie in the hall. One said, "That's what she's wearing?" The other raised one of her hands. As they passed by, the first one shook her head. "Girl," she said. "You better than me."

"Tyler," Mr. Shephard said. "Have you given thought to where you'd like to live next semester?"

"Oh, I've given it a lot of thought, ha," she said. "I'm not sure what to do. They're offering me a spot in another dorm. Did they do the same for you, Peyton? See, yeah. But I'd rather not live in the dorms if I don't have to. Especially because . . . I *really* want a dog."

Peyton's parents laughed as if this were a rare condition.

"She doesn't just want one. She *really* wants one," Peyton said.

Mrs. Shephard said, "Good thing you aren't allergic then, huh?"

"Yeah," Tyler said. "An apartment would be amazing, but I might try to go back to Pi Phi."

"See, Peyton?" Mrs. Shephard said. "The houses are just like the dorms but better."

"I don't think the Black sorority even has a real house," Peyton said.

"Tyler?" Mr. Shephard said. "Any idea if there's an AKA house?"

Tyler let out a thoughtful hum. "That's a good question. I can look into it."

From around the corner, a nurse wheeled an elderly man. And then, at the other end, Joanie entered through the automatic doors.

"Oh, hey," she said to Millie. "No way. Good timing. What's up?"

Millie stood up. "Hey, hi. Do you have a sec?"

Joanie wore athletic shorts, a hooded sweatshirt, a large backpack, and a tote. They walked back through the double doors and down another wide hall. There were benches and windows lining one side. Joanie set her bag down and took a seat.

"Last night sounded crazy," she said. "I wasn't even on campus. My team took a bunch of kids camping for a night."

Millie sat down next to her and said, "I hope it didn't cut into your trip."

"Nah, we were all done by then. But yeah. How are you? Are you good?"

"Oh, yeah. I'm okay." Millie looked behind her. "Well, I wanted to see Peyton but she's having family time. Is Kennedy seeing people?"

"Yeah, she is but she's asleep. I just came from there. And I'm an idiot because I forgot to give her stuff to a nurse." Joanie dipped the tote bag on her arm. Inside was an eyeglass case, a light blue sweatshirt, a toothbrush wrapped in tissue, and a paperback book.

"I could take that to her," Millie said. She touched the flowers on her lap. "Any chance you could bring Peyton one of these?"

"Oh, for sure." Joanie gestured to the flowers; her fingers went in and out. Once they were in her arms, she made a goofy pose. "Ha. These are awesome. Do I look like a beauty queen?" With dreamy eyes Joanie did a flat-hand wave to a large crowd.

"Ha, yeah. You look great," Millie said, feeling embarrassed and cruel. "So I just wanted to say"—she tried to recover—"that I'm really sorry that you had to kind of cover for me."

"Oh, no sweat! It's actually all good. All my finals aren't till next week. And Aimee's giving me a little bonus." Joanie placed her hand to the side of her mouth. "A hundred bucks. I know. Cool, huh? So yeah, no sweat. It all worked out."

Millie tried to blink away the sting. "Oh great. That's good. I'm really glad they did that. But yeah, still. I'm really sorry."

"No worries. It sounds like you had your hands full."

"No, I know. But I kind of assisted in all of this, so . . ." Millie knew, a second too late, that she should have moved on. She shook her head and covered her nose with one hand. She blinked and said, "I'm sorry."

"Oh hey. Oh no. You're okay." Joanie scooted toward her an

inch. Millie wiped her face as Joanie patted her sweatshirt pockets. "I wish I had a tissue. I'm sure they have some here."

"No, I'm fine. I'm sorry. It was just like . . . a lot."

"No, yeah. Of course. I heard it was super intense."

Millie exhaled through rounded lips. Having cried, she felt slightly better; she didn't have to wonder if she would. "I haven't made a mistake that big in . . . well. That might be my biggest mistake."

"Dude, I get it. But things happen. And if someone is unresponsive, all you can do is make the best call you can. You can't blame yourself. And everyone is okay."

The double doors behind them swung open. Millie was relieved to see what looked like a father and daughter she didn't know. The girl was swinging a white plastic bag. The father looked like he hadn't slept in days.

"I should go." Millie partially stood. "But you've been really nice. So thank you."

"Hey, really quick, do you wanna pray about it?"

Millie said a light "Oh."

"Real quick, I promise. Unless that's not cool."

"No no, of course." She sat back down.

Joanie held out both her hands. "Cool. And my hands are wet because I just washed them."

Millie said, "That's okay."

"Heavenly Father." Joanie closed her eyes, and somehow, they were praying. "We just want to lift you up here in this hallway. I thank you for my Res Life sister here"—a squeeze—"and I ask you to come into her life today and just let your presence be known."

Millie's back was painfully upright. She was uncertain as to whether she should close her eyes. She hated how embarrassed she felt. No one was around, and Joanie wasn't doing anything wrong. But something was missing, which Millie identified as the ability to talk about it with Colette.

Joanie went on, squeezing Millie's hands on specific words. She was one of those prayers who repeated the same appellation, over and over. "Father God, we know that you don't place anything in front of us that we can't handle. And we thank you for every inch of *your* design. And as Millie goes into the holiday season, shed light on her, Father God. Give her perspective . . ."

At this, Millie slightly averted her gaze.

"Surround her with people who call her *up*, not out."

Millie closed her eyes for fear of smiling. Ryland would love to hear this part. But then Millie caught herself again. Wait, she thought. This is so sad.

Joanie began to wrap things up. She asked Jesus to give Millie discernment, and then she said, *Amen.*

"Thank you, Joanie. Honestly."

"Anytime, Millie. For real."

"Good luck with finals. And your Christmas shopping, too."

"Hey, you too. But you know what? One last thing. You might want to talk to Tyler. Just whenever you have the chance."

Millie had stood. She touched her neck and said, "What's that?"

Joanie stayed on the bench. "Yeah, she came down to my room this morning and she was real fired up. Saying she wants to talk to Residence Life and the dean . . ."

Millie looked out the window, down to a parking lot below. "Man. Okay. Yeah . . . that sucks."

"You know what? If I were you?" Joanie stood. "I'd take her somewhere out of the dorm. Get on her level. Hear what she has to say. And actually—don't know if I told you this—but I've gotten to know Tyler a little, and she's actually pretty rad. I lofted her bed one night—oh yeah, you were there, I think. I invited her to stop by my clinic and she actually came through. By herself. And she's pretty strong! So yeah. Anyway. It sounds like you two just need to hash it out."

It was a Colette thing to say, but this time, on her own, Millie thought, Wow. What an absolute little shit. She understood it now. This was Tyler's thing: doing pranks, taking naps, collecting Peytons and Joanies along the way. To Tyler's credit, the latter was something Millie had been unable and unwilling to do herself. Perhaps that was where she first went wrong. Joanie looked happy. She always did. She looked like the kind of person who slept eight hours every night. Millie actually wanted to lift weights, too. And she felt she should learn how to run at some point. But get on Tyler's level? She would not. Tyler sucked. But she probably didn't suck around Joanie, because why would she. Joanie was nice. Millie considered something that depressed her to no end. Maybe she wasn't that nice. And maybe Joanie should RD.

"I'll definitely reach out," Millie said. "Thank you. Really."

Joanie said, "Right on. Take care," and they performed what could loosely be called a hug.

KENNEDY'S ROOM WAS on a different floor and in a separate wing. When Millie reached the door, she made herself walk right in. She hoped that Kennedy's mother would be there, assuming she was personable and nice. But no one was there but Kennedy, asleep with blood still in her hair. Her wrist was bandaged and resting on her hip. The room smelled a little wet.

Millie set the flowers on a chair. The kraft paper crinkled, and Kennedy opened her eyes.

"Oh," she said. "Sorry. Hi."

"Hey. Hi. Sorry to wake you."

"No, yeah . . ." Kennedy looked around. "I should probably get up."

Millie felt the urge to give herself a chore. "I actually have some of your stuff," she said. Kennedy said thank you and received the tote. She placed it between her knees. "Well, Joanie got it for you," Millie said. "But yeah. How are you? How do you feel?"

Kennedy used her good hand to sit up. "Thank you. I'm good. Or like . . . yeah, I'm fine. I'm on painkillers so it's not that bad . . . not a lot or anything. Just a normal amount. And yeah, I actually feel okay since I got so much sleep. Which sounds really weird but yeah. That was like, the best sleep I've had in a while." She laughed. "And it's Friday, right? Okay, good. Or not good. I have a final today but the teacher is nice."

"You'll definitely get a pass."

"That's what I thought," Kennedy said. "Okay, good. Sorry. I'm like, still waking up."

"That's okay."

Kennedy looked at the flowers. "Those are so pretty. Did you bring them?"

"Yeah, I did."

"That's so nice. I love flowers. Ohmygod, that sounds dumb. I'm all, 'I love flowers.' Everyone does."

"That doesn't sound dumb," Millie said. She lifted her shoulders and looked around the room.

Millie asked if her mom was there yet. Kennedy said that she was on her way.

"Sorry, can I ask you something weird?" Kennedy said. "Well, I guess there's two things."

"Oh, yeah sure."

"Okay . . . did you tell Peyton to put my dishes on my bed?"

To imply she hadn't heard or understood, Millie squinted and turned her head.

"No, of course you didn't," Kennedy said. "Sorry. I don't think she gets what people are saying all the time."

"I told her to talk to you," Millie offered.

"No, I believe you. Sorry. I knew that wasn't true."

"Okay . . ." Millie rocked back on her heels. "Yeah, no. That's not . . . yeah."

"And also?" Kennedy said. "Okay, I know this sounds weird, but who was like, all there last night?"

Millie pushed her shoulders back. "What do you mean?"

"Well, I remember you there, which—thank you. And I remember my suitemates being there, too. And . . . I know I sound crazy, but was there someone else?"

Millie tucked her hands in her pockets. "You mean like . . . the paramedics?"

"No, never mind." Kennedy looked at her bandaged wrist. "Sorry . . . I don't remember what happened before. Well, I kind of do? I don't know."

Millie wanted to sink down. She wanted to touch the railing on the bed, fight off her nausea, take deep breaths. She felt like maybe, possibly, that she was a bad person. "No, yeah. Don't worry," she said. "There was a lot going on."

"I don't want to like . . . I don't know." Kennedy struggled. "I don't wanna put all this on you. But I guess you're my RA, right? Is it okay if I say this? It's embarrassing, so please don't tell."

"No, yeah. Of course I won't."

"Okay. So I got rejected from this class that I wanted to take? Which really sucked because it was one of the reasons I'm here. And the person teaching it, I read her book and I really loved it, and I just like . . . yeah, I don't know. But then, when everything was happening, I saw her. Not just a little, but a lot. I don't even know her, but she was like, there. It didn't feel like a dream or anything. And I know I've been really sad and not sleeping great, but . . . if I'm like, *seeing* people? Then that's not good, right?"

As Millie tried to find her words, she stared at a tray in the corner of the room. A plastic wrapper was left on top. The side of it said *Mini-Muffin*. That Agatha hadn't been just hers alone felt like she'd been decieved. Like she'd been doing something intimate in her room, thinking that she'd been alone. Kennedy was waiting for her to speak. Wow, Millie thought. I could make all of this make sense for you right now. But she knew she wouldn't. Agatha was still too big. Her eyes filled with tears. "Sorry," she said. "I felt like I was going to sneeze."

"That's okay."

"No, yeah. That sounds really, really hard," Millie said. "It sounds like you've been through a lot."

Kennedy rubbed her pointer finger under her nose. "I just feel really stupid. I literally *saw* her, and I felt like, Ohmygod. She's here to like, save me somehow. And then I woke up. And I was here. And they asked me if I needed anything from my room. And I was like, oh maybe she really was there somehow, and she'll visit me and I should have her book just in case." As she spoke, Kennedy pulled a paperback out of the tote. "Oh my God," she said. "There's blood on this now." She turned the book over and back. There on the back cover was Agatha's face. There were splotches of brown blood along the spine and where the ends of the pages met.

The way Millie felt then, it didn't make sense to her. She found no other word for it—she was completely grossed out. She knew she should have been unnerved; Kennedy was on the edge of getting it. But Millie was viciously repulsed by the idea that while she'd been thinking of Agatha, Kennedy had been doing the same.

"Well, that's just great," Kennedy said. "I've had this copy forever and . . . ugh. That's so frustrating. Sorry, I'm not trying to be weird. But everything has just sucked for me for an entire year, and I just want a teeny break, you know?"

"Yeah, of course."

"And maybe it's my fault but I kind of feel like it's not. And it just doesn't seem fair that I made *one* mistake. But then it's like, welp? You killed a dog, so now you're the worst person who ever lived. And you have to change schools and stop twirling and you get the roommate who won't shut up about dogs. And your other roommate is like, 'Excuse me, are you doing your dishes? You still have dishes. We said no dishes in the sink—'"

"How—" Millie shook her head. "Sorry . . . who killed a dog?"

"It wasn't— Ugh." Kennedy held her face in her good hand. "Sorry. I'm not talking right. If you have to go, that's fine."

The way she said it sounded like she wanted Millie to go; that if Millie left the room, she could save Kennedy from herself. "Yeah, I do have a final," Millie said. "I'm sorry you feel like you can't catch a break."

"It's okay."

Millie used to be so good at this, talking to young women

about classes and friends and how they felt. "Kennedy," she said. "If there was something I could have done, or if I didn't check in with you enough . . ."

"Oh, no no no." Kennedy said. "You were a great RA. Your bulletin boards were always so cute."

"Oh. Yeah, thanks."

"Yeah, no, you were great." Kennedy fixed her covers. She folded them like they were a napkin on her lap. "If anything," she said, "I should be apologizing to you. I'm sad that I didn't like . . . participate more."

MILLIE EXITED THE hospital and pulled her phone out in her car. She clicked the one recent contact who she knew might answer.

Glory said, "Hi, Mill."

Millie sniffed and held her nose.

"Oh lord." Glory sounded like she was taking a seat. "Okay. I'm ready. What is it? Are you pregnant?"

Millie bent and placed her head on the curve of the steering wheel.

25.

EVERYTHING WITH ROBIN WAS ACTUALLY SOME-
thing else. The Thai food they had for lunch was "actually
very good." The houses and public library were "actually
really nice." Agatha drove to where they could see horses and
cows. It felt like a vacation; they had so much to catch up on. It
was a relief for Agatha to distract herself from the previous
night, and the matter of how and when she'd reach out to Millie. Agatha told herself that if she was going to be contacted by
anyone official, it would be that day, before five p.m. After lunch,
horses, and cows, she and Robin went back to bed. In the sheets
Agatha looked at her watch. Only three more hours to go.

Agatha had gray underwear on. Robin was very much Robin,
long and bare in the old white sheets. Robin rolled over, her
hand in Agatha's lap. "I'm almost hungry," she said.

"I was about to say the same. We could—"

The nightstand buzzed. Agatha took up her phone. The
caller ID scrolled with the words *University of Ark*.

She pulled a shirt over her head. "Sorry. I'll be right back."
There was another small bedroom down the hall but Agatha
took the stairs.

She went through the kitchen and stood at the washing machine. "Hello?"

"Professor Paul? This is Aimee Pearson, director of university housing. How are you?"

Aimee Pearson was a better option than the ones she'd feared most (Someone from her department. Someone from HR). The previous night, after showering blood from her hands, Agatha had sat down at her laptop. She'd written a letter that was now in her drafts. It was addressed to two superiors in the English department and it detailed what had occurred. She didn't know whether acknowledging her presence would draw more or less attention to the fact that she'd been at an undergraduate dorm at ten p.m. on a Thursday night. But regardless of why she'd been there, she'd helped more than she'd harmed, yes? Of course, now, she did realize that had she not been with Millie, Millie would have answered the phone. Looking back on her breakfast with Robin, it was as if Agatha had wanted to be seen in public. Out and about, above reproach, with someone closer to her age.

"I'm fine, Aimee," Agatha said. "Thanks for reaching out. I'm so glad you called."

"We're so glad you were there last night. I wanted to check in to see if there's anything you need."

"No, that's very nice of you. Are the girls doing okay?"

"They are. Peyton is with her parents and doing well. And Kennedy is still at Washington Regional. She'll be just fine."

"I'm so glad to hear it. And—is she accepting visitors? I'd love to drop off some flowers." Agatha threw up a hand. She was so nervous. She didn't mean to say it. She did not want to drop off flowers.

"Yes, she is accepting visitors. Do you have a pen?"

"I do." In the kitchen, Agatha wrote the room number down.

Aimee told her how kind the gesture was. "If you need any-thing, call me. Or call Josh. And . . . huh. Well, I'd give you Millie's number, but I guess I don't need to?"

In bare legs and feet, Agatha said, "Oh, right. I do have her email, yes."

"Mhm."

"Is she doing okay?"

"A bit shaken up but she'll be fine. But I don't want to hold you. I'll let you go."

Agatha walked back upstairs. She imagined Millie at the hospital, sleeping on chairs, eating from a vending machine. Ai-mee's call had served as a reminder that no amount of daytime sex could erase that evening, or turn the weekend into a vaca-tion. Agatha returned to the bedroom, where Robin was on the bed, inspecting a nail. She picked her pants up from the floor. "I'm sorry to be abrupt, but I actually have to go down to the hospital and see the girl from last night."

"Right now?" Robin said. "I can get dressed."

Agatha pulled a blouse from a hanger. "Oh no. You don't have to go."

"No, I can be ready. I can just sit in the hall."

Agatha watched Robin don high-end, camel-colored sweat-pants. "Robin, wait. I'm so sorry. But you actually shouldn't come with me."

Robin pulled her bra down, tiny folds of skin beneath. "Why?" she said. "I can be nice."

"It was just really messy. I think you should probably stay."

Robin sat and her foot made an *L* shape between her legs. "I'm not going to go like . . . in the room."

"No, I know. It would just make me anxious."

"You'd be anxious?"

"A bit. Yes."

Robin had an odd expression then, like she couldn't remember why she'd walked into a room. "Okay. Well. Can I shower while you're gone?"

"Yes, of course. And I'm sorry."

"No, that's fine. Is there a towel?"

Agatha pointed into the bathroom, the space beneath the sink. Downstairs she retrieved a spare key from a drawer. She brought it back up; set it on the dresser top. Robin could be heard in the en suite bathroom. Agatha opened a top drawer and retrieved a bundle of white socks.

"So the key is on the dresser."

Robin was wrapped in a towel. Her sweatpants and underwear were on the floor.

"It's the black one and it's for the top and the bottom lock," Agatha said.

Robin bent into the tub. Water began to pour.

"I won't be long," Agatha said. "Eat whatever. And please be careful. That can get very hot."

"Can I ask you something?"

Agatha stopped.

Robin sat on the toilet lid. "And if the answer is yes, then that's fine," she said. "But are you seeing someone else right now?"

Agatha separated the two socks in her hands. "What made you ask that?"

"I'm just curious."

The medicine cabinet mirror was starting to cloud. Agatha hadn't planned on telling Robin about Millie, but she hadn't planned on Robin being there at all. The idea of saying anything seemed premature, but Robin's lightness, her curiosity, the Cadillac out front, it put everything else in fair play.

"Very loosely," Agatha said. "And it's more of a casual thing."

Robin made a noise like she'd known it all along. "Is it the person you were just speaking to?"

"Oh. No no. That was someone else."

"So you *are* going to the hospital right now?"

"Yes. Did you think this was all a ruse?"

Robin smiled and put a fist to her chin.

"Robin, no. No no no. The person I was on the phone with is the director of student housing. She just gave me the information. But, to answer your question . . . the person I'm— We're not seeing each other seriously. It's very complicated but she was there last night, too. And she might be at the hospital, which makes you coming not a good idea. She definitely knows it's not serious, but I think it would be a little mean . . . if I were to show up there with you."

Robin blinked twice. "She was there last night?"

"She was." Then Agatha said something that she hated. "Which, I know. But it's a small town."

Robin said, "Huh," and she stared into the tub. "And you'd feel mean seeing her, if I was there."

"I would."

"Why would you feel that way?"

They were both smiling now. Agatha said, "Robin, please."

Robin nodded several times.

"I'm sorry," Agatha said. "I know this is all very strange."

"I wasn't trying to go deep," Robin said. "And I do get it. I was supposed to come here and I didn't. And you have to live your life. Do I love it? Not at all. But it is what it is."

Something billowed in Agatha then. *Do I love it? Not at all*,
she'd said. How special it was, even after all this time, to hear
Robin's admission of jealousy, especially in terms of Agatha herself.

Agatha bent and put her socks on her feet. "Are you seeing
anyone right now?"

Robin made big lips, meaning *Barely*. "No. I went on one
date. I kissed someone but that was it. I really am just focused
on my body and getting better."

"Robin, I think that's great."

"No, I know. And it is. But I know you have to go."

"I do. I'm sorry. Okay. The water does get very warm so
watch out."

Agatha took up her jacket from the arm of a chair. It's already December, she thought. Only five months until she'd be
home. Or maybe Robin could stay longer. It would be fun.
They'd buy her all new clothes. They'd go for long walks and
explore. Yes, they'd say later. No, it was actually really great.

Agatha watched the steam leak from the bathroom door.
She leaned back in. "Can I say one more thing?"

Robin returned her gaze.

"To be clear, it truly is just casual . . ."

Robin said, "Okay." The way she said it was familiar and
sweet. Hello, earrings. Okay, work pants. She tucked the towel
underneath her arm. "That doesn't sound like you at all. Do you
work with her?"

"I don't."

"Is she from here?"

Agatha sighed. "Let's not do that."

Robin smiled. "You are very red right now."

"I don't think I am."

"Not even your tan can save you."

"Okay . . . goodbye. I'll see you soon."

"But wait." Robin looked as if she'd heard her name in another room. "If you don't work with her, then why was she there? I thought it happened at a dorm."

Agatha centered herself in the doorway. "No, it did. That's correct."

"But she doesn't work with you."

"No, she doesn't."

"Then how was she there for all that?"

Agatha raised her chin as if she finally understood. "Oh oh, yes yes. She actually works there."

"The hospital?"

"No, the dorm."

Robin flexed and bent her right foot. The arch of it was perfectly round. It looked like a cursive letter *C*. "What?" she said. "She works there how?"

Agatha retrieved her keys from her pocket. "It's complicated because she's a bit older, but she works there as an RA."

From Robin's mouth came a sharp little gust. She placed her foot back on the ground. "Like a student RA?"

Agatha moved her head side to side. "Yes, but she's a bit older. Robin, I do have to go."

Robin's eyes widened and recoiled. "Am I hearing this right? She's a student student? Not a graduate student?"

"She's not *my* student. No no no."

"But you're messing around with an undergrad? Is that what I'm hearing?"

Agatha exhaled. She fingered her keys.

Robin let out a terrible, one-syllable laugh. "Agatha. How old is she?"

"Alright . . . this doesn't seem quite fair. I haven't asked about the people you've seen."

"You can ask me when we're done. I'm asking you. How old is she?"

Agatha recognized Robin's contempt, and it did something to ignite her own. With smug overarticulation, Agatha said, "She's twenty-four."

Robin nodded, furious and bemused. "Well, that's big of you."

"Come again?"

"No, I'm honestly a little concerned. Because the way you are right now, the way you're standing, it seems like you don't realize how this sounds."

"Please explain it to me, then."

"She's a student. You're a professor."

"For the second time now, I'm not her professor."

"It doesn't matter. Agatha. What do you think you're doing? There's a fourteen-year age gap and you work at the— Ohmygod." Robin held out a hand, distancing herself. "Did you interview her?"

"Okay, you are deliberately twisting things around. A colleague recommended her. She set *up* the interviews."

Robin framed her face with her hands. "This is unethical. How do you not see that?"

Agatha almost spat on the floor. For their entire relationship, Agatha had watched Robin claim to be a graduate student in service of discounts and deals. Movie theaters, museums, American Apparel. Robin had no qualms shopping at stores that were flagrantly homophobic. She had a specific way of stealing from Home Depot: she placed small items into a trash can and purchased the trash can through self-checkout with the lid. When several dancers in her cohort refused to work with a verbally abusive choreographer, Robin continued to show up to rehearsals. "Well, they don't have solos," she'd said. "He can call me whatever he wants."

Unethical. Agatha found herself preparing callow responses to this claim. She flinched at her instinct to use the language she'd been inundated by at Belgrade. Ohmygod, so you're an ethics professor now? You need to grow up. Sorry that she's twenty-four.

"Robin, I'm having a hard time keeping up. First, it's that she's a student, not mine. Then it's about her age. All this coming after, 'Oh it's fine. I was supposed to be here. If you're seeing someone, it's completely fine . . .'"

"I thought she was a grown-ass woman."

"Explain to me how she isn't."

"When I was twenty-four, I was an idiot. I was still sleeping with men."

"Ohhh. I get it now." Agatha laughed, hands to hips. "You just don't like that she's younger than you."

Robin's head began to slowly inch back. Tiny wrinkles formed at her jaw. Agatha could see Robin's tongue in her mouth, perched for a click that never came.

"I need you to listen. This ain't about me. What you're doing to a twenty-four-year-old girl isn't fair, and—"

"Doing to her? Robin, come off it. They can't be 'girls' when I'm with them and grown women when you want a job."

"Wow."

"Wow yourself. How dare you? She doesn't work for me. I'm not her teacher or her boss."

"Agatha, have you met you? You're everybody's boss. There is no way this is just a fun thing for her."

"Okay, Robin? You just fucking got here. You don't get to just drive up in some Cadillac and tell me about how things are and how they aren't. She's a grown-up. There's absolutely nothing I could give or take from her. Not to mention, she approached *me*. And it's unbelievable that you're suddenly the standing authority on what a grown person does. She's an adult. She's trying to buy a house. No one is helping her out. She also has something called a savings account—"

"Wow . . ." Robin said. "You can fuck right off." Then she was laughing, clapping her hands. "Why yes," she said. "What a feat. How much is the house? Nine dollars? I'll buy it for her myself. But sure. Let's give it up for a little white girl in Arkansas with goals and a savings account—"

"Oh my God. She's not—"

In stopping herself, Agatha set the room off-balance. The water in the tub was still coming out. Agatha experienced a visceral desire to reach in the tub and turn it off.

"She's not what?" Robin asked.

"Can we just stop?"

Robin took a step back. "What is her name?"

"I'm not doing this with you."

In a new register, Robin asked, "Is she Black?"

Agatha swallowed but held her gaze.

"Is this the girl from your . . . wow."

And then Agatha thought, So you did read them. This felt like a tiny win. And the fact that it did leveled her so hard and fast that she became light-headed. She reached and touched the wall. For possibly the first time, Agatha saw what she had done. She swallowed and held up a hand. "I'm sorry," she said. "I think we should take a break."

Robin turned off the water and walked past Agatha, turning

her body so as not to touch. She gathered her charger and her phone. Agatha watched her for a full ten-second count. Then she looked down at her own phone. An email from the chair of the English department was on the screen. The subject line said *Checking in.* Robin took up her toiletry bag and a pair of long socks. "Do your thing. I'm good," she said.

Agatha said, "Robin," and Robin shook her head. She held her towel closed and folded a sweatshirt on the bed.

"Just leave me the key. Go ahead," Robin said. She'd lock up when she was gone.

———

KENNEDY'S HEAD WAS back on a pillow, her face up to her right as if she were trying to decipher a smell. Her eyes were closed and her left wrist was bandaged in gauze. A plastic chair against the wall held a bouquet of flowers. Agatha gently laid her own bouquet on top.

She stared at the young woman. *Why are you here?* she'd said. Agatha quietly slipped out of the room. Back at home, Robin was gone. Agatha packed up her things, too. She texted Millie one last time and asked if she could meet and talk.

26.

ILLIE WAS LYING WITH HER HEAD AT THE FOOT of her bed when Josh phoned her cell just after four p.m. It was somehow still Friday and Millie could smell the hospital on her, but she didn't have the will to shower or change her clothes. She was on call for the weekend; she couldn't leave the dorm. She'd told herself that if they were to fire her, they would do it before five p.m. It was 4:02, and here was Josh calling. She'd almost made it. This was it.

"Hey, Millie, it's Josh, how are you?"

"Hi. Yes, I'm okay." Millie knew that if things had been different, she would have found this cute, him saying who he was whenever he called. "How—is everything okay?"

"Are you at Belgrade right now?" he asked. "Okay, great. I'd love your help."

Peyton's parents and Tyler's mother were downstairs. Tyler and Peyton were moving out. The parents had asked Victoria if someone could assist. "They have keys," Josh said. "They should be going up right now. If you could meet them and help them out with their bags, that'd be great."

Millie swung her legs off her bed. Please don't make me do

that, she thought. I don't even have a shirt. "No, yeah, that's fine." She opened a drawer. "I can go over there right now."

"Okay, great. Colette will meet you. She's grabbing the cart."

Millie had RA shirts from previous years, but the idea of wearing one felt like a pathetic attempt at appearing in charge. So she put on an Arkansas sweatshirt, hunter-green shorts, and her lanyard. Behind her door, she heard adult voices in the hall. Then there was a key in a lock. Mr. Shephard said, "There we go."

A woman's voice, not his wife's, said, "Alright. I was nervous, but it looks like they kept it nice."

Mrs. Shephard said, "I know they better."

Millie wanted to wait as long as she could. Till bags and boxes were zipped and sealed, till she could bend down to avoid eye contact. In the anteroom of her dorm, she listened to the parents talk and move. Tyler's mom was wearing some kind of sneakers. "Oh lord," Mrs. Shephard said. "This must be from Simi."

Millie assumed Colette would take her time as well, but there was the ding of the elevator; the screech of uneven wheels. She checked herself one last time and left her room. Colette rounded the corner with the move-in cart. Checkered Vans and red polo.

"Hi," Millie said.

Colette said a clipped "Hey." She reached and pulled her pants up in the back.

"They're already in there," Millie said.

"Yeah. That's what Josh said."

From inside the suite, Tyler's mom laughed. "Oh, I know that's Tyler's," she said. "She won't go anywhere without it."

Colette scratched the space behind her shoulder. "So, it sounds like both of them are okay."

"Yeah," Millie said. "They're both okay. Considering."

"You went to the hospital?"

"Yeah, I just dropped off flowers."

In the suite, Mr. Shephard said, "Monica, gimme that."

"No no, Wally. I'm stronger than I look."

The move-in cart drifted toward a wall. Once again, Millie wanted to squat and cry. She wanted to make up. She hadn't meant half the things she'd said. Had they not been fighting, Millie knew Colette would have said, Monica? Of *course* that's her name.

Colette put her sneaker in front of the cart's wheel. "Welp," she said. "Wanna do this?"

"Yeah, sure."

But then Millie heard the unquestionable sound of Command strips being removed. Tyler's mom said, "Good thing I grabbed a trash bag." Mrs. Shephard told her husband to watch out for his back. Millie froze, her fears back in full force.

Colette touched the wall. "Did you meet them already?"

"No."

"So they don't know who you are?"

"I guess they're about to."

"Yikes," Colette said. She whistled with "Well, okay."

Millie stood in front of the suite door. Inside, Monica asked if they were double-parked. Mrs. Shephard said, "No, no, we found a spot." Millie took a breath and raised her hand to knock. But then Colette stopped her. She closed her eyes and shook her head.

"Ugh. Just go to your room," she whispered. "I got it. It's fine. Just go."

"What?" Millie said.

"You don't even have a shirt."

Millie touched her lanyard. "Are you sure?"

"You wanna go in there? Yeah, that's what I thought." Colette pointed to a hair tie on Millie's arm. "Gimme that," she said. She slipped the tie onto her wrist.

Then Colette bent over completely at the waist. Millie watched her twist her hair with a curious precision. After a few manipulations and tucks, Colette stood upright again. On her head her dark hair was poised in a darling, messy bun. She gently plucked some strands from her hairline; they came down sweetly around her face. It was as if Colette were respectfully following the customs of another culture. She looked like she was going out to meet up with some friends.

"Wow," Millie said.

"Okay, chill out," Colette said. "Gimme your lanyard, I need a fob." She applied a loose tuck to her polo behind her jeans. She stepped up to the door and Millie went to her room. "And just to be clear," Colette said, touching the cart, "I'm not . . . I'm still kind of mad."

"I know."

"But I told Ryland that what he said was racist and he feels really bad."

Millie said, "Okay," and she went inside her room.

She leaned her ear against the wall. Three rosy taps came through like a bell. Colette called, "Hello?" The suite door opened. "Hey, y'all. How are you? Ah'm an RA and Ah'm here to help out."

Peyton's dad called her "young lady." Mrs. Shephard said she thought they'd been forgotten. "No no, Ah just had to grab the cart right quick. But Ah'm ready whenever you are. Oh man. Y'all are quick."

Millie listened to the lifting of containers. There were suit-cases, milk crates, paper and plastic. Colette made her way from the double room to the hallway and back. "Okay . . . oops. Lemme grab that . . . yep. Ah think that'll fit right there. Per-fect. Cool beans."

The Shephards went downstairs and then it was just Colette and Tyler's mom. They talked about the decent closets, how the size wasn't bad for a dorm. Then Monica said, conspiratorially, "Can I ask . . . were you there last night?"

"No, ma'am," Colette said. "Ah have mah fellowship group on Thursday nights. We tend to go pretty late."

Millie sat and hugged her knees to her chest. She stayed there even after they'd packed up and left. The sun was low and pretty outside. There was a knock at the door. Millie reached up and pulled the knob.

Colette waited a beat and then she gently pushed. The door hit Millie's thighs. Colette squeezed herself in. She'd taken down her hair. "Have you just been sitting here?"

Millie said yes.

"Did she like . . . is she fired?"

"I don't know."

Colette took the lanyard off, threw it on Millie's desk. "Are you super depressed now?"

Millie said, "Kind of."

Her phone buzzed. It was sitting on her knees. The screen said *Agatha. Millie—let's meet and talk.* There was also an email from Aimee on the screen that she hadn't seen before. The sub-ject line read *Meet Monday?*

"Is that her?" Colette asked. She bent and saw for herself. "Yikes," she said. She handed Millie her hair tie. "Are you on duty right now?"

Millie touched her palms to her head.

Colette dragged two fingers through her hair. "Millie, it's fine. Just don't be too long." She kicked Millie's sandal and held out a hand. "Here. Get up. Gimme the phone."

"Really?"

"Yes, I'll even answer it if someone calls."

27.

T HE PARKING LOT OF HARPS GROCERY STORE was spacious and forgiving, the kind where parents teach a teenager how to drive. Agatha parked her car around the side of the building. Millie appeared in her RAV4. Her hair was pulled up like when they had first met. Through the rearview mirror she hustled across the lane, even though no other cars were coming. Agatha unlocked the doors with a click. Millie sat down, holding her lanyard and her phone.

"Hi. Are you alright?" Agatha asked.

"Yeah. Sorry, hi. I'm fine."

Millie looked like she'd recently cried. She was about to say more, but then she glanced at the back seat. "Wait," she said. "Are you leaving?"

Agatha let her face fall into what she hoped was an apology. There in the back seat was her purse, a carry-on bag, and two paper bags filled with food. In the trunk were her two large suitcases, filled with forty-eight items. Millie touched her eyebrows and said, "Ohmygod." Her belongings jingled together between her thighs. Agatha placed her hand on the steering wheel. You are so nice, she thought. I should not have done this at all.

"Millie, hey." Agatha touched her back. She hated what she thought then, which was, Don't. Someone might see. "Hey. Listen to me. This is going to be fine."

"Did you get in trouble?"

"Don't worry about me. I'm always fine."

Millie wasn't wearing a jacket. There were goose bumps on her legs. "I feel like you wouldn't be leaving if everything was fine."

"Listen to me. No one's in trouble. I resigned. I have a job and an apartment. Do not think about me. I feel like you're freezing. Should I turn on the heat?"

"No, I'm okay."

They sat for a long while. Millie stared at the dashboard, and then she laughed a single time. "I feel terrible," she said, her voice clear and bright. She looked at once very pretty and tired. "I feel so completely awful. And I know I didn't say it earlier . . . but yeah. I don't know. I liked you a little bit."

Agatha exhaled through her nose. "I know."

Millie flinched the tiniest bit; items rustled in her lap. She looked out the window then, and she did a very cute thing. She raised her eyebrows and looked down. She mouthed *Yikes* to herself.

"And that's . . ." Agatha stopped herself, thinking, Jesus Christ. "If I should have done something to—"

"No, I'm not saying that."

"I know you're not. But it's . . ." Agatha looked at the dashboard and her heart atomized with affection and regret. She was terrible at this. She didn't want to mess it up. You're lovely, she wanted to say. And I'm so selfish and unfair. And I was being really careless. And I wish I could tell you more, but that would be unfair, too. It would be mean to tell Millie how good she was at sex. It would be odd and weirdly timed to say that she was a good actress, too. *I wasn't thinking properly,* Agatha wanted to say. *And no, I don't exactly regret it either. But this is it, it has to be. Please don't ask if you can call me sometime.*

There was nothing left to do but the best and worst thing she could. Agatha leaned and reached into the side of her bag in the back seat. "Millie," she said. "I wish there were a better way to do this . . . What's the down payment on your house?" An envelope was in her hand.

28.

MILLIE EYED THE ENVELOPE AS IF SHE'D UNCOV-
ered a weapon. "My what?"

Agatha looked almost annoyed. "Let me do this.
The down payment. How much?"

"But why are you—"

"Millie, how much is that house?"

She touched her knees. "It's one-oh-two."

"And she's letting you do ten percent down? Okay, great. I
thought it was one-twelve so I got you twelve thousand. Look at
me. Take this. Don't think about it. It's yours."

The money felt fat and illicit in her hands. Millie's keys
scraped the inside of her leg. "But why are you . . ."

Agatha shook her head. "Don't think about it. It's yours."

"But that . . ." Millie felt hot and sick and strange. "I mean,
I ruined your entire time here. This doesn't seem to—"

"No no no. I made decisions, too, okay? None of this is your
fault."

Millie forced herself to look out the window. There were
used cardboard boxes propped against the grocery store. The
weight of the envelope was shocking and bizarre. She looked
down at it and laughed. "This is like, completely insane."

"Don't think about it," Agatha said. "Take it and go straight to the bank. And if you don't want a house? Great. Take a year off. Go to Mexico. Use your Spanish. It doesn't matter. You—" She adjusted the sunglasses on her head. "Millie . . . I'm just incredibly sorry. And I'm also very sorry that this is how I'm saying it."

Millie bent and rubbed her ankles. She wished she'd said yes to turning on the heat. Agatha was really leaving, and Millie wanted to absolutely die. There were many things she wanted to say, many of which had no beginning or end. How am I supposed to. Because this feels *bad*. A complete nightmare. The way I feel for you. But I speak differently now. I don't go up at the ends. I bought a *vest*, she thought, humiliated. It was so expensive but I did it just because of yours. And yeah, I'm kind of good at Spanish because of you, but you also like, told all my business? In *Teen Vogue*? Very quickly, a flash of anger rose up in her chest. This feeling—she was certain—was just the tiniest bit of how she was supposed to feel. Did you pick Becca because you think I'm dumb? she thought. How do I just like, walk back to my car?

"Is this . . ." Millie swallowed. "Can I say something else?"

"Of course."

She looked down at the envelope and poked the corners with her palms. "Is this you saying sorry for the article, too?"

Millie looked up to find Agatha's eyes alert in a way she hadn't seen before. She would think of this expression far into the future whenever she saw a sign in the woods that said CONTROLLED BURN. In her periphery she saw Agatha's chest go up and down with meticulous restraint. Then she made the smallest nod Millie had ever seen.

Millie twisted her lips to the left. "I thought you were asking me things so you could look them up later."

Head to her hand, Agatha said, "I was . . ."

"But you didn't say it was for something online. And why did you pick the name Becca? I feel like that was kind of mean."

Agatha ran a hand through her hair. "I can see how you would think that. And I'm sorry. The name had nothing to do with you. Please believe me on that."

The way Agatha looked at her; she was doing it again, making Millie feel very important. "See, that's like, ugh"—Millie made two fists—"I hate this because the bigger problem is that I should be more mad and I'm just not."

A guy came out the side door of Harps. He had a denim hat on and an apron at his waist. He went to light a cigarette, when he saw Agatha and Millie. He finished lighting it and then he walked away.

"If you had asked me," Millie said, "I probably would have said yes."

"I know."

"But I also would have said different things. I don't know." Millie crossed her legs. There was the rustle of paper. She'd almost forgotten the money in her lap. "Geez," she laughed. "How do you just have twelve thousand dollars? That's more than I make in a year."

Agatha closed her eyes again; for a second, she looked unwell.

"Sorry, I'm . . ." Millie went on, "I'm not trying to make you . . . I don't know. I know most of this is my fault. And I obviously more than liked you, which I guess you knew, but now you're leaving and . . . sorry. I don't even know why I'm saying this to you." Millie laughed at herself, but she was crying somewhat, too. "Like, I don't want you to leave, but ever since you got here . . . I don't know. Maybe this is a good thing. What you did wasn't cool to me. And I don't think that I should feel this way.

Actually, I know I shouldn't. Like, you shouldn't get to do whatever you want and then I'm all, 'Oh, okay, that's fine.' And you *did* do whatever you wanted. Like, you definitely should have told me all that stuff was for *Teen Vogue*. Which is *so* random but yeah, I don't know. You could have been like, 'Hey, can I use that thing you said?' But when I saw it, I was like, 'Oh, I must have told her that that was fine.' So yeah, that's . . . that's probably not great. But even that's a bad example. It's way, way more than that. And even though I know it's not good in my mind, I still don't like, know how to know it in the moment. You know what I mean? Like right now. I'm so sad that you're leaving that I could literally punch myself in the face. But if you tried to like, I don't know, murder me or something, I'd probably be all, 'Oh, okay,' and just like . . . offer to help—"

"Millie . . ."

"Okay. Just gimme a second." Millie held her temples in her hands.

Agatha touched the envelope in her lap. "I messed up," she said. "And this doesn't make it better, but I do want you to take it."

Millie exhaled with a tiny cry, the type of noise one makes when they're sleeping.

Agatha rested her elbow on the door. "Are you in any kind of trouble?"

Millie exhaled and said, "Yeah."

"Really? How much?"

"I'm not sure. A lot. They're both fine, the girls from last night. But Tyler is trying to get me fired."

"She's what?"

Millie uncapped her sanitizer and then sealed it back. "It's so stupid, but it's my fault. She gave me twenty bucks to help her switch her rooms, *months* ago, and now she's saying she did it to get away from Kennedy, which is false. And I was just like, saving everything for the house so I was stupid and I took it. But yeah. Tyler is having a meeting with Aimee. And Aimee wants to talk to me on Monday, too."

Agatha's eyebrows went up into her head. Then she laughed, a real laugh, a *hahaha*. The sound of it was so mature, it made Millie want to stop time. "You're kidding," she said. "What a little shit."

"I know. But it's my fault."

"No . . . Millie. You don't, hmm . . ." Agatha looked out the window, as if she were trying to recall the word. "You are a very nice person," she said. "And that's great. Most people aren't. But you don't have to be nice *all* the time. You can do whatever you want. Or you know what? Don't," she laughed. "You're smart. Don't listen to me."

"Are you really leaving right now?"

Agatha said nothing.

"Wow," Millie said. "This really sucks."

"I know."

Agatha looked so cool and ready for travel, her right leg bent in a way that felt smart. Millie could feel it with certainty now, that it was over, and that she should be leaving, too. Quite possibly the saddest sensation Millie had ever known was this: that someone cared for you but not like you cared for them. That they were leaving for good this time, and wanted you out of their car.

"Well?" Millie said. She squinted with one eye. "I don't know . . . I had a good time?"

Agatha touched her arm. Her hand was formal, but it was there. "Look at me," she said. "I did, too."

29.

AGATHA COULD MAKE IT TO EUREKA SPRINGS by dinnertime. In her car, she had what she felt was an adolescent thought: she wanted to drive down Dickson one last time. She passed the post office, the white steeple of a church. A drugstore she'd never been in; it always looked empty. There were new signs on the lampposts that were bright orange. They said *Experience Fayetteville*. Some said *Exp Fay*. She passed a sign for a place called US Pizza Co. A bookstore called Nightbird. Then she saw a blue baseball cap and a braid sticking out the back.

There was just enough time for her to safely turn into the parking lot of Puritan, a coffee shop she'd been to once. Tyler descended from the restaurant patio, several items in her hands. She was going to a car. Agatha wondered if it was hers. She pulled up behind it and rolled her window down. "Hi, Tyler?" She took her sunglasses off. "Hi. Can we talk for a second? Hi."

Tyler was wearing leggings, Birkenstocks, and a sweatshirt featuring an illustration of an ocean and the year 2016. Draped in her fingers was one of those phone-wallet-key chain combinations. In the other hand she held a Texas Instruments calculator.

Tyler stopped walking. She gave Agatha a puzzled and slightly offended glance.

"Do you remember me? Hi," Agatha said.

Tyler squinted and said, "Hiii?"

"I need to talk to you. It won't take long."

Tyler looked behind her. On the patio there were people drinking out of tumblers and mugs. A loose hair floated into her mouth and with one finger, she pulled it out. "This is really weird," she said.

"It's very important. It's about last night. Can you get in?"

A car appeared behind Agatha's and politely honked. Tyler closed her mouth and reached for the car door. She sat down and she smelled masculine, like a tropical Old Spice cologne.

"Just so you know," she said, "I'm sharing my location with my friend Casey."

Agatha looked at her, and said, "Okay, great."

She drove down the street to yet another parking lot, this one featuring a U of A Laundromat and Clubhaus Fitness. Once again, she felt guilty for noticing a few surveillance cameras, and for parking away from them. Tyler clutched her belongings like someone might take them. She, like Millie, could have benefited from a purse. Agatha pulled her key from the ignition and touched her finger to the place beneath her mouth. "Alright," she said. "I need to talk to you about Millie."

Tyler said nothing. Her face stayed impressively still.

"Why are you trying to get her fired? Is that your ultimate goal?"

Tyler's keys ticked against her calculator. She looked out the window, seemingly disappointed by where she'd been driven to. "Who told you that?" she said. "I'm not trying to get anyone fired."

"Okay, then whatever you told her boss, that you paid her? You need to take it back or she's going to lose her job."

Tyler smiled. "But I did pay Millie."

"Not the way you said you did."

Tyler sat up and adjusted the rim of her cap. "This is so random. How would you know? And I don't even care that Millie took my money. I'd had a bad feeling about Kennedy and last night kind of proves my point. And—you know what? Millie isn't as innocent as she makes herself out to be. She's been a pretty bad RA. So yeah." Tyler took up her things. "Sorry she had bad judgment, but I don't really see how that's my fault."

"Alright." Agatha stopped her. "Can you just tell me why?"

Hand on the door, Tyler said, "Why what?"

"I'm trying to understand why jeopardizing Millie's future is worth it to you."

Tyler's top lip dipped in the middle. "What does that even mean?"

Agatha took her seat belt off. In doing so, she got another whiff of Tyler's cologne. "Tyler, I need you to tell Aimee that what you said isn't true. Millie has a job lined up for next year. This puts her at risk."

"Okay. Once again. Not my fault."

"This is absurd. Why do you care?"

Tyler's face mushed together in confusion. Then, between her eyebrows, was cavalier intrigue. "Why do *you* even care? Ohmygod, wow." Tyler's face brightened and her chin went toward her neck. She laughed and said, "I *knew* it."

"You don't know anything."

"Yes, I do," Tyler said. "This all makes perfect sense. You weren't doing interviews at ten o'clock at night. And yeah. See? Bad RA."

Agatha exhaled and cracked her neck to the side. "Okay, how can we get to the point where you can tell Aimee the truth? It looks like bribery. Do you understand that?"

"Once again, that's not my fault. And I don't even care. About any of this. I'm moving out. I have an apartment now. *And*," she laughed, "obviously you care, which seems inappropriate to me . . . but I'm not just gonna do something for you and not get anything in return."

Agatha smiled, almost enjoying Tyler's reasoning. "What could you possibly get from me? Do you want me to pay you?"

Tyler's items jingled on her legs. "I mean, I can be bought," she said. "Ohmygod. I sound crazy. I'm all, 'I can be bought.' But yeah. I don't know . . . Make me an offer? Ha ha. I mean, *technically* . . . I could make this bad for you." Tyler raised her eyebrows in a specific way. It was like she was posing for a group photo. Like someone had said, Let's do a fun one.

Agatha had always liked Tyler. Her meanness and decisiveness were remarkably pure. Seeing her this way felt like she had a celebrity in the car; it was exciting and disappointing. Tyler had terrible posture that Agatha had never deciphered from her tone. And now, with a threat in the air, the scent of her was annoying and odd. Tyler smiled at her again. She was being her most immature self. Of this, Agatha knew, she was completely deserving.

"You know what? Fine. What do you want?"

Tyler slumped. "I don't know. Make me an offer."

"I'm not playing that game. What do you want?"

She let out a puff. "Okay, no. You know what? I want fifteen hundred dollars."

"Wow," Agatha laughed. "You're a little shit."

"Okay, aren't you supposed to be a professor?"

Agatha stuck her keys into the ignition. "Put your seat belt on."

"Why?"

"Because we're going to a bank."

"Eww, no. Just Venmo me."

"Are you—" She almost said it. Agatha almost said, Are you dumb? No, she thought. You, Agatha, *you* are dumb. She touched her chin with her fingers and blew out through a small O. Agatha had no idea when it had happened, when this had become her life. That she was frequently in the position of giving other women money.

"We're going to the bank so I can give you cash." She released the emergency brake and pushed her sunglasses up her nose.

Tyler looked down at her belongings, as if someone had put them there. "Great. I have no way of carrying that much cash right now, but cool."

The bank was on the same street, possibly five hundred feet away. Agatha's last drive down Dickson had become one of staccato stops with Tyler Hanna in the passenger seat. Once parked, she reached for her purse and checkbook. Then she retrieved a pen.

"You're doing a check?" Tyler asked. "Don't you need to know how to spell my name?"

Agatha, eyes down, told her, "No." For reasons she couldn't articulate, she didn't want to fill out a withdrawal slip. On the memo line of her check she wrote *Research*, so she could later write it off. "I'm making a check out to myself. Then I'll cash it and give it to you." She wrote out the words *fifteen hundred* and exhaled. "Jesus. What in God's name are you spending this on?"

"That's really none of your business," Tyler said.

Agatha signed her name. "Ooh, something special, huh?" She ripped the check from its perforated edge. "Are you getting a big gift card to Pinkberry?"

Tyler looked as if she'd been spat on. "It's actually for a dog."

"Well la-di-da."

"And I'm pretty sure the nearest Pinkberry is in Texas but good try. And I don't even like sweet things, you psychopath."

Agatha received this comment like she'd heard a loud noise. "Stay in the car, please."

Tyler held up a hand. "Literally where else would I go?"

The bank teller was the same one who had joked months ago about the government only giving them one-size bills. Agatha slipped the cash into an envelope and sealed the top on her way out. She was surprised to find Tyler staring out the window and not looking down at her phone. Tyler's distant gaze made Agatha walk faster. She suddenly felt like she'd kidnapped her. She needed to get out of town.

"Okay. This is for you." Agatha closed the door. "But first, you're going to call Aimee and you're going to cancel your meeting."

Tyler made a noise at the back of her throat. "No, I'll just email her."

Agatha's phone was already out. "No, you're going to call her. Here, I have the number."

"No, that's so awkward. I'll just email now so you can see."

"No," Agatha said. Millie flashed into her mind. "I want you to say it to her. Call her. Right now."

Tyler slowly reached for Agatha's phone. "This is getting really intense."

"We're not using my phone. You're going to use yours."

"Okay, I'm going. Stop being so intense."

In the end, Agatha was quite impressed with Tyler's reformatting of the events. "So yeah," she said. "When we switched rooms, I'd had a bad feeling, but it was mostly because she had so much stuff . . . Yeah, and I didn't—or I did offer to pay Millie, but she actually slipped it back underneath my door . . . Yeah, I actually found it when I was packing up just now . . . Exactly. So yeah. Just wanted to clear that up."

Tyler hung up the phone with Aimee. She did a *Welp* with her shoulders, and then she held out her hand. She accepted the envelope as if she were doing Agatha a favor, watching over her things while she used the restroom. Agatha was mystified by their two interactions together. *You dress how I want to dress when I'm older. I don't even like sweet things.* Agatha felt certain that this moment would be shaped to Tyler's liking. She would become part of a story Tyler told whenever anyone asked how she got her dog.

Tyler put her hand on the door and stopped. "I'll probably never see you again, so I might as well just ask. Why didn't you do one of those *Teen Vogue* things about me?"

Agatha turned and looked at her.

"I saw that you did one of Jenna and Casey," Tyler said. "Actually, I saw you did two of Jenna. Or it sounded like you did."

Agatha's head felt incredibly heavy. She rested her chin on the base of her hand. "Do you read *Teen Vogue*?" she asked.

"Not really, no. But I googled you after last night. You should have just come in our room instead of like, spying. I could have told you way, way more."

"That's . . . hmm." Agatha stared straight again. She didn't feel moved to cry, but she did have tears in her eyes.

"Also," Tyler said. "If you and Millie are together, I don't care. Well, I do think it's weird. But not because you're women.

My mom dated a woman once. Which was weird because she's my mom. But the lady was nice."

Agatha looked at Tyler again. It was the second time that day when she'd been told she could have gotten what she wanted. That she really should have just asked. Agatha felt hot then. She wanted Tyler out of the car so viciously that she almost handed her the keys. "Do you want me to drop you off somewhere?" she asked.

Tyler looked down at her phone. She opened the door and looked around. "No, I'm good," she said, but she didn't sound that way. "Yeah, okay. I think I'll just get out here."

30.

ON MONDAY MORNING, MILLIE WENT TO Aimee's office, after her Spanish final, before she'd eaten lunch. Aimee said, "Hey, girl," and "Go ahead and shut that door." Millie did so and set her backpack by her knees. She'd done her hair and she wore a zip-up fleece and jeans. Over the weekend she'd decided to never again receive bad news in shorts. Her good haircut was still good and it sat on her shoulders. Her waves and a scarf warmed her neck.

"Okay . . . hi." Aimee smiled. She wheeled her chair to the middle of her desk. Her hands were folded together. Her shoulders hunched like a coach. "So there's a lot we need to talk about. But let's get a few things out of the way . . . Number one. Tyler called . . ." She made wide eyes. "And she confessed—or—explained what went down between you two."

Millie crossed her legs in a way that implied she understood. Then she said something that she felt was very Agatha. Instead of saying, She did? Millie said, "Did she."

"You know I never doubted you," Aimee said. "It was just messy for a minute. But she's out. She's in an apartment. She hated the dorms and she's not the first. As for you . . . do you want the good news or bad news first?"

Just as Millie was saying "Bad," Aimee cut in and delivered it.

"I can't have you RD next year. I gotta give the Belgrade spot to Joanie."

Millie, unprepared, said a light "Oh."

"I know, Mill. I'm sorry. She asked me before the year started up. But here's the real reason . . . Peyton likes Belgrade." Aimee raised her hands. The gesture looked strangely Catholic. This was to signify that she didn't understand why. Millie felt air go through her nose, into her chest. I lost it, she thought. I lost it and it's gone.

"So," Aimee went on, "Peyton's gonna be at an apartment with Tyler—odd pairing, that one is—and then she'll be back in Belgrade for her senior year. But her parents are still a bit miffed and it just doesn't work to put you back in there so soon. Do you understand what I'm saying? I'm sorry, Mill. We're giving her and another student an entire suite, which . . . I don't know who it is. Simi? Do you know who Simi is?"

"No, I don't."

"I think it sets a terrible precedent, but I was overruled. Peyton's parents made a donation once. Her dad works at— Anyway. Listen, Mill. This is a not-now, not a not-ever situation. I think Marissa in Hampden is about to leave. The second she's out, you're absolutely in. Does that mess up all your plans? It's just a delay. It's not a no."

Millie put her shoulders back against the chair. She felt dumb and incredibly resigned. It was unbearably humbling that because Peyton would be at Belgrade, Millie would not be allowed to do the same. Millie's face had indicated agreement when Aimee implied that wanting to live at Belgrade was strange. But she completely understood why Peyton would want to come back. Belgrade was plain and unfussy. The rooms were functional and small. It was uncomplicated to a fault, and just south of sorority row, which could be loud; but mostly, it was collegiate-looking, like it was from a movie or brochure.

Millie said, "Okay. I understand."

"Are you mad at me?"

"Of course not, no."

"Okay, good. Oh, one more. Just a tiny thing," Aimee said. "Going forward, you're gonna do your check-ins with me on Tuesdays, okay?"

Millie touched her tongue to her bottom teeth. "Oh. Okay, that's fine."

"Just easier that way. Josh has a lot going on."

"Right," Millie said. "No, that makes sense."

This stung less than she thought it would. Millie liked Josh, but more than she liked him, she wished she'd done things his way. Josh had looked out for himself. He'd understood that he could lose his job next year.

"Okay okay okay. Enough of that for now." Once again, Aimee gestured with her hands. This time, like she was saying, *No more bids.* "Do you want the good news? The house is yours if you want it."

Millie's head went up and to the right.

"The train saved you," Aimee said. "They were in town and it went by twice when she was there. She asked me if it was always like that and I said, 'You know . . . I'm not sure.'" Aimee winked. "So that's it. It's yours if you want it. But I realize this is sooner than we discussed. And I'm setting you up with no job and a mortgage, so tell me how we feel about all that."

Millie hated the chemistry that was happening—fusing the house with Agatha this way. It felt more real now than it had with the envelope of hundreds in her hand. When she'd depos-

ited the money into her account, Millie had a fantasy where she'd
get the house in the spring. But the money she'd put down
wouldn't be from Agatha. She'd have done it on her own. But
because of a train—one she'd come to know intimately—Millie's
days at Barnes & Noble Café were rendered completely unnecessary. That whole summer. Her entire year at home. She could
have gone to the gym more. Run errands with her mom.

"I'll be fine," Millie said.

"You sure? Are your parents helping you?"

"No, but it's fine. I got it."

At this, Aimee gently mocked Millie's *I got it*. She pouted,
like it was none of her business, but that she was still duly impressed.

"Okay. Then I'll connect you. She's a lot so get ready."

"Okay. Thank you, Aimee."

"You are very welcome. But, Millie. One last thing . . ." Aimee looked upward. Her lashes fluttered with what looked to be
obligation. "And this is neither good nor bad, but let me say
for just a second . . . I'm sure you know Professor Paul has resigned."

Aimee was stating a fact, but it was clear she was asking a
question. Millie answered with a careful "I do."

"Okay. Is there anything . . . well, you're, how old are you?"

"Twenty-four."

Aimee nodded and looked everywhere but at Millie's eyes.
"Right. So technically . . . there's nothing you *need* to tell me. I
don't know where I was going with this. Here's the last thing I'll
say. You know how you're not supposed to do work on your bed?
'Cause it messes with your sleep? Okay. I do think there's something to that. And *generally*"—she overarticulated the word—"it's
a really good idea . . . to not go to sleep where you work. Or work

where you sleep. Either one, really. Are you hearing me with this?"

Millie had heard that before. She did it anyway, all the time. She did homework on her bed. She slept with her phone underneath her pillow. If she woke up at night, she checked the time on the screen. She did and often would, far in the future, wear her RA polo to bed. That was how she slept best.

"Does that make sense?" Aimee asked. "Are you mad at me for saying that?"

"No, sorry." Millie smiled. "It's . . . yeah. I have heard that. Sorry. I'm not laughing laughing. I've just always slept where I worked."

Aimee looked concerned. "What do you mean by that, Mill?"

"No, not like, figuratively. I literally sleep where I work. Like at the hotel or when I was a camp counselor . . . And yeah, as an RA."

"Oh oh oh. Well, good point."

"But no. I do get what you're saying."

"Okay, good. And . . . well. You're twenty-four. And you're okay?"

Millie felt like crying. "Yeah, of course. I'm always fine."

———

THAT EVENING, RYLAND was on duty. While doing rounds, he discovered that the suite next to Millie had been cleaned and left unlocked. He summoned Colette and they knocked on Millie's door. In Peyton and Tyler's old bedroom, the three of them lay across the shiny floor. Ryland apologized and Millie said it was okay. Colette showed Millie something she'd found: the social media account of Josh's girlfriend. They'd been together for at least two years. She had long, thick box braids down her back. She spoke German and there were pictures of her climbing, a large harness at her waist. "You're way cuter," Ryland said. Millie knew that wasn't true.

The next day Millie asked Colette if she wanted to take a walk. They went to the Frisco Trailway and took it down over the stream. They stopped at the little yellow house. Millie pulled out the keys. The way the light came into the kitchen made her excited and terribly sad. She had not gotten the house the way she'd wanted, but she still had someone to show it to. Colette touched the walls and opened the cupboards. She looked at one of the transom windows and said, "I like that a lot."

Since Agatha's departure, Millie had been consumed with an unease that mimicked the sensation of an early sore throat. It was something she couldn't quite articulate or shake. She felt as though her entire personality were leaving the pull of gravity. What Millie kept coming back to was the night in Agatha's kitchen, the two stacks of papers on the island counter. Kennedy's cover letter sat on top of the bigger pile. Agatha had discarded her at *My name is.* The old Millie would have gone to check on Kennedy a couple of days later. Hey, how's it going? How's your semester? But instead, she'd laughed and watched Agatha grind her coffee for the next day.

Millie wasn't certain that she'd recover from it: crying in Agatha's car; losing a job because of her behavior; being caught, so publicly, stealing Colette's verbal turns of phrase. But she did have the house—how she got it notwithstanding. And perhaps, if she continued to scrub, she'd find herself again, somewhere underneath.

Colette walked over to the refrigerator. She eyed the unfinished grocery list. "I bet the last one was 'chicken,'" she said.

Then she stepped up near the sink. "Oo," she said. "Can you feel that?"

Millie waited in the silence. "Feel what?" she asked.

Colette lifted her head. "Someone died in here," she said. "Not in a bad way. But someone definitely died."

31.

WHEN KENNEDY WOKE UP, SHE FOUND HER arm wrapped and bandaged. She smelled like antiseptic and hair in need of a wash. She bent her fingers slowly; they were a sick brown and faded blue. She was in a hospital gown, which was weird; she hadn't remembered taking off her clothes.

A young man in scrubs checked on her in the night. "Hi there. Everything okay? You press that button if you need anything." She was placed on something called EOC, which she learned meant *emergency officer commitment*. A woman came and asked her questions about how she felt. She wrote things down and that was kind of it.

Her mother's flight was delayed because of a snowstorm, so Kennedy had a lot of time to herself. For breakfast she had an omelet and some wheat toast. A mini muffin and a fruit salad. For lunch she had a turkey sandwich with a side salad and some chips. She ate everything very slowly, using only her good hand. It seemed like every time she fell asleep someone came in and checked her vitals. Millie came, which was embarrassing. Kennedy had asked too many questions and cried. But Millie had brought flowers that made the room smell nice. After she left,

Kennedy fell asleep again. When she awoke, the room felt warm. On the chair were two bouquets. The second one didn't have a card.

Around three p.m., Kennedy heard her mother approaching. There was the sound of bags against her coat, the rolling of a carry-on. When Nichelle came in, it looked as if a large moth had landed on her face. Like it had left a red mark on her skin. She stood in front of the bed. She pouted and said, "Hi, sis."

Kennedy said, "I'm okay."

Nichelle kept saying, "Ohmygoodness." Kennedy pressed herself into her mother's shoulder; held her bandaged arm above her purse. "I'm okay," Kennedy said again. "It's really not that bad."

Kennedy didn't want to talk about Peyton. Or the rejection letter. Or how she'd thought she'd seen Agatha Paul. But strangely, Nichelle didn't really ask. She wiped her eyes and rolled her bag to a corner of the room.

"They won't let us leave just yet," she said. "They have to . . . decide you're ready."

"Okay. If you want to go get lunch or something I won't be mad."

"Don't be crazy. I'm staying right here."

Kennedy lay back against her pillow and smiled. "I can't believe you flew," she said.

Nichelle blew upward. The hair above her forehead took flight. "There's so much snow. Don't be mad at me, Kens. I'm sure you know how I got a flight."

Kennedy looked up. "You asked Erin's mom?"

Nichelle had only flown a handful of times. Erin's mom, a commercial pilot, had helped her secure the last two flights she took. The most recent had been to Fort Lauderdale with some girlfriends. There, Nichelle saw the ocean for the first time.

"Sweetie, I had to," Nichelle said. "She got me a flight out of Moline."

"So Erin like . . . knows I'm here?"

"Sis, I hope you're not mad at me."

"No, I'm not mad." Kennedy could smell herself. She wished she could take a shower.

Nichelle pulled a chair up to the side of the bed. "Did they feed you?"

"Yeah. It wasn't very good."

Nichelle hung her purse on the back of the chair. "Remember when Dad was at Genesis? And you loved to eat those peaches?"

Kennedy nodded, bent her knees. "I don't know if I'd still love them now." She looked around the room. There was television in the corner. A remote was Velcro'd to the side. "Should we watch something?" she asked.

"Oh, sure." Nichelle stood. "Do you wanna pick?"

Kennedy said, "No, you."

Nichelle flipped over sports channels and the news. Then the fun stuff started to appear. Bravo. Oxygen. There was a fixer-upper show with a southern couple; the woman had a pixie cut and the man had a beard. Nichelle looked back at Kennedy. Kennedy sat up and said, "Yeah."

THEY STAYED AT the hospital till Saturday afternoon. A nurse taught Nichelle how to keep the wound clean. Kennedy watched the Cooking Channel while Nichelle went to Belgrade. Nichelle got a U-Haul cargo trailer and moved everything out of the suite. Around noon she called and asked, "Did they give you lunch? Okay, good. Tell them no thanks." Nichelle brought back bowls from Chipotle. Kennedy liked to eat hers using chips instead of a fork.

Around three, she was discharged. Outside, the light was overwhelming but nice. On the way to the rental car, Kennedy asked, "We're going home?" Nichelle said yes, that that was the plan.

At a gas station, Nichelle asked if Kennedy wanted to come in or sit. Kennedy wanted to sit. Out the window, she said, "Wait. Mom. Is it okay if I have my phone?"

Nichelle paused. Her lips parted.

"I haven't had it in like, two days."

Kennedy could tell what her mother was thinking. That this might be like Iowa again. Messages she shouldn't see. But then Nichelle said, "Yes." She opened the car door. "Yes, but you can't be on it the whole drive."

"I know."

"And Kennedy?" She handed her the phone. "Don't do anything about whatever you see. Let's let everything sit for now until we can get ourselves right at home."

The battery was at two percent. Kennedy reached into the console box and found her mother's portable charger. She clicked on her text messages—there were seventeen new ones—and the app refused to open right away. In her lap she turned the phone over and over and over again.

Finally it worked. The most recent text was from her twirling coach back in Iowa. *Hey Kiddo. We're thinking about you. We love and miss you. Would love to hear your voice.* There were a few messages from numbers that were not in her phone. They started out like this: *Hi Kennedy, this is Jessie from Belgrade. I think we have American Lit . . .* There was a message from Casey, and it was quite long. *Dear Kennedy, this is Casey. I've been thinking of you and lifting you up* . . . The next one was from Leanne, her old friend and trumpet player. Leanne had left a voicemail, too. The next one was from Erin and it made Kennedy touch her mouth. *Hi. Are you okay? I was wrong to cut you out. Please talk to me. I'm so sorry.*

Nichelle came out of the gas station with a bag on her arm. Through the plastic, Kennedy could see the colors of Vitaminwaters and Lay's chips. As Nichelle pumped their gas, Kennedy moved on to emails. She had one from her creative writing teacher, the one who had helped her write her essay. Everyone was being so formal. There was no mention of Peyton. People were acting like she'd done something to herself. Well, maybe . . . Kennedy touched her ear. She really did remember Agatha Paul being there. She was certain of it. She had seen her face. But Agatha hadn't been there. Of course she hadn't. Perhaps Kennedy misremembered other things, too.

Nichelle got back in the car but something in her eyes had changed. Kennedy asked, "What's wrong, Mom?" and Nichelle shook her head.

"I'm trying to be strong here." She shook her head again. "This is hard. Ken, look at me."

"Mom. I'm fine—"

"No, I mean this," she said. Nichelle looked like she was saying something for the first and last time. "Look at me. Don't do anything like that ever again."

For a moment, Kennedy looked down at her arm. She took a breath, no longer confused. She looked back up, and told her mom, "Okay. I won't."

Nichelle looked down at Kennedy's fingers. They were still

bruised at the joints. "They told me that we can get a plastic surgeon to look at it."

Kennedy pushed her hair back. "No," she said. "That's okay."

They drove for an hour and they listened to the radio. In Missouri they passed a sign for an exit up ahead. Advertised were gas stations and fast-food restaurants. And then there was a sign featuring the red-and-white bull's-eye.

Nichelle must have seen it, too. She asked, "Do we have everything we need?"

Kennedy said, "I think so," but Nichelle followed the signs.

And there it was: the white building, the Target sign. Big gray parking lot. Bright red windows and doors. It was weird how similar they all looked, no matter where you were. Rolling into the parking lot, Kennedy felt like she was home.

Nichelle parked and turned off the car. She pushed her sunglasses on top of her head. "Alright," she said. "Let's stretch our legs. We can just look around."

ACKNOWLEDGMENTS

I am deeply grateful for the support and expertise of my agent, Claudia Ballard. My editor, Sally Kim, has a brilliant ear and eye, and I am profoundly thankful for her patience. So many thanks are due to my team at Putnam: Katie McKee, Alexis Welby, Ashley McClay, Nicole Biton, Jazmin Miller, Tarini Sipahimalani, Brennin Cummings, Emily Leopold, and Samantha Bryant. Thank you to the production team, Emily Mileham, Claire Sullivan, and Ashley Tucker. Thank you to Sylvie Rabineau, Laura Bonner, Camille Morgan, and Oma Naraine. And thank you Vi-An Nguyen and Anthony Ramondo for a book cover I adore.

I'd also like to acknowledge the support I received while working on this book. My sincerest thanks to the Maryann Evans Postgraduate Fellowship.

I'm very grateful for the three books that inspired the three main characters in this novel. I discovered Agatha Paul within *Paying for the Party: How College Maintains Inequality*, by Elizabeth A. Armstrong and Laura T. Hamilton. Kennedy came about from F. S. Michaels's *Monoculture: How One Story Is Changing Everything*. And Millie arrived via Lester Spence's *Knocking the Hustle: Against the Neoliberal Turn in Black Politics*.

ACKNOWLEDGMENTS

For two years, Isabel Henderson provided vital research, editing, consultation, and transcription. This novel is vastly richer because of her capacious and quick mind. Kelsey Kerin also provided pivotal research and perspective. You two are brilliant readers and friends.

This novel was greatly enhanced by the thirty interviewees who agreed to share their lives and experiences with me. While their names are not included, I am deeply indebted to them for their generosity and time. Thank you to the residents of Iowa City, Joplin, Chicago, and Fayetteville. To several students and alumni from the University of Iowa, Amherst, and the University of Arkansas. Thank you to the collegiate featured twirler and fire girl, and the coordinator and coach of a Southern U. step team. To the dance coordinator, ex–River North Dancer, and a frequent 100 Nights Chick-fil-A participant. Thank you to the journalist, the optometrist, and the Starbucks manager, and, of course, the many resident assistants and resident directors. Lastly, thank you to the student who shared with me that she received "practice paychecks" from her dad's dental office.

I'd like to acknowledge the medical professionals who kept my body going despite a career of sitting and screens. Thank you to Dr. Zach Molland, Dr. Robert Abbott, Lora Richardson, and Dr. Lauren Brindisi.

Many thanks to early readers and friends: Christina DiGiacomo, Melissa Mogollon, Megan Angelo, Rachel Jacobs, Holly Jones, Jade Jones, Mindy Isser, Alycia Davis, Loren Blackman, Njoki Gitahi, Julie Buntin, Liz Moore, and Caleb Way.

And lastly, endlessly, thank you, Nathan. Thanks for taking me to Arkansas and especially for AO.